FIRE AND TEARS SERIES

Brightarrow Burning
Darkness Singed
Dawn Ignited

Fire and Tears: Series Collection Books 1-3

FIRE AND TEARS

SERIES COLLECTION BOOKS 1-3

ISABO KELLY

T&D PUBLISHING

FIRE AND TEARS

CONTENTS

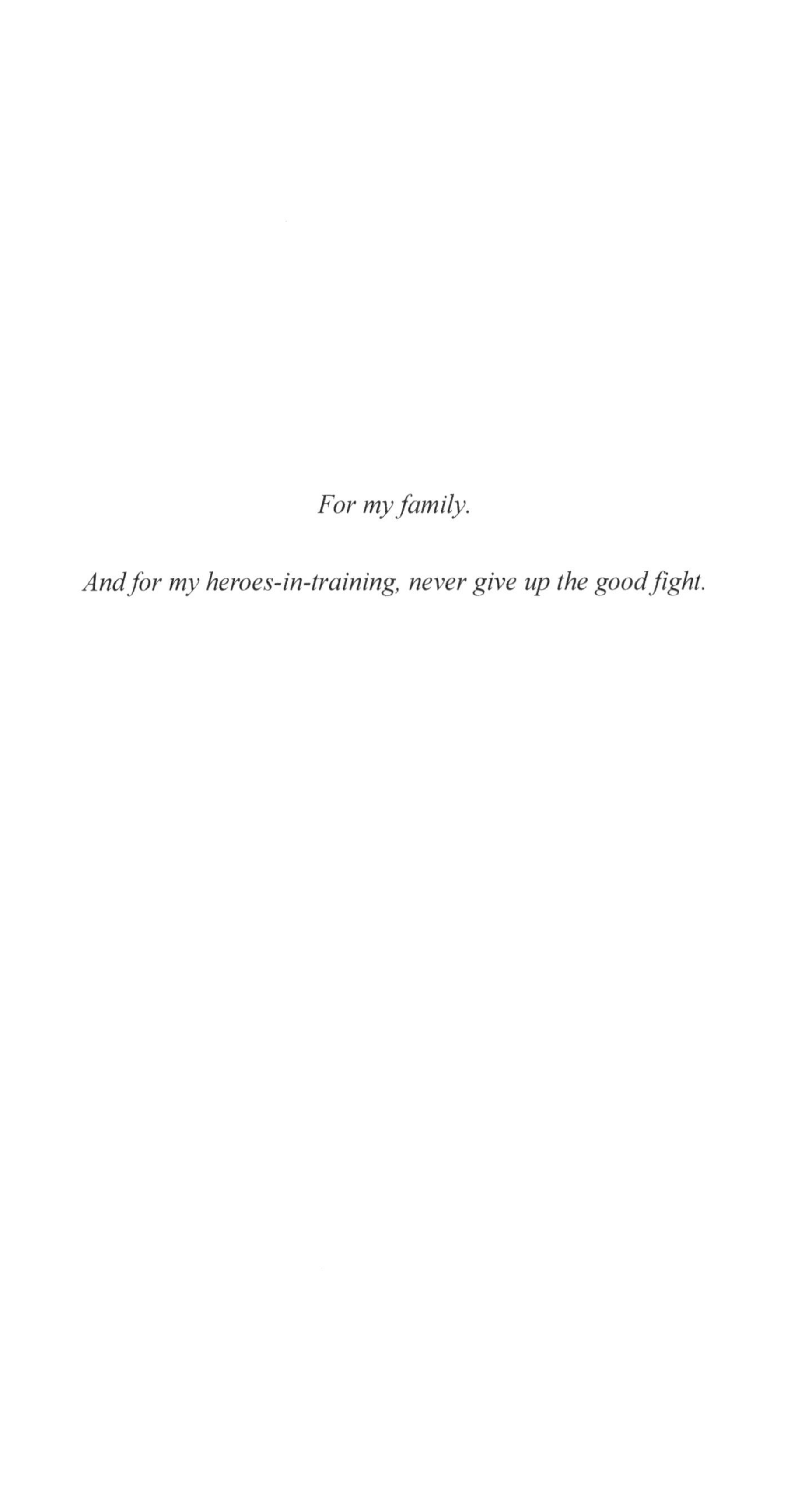

For my family.

And for my heroes-in-training, never give up the good fight.

BRIGHTARROW BURNING

ISABO KELLY

BRIGHTARROW BURNING

FIRE AND TEARS BOOK ONE

THEIR WORLD AT WAR

Layla Brightarrow's world fell apart the day the Sorcerers invaded her city. Abandoned by the neighboring elven kingdom, Layla must forsake all hope for the man she loves, a powerful elf lord now forever beyond her reach. But when some of the elves break the neutrality to side with the Sorcerers, Layla is sent to assassinate one of the traitors. Her mission forces her to confront the very man she never thought she'd see again—and face a desire she thought long buried.

Ulric of Glengowyn is determined to protect Layla from his traitorous brother, and he'll do whatever is necessary to keep her alive, including using her feelings against her. But his game of seduction cuts both ways, endangering both their lives. To save her, Ulric must convince Layla to trust him, an impossible feat when her mission is to kill his brother.

For Layla, Ulric is a temptation she can't resist, and a risk she doesn't dare take. Years of denial and betrayal hang between them, leaving Layla caught between duty and a love that could be her destruction. Or her salvation.

CHAPTER ONE

"J knew I'd find you here."

Layla Brightarrow flicked a glance over her shoulder, then returned her stare to the labyrinth of cobbled streets below. "What do you want, Ulric?"

"I'd like to know when you're going to stop trying to kill my brother."

"When he stops luring, capturing and selling my people." She felt Ulric move up close behind her but refused to flinch. Her every sense, however, focused on his presence, his movements, his breathing. Her muscles instinctively tensed, preparing for action, but she forced her body to relax.

"You know I don't condone what he's doing..." Ulric murmured.

"So you've said."

"But this is dangerous. For you."

She snorted, still refusing to face him. Ulric of Glengowyn was beautiful, sexy, and the man she'd been in love with since she was old enough to understand what those strange feelings in her gut meant whenever she looked at him. He was also an elf, and while he wasn't exactly an enemy now, he wasn't an ally either.

"Go away, Ulric."

"No."

"If you're so concerned about your brother—"

"I could care less about that traitor, and you know it."

She turned her head just enough to glance at him from the corner of her eye. "Do I?"

"Don't play games, Layla. You know I don't support the traitors."

She made a vague noise in the back of her throat to keep from giving him a direct reply and looked out over the cityscape again. From her perch atop the abandoned tannery, she could see several blocks into the Sorcerers' territory.

She tried to ignore the part of her heart whispering she could trust Ulric. The truth was, she couldn't be certain if he sided with Althir or not. They were brothers, after all. And when Althir, along with a number of other elves, broke Glengowyn's neutrality to side with the Sorcerers, he forced her to guard herself against Ulric's motives as well.

"Why are you here?" she asked on a sigh. "If you don't care if I kill him, leave me be."

Hard hands clamped onto her shoulders, and Layla found herself facing a very angry-looking Ulric. Her breath caught at the sight of him, as it always did. His dark hair silky and straight against his angular, pale face. She could just see the points of his ears poking out from his hair. His body was broad and well-muscled, bigger than the average elf, and so perfectly formed he'd been the fuel for her fantasies for years, even when she'd taken other men to her bed in an attempt to forget him. But in that moment, with the heat of his breath against her face, his eyes captured her completely. Dark blue and as sharp as lightning.

"How many times do I have to tell you this, Layla? I care if you get killed."

His hands tightened almost painfully for a moment, then loosened. For the sake of self-preservation, she took a step away from him. "I'll be fine."

"He almost killed you once already." Pushing the strands of her bangs aside, he fingered the jagged scar on her forehead.

She knew it was still an ugly red welt against her pale skin, adding to the many imperfections of her face, and she hated having him look at it. She jerked her chin to one side, dislodging his touch, then brushed her short hair forward again to cover the mark.

His jaw tightened and his voice deepened. "I don't want him to succeed next time."

"He won't. I know what to expect now."

"Do you?"

His mocking tone brought out her anger, which was so much better than her uncertainty and self-consciousness that she embraced it fully. "I learn from my mistakes, Ulric. I will kill Althir this time."

"But not tonight."

"Why?"

"Because he changed his plans."

She narrowed her gaze and studied him closely. "Why?"

"One of the Sorcerers summoned him and he couldn't refuse."

"How do you know?" But she'd already guessed. "You're still in touch with him. You still talk."

"He's my brother."

He glanced away, not meeting her gaze, and Layla's instincts leapt. She hadn't trusted him before, but now…

All the other elves had broken ties with the traitors, even if they were family members. Yet Ulric hadn't. He claimed he didn't care if she killed Althir, but he still spoke with him often enough to know his plans had changed? Why would he do that if he so disapproved of what his brother was doing? The only thing she could think was that he was helping Althir.

She clenched her teeth in an attempt to hold in the fury brought on by that possibility. Even if he wasn't directly helping his brother, Ulric was still in contact with one of the elves responsible for hundreds of human enslavements and deaths. That reality was betrayal enough.

"Leave, Ulric," she said, struggling with her disappointment. "Before I kill you, too."

He laughed, the sound so unexpected Layla actually jumped. She cursed herself for her idiotic behavior. Worse still was her body's reaction to his laugh. Her thighs clenched, her heartbeat sped, and her nipples tightened. Despite her distrust, despite everything, she wanted him so badly it hurt.

"You won't kill me," he murmured and closed the distance between them again.

"Don't be so sure. You've betrayed us—"

"I have not!" He gripped the back of her neck hard, bringing her face close to his. "Is that what you think? That I'm working with Althir against the Sinnale?"

"What am I supposed to think when you're still talking to him?"

"I do that for you."

She sucked in a breath. "That makes no sense."

"It does if you'd just believe that I don't want you to die. If I know what he's doing, where he's going, I can keep you safe."

"It's not your place to keep me safe. The elves chose their neutrality when the war began. You agreed with that position. You took your weapons and left us to our fate." Elven weaponry was their only defense against the Sorcerers. But after the invasion, Glengowyn broke off all trade with Sinnale, including those vital weapons. "Why would you care if I lived or died now?"

His voice dropped to a whisper. "I've always cared."

The grip on her neck softened, coaxed, drawing her closer so only a breath of space separated their bodies. Feeling the heat pumping from his skin, through his tunic and her heavier shirt and cloak, left her momentarily helpless. The air was damp, threatening rain, and she was cold after spending so much time on this rooftop waiting for Althir to appear. Ulric's heat drew her more surely than any fire. His fingers stroked lightly where her now short hair met her neck, and Layla shivered.

She didn't trust him and yet she found resisting him one of the hardest things she'd ever done. More difficult even than her first kill.

"I hate that you cut your hair," he said, his gaze traveling over her face. "You're still beautiful. But I adored your long hair."

"Long hair is a hindrance during war. And I know full well I'm not beautiful."

Just weeks after she'd nearly killed his brother, and almost died in the process, Ulric started to show up everywhere she went in Noman's Land, following her and trying without any subtlety at all to get her into bed. After years of treating her as no more than a friend, the daughter of merchants he regularly sold elf-weapons to, suddenly he was plying her with compliments, touching her, teasing her. As much as his continued communication with his brother, his attempts to seduce her roused her suspicions and heightened her distrust.

"You never believe me," he said, shaking his head. But his tone was teasing now, as if scolding a naughty child.

"Why do you keep the scar hidden?" he asked.

She glanced away. "It's ugly." It wasn't the only ugly thing about her. But it was the one thing she could cover. The gap between her two front teeth could only be hidden if she kept her mouth closed and she was too outspoken for that. Her nose was too sharp, her face too long, her eyes too far apart. Her skin was splotchy and her figure much too thin. Two years of war had taken their toll on a body and face never perfect enough to compete with the beauty of the elves anyway.

Now she had a scar to add to her imperfections. Yet another reason she didn't believe Ulric could really want her.

He brushed her hair aside again, catching her hand when she reached up to stop him. "It's a mark of your courage," he murmured. "You shouldn't be ashamed."

"Easy for you to say." How could he understand? He was a warrior without a single scar, not one imperfection, though she knew from her father that Ulric had fought in at least two wars during his long life. He was battle-hardened and yet still looked magnificently flawless.

"No. I hate that you have this."

He ran his finger over the rough skin and Layla trembled in response. The slight contact sent heat radiating throughout her body. She started to lean into him, catching herself only at the last minute.

"It reminds me you were nearly killed. Every time I see it…" He paused and swallowed visibly. Layla raised her brows. He sounded and looked so sincere.

"But you shouldn't be ashamed of the mark." His voice dropped to a whisper. "And I need the reminder."

She frowned. "Why?"

He used the hand he still held to tug her a step closer. With only a couple of inches of air between them, his scent overwhelmed her. She'd always liked the way Ulric smelled. She used to make excuses to be near him when he came to negotiate with her parents and later her, just so she could revel in that scent. But now, there was a heady intensity that blocked the harsher smells of Noman's Land—the rubbish, the sewage, the ash of burnt fires and other things she tried not to think about, the hint of magic that was as impossible to describe as the scent of a baby's head but just as distinct, though much less pleasant.

With Ulric standing so near, with his eyes staring directly into hers and his hand gripping her, warm and strong, all those other things faded under the spicy, subtle aroma of him.

"You aren't answering my question," she managed to say, but her throat was tight.

"I've forgotten what you asked."

She was pretty sure that was a lie. He couldn't possibly be as overwhelmed by her nearness as she was by his. But for the life of her, she couldn't see the lie in his expression.

She tried, gods help her, she tried to tug her hand free of his. She needed to step back, to put some distance between them. Instead, she leaned ever so slightly forward and her gaze dropped to his lips. A mouth she'd studied more often than she cared to admit.

"Please come away with me," he whispered.

The *please* almost had her. He'd never sounded so sincere, or vulnerable. Or quite so desperate.

But a very small and quiet part of her whispered, *He's still in touch with his brother. And you are trying to kill Althir.*

She eased back, using every ounce of strength she'd honed in the last two years. "I have a job to do tonight."

"Not tonight. Damn it, Layla, he's not going to be here."

She cocked her head to one side, studying him. Seduction had been replaced by anger—but there was still that edge of desperation. "Then I'll go looking for another elf."

She took another step away. When her back touched the parapet, she reached out and gripped the wood of her bow from where it rested always within easy reach. She held the weapon as a type of talisman against the draw she felt toward Ulric.

"Are you determined to get yourself killed?" he hissed. "Do you really want to die?"

"No. But I don't want my people to die either. The traitor elves are helping that happen. I intend to stop them."

He shook his head, his hair whipping around his face as his hands clenched into fists. "If I could kill them all myself, I would," he spit out. "This is too much."

"But you can't kill them. Any more than any other elf can. That's why I'm here."

"I know my king and queen have come to an arrangement with the human council. Your fresh quiver of elf arrows is more than enough proof."

She already knew he'd guessed his government was now working with hers, despite their initial call of neutrality. But they'd never discussed the situation. She had no idea how he felt about the deal.

"Do you disapprove?" Now that they were talking about the previously unspoken subject, she couldn't stop from asking, though she warned herself he might well lie. He was here trying to seduce her to keep her from killing his brother.

"I approve," he said without hesitation. "I never thought we should remain neutral. What's to stop the Sorcerers from turning their attention to Glengowyn once Sinnale falls?"

"Your weapons. Your magic."

He scowled at her matter-of-fact tone. "Only for so long. With the strength gained by conquering Sinnale, the Sorcerers would be formidable enemies."

"Then why did your people choose neutrality?"

"They believed in the strength of their magic and weaponry."

She turned away to look out over the battered buildings surrounding them. "And the defection of some of their own people changed this belief?"

"It brought us into the war."

"Yet the king and queen are keeping their cooperation with our council secret."

"There are still those in Glengowyn who want to remain neutral—most of the elves wish to remain that way. They've…disowned the traitors. It's a handy way of disavowing any part in their duplicity."

She sucked in a deep breath as she listened. The air was sharp and humid in her mouth, tasting faintly of ash and mist. "So most of the elves would still leave us humans to die." He was silent for long enough she knew she'd hit a soft spot.

"I'm not one of them, Layla," he murmured. "I believe we should be involved."

"But on which side?"

His hands clamped down on her shoulders and she was whipped around so fast her feet twisted beneath her, costing her balance. He brought her up flush against his body before she could regain her footing.

"How can you ask me that? I'm betraying my own brother to protect you."

The feel of his hard muscles pressed against the length of her body made her stomach tighten. Blood pumped faster through her veins. Swallowing to rewet her throat, she opened her mouth to speak, closed it, swallowed again, then forced a few words out. "You expect me to trust you?"

"Yes," he hissed.

"Yet you still talk to Althir."

He brought his face closer, his breath brushing hot against her mouth. Her lips parted without her permission and need welled up to flow through her. His scent was impossible to ignore now. Something about it called to her, and she found it harder to resist the longer they stood this close.

"I talk to my brother to keep you safe."

"And that's the part that makes no sense," she said, her voice low and harsh from a lust she could barely control. "Why would you work so hard to protect *me*?"

"Because I care about you, damn it."

Her head spun as tension tightened in her gut. She blinked to force back the dizziness. "But only after I nearly killed Althir," she pointed out, as much a reminder to herself as to him. "Before that, you weren't here keeping me safe."

"I was forbidden by my king and queen."

She frowned, trying to see the lies around the haze of want fuzzing her brain.

His voice softened. "I tried to leave Glengowyn. To help you. King Varim forbade it. Until the other elves defected, I was stuck by their ruling."

His grip relaxed and he cupped her face in his palms. A shiver raced along her arms and up the back of her neck. *Step back*, she thought. *Get away while you can.* Instead, she dipped a breath closer. She barely felt in control of her body. So easy to just let go, to allow him to seduce her, to give in to what she'd wanted for more years than she could bear to think about.

"Layla." His voice dropped an octave. "They had to physically keep me away."

She shook her head and shifted her gaze from his, though his hands stayed in place. She couldn't bring herself to dislodge his hold. "No. That's...that's wrong. You never... Not before. I can't..." Why wasn't her brain working? Now she couldn't form a coherent sentence? She faced him again, intent on arguing, but as soon as her gaze met his, all the words evaporated.

Her pulse sped, and as she watched, his pupils dilated, nearly overtaking the blue of his eyes.

Suddenly she understood. Elf-fire. The pheromone that elves exuded whenever they were about to have sex, or at least wanted to very badly. The drug that drew humans to elves and was said to make the sex so amazing, humans often became addicted—which was why the pheromone was also nicknamed elf-tears.

Elf-fire couldn't be faked. It was a physical response, completely out of an elf's control. But they had to actually be attracted to their partner. While elves could have sex without attraction, though they rarely did, they could never pretend to have an elf-fire reaction.

Which meant, whatever else Ulric was after, he wasn't pretending to want her.

As she studied his eyes, watched the black widen more, the reality of the moment pierced her resistance. He was as affected by her as she was by him. She wasn't sure why. She just couldn't imagine what he saw in her to invoke lust. But in that moment, it didn't seem to matter. She'd dreamed about having him for so long. Even if it was just this one night. Even if she couldn't trust his other motives. She could trust his desire. And for a few hours at least, she could give in to her own.

"Elf-fire," she murmured aloud. She raised a hand to his cheek, then trailed her fingers along his neck, watching in satisfaction as he sucked in a breath. His hands tensed on her jaw, edging her closer. "Now do you believe me?"

"I believe you want me."

A low growl escaped as he stepped forward and wrapped his arms around her waist. "It's about damn time.

CHAPTER TWO

Ulric's mouth closed over hers. For a fraction of a second, his kiss was gentle, a silent plea for permission. But before she could suck in a breath or even accept the reality of Ulric's lips on hers, his kiss went from asking to demanding. His hold tightened around her waist, his head tilted to one side, and he kissed her with so much intense urgency, she was reminded of a dying man grasping for the one thing that might keep him alive.

Desperation overwhelmed any remaining sense of self-preservation. Her bow slipped from her fingers and both her hands found purchase on his solid frame. She couldn't have refused him then if the entire army of Sorcerers marched up to that rooftop. Pressing against his hard body only increased her insanity. Gripping at the muscles of his shoulders, the silky lengths of his hair, made her want more. Naked bodies, sweat and pounding flesh. There on the rooftop. Anything, everything he would give her. She wanted it all.

Only the barest remaining shred of sanity kept her from tearing his tunic from his body. "Somewhere else," she moaned against his neck as she tasted the salty tang of his skin. "A bed. I want you on a bed."

"The woods, Glengowyn…"

"No." She rubbed her breasts against his chest and sighed at the feel of his body tensing in reaction. "I have a place. Closer."

"Closer is good. Now would be better."

But closer was good. And closer was a place he couldn't know about, a place she'd never used before but had set up just in case. A safe house she'd never be able to use again after tonight. That didn't matter. The small, simple set of rooms would serve their purpose, giving her a secure haven to indulge for just this one night. And gods help her, she wanted to indulge, to taste and feel and suck and fuck until her body ached. And then she wanted to do more. One night. Just this one night. After, she'd be able to put this long obsession behind her and move on with her mission. Elves rarely slept with human partners more than twice anyway because of the side-effects of elf-fire. This was all she would ever get from him, so it had to be enough for her lifetime.

Nothing else mattered but quenching her need, answering the lust. And tomorrow she would walk away.

Because she'd have no choice.

Even that much reality was quickly overwhelmed by passion when his lips captured hers again. "Where?" he grunted before kissing her, making it impossible to answer.

When she could force her mouth from his long enough to speak, she said, "I'll lead." She tried to pull away, but he jerked her close again and kissed her. As her fingers tangled in his hair, she forgot what they'd been talking about or why she'd thought space between their bodies was necessary.

Then she felt him tug at her quiver strap. "No." She grabbed his hand to prevent him from disarming her here in the open. "Not here." Barely avoiding his next lunge, she snatched up her bow, then dropping it over her head to hang across her back, she spun toward the doorway and the stairs that would take them out of this building into the streets of Noman's Land. Her rooms were only a few blocks away, just outside the edge of Sinnale-held territory.

Tension vibrated from his hand up her arm as they made their way through the dark shadows, avoiding the infrequent pools of light cast by the few remaining working gas lamps. The Sinnale kept the lamps doused in and near Noman's Land. But Layla was comfortable in the dark. She'd traveled these streets frequently enough that even on a moonless night she could maneuver by feel alone through the twisting lanes and alleyways.

Darkness was her friend. And tonight it helped make the situation seem unreal, a dream in which she didn't have to worry about Ulric's true loyalties. In this dream, she could have him without fear or consequence.

The haze of lust filling her head didn't dim as they trotted toward their destination. In fact, it grew stronger with each step. She realized she felt drunk, out of control, loose and giddy all at once. *So this is what elf-fire does.* As the sensations continued to intensify, she thought, *No, this isn't quite like being drunk.* This was better, higher, brighter and more intoxicating than anything a man or elf-made liquor could conjure.

Unable to resist, she turned into Ulric and kissed him, her movement sending them both stumbling into a wall. He didn't stop her. He fell into the kiss, bracing one hand against the brick at her back to hold them both up while his other arm tightened around her waist. She'd barely found her footing again when he lifted her up onto her toes to better align their bodies. His hard cock poked at her lower abdomen, and she clenched in reaction as wetness seeped into the worn material of her undergarments.

"How much farther?" he hissed.

"Not…not far. Two blocks."

"Not close enough."

He ground his hips against hers and she nearly gave in. Against the wall of an abandoned building facing out onto the main street was fine by her. She didn't care if someone saw them. She wanted him inside her, fucking her hard and fast and now. Even the discomfort of her quiver and bow pressing tight into her back barely registered. All she could think about was Ulric.

He was the one who resisted this time. "A bed." He breathed through his teeth. "You deserve a bed."

She nodded, even if she couldn't quite make sense of what he was saying. Then she tugged him back onto the sidewalk, stumbling on weak legs for those last two blocks.

She pushed him into the alley, past piles of stinking garbage which she hardly noticed under the influence of the elf-fire. Or maybe it was just Ulric. When they reached the wooden side door into the building, she broke away from another kiss long enough to pull the key from a hidden pocket in the sleeve of her tunic and shakily insert it. The lock gave without a sound. They slipped into the dark stairwell, their hands reaching for each other again.

In the pitch blackness, Layla led Ulric up the stairs—she'd practiced here and knew the layout by feel. On the fourth floor, she eased open another soundless door, tugged him into a dimly lit hallway and managed to stagger to the fourth door on the left before diving into another kiss.

"Should get inside," she mumbled against his mouth, then immediately prevented his answer by licking her way past his lips to tangle her tongue with his. Only the sound of metal hinges creaking under pressure brought her up for air.

When she glanced behind her, she realized he'd been pushing at the door knob hard enough the wood frame was buckling. "Gods, you're strong," she whispered as a thrill of excitement tightened her stomach. She fumbled open the lock with the same key she'd used downstairs, then nearly fell inside as the solid wood which had been holding her up moved.

Ulric didn't wait for her to recover her footing. Instead, he followed her in, catching her up in his arms and slamming the door closed behind him with his foot. The reverberating bang made her cringe. It was late and the few people squatting in this building would be asleep. But any concern she might have felt was washed away as Ulric's lips covered hers again.

The darkness was lit only by light from the street filtering past a dirty window. They tripped and staggered through the small main room to the rudimentary bedroom. She finally allowed him to remove her quiver and bow, even smiled when he set them gently aside before roughly grabbing her up again. She had thought she'd feel more vulnerable without her weapons, that the spell of lust and need would weaken under her instinct for survival.

Instead, she felt freed. For the first time since the war started, she felt able to relax her guard and simply enjoy the exquisite sensations thrumming over her nerves. She didn't even worry that her survival instincts seemed to have shut down, because Ulric's hands were on her skin, under her tunic, and that made everything right.

Layla's breath caught when she landed on the soft mattress with Ulric's weight on top of her. The feeling was so perfect, so often imagined, that in the dark she could convince herself this was a dream. The strong, rich scent of his skin overpowered the musty, damp smell of the room. The feel of his hot, hard body against hers warmed her in the chilly air. Only then did she realize he'd removed her tunic as well as his own, leaving the thin material of her shift as the sole barrier between them. When had he done that?

"I should be nervous," she whispered as she trailed her fingers up his spine.

"Why?"

"I can't remember."

His grin flashed white in the dimness. "I've wanted this for a long time. But I'll stop if you tell me to."

Her snort of shock and disbelief echoed in the small room. "Right. That's going to happen." Wrapping her hands in his hair, she pulled his face to hers and kissed him again, allowing herself to fully fall into the sensation now that they were ensconced in the security of her safe house and the softness of a bed.

She couldn't taste him enough. Her hands raced over his bare back, testing his muscles, learning his body. She gripped his ass through the soft, pliant leather of his trousers and smiled when he groaned. His mouth moved to her neck, and she gasped. "Take these off." She tugged at his trousers. "I want to see you."

He left her long enough to remove his boots and trousers. When he rejoined her on the bed, her hand went right to his cock. She'd wanted him in her hands, in her mouth for so long she could barely believe this was real. He was hot and hard and pulsing in her palm. Without hesitation, she shoved him onto his back and leaned over his erection, letting her breath caress him. The muscles across his abdomen rippled and clenched. She met his gaze, smiled and licked the very tip of his cock. He hissed in a breath and his hips bucked upward. More than willing to oblige him, she took the full length of him into her mouth. Need and lust drove her to suck him hard and slow, savoring his salty taste.

His moans guided her, and she licked and sucked until she was sure he would come in her mouth. She wanted him too. She wasn't thinking of her own pleasure—she knew he wouldn't leave her wanting. But in that moment, with Ulric completely at her mercy, she wanted him to lose control. Cupping his balls in the palm of her hand, she fondled and squeezed, eliciting more of his groans. Her own body reacted to his pleasure. Wetness seeped down her thigh, reminding her that she still had her trousers on. Her shift was in the way as well, preventing her bare breasts from rubbing against his leg, but the tease of material against her nipples made up for the frustration. As she brought him closer and closer to the edge, she thought she might come too, purely from the pleasure of controlling his body this way.

"Stop," he muttered, reaching down to clench his hands in her hair.

She raised her head only enough to meet his gaze. "No. I want you to come now." And she returned to his cock, sliding her lips over him in a long, firm stroke. His head dropped back against the mattress. The tension in his hands remained but he didn't try to push her away. His hips bucked, flexing up to meet her downward movements. And then she felt his entire body stiffen. A moment later, her mouth was flooded with hot liquid. The sound of his cry echoed in the quiet room. She swallowed and continued to suck gently, drawing out the last of his release as his cock pulsed in her mouth. Finally, when his body relaxed, she gave him one last lick and crawled up the bed beside him.

"Did you enjoy that?" he growled, his voice breathless.

"Oh, very much. Did you?"

"Obviously. But that wasn't exactly the start I'd planned."

"What did you have in mind?"

He rolled her onto her back and stripped off her shift. His gaze fell to her breasts and she arched under the scrutiny.

"Shall I show you?" he said.

"Yes, please." The elf-fire raged through her system, heightening her senses. When his tongue touched only the very tip of her nipple, a sharp shock of pleasure raced through her.

"Oh," she gasped, amazed at the intensity. Then her breath left her as his lips closed over her nipple, sucking her hard into his mouth. Her insides clenched and quivered and she felt very close to coming from the movements of his mouth against one breast. Then his hands joined the effort, massaging and squeezing her other breast, pinching her other nipple until she gasped in near pain. She moaned and held his head closer, wanting more of this treatment.

When his mouth left her breast she wanted to protest, but his lips were moving across her ribcage, down her waist, and that felt so good she nearly screamed. Everywhere he touched felt overly sensitized, her nerves ready to burst. Sounds she never imagined herself making filled the small room as his tongue dipped just beneath the waistband of her trousers to flick the skin between her hipbone and her pelvis. He stripped her boots and trousers off without his mouth leaving her skin. As he pulled her underwear down her legs, his tongue trailed over her inner thigh, and she clenched in reaction.

Then he flicked her clit with his tongue and her body arched up, tension unlike anything she'd ever experienced seizing her muscles, controlling her.

She jerked against his mouth. "Oh gods," she groaned. "This is too much. Was this…was this how you felt?"

"Yes." His breath was hot against her damp curls.

"How could you stand it?"

"See for yourself." And his lips closed over her clit, sucking her hard.

She didn't hold out even a fraction of the time he had. She came instantly, crying out at the burst and pulse of a release that shook her to her core. The orgasm went on for a long time, longer than any other she'd had. Ulric refused to relinquish his hold, forcing even more sensation from her and she thought she might lose her mind as she screamed with her release.

When the tension finally eased, she was panting and trembling.

Ulric released her and moved slightly away. In the cool room air, her nipples peaked and her body quivered, muscles jerking in after-effect. She only realized Ulric had been holding her hips down after he'd let them go. Every inch of her body felt both satiated and still wanting. It was the continuing need that surprised her. How could she possibly want more? How could she take any more?

She glanced down the bed to meet Ulric's stare. His eyes glistened in the dark room, still full of heat and desire. Before she finished catching her breath, he gripped her hips again and flipped her onto her stomach then pulled her up to her hands and knees.

"More," he ground out.

"But…" She'd never known a man who could get erect again this quickly after orgasm. Unless she'd taken longer to come than she realized, but she doubted that.

"Elf-fire," he said, answering her unspoken question. "And I need more of you. Now."

His fingers dipped between her ass cheeks and slipped down to her dripping entrance. She jerked, her body so tender she could barely take his touch.

"More," he said again, and replaced his fingers with his cock. In one hard stroke, he plunged into her.

Layla's back arched, forcing him deeper. She was beyond making any sound now, too overwhelmed by the feel of his thick cock stretching her walls. But the sound of skin slapping against skin filled the room. Each thrust of his hips pounding against her ass made her tighten and clench around him. His fingers bit into her hips and she savored the feeling. Sweat dripped down her cheeks. For the first time since she cut her hair, she was glad to be free of its tangling presence. It would only get in the way when she looked back over her shoulder to watch Ulric fuck her.

He met her gaze and pounded harder. The muscles in his jaw clenched. He was sweating as well, the moisture dripping down the smooth pale muscles of his chest. The sight of him only increased her pleasure. Reaching between her legs, she fingered her clit, adding just enough pressure to push her body the rest of the way to orgasm. In the storm of release, she found her voice again, crying out his name.

A moment later, she found herself on her back and Ulric was inside her again. His hips jerked against her as he pulled her legs up to circle his waist.

"More," he repeated.

With his heated word, another wave of sensation washed through her, firing her blood and making her pulse race. She realized this was the elf-fire at work but was beyond caring. She'd never experienced anything like this and knew she never would again. This was more than just elf-fire. This was Ulric.

She came again, and again. Until she could barely breathe and spots danced before her eyes. She'd never orgasmed like this, didn't even think it was possible. And still he demanded more.

"No, no. I can't. Not again. Please."

"Once more," he insisted. "Come. Now."

And she did, instantly, on his command. Her body was so far beyond her control, so full of pulsing reaction, she only knew he came again because his movements stopped. She looked up to see his face, tense and stiff, his eyes closed tight, his lips pulled back. She'd never found men attractive when they came. But the sight of Ulric's release filled her with awe. And what love she'd felt for him before seemed a pale thing to what she felt now.

He collapsed to the side of her and pulled her tight against him, wrapping her in his arms. She sighed, wondering how long she could remain in this blissful state. Elf-fire still coursed through her system, but the intensity had dimmed. Physical exhaustion slipped in, making her limbs heavy. With a sigh, she rested her head on Ulric's shoulder. There didn't seem to be anything to say. Words were a crude way to communicate after what they'd just shared, and so by some silent, mutual agreement, they remained quiet. His hand slid lazily up and down her arm, raising faint tingles in its wake. She concentrated on that feeling, wondering if her body would allow her to make love again tonight.

Before she had a chance to test her limits, though, her eyes drifted shut and sleep took her.

CHAPTER THREE

ayla came awake suddenly and completely. Out of habit, she listened to her surroundings before showing any signs of being awake. Then she blinked her eyes open and stared up at the dark ceiling. She could feel the heat and weight of Ulric beside her and wanted to roll into him. But reality was setting in, and though daylight hadn't invaded their privacy yet, it was on the way.

She'd made more mistakes in one impetuous moment than she knew how to fix. Why, why had she given in? She could try to blame the elf-fire, and that was definitely a valid excuse, but when she got right down to it, she'd wanted a night like this for years. The fact that she still couldn't trust him only made the moment more bittersweet.

As quietly as she could, she rolled out of bed and gathered up her clothes. When Ulric shifted, she froze, waiting. After he settled, she realized how accustomed she'd grown to holding perfectly still and waiting for a safe moment to move. She hadn't always been this way. In her youth, she'd been full of impatient motion, never settling in one place for long. Ulric had actually started her on the path to controlling that restlessness when he'd taught her how to shoot a bow. Unfortunately, the war had done the rest.

She had to get out of here before he woke up, before the elf-fire caught her in its spell again and she completely forgot herself. She'd allowed him to lead her away from a possible target last night. His brother could still have shown. Ulric might have been lying about Althir's changed plans. She should have remained at her post and waited for her opportunity to kill the traitor she'd been sent to kill.

Pulling up her trousers, she clenched her jaw to hold in a disgusted snort. Instead of doing her job, she'd dragged Ulric to one of her few safe houses inside the relatively deserted section of city between the Sinnale border and the Sorcerers' border. This room was useless to her now, and with the coming day, she regretted that loss. Finding safe places to hide inside Noman's Land was difficult. Both her people and the Sorcerers' minions roamed these streets, each looking for weaknesses in the other's defenses. She'd sacrificed this rare haven for one night of sex.

Worse, she felt as if she'd betrayed her people merely by being with an elf. She had no idea of Ulric's true loyalties. Though she desperately wanted to believe all he'd told her last night. She was so giddy in love with him that if no other lives were at stake, she would hand herself into his keeping, the results be damned. A terrifying truth.

She stuffed her feet into her boots and dropped her quiver and bow over her head, adjusting the quiver strap across her chest. Glancing back toward the bedroom, she swallowed hard. She loved him. Damn it all to the sacred hells, she loved him. She wanted him again, even now. And yet, she knew better.

Or did she? Could she trust him? He'd been trying to convince her for weeks that she could. And the elf-fire was real. He couldn't fake that.

But she couldn't afford to trust him, even if she wanted to. He was still in contact with his brother. There was just no way to be sure he wouldn't hand her and her city over to Althir and the Sorcerers. At least no way she dared risk with so many lives at stake.

Which meant she could never see Ulric again.

She left the safety of the building and slid into the predawn air, keeping close to the shadows out of habit. Turning at every sound, scanning the streets for any signs of minion patrols, she made her way to the nearest Sinnale guard post. From there, she'd go on to the council and hope her mother and father didn't realize she was lying when she explained why she didn't complete her mission. They'd always been honest with each other—she was an only child and her parents doted on her. Keeping secrets from them was going to hurt. Though, she'd been keeping her feelings for Ulric a secret all her life so perhaps this wasn't so unusual.

Thinking about him again made her chest ache, both guilt and longing twisting her emotions into a ragged mess. She would have to avoid Noman's Land for a while. She couldn't risk seeing Ulric again so soon. Time had to pass before the effects of the elf-fire wore off. At the moment, she was even more vulnerable to him than she'd been before the elf-fire.

The sound of booted feet sent a jolt of adrenaline through her system. She melted against a nearby alley wall, tucking as far into the darkness as she could. As she scanned the street, she pulled her bow over her head, then slid an arrow from her quiver. The weapon would do her no good in a close fight. But she could use one well-placed shot to cause a little chaos and gain a few seconds' head start to run away.

The harsh stomp of a marching group neared. Minions. Her

people moved more quietly. The Sorcerers' soldiers were too confident and cocky to hide their whereabouts. There weren't enough elven weapons left in Sinnale to harm them. Or so they thought.

She held her bow in one hand and silently nocked the arrow into place as a group of five minions came into view not two blocks away. They were heading back toward their own territory, swords in scabbards, gazes scanning the streets. Each had the sickly yellow hue to their skin that came from being in thrall to a Sorcerer. Even in the dim light of the approaching sunrise, she could see the dark circles around their sunken eyes and the glitter of red over their irises. They'd been human once, Sinnale citizens. Now they were enemies, so changed by the Sorcerers' magic, they were forever lost to humanity.

As they passed her hiding spot, one turned to gaze into the alley. He paused, falling a step behind the others. Layla remained motionless, her bow lowered but ready to be raised and fired in an instant. She held her breath even though she told herself to breathe. He was so close she could smell the faint scent of decay that clung to all minions.

After an agonizing moment, he moved on.

"You see something?" one said, his voice a wasted, harsh grunt.

"Probably just a rat," the minion who'd looked into her alley said.

"Check?"

"No," a third man, this one at the head of the group, said. "No time. The elves brought four more across the border last night. We're needed at the citadel."

They vanished down another street and Layla heard no more. But what she'd heard was enough. Sickness welled in her throat. Four more of her people, lured by elvish glamour and magic, taken by the traitor elves. And she'd spent the night fucking an elf.

When she was sure her way was clear, she hurried on to the relative safety of her border. Disgust swirled through her. Because even now, even with the guilt clogging her throat, if Ulric caught her, she'd go with him. Her only hope was to avoid him, to never see him again. The problem was, if he wanted to find her, he would. And she knew she was no longer strong enough to resist him.

CHAPTER FOUR

*L*ayla managed to avoid Ulric for nearly a week. She stayed out of Noman's Land, using the excuse that she wanted to help her parents and the council improve border security. But she could avoid her real responsibilities for only so long. Inevitably, the council sent her back to the edge of the Sorcerers' territory, back to hunt the traitor elves.

At least she wasn't after Ulric's brother this time. That was something.

She stood on yet another rooftop, behind yet another parapet, in the blackness of Noman's Land, watching the well-lit streets of the captured section of the city. Her lip curled. The Sorcerers didn't bother to hide in the dark, the way her people had to. Their border was protected by sporadic and impossible-to-detect spells. Every time Sinnale spies infiltrated their territory, they risked triggering one of those spells. And even if they didn't, getting caught in enemy territory meant a death sentence. Humans had no real ability to kill the Sorcerers either—not without the needed elven weapons which were so scarce now as to no longer be a threat. So of course they didn't bother skulking around in the dark. They were winning the war.

At great expense to the spies who'd gained the information—four had been captured and were presumed dead—she knew that three of the traitor elves would be traveling close to Noman's Land escorted by a single Sorcerer. She was good with her bow. Even before the war, she'd practiced enough to become an expert archer so she could help her parents in their weapons negotiations with Ulric and the other elf traders. She could fire three arrows before the Sorcerer could find her. Killing all three elves was unlikely, but she would kill at least one. Maybe even two.

Chances were good she'd be injured too. Even killed. The Sorcerer *would* pinpoint her location before she could avoid his attack. But it would be worth it to take out at least one of the elves. And if she was killed…well, that was penance for giving in to Ulric and endangering her people.

She took a deep breath and calmed her nerves. She didn't want to die. But from the moment the Sorcerers had arrived, she knew it could happen any time. And if she was killed, she wanted it to be during the execution of a worthy mission for her people.

She stared at the brightly lit street, keeping well to the shadows. She had her bow in hand but hadn't pulled an arrow yet. The time was drawing near.

Even as her body took on the stillness of a statue, she heard the sound of the approaching carriage. It rolled around a corner, clattering against the cobblestones, the horses' hooves clicking loudly in the still night air. The window shades were pulled tight. The Sorcerer and the three elves were inside. She was certain of that, even if she couldn't see them.

She raised a small palm-sized mirror and signaled the team ahead of the carriage, the group that would cause a distraction so she could attempt the assassinations.

The Sorcerer would know what they were trying to do, but he wouldn't be able to find her until it was too late. Thanks to the elf king and the charm that hung around her neck, she would remain hidden to magical senses until she released her first arrow.

A section of building ahead of the carriage exploded, throwing debris and rubble into its path. The horses squealed in protest and reared back. The coachman had them back under control quickly—he was a human slave, she noticed—but their path was blocked, and the narrow road didn't allow them to turn the carriage easily to take another route.

As anticipated, the Sorcerer immediately stepped from the carriage and signaled those inside to remain. He closed the door, but the moment's exposure was enough. She knew the elves' positions inside the carriage. Her arrows would slice easily through the shades, slowing fractionally, but not enough to keep from being deadly.

She watched the Sorcerer scan the rooftops. She remained in shadow as she pulled out her first arrow. Those years of practice ensured she could fire each quickly and accurately. She steadied the first against her bow and drew the string back.

The Sorcerer would have put a protective spell on the carriage, but it was no good against elf arrows.

She sighted, aiming for the point at which she was certain one of the traitor elves sat, and fired. She pulled the next arrow, nocked it and fired again, then a third time, so quickly the first arrow had only just sliced through the shade when the final arrow left her bow.

An instant later, the parapet not four feet from her exploded in a molten blast of magic flame.

She dove for cover, away from the first shot, but obviously the Sorcerer had anticipated that because the wall two feet in front of her also exploded.

Crawling as quickly as she could, she made her way to the

opposite side of the rooftop. The building shook beneath her, forcing her to her stomach. She glanced back and realized the area where she'd stood had turned into a blazing, melting tumult.

And the building was going to collapse out from under her before she could reach safety.

With a renewed sense of desperation, she scrambled toward the still solid end of the roof. If she could just make the next building, she could escape.

The sides of the building started to melt, blocking the easiest exits. Amidst the stench of sulfur and the air-stealing heat, she scrambled to the only safe edge. But that side of the building was farther away from its closest neighbor. Escape was a long jump and she'd have to get a running start to make it.

Unfortunately, she was quickly losing room to make that needed run.

She stood, despite the fact that it exposed her to the still-falling rain of magic fire, and started to sprint. The wood floor beneath her was quickly melting away. She slipped, slamming onto her hands and knees, as the building shuddered again.

Too late, she thought, even as she scrambled back to her feet and dove for the edge of the roof. She couldn't make the leap now. It was too far. She looked down frantically for a railing she might drop to, but this side of the building was smooth brick, not even a window ledge to aim for. Behind her, the fire roared, sucking oxygen from her lungs and coating her in sweat.

She cried out in frustration and fear. A slow death by fire was too horrific to contemplate. There was no smoke to choke her first, to send her into unconsciousness before the fire caught her. No, the Sorcerer made sure she would burn, horribly and fully conscious. Her only consolation was the building would probably collapse quickly and she would die in the fall.

She looked at the rapidly approaching lava-like roll of fire and heat. She could jump, take her death into her own hands. Would slamming into the cobbles below be easier than flame? Probably not. But it might be quicker.

Still, she hesitated. It wasn't in her nature to commit suicide, despite the job she did for the war effort.

Her brain and body balked at taking that last leap.

She watched the melting roof drip away, watched the last few yards of safety evaporate.

And then she heard something over the roar of magic flames, the sound of her name. She looked to the neighboring rooftop, thinking it was one of the other team members. The sight of Ulric, magnificent in his rage as he signaled to her, took her breath away. She looked down and realized he'd pushed a plank across the gap between buildings.

She didn't hesitate. The flames were too close. She crawled onto the thick wood and scrambled toward safety. When the building behind her shook, her precarious hold teetered. She clung to the wood, her eyes closed for an instant. Then she pushed back to her knees and crawled as fast as she could.

Ulric swept her off the plank and into his arms just as the other end started to burn. He pushed away the part he'd been bracing, letting it topple in a fiery line to the cobbles. Then he wrapped her close and gave her a quick, fierce hug. She barely had time to register the hug before he was pulling her across the rooftop to yet another building. This time, the jump was easy, only a foot of space to leap. From there, he led her down an external stairway and into the dark streets. Her night vision shot from the fire, Layla clenched Ulric's hand and fought to keep her feet under her as she ran blindly behind him through the alleyways.

When they finally stopped, she could barely draw a breath. She bent over and worked to get oxygen into her straining lungs. She could still taste the sulfur in the back of her mouth.

When her breathing finally started to return to normal, the reality of being alive sank in. She glanced up to see Ulric standing over her, breathing normally, his face a stone mask of anger as he glared.

She met his gaze, then threw herself into his arms, hugging him tight. She was sure it was the adrenaline, the near-death experience, but she wanted nothing in that moment so much as to hold him. She wasn't even sure how to thank him for her rescue. She'd have to figure that out later. Now, she needed the solid reality of his body against hers, a confirmation of her survival.

His arms locked around her, keeping her close. And then his mouth found hers. She didn't resist, didn't question. All her self-talk about never seeing him again, never allowing him to seduce her, went out the window in that minute. It didn't matter if he was working with his brother or not. He'd just saved her life. After a week of her avoiding him, he'd still found her and helped her. And she'd never wanted a man more in her life.

Their kiss was fierce and hungry. His lips hard against hers, almost bruising, fired her need. She devoured him, soaked him up, melted into him. And it still wasn't enough.

She felt the rise of the elf-fire, felt it intensify a desire that was already overwhelming. She ripped her mouth from his and cried out at the sensation. Her alert nerves screamed. A part of her wanted to push away. This was too much, too strong. She needed to calm down a little first so she could handle the power of the pheromone's effect.

But Ulric wouldn't let her. He ran his lips over her throat, more gently, but the feel was a line of ice and fire, making her insides shake.

"Please," she panted out, "I…I can't…it's too much."

But he didn't stop. His hand cupped her breast through her

tunic, kneading her firmly. His touch was solid and gentle at the same time, as if he was trying to control the excess of sensation.

"I have to…" he muttered against her neck. "I can't let you go."

She moaned, unable to stop herself. His words were more delectable than any of the physical feelings. Her reaction seemed to intensify his hunger, though, because his gentle touch turned rough again, desperation in his groan.

"Layla." His mouth descended on hers.

Her body shook against the need. Too much. And not enough. The sense of being overwhelmed, the almost painful brush against her sensitive nerves, became welcome. Needed. She felt him everywhere. His hand moving along her spine made her arch. He squeezed her ass with his other hand and she rubbed against his erection, desperation riding her hard. She needed relief and she wasn't sure where to turn. To get away. To get closer.

Ulric took the debate out of her hands. He worked the lacings of her trousers loose and pushed the soft leather down her hips until they pooled around her ankles. Her feet were trapped, but that didn't stop him. He lifted her and she braced her thighs against his hips even as her feet stayed linked near his knees. She glanced down to see he'd already freed his erection from the confines of his own trousers and the sight of his straining cock made her overheated blood erupt.

Holding her around the waist with one hand, he moved her hips forward, positioning her so his tip nudged her opening. Liquid seeped down her thighs. The feel of him was a tease that only heightened her passion. She had a moment to be impressed by his strength—he held her entire weight without bracing against anything—then he pulled her hips down, ramming into her. And Layla screamed. He felt so good and thick and so damned right.

She let him take control of the rhythm because she could barely focus beyond the friction of his cock pumping into her and the bump of her swollen clit against him. Her orgasm rose quickly, painfully, and her body started to move of its own accord to reach that exquisite peak. With her shins braced against the tops of his knees, she had enough leverage to follow his movements and meet him stroke for pounding stroke.

He murmured her name against her neck, the warmth of his breath washing another wave of heat over her skin. And when his hands tightened on her waist and ass, her body finally broke. She came with another scream, a sound Ulric swallowed in a kiss. A moment later, she tasted his own groan as his every muscle stiffened. She clenched at his shoulders, holding him until she felt him relax again. Then she pulled back from their kiss to look him in the eyes.

What she saw there devastated her. Tenderness and fear all swirling together with a look of wonder. Did she look that way? She felt those same emotions. Could he see it in her eyes too? Did he know she loved him?

And was she just seeing what she wanted to see?

As she held his gaze, she knew she wasn't imagining the tenderness in his look.

"You came for me," she murmured, still amazed by that fact. "You saved me."

He didn't speak at first, just stared at her. Then he raised a hand to touch her cheek. He ran a finger along her face and up to the scar on her forehead, tracing the bump. "That's twice now you've nearly died.

I don't think my heart can take a third."

His words warmed her more than his body heat. "Thank you."

He touched her cheek again. Then loosened his hold so that her feet eased to the ground. "Come on, we need to get somewhere safe." He patted her bare butt once before letting her go. "We have some things to discuss."

CHAPTER FIVE

*L*ayla didn't want to talk. She didn't want the moment to end. But as she pulled her clothing back into place, she knew she owed him this conversation. If for no other reason than that he'd saved her life.

As he led the way through Noman's Land, though, a part of her started to doubt his motives again. He could have saved her life merely to earn her trust. Even after their last night together, he must know she still didn't trust him fully. Perhaps he'd come to her rescue to gain her confidence, to encourage her to give away valuable information.

She swallowed hard as he opened the front door to a relatively intact building. It had once been a travelers' hotel, with a popular commons for locals and travelers alike. She followed, despite her instinct to stick to places she knew were safe. If he wanted her dead, he wouldn't have saved her. He could still be turning her over to the Sorcerers. But at the moment, she was willing to take the risk.

She didn't want to believe Ulric would save her life only to hand her over to the enemy. She didn't want to have these suspicious thoughts. She wanted to trust him, to love him freely. But she couldn't stop the wary voice whispering in her mind that all Ulric's actions were part of a more nefarious plan.

The idea hurt now more than ever before. And if he did end up betraying her, she thought she probably deserved it.

He took her to a small room on the second floor, one of the guest rooms. There was a ceramic heater in one corner, a wash basin and pitcher in another, and a large bed filling most of the room.

He walked directly to the single window while she closed the door behind them. The lock was still in place so she flicked it closed. At least this way, if someone tried to enter through the door, she'd hear them coming. After studying the street below, Ulric pulled the thick curtains across the windows and turned to the ceramic heater.

He pulled out a flint and steel from behind the heater and she raised a brow. "Most of the basics have been looted. Anything that could be used for heat and starting fires was taken over a year ago."

Without comment, he opened the door in the side of the heater and proceeded to light the pile of wood and tinder inside, monitoring it until a steady flame burned. Then he closed the door and faced her.

She narrowed her eyes and studied the room more closely. The bed was made, the sheets looked fresh, though it was hard to tell in the dark. As she stared at the mattress, a subtle light rose in the room. She glanced back at Ulric to see a small ball of white light floating above his left shoulder. An elf trick she'd always envied.

"You aren't worried about anyone seeing that light?" she asked as she walked to the washbasin. The pitcher was filled with clean water, and fresh towels were folded on the lower shelf of the basin stand.

"You planned this," she stated as she turned to face him. He still stood silently by the heater. Since he hadn't answered her question yet, she met his gaze and waited, refusing to speak until he explained.

"The curtains are thick enough to hide this small amount of light," he finally said. "And I've kept this room ready and safe for the past week. I wanted us to have somewhere comfortable to talk. I assumed after you left without explanation that your safe rooms wouldn't be an option."

"There aren't any chairs," she commented. "If all you wanted to do was talk, shouldn't there be something to sit on besides the bed?"

A smile broke through his serious expression, the first smile he'd given her all night. "I never said all I wanted to do was talk. But we do have some things to discuss first."

"First? You're assuming a lot."

"I think I have the right to those assumptions after what just happened."

"You saving my life or you fucking me in an alley?"

"Both. And the fucking was mutual. Now would you like something to drink?"

He gestured to a table by the bed and the bottle of wine. She nodded, wondering if he might actually drug her, then hating herself for the thought.

He poured two cups, took a drink from one, then handed that one to her with a mocking expression. The fact that he read her so well was humiliating. She took the ceramic cup begrudgingly and gulped the deep red wine. It was sweeter than she'd anticipated and went down very easily. Given the events of the night, her near death, the run through the streets and the passionate sex, she realized she was parched. She finished off the cup and held it out for a refill.

Ulric chuckled and poured. "Trying to get drunk?" he asked. "That won't save you from my questions."

"Just thirsty," she muttered before taking another slower sip.

"Of course. Understandable." He took a drink from the second cup, then motioned to the bed. "Make yourself comfortable. I'll stand." His smile turned self-mocking. "And keep my distance so the *Shaerta*, the elf-fire, remains at bay for the time being."

"That would be good."

She climbed onto the bed and settled against the headboard, staying on the side farthest from the door, closest to the window. Just in case.

Then she waited. He was the one who wanted to talk. He was the one who would have to start. She'd as soon finish her wine and slink off somewhere to sleep. Inside, she snorted at her own lie. She didn't want to go anywhere. She wanted Ulric on the bed with her, she wanted to lose her mind again to the passion and the elf-fire. She didn't want to think about their situation or the war or anything else that reminded her a real world existed outside this room. She most certainly didn't want to keep thinking about the ways he might even now be betraying her.

Finally, he leaned against a wall and folded his arms over his chest, cradling his cup of wine in one hand. "Why did you leave without saying anything?"

He didn't have to clarify. She couldn't pretend not to know what he was talking about. She started to tell a convenient lie, then thought better of it. He would know and he wouldn't let her off with anything but the truth. "I didn't want to talk to you. I didn't know what to say."

"You regretted that night?"

"Of course."

His brows lowered and his eyes narrowed. "Why 'of course'?"

"I gave in to the elf-fire. It was chemistry, hormones. I wouldn't have done that otherwise."

"Because you don't want me? You can't tell me that."

"You know I want you. I've wanted you for years."

Now his eyebrows rose. "Years?"

"Don't pretend you didn't know."

He tilted his head and his arms relaxed. "I didn't, actually. You never seemed…affected by me."

She laughed, a harsh sound even to her own ears. "I was always *affected* by you. Maybe because you never saw me any other way, you didn't know the difference."

"But I saw you with others, other elves, other human men."

"If you didn't notice, it was because you didn't want to, then. I'm not that good at hiding my feelings. At least I wasn't."

He glanced at the heater and took a sip from his cup. "Maybe I didn't want to notice," he murmured, very quietly. He met her gaze and said louder this time, "Human/elf relationships don't… Well, they aren't common."

"Yes. Your people don't have a very high opinion of mine outside of trade."

"Is that what you think?"

"Isn't it true?"

He shrugged. "Maybe for some. But not all."

"Why then? Why do elves refuse to spend more than a few nights with a human before ending the connection? Because the elf-fire is addictive for humans?"

"That's one of the reasons. Probably the most common."

"And what are the others?"

He held his silence for long enough that she wasn't sure he'd answer. Finally, he pulled in a deep breath and held his arms out in surrender.

"Your lifespans," he said. "They're considerably shorter than ours."

That was true enough. But there was something else, something he wasn't saying. She opened her mouth to ask more, but he cut her off.

"That's not what I came here to discuss. We'll have time to talk about the implications of a human/elf relationship later."

She raised her brows in surprise, but he hurried on.

"What I really want to know is how you could leave without so much as a goodbye?"

"I told you, I was…embarrassed that I'd allowed the elf-fire to overcome my common sense."

"But you just admitted you've wanted me for years. Why resist?"

"Don't be obtuse, Ulric. We're on opposite sides of a war."

"I am not your enemy," he ground out. "I never have been." He pulled away from the wall and started to pace, dropping his nearly full cup onto the bedside table so abruptly some of the wine spilled out.

"I just saved your life and you still don't trust me? What do I have to do? Die for you?"

She turned her head, not wanting to see the hurt he tried to hide with anger. What right did he have to be hurt by her distrust? "You've just admitted you never knew I wanted you, or at the very least you ignored it. Then suddenly, after I nearly kill your brother, you start trying to seduce me. And you expect me to believe you didn't have an ulterior motive for that?"

"You know I want you. The elf-fire doesn't rise otherwise."

"The fact that you want me has nothing to do with the reasons you started trying to seduce me."

"I beg to differ," he said dryly. "I would not have attempted to seduce you if I didn't want you."

"And what made you suddenly decide I was worthy of your attention? When you'd shown no interest over the many years we've known one another? Lust and desire can arise after the fact. But that's not *why* you started to pursue me. Once the war began, I never even saw you until after I started hunting Althir."

"I've explained this to you. On more than one occasion."

"And yet I still doubt your motives. Why do you suppose that is?" She hated herself for what she was saying. She hated that she even remotely believed these suspicions. And she detested that, because of the war, she couldn't trust him. But then, if not for the war, would he ever have seen her as a lover?

"I knew from negotiating with you that you were stubborn. But I never realized how obstinate you could be." He stopped pacing and faced her. "You want the truth? I wanted to seduce you so I could convince you to give up trying to assassinate the traitor elves."

"Exactly. You were trying to save your brother."

"No," he hissed, closing the space between them and dropping his face close to hers. "I was trying to save you. To keep you from getting yourself killed. As you nearly did tonight! I don't want you playing assassin, period. If I had my way, I'd sweep you off to Glengowyn and keep you hidden away and safe until the war was over."

He snatched the cup from her hand and tossed it aside. The ceramic shattered against the stone wall near the window. Then his hands were on her face, holding her gaze. "I don't care if the traitor elves burn in sun-lava for eternity. I don't even give a damn about the war. All I care about, all I've ever cared about is you, Layla."

"But why now?"

"Not just now, damn it. Years. For years you've been there, in my life. And when you were nearly killed, I knew just how much it would hurt to no longer have you there."

His grip gentled, but he didn't release his hold on her cheeks.

Shifting so he was sitting next to her on the bed, he drew her closer. "Layla, don't you understand? How can you be so clever and so daft all at the same time?"

"Daft?" She straightened, offended by the insult.

"I love you, Layla. I love you. How can you not realize that?"

Her bottom lip started to tremble. She bit down hard on the inside of her cheek to stop the emotional tell. "That's not funny, Ulric. And that's not very nice."

"I'm not trying to be funny or nice. And I'm not saying this as part of some convoluted plan to betray you. I love you."

Her whole body started to tremble then. And an actual tear leaked from the corner of her eye, rolling across her cheek. She shook her head. "Elves and humans don't have relationships. You just said the aging and the elf-fire addiction make relationships impossible."

"I didn't say impossible. Nothing is impossible. And what does that have to do with the fact that I love you?"

"You…you can't…"

"Why not?" He kissed her, a soft brush of lips, full of tenderness and question. "Layla, the *Shaerta* is only ever this intense when love is involved."

At his mention of the pheromone, she realized her skin was tingling and her nerves were sparking under its influence. "Really?"

"Without love, the effects are still impressive and addicting for humans. But nothing like what's happening between us." He pulled back to meet her gaze, a strange little smile hovering around his lips. "You've never experienced elf-fire with anyone else, have you?"

She shook her head. "I'm not attractive enough to draw the attention of an elf lover, even a temporary one."

"You're beautiful," he murmured. "Any man, elf or human, would be lucky to have you."

For some reason, in that moment, with his blue-eyed gaze steady on hers, she believed him. She believed everything he said.

"You love me." She heard the wonder in her voice even as another tear dripped over her cheek. "How is that possible?"

He chuckled. "I have no explanations. All I know is it's the truth. I never realized how much I needed you until I almost lost you. And then tonight… I would have gone mad if you'd been killed."

She touched the hand cupping her cheek. "Thank you again. I don't want to die, you know. Especially now." She brushed her lips against his. "But how can this work?"

"We'll figure that out later. Now, I just need you, Layla. Stay with me tonight, here. Don't sneak out in the morning. I want…I need to wake up with you beside me."

"Ulric," she sighed. "This is impossible."

"Do you believe me? Do you believe that I'm not trying to betray you now?"

She swallowed and tried to think past the rising heat of the elf-fire. And she realized with some surprise that she did believe him. She fully and completely believed what he was telling her. He loved her.

The wonder of it must have shown in her expression because he smiled and pulled her close, finally allowing his passion freedom. His kiss was deep and hungry, his tongue eager against hers. She wrapped her arms around his neck and fell back against the mattress, taking him with her.

CHAPTER SIX

His lips were soft as they glided over her cheek, across her jaw and down to her neck. With tiny nibbles on the tender skin, he brought shuddering sighs from her, and she clenched in reaction. The elf-fire was pumping through her, heightening her senses, making his every touch more intense. Yet with his slow, gentle movements, the effects of the pheromone were somehow different. The overwhelming need still rode her, but there was no longer the frantic element, the need to devour him instantly. Instead, every nerve screamed for the slow, deliciously thorough torment he was inflicting. She didn't want fast or frantic. She wanted, no she *needed*, this slow burning ache.

"Do you feel it?" she murmured as his mouth traveled to the edge of her collar.

He nudged aside the top of her tunic and ran his tongue across her collarbone. The move made her gasp and dig her fingers into his hair.

"Yes," he murmured. "Still intense, but…"

"But…" She didn't have the words any more than he did. She

only knew this time, the elf-fire was driving them to a different pace.

"I've heard of this. But never experienced it."

His whispered words heated her damp skin, raising chill bumps, and her muscles clenched again as wetness seeped between her legs. "What's different? Why...? Why is it affecting us like this? Because we made love earlier?"

"Because we're in love," he murmured.

She raised her head and met his gaze. "You know?"

"I do now."

"You were telling me the truth. You do love me."

"Yes. And you love me."

"I always have."

"I'm very glad to hear it."

She smiled. "Love really does make a difference?"

He nodded even as his fingers went to work unlacing her tunic. "Which is another of the reasons elves avoid relationships with humans."

"I don't understand. Why is this time different from the other times we've made love?" She shivered as he parted the material, exposing her breasts to the warm air. His gaze dropped and so did his mouth, taking one peaked nipple between his teeth. She gasped as the shock and pleasure of it tore through her.

He lifted his mouth to say, "Maybe because we've declared it? I don't know. I've never been in love before." His lips returned to her nipple, his tongue teasing the hardened tip.

"You've never been in love before?" The idea was enough to override almost all other thoughts.

"We'll talk about it later," he muttered around her skin, then sank against her, suckling hard even as he kneaded her other breast with his clever fingers.

She wanted to argue, but her body took over for her mind. They could talk about this later. Now, she wanted nothing more than to feel, to experience this new level of intensity and to wallow in his devoted attention to her pleasure.

Her skin hummed as his hands moved down to her stomach. The muscles contracted and her core tightened in anticipation. She could barely wait. Despite her earlier orgasm, she felt as if she might explode with just the faintest brush of his fingers.

He unfastened her trousers, more gently this time, and after removing her boots, slid the rough leather down her hips, over her thighs, trailing his fingers across her skin as he stripped her. Her muscles quivered. Her toes actually clenched, all for the anticipation of his touch which continued to sweep slowly and gently across her skin.

He moved up between her legs, gripped her thighs and settled his mouth over her. He flicked her clit ever so softly with the tip of his tongue. Layla arched up off the bed. She lost all track of time at that stage, washed in sensation, each tap of his tongue tightening her muscles. He increased the steady rasp of pressure with her rising tension, taking her toward a peak she could barely fathom. And just when she thought she'd explode, he eased his touch, letting her muscles unclench just a bit before once again driving her higher. Each tease only intensified her desperation, so that when he finally sucked hard and slipped one finger inside her, her orgasm hit with the force of a battering ram. Wave after wave pulsed through her, going on and on. Surpassing even the previous, intense, elf-fire-driven orgasms.

She came down as slowly as she'd reached her peak, blinking her eyes open when she realized they were closed. "Ulric..." she murmured.

He'd eased up her body and was staring into her face. He cupped her cheeks between his palms and slipped into her in one long, steady stroke. His thickness filled her perfectly. There was no other way she could describe it. He felt right, as if he'd been made for her.

Despite their previous encounters, this sensation was completely new. Before, he'd felt wonderful and she'd been relieved to finally have him inside her. Now… Something had changed, and everything was better, richer, more perfect. That shouldn't have been possible. She'd thought each time he'd fucked her had been perfect.

"The elf-fire?" she asked when she saw his eyes widen.

He nodded, eased his hips back and stroked into her.

She arched and sighed. "Why didn't I know this was possible?"

"Because it isn't possible with anyone but me," he whispered in her ear as he slid into her again. "No one else will feel this good to you. No one else will ever be able to satisfy you the way I can. You're mine, Layla. You belong with me."

"Yes." She said the single word so quietly, she wasn't sure he heard her. But she kissed him to show what she couldn't say out loud. She was his. She'd belonged to him for years. And there never had been anyone else for her but him.

He made love to her with his cock as slowly as he had with his mouth, kissing her until she couldn't breathe. She came once, a fast, sudden peak that surprised her. But when the orgasm ended, rather than coming down she continued to tighten toward another. Panting, her hands clenching his shoulders, she pumped her hips against his harder, faster, reaching for more. His breathing sped as he matched her pace. And when she came again, he followed two strokes later, groaning against her neck as his cock pulsed inside her clenching passage.

They lay in each other's arms for a long while, Ulric lazily stroking his hands across her skin. Each flutter of his fingers sent frissons of sensation through her already exhausted body, but his touch felt so comforting she didn't ask him to stop. She wondered if he was feeling the same sense of wonder and the almost painful over-sensitivity.

"I love you," he murmured into her hair.

He sounded sleepy and sated, his voice deeper than usual. She smiled into the darkness and hugged him close. "I love you too. We have a lot to talk about still."

"Yes. But later. No reality now."

"Yes." Relief sighed out on her next breath. She didn't want to abandon this euphoric contentment for reality either.

"Stay with me. Be here when I wake up."

Despite the exhaustion in his voice, his tone was pure command. A command she was inclined to obey.

"Yes," she murmured again. When she angled her head up to look into his face, his eyes were already closed. His hands stilled as his breathing deepened. She watched him sleep for several minutes, awed by the moment. She didn't want to sleep only to wake up and find this was all a dream. He loved her. He wanted a future with her. At least, she thought he did. They hadn't had a chance to discuss the future. But they would in the morning, she was sure. She didn't know how they would manage being together. The war made their situation difficult at best. But they'd find a way.

He loved her. As sleep finally dragged her under, she thought, with his love, she could do anything.

A KNOCK ON THE DOOR STARTLED LAYLA AWAKE. SUN LEAKED IN past the curtains. She blinked and rubbed at her gritty eyes, for a moment disoriented and unsure where she'd spent the night.

Then the bed creaked beside her and she remembered. She rolled over to see Ulric climbing to his feet. "Who's that?" she asked, worry sending her from the bed to snatch up her clothes.

Ulric frowned as he pulled on his trousers. "Not sure."

"Who knows about this place?" She'd assumed this was a secure room. Gods, she'd slept as if safely ensconced in her apartment near the council in the Sinnale-held territory. Anyone could be at that door.

She pulled her tunic over her head and then snatched up her quiver, pulling the knife that was tucked into a side pocket of the leather case. Since she'd lost her bow running from the Sorcerer, the arrows and the knife were her only remaining weapons. In the confines of the apartment—and with no bow—the arrows were mostly useless. The knife wouldn't be much use against a Sorcerer either. But at least it was something.

Ulric glanced at her, still frowning. He noted the knife without comment, then crossed to the door.

Before he could open it, a fist hammered hard against the wood, shaking it in its frame.

Layla's heart started pounding. Whoever was out there wanted in pretty badly.

Over his shoulder and without looking at her, Ulric said, "Stay back." He motioned her toward the ceramic heater. It wasn't much cover, but it would be something.

She put the bulk of the heater between her and the door just as Ulric released the lock and let the door fall open. And suddenly, Layla couldn't breathe. Her heart raced, her brain screamed to run, her fingers clenched the knife, but she couldn't suck in enough air to make any noise, not even a gasp. In the dim hallway stood Ulric's brother, Althir.

He smirked as he strolled past Ulric into the room and met her gaze. "Hello, Layla."

CHAPTER SEVEN

*L*ayla looked between Ulric and Althir, barely able to comprehend what she was seeing. Ulric looked annoyed but not surprised. Althir looked smug, self-satisfied.

Her heart plummeted in that moment. After all her suspicions, after all Ulric had done to earn her trust, after *last night*, she'd finally accepted that he wasn't going to turn her over to his brother. Only to come face to face with how wrong she'd been to trust him.

"I knew it," she hissed, holding the knife against her forearm, prepared to fight her way out of the room. "I knew I couldn't trust you!" She spit this last at Ulric, whose expression darkened further. Althir laughed which made her want to cry. But she didn't have time for tears. She had to get out of here.

"Where are the Sorcerers?" She spoke directly to Althir, no longer able to look at Ulric.

"The ones I brought with me?" Althir asked in that smug tone. "Why would I tell you that?"

"Althir." Ulric spoke for the first time. His voice was deep and dangerously quiet, the single word holding a note of warning.

Althir's smile dropped away and he looked almost sheepish.

"Why are you here?" Ulric asked. "How did you find me?"

"You think the Sinnale are the only ones with spies?" He nodded to Layla. "You tried to kill me. You. Of all people. We've known each other for years."

"You've been luring my people into slavery and death. You expect me to ignore that?"

"You're fucking my brother. What of his part?"

"My mistake."

"Don't," Ulric barked.

His tone was so sharp Layla jumped.

"Don't call this a mistake. Don't ever say that again."

"You're about to turn me over to your brother and you want me to be pleased about being betrayed? You still want me to love you?"

"I am not turning you over to my brother," he ground out. Then to Althir, "I'll ask again. What are you doing here?"

"I thought that'd be obvious." He chuckled and looked Layla over. "Does she share? You've had her what, two, three times now? Can't fuck her any more without consequences. I can take her off your hands if you like."

Layla didn't even see Ulric move. She blinked and he was standing behind his brother, a knife to his throat. She hadn't even realized Ulric had a knife. She gaped at the scene. Elves couldn't kill other elves. It was impossible. That was the reason the king and queen had come to the Sinnale to take care of the traitor elves. But still Ulric held the sharp blade against his brother's jugular as if he fully intended to use it.

"You will apologize to Layla now, brother. And then you will answer my question, and hers regarding the location of the Sorcerers."

"Why should I? You can't kill me."

A thin line of blood appeared on Althir's neck. Layla never saw

Ulric inflict the cut. One moment Althir's throat was a pristine, flawless white, the next a well of blood opened and dripped slowly down. Althir's eyes widened in surprise, a shock he couldn't have faked. He reached up to touch the wound but Ulric warned him off with a grunt.

"What are you doing?" Althir demanded. "I'm your brother. Your own fucking blood."

"You gave up the right to my loyalty the day you turned traitor. Now, apologize to Layla, or I swear by all that is sacred, Althir, I will slit your throat open and watch you die."

"You can't. It's not possible."

"You know better than that."

Layla's gaze narrowed. "What do you mean?" she asked Ulric. "You can't kill him. Can you?"

"Of course I can. And I will if I have to."

"But… But… It's impossible."

"No. It's taboo. It's socially unthinkable. It's so much a part of our social order that even some elves have forgotten it's physically possible. But we *can* kill each other. Repugnant though it is for us." He leaned in close to his brother's ear and murmured, "But I would not find killing you so difficult, Althir. Remember that. For what you've done, and what you intended to do to Layla, I would kill you."

She felt her mouth gaping open and snapped it shut. Ulric looked and sounded as serious as he ever had. Before her stood the warrior elf, the soldier and leader he'd been at one time. And she understood now why her father had whispered the tales of his ferocious valor in battle. Deadly intent suffused his every muscle. If this was an act, it was an impressive one. Althir looked terrified, truly worried his brother would slit his throat. She could actually see his hands trembling even though she was the length of the room away.

She met Ulric's gaze then. "Would you really?"

"Absolutely. And I wouldn't regret it."

"For me?"

"Only you. I haven't been playing games with you, Layla. I didn't bring him here. And I have no intention of letting him hurt you or turn you over to the Sorcerers. I do love you. And I will kill to protect you."

Althir opened his mouth to speak but closed it when Ulric moved the knife slightly against his throat. He swallowed visibly and remained silent.

Layla straightened away from her place behind the heater and continued to stare at Ulric, trying to gauge his sincerity. Could this be yet another convoluted trick, a way to get her to the Sorcerers without a fight?

He held her gaze, looking serious and steady. He didn't flinch or turn away. He didn't blink. And she knew the truth. He would actually *kill* Althir. He would kill him to save her. He loved her.

Her shoulders relaxed and she let out a long, low breath. He raised a brow and she nodded. "Okay. Okay. I believe you."

The smile he flashed was full of relief too, and she realized a lot of his tension had been caused by her reaction, not his brother's presence.

"Shall I just kill him and get it over with?" he asked, sounding almost jolly now.

"Shouldn't we find out why he's here first? If the building is surrounded, it would be good to know by how many and where they are."

"Right. You've a point." He angled his head to look at the side of his brother's face. "Well?"

Althir swallowed again. "Are you going to move the knife?"

"No."

"There are no others. I'm here alone."

"Don't lie to me, Althir."

"I'm not. I'm not." He held his hands up toward Layla as if pleading for her intervention. "I swear on all that's sacred. I'm here alone."

"Why?"

His gaze flicked around the room, then settled on Layla again. "I need your help."

"Mine?" Ulric asked. "Or hers?"

"Both really, but hers specifically."

"You need *my* help? The woman who tried to kill you? The woman you were just threatening to turn over to the Sorcerers?"

"I didn't really… You just assumed…" He shrugged. "I said all that to piss off Ulric."

"That wasn't a very wise idea," she said, nodding to the knife still resting against his throat. "Why would you do that?"

"Maybe we should go back to the reason he's here?" Ulric said.

"I never thought he'd try to kill me," Althir muttered. "Just thought you were a toy to him. That's why I was taunting you. I wanted to humiliate him."

"Him? Why?" She studied both men as they fell silent. And her eyebrows rose. "All that was some kind of sibling rivalry? You want my help and yet you made me think he'd betrayed me because you don't like him?" Her voice rose on that last comment. "I don't believe this. I didn't think elves were supposed to engage in that kind of petty behavior toward each other." She almost laughed. "And here I was putting you all on a pedestal. Thinking you were all so flawless."

"You should have known better than that already," Ulric said. "If we were flawless, you wouldn't have been sent to kill the traitors."

"True. Which brings us back to why you're here," she said to Althir, though she was still a little bemused.

She'd seen Althir and Ulric together and had always thought they got along. She'd had more dealings with Ulric—he was the one who negotiated with her parents and her. Althir didn't have the same talent for bartering and didn't enjoy it like they did. He spent most of his time flirting with the local women and directing the weapons deliveries. She couldn't recall having ever seen the brothers fight, though. In hindsight, she realized she'd rarely even seen them speak to each other.

Obviously, there was no love lost between them. No wonder Ulric didn't particularly care if she killed his brother. But… "Why have you two been in touch all this time if you don't even like each other? If Ulric is willing to kill you, Althir, and Althir wanted to humiliate you, Ulric, why were you two still communicating after Althir turned traitor?"

"Tell her," Ulric ordered when Althir didn't speak right away.

"After you nearly killed me, I got in contact with Ulric," Althir said reluctantly. "I wanted confirmation that the king and queen were behind the assassination attempt. I knew the Sinnale didn't have enough elven arrows left. It shouldn't have been possible for you to attack us."

"Is that why you turned traitor?"

Althir held his tongue until Ulric gave him a forceful nudge in the kidneys. "Power, all right?" he spit out. "We wanted power. The Sorcerers promised us… Well they promised a lot. Most of which they didn't deliver. But by the time we realized they were using us, it was too late. The king and queen had already gone to the Sinnale council. You already had the weapons and the leave to kill us."

"You're here to beg for your life," she realized.

"I'm here to make a trade." Althir raised his chin, as if offended by her wording. "I'm not afraid to die."

She wanted to disagree with that comment, but she held her tongue and let him finish.

"What scares me is the wrath of the king and queen."

She glanced at Ulric. "I don't understand. Isn't death the ultimate threat?"

Ulric let out a breath. Then he said, "You want proof of my love and trust, what I am about to tell you is one of our most guarded secrets. Death isn't the end for an elf. We continue on in an afterlife."

"All cultures believe in some sort of afterlife."

"Yes, but an elf's afterlife is…proven. We know it exists. We know what happens when we finally, eventually die. We know what our next plane is."

"What is it?"

"That will take some time to explain. For now, just know we do experience another existence after this one. Unless, of course, the king and queen prevent our continuation."

"They can keep you from your afterlife?" She wasn't sure what was more shocking, that they had proof of an afterlife or that their passage into that afterlife could be prevented by their leaders.

"The royal couple is in possession of a…you would call it a curse. The *Or'roan*. If it's inflicted on an elf and he dies, he ceases to exist. Period. His essence is destroyed utterly. It is the worst possible punishment that can be inflicted on one of our kind. Even death is less feared."

"And my dear brother," Althir sneered, "favorite of the royal court, confirmed that the king and queen invoked the *Or'roan* on all the traitors before they made arrangements with the Sinnale to kill us."

"So if Ulric killed you now, you would stop existing? You would no longer *be*?"

"Exactly. There would be no future lives for me, nothing. I would be over. And I do not want that to happen. After last night, I knew I couldn't wait any longer to seek your help."

"Last night? Did I kill any of those elves?"

"I'm not sure how you did it, but you killed two and mortally wounded the third. He won't live for long." Althir cursed in elvish. "They promised us, the Sorcerers *promised us* that they would keep us safe from the assassins. If we continued to help them, they would protect us. Some help they proved to be. One man to guard three elves?"

"They didn't think we would prove as great a threat as we are," Layla said with no small amount of pride. "They underestimated our resolve and our commitment."

"Layla was nearly killed last night," Ulric murmured in Althir's ear. His knife moved ever so slightly against Althir's neck.

"Don't, Ulric. I want to hear what he has to say before we decide whether or not to kill him."

"Those elves you killed," Althir continued when Ulric eased the knife back, "they have ceased to exist. After their long, long lives, after all the lives they've lived before this one, they no longer are. I don't want to end like that. I don't want to end."

"How do you think I can help you?"

"Your parents are on the council."

She stepped forward. "The identity of the council members is supposed to be secret."

"What do you think we took to the Sorcerers as bargaining chips?" he said with some disgust. "The council came to Glengowyn to solicit our help. They were refused. But their identities were revealed to a select few. A few of those turned to the Sorcerers."

"Did you know about this?" she asked Ulric. Even she hadn't known the council had revealed their identities to the elf leaders before the traitor elves defected. She'd assumed the king and queen discovered who the council was only after they'd come to the Sinnale for help.

"I was one of the few who knew," Ulric confirmed. "Their identities were safe with me, however."

After all that had happened, and all he'd done, she believed him. She nodded and motioned for Althir to continue.

"I want you to persuade your parents to intercede on my behalf with the king and queen. I'll suffer any other fate—banishment, a clean death, anything they choose so long as they lift the curse."

"Why would I do that? Why would my parents? You've been responsible for the deaths and enslavement of hundreds of my people."

"I'll give you information in return. Information you could never get through conventional spies. The kind of information that could win this war for you."

That was a tempting offer indeed. "How do I know this information is so valuable?"

"The king and queen could always reinstate the *Or'roan* if his information proves useless." Ulric finally lowered his knife and stepped away from Althir. But he moved to stand between her and his brother when he did, still protecting her.

His gesture made her smile. "True. Can we trust this isn't a trick, some way of getting information back to the Sorcerers about our internal workings?"

"It could well be a trap of some kind. But if so, Althir will die under the *Or'roan*. We can make arrangements to prevent information from getting out."

"A spell? He could have a spell on him that we can't detect."

"I don't," Althir put in.

But Ulric stared at him, considering for a silent moment. "That's possible. It would take a lot of power, though. And I think the queen would still be able to sense such a spell. It's her unique talent."

"What about an assassination attempt, then? Could he be trying to get close to the council, only to trigger some spell that would kill everyone?"

"He'd get killed himself in such a case, and he'd still be cursed."

"None of that will happen," Althir insisted. "I'm here in good faith. I want to make this trade."

"You're a traitor," Ulric said. "We aren't going to take your word. I'm still not convinced you don't have Sorcerers waiting for us."

"I swear, Ulric. I swear on the heads of the king and queen. I am sincere."

Even Layla understood that giving one's word that way meant something to an elf. But this was a man who'd turned his back on his people for power. And yet, if he was sincere, and if his information could bring an end to the war…

"I have an idea that should mitigate the dangers," she said.

Ulric turned enough to look at her while still keeping Althir in his line of sight.

"If he's telling the truth," she said, "it could mean an end to the war. We have to risk that."

After a long, silent moment, Ulric nodded. "What do you propose?"

"I'll need to leave. I need to make contact with my people."

Ulric stared hard at Althir. "Can she leave here safely?"

"Yes. I told you, I came alone."

"No one followed?"

"No. Believe me, Ulric, I do *not* want the Sorcerers knowing my plans. They would do much worse to me than the Sinnale."

"Know this, brother, if Layla leaves here and is harmed in any way, I will make you wish the Sorcerers had found you first."

Althir licked his lips in a quick, nervous gesture. He believed Ulric's threat. She did too and it warmed her heart.

"I'll be back by midday. If the council wants to accept your offer, I'll tell you then and we'll make arrangements for your passage. But you will be examined first. You'll have to submit to that."

"I understand," he said, though he didn't look happy about the prospect.

She gathered up her quiver and dropped it over her head so it angled across her back. Then she pulled on her boots and took one last look around the room. When she was sure she had collected all her gear, she started to the door. Ulric stopped her at the threshold.

"Be safe," he murmured. "He may still be lying."

"I'll be careful. I've been doing that for a while now."

"I wish I could go with you."

She smiled. "I need you to keep an eye on him. I trust you to make sure he doesn't do anything to compromise my people."

"You do?"

She nodded.

"Good. It's about time."

He leaned in and kissed her, a slow, deep, passionate kiss that promised more when they had time.

"Can you two save that?" Althir said dryly. "I don't want to watch if I can't take part. Unless, of course, you're willing to include me."

Ulric lifted his head, cupped her cheeks and said, "I will kill him slowly and painfully if anything happens to you. I may kill him even if nothing happens to you."

She chuckled. "Try not to until I get back with the council's decision." She gave him one last quick, hard kiss and left the room. Despite the danger and the possibility that Althir was involved in some kind of elaborate trap, she felt lighter and happier than she had in years.

CHAPTER EIGHT

*L*ayla crossed the treeline border into Glengowyn. This was only the second time in her life she'd been to the elven city. Most of the negotiations for weapons with her parents had taken place in Sinnale.

She followed a rock-lined path, marveling at the rich greens and browns of the trees and soil, the smattering of colorful flowers along the edge of the path, the quiet call of birds and bugs, the scents of fresh earth, moisture and a faint perfume that was unique to the elven city.

Everything was so peaceful, clean and beautiful. Such a contrast to what had happened to her own home.

But now, for the first time since the start of the war, there was hope for Sinnale, hope that they could get back to the beautiful place she'd grown up in.

She turned down another path, following the directions she'd received in a note carried to her by one of the elves' carrier owls. Outside of the council coming to Glengowyn to ask for help, no human had been allowed into the city since the invasion. This trip was a testament to her trust in Ulric. He promised in his note she would have safe passage. If he was wrong, she would be arrested by the elven guard any moment.

But the path remained clear. She soaked up the peace and quiet and tried to calm the tingles fluttering in her stomach. She hadn't seen Ulric since the day she'd brought a group of Sinnale soldiers to collect his brother. Althir's story proved true. There were no tracking or assassination spells on him. No Sorcerers or minions had waited for her to appear from Ulric's hideaway. And over the last two days the information Althir had been providing was proving extraordinarily beneficial. He gave them inside information on the vulnerabilities and resources of the enemy, and it was enough for them to arrange a counter-offensive. Up to this point, they'd been defending, retreating, giving way. Now they could push forward and attempt to take their city back. There was a renewed vigor among the Sinnale, hope for a future.

And the elves had agreed to start trading weapons again. Not just the weapons needed to assassinate the traitor elves, but enough to resupply the entire resistance.

They even offered a few special weapons they'd never allowed into human hands before—despite her mother's best bartering efforts. Magical weapons which would give them an advantage the Sorcerers couldn't predict. Even the traitor elves wouldn't expect the king and queen to hand over these particular tools.

The war would turn. It would end. And with luck, the Sinnale would come out on top to rebuild their city.

As she neared the location indicated in the note, her surroundings began to change. A small, blue stream trickled across the path. The green of the trees seemed to take on a slight glow. It was late in the day, approaching sunset. But the glow gave plenty of illumination within the forest.

As the external light continued to lower, the glow got brighter, the green turning a translucent blue, sparkling with pinpoints of white light. By the time she reached the white stone structure twined with the giant tree trunks, the only light was the blue glow and the dancing of white sparks within the glow. The structure was a rolling wave of smooth stone, interrupted by tall, narrow windows and walkways bracketed by golden marble columns. Stained glass covered every third window, while the rest of the panes were made of such flawlessly translucent glass, they were barely visible. A faint scent of honeysuckle painted the clearing in front of the house, the plants themselves climbed the low walls enclosing the clearing. She loved honeysuckle. It was her favorite smell next to Ulric's natural scent. Funny, she'd never noticed if Ulric smelled of honeysuckle. It would be amazing for him to avoid it given the strength of the scent around his home.

She stood just outside the low wall and took a deep breath. She'd never seen Ulric's home before. The sight was a little overwhelming. But more than the house, it was the thought of seeing the occupant that held her in place. She wanted nothing more than to see him. But a treacherous part of her was afraid he brought her all this way to tell her he'd made a mistake. He didn't really love her. He wasn't willing to enter into a relationship with a human who would die centuries before him.

The quiet forest music soothed her enough to get her moving again. She crossed the grassy clearing and walked up a short flight of white stone stairs to the dark wooden doors. Before she could raise her hand to the knocker shaped like an owl, the doors parted and swung open.

Ulric stood on the threshold, looking stunning in a deep purple tunic and black leggings. His hair was pulled back from his face, framing the strong, angular lines and highlighting his masculine perfection. Her breath caught. Would it always take her by surprise, just how gorgeous he was? And would she always feel inadequate and ugly by comparison?

He didn't move toward her and she didn't step inside. She couldn't seem to make her feet move. The silence stretched as they stared at each other. Nothing in his expression gave away his thoughts. And when he continued to stand still and not talk, she started to fidget, pulling down the edges of her cream tunic and picking at the soft cotton of her tan skirt. These were her best clothes, an outfit she hadn't dared wear since the beginning of the war, but her best was still a far cry from the splendor of his clothing.

Her movements seemed to snap him out of his silence. "You look beautiful," he murmured and finally closed the distance between them.

She touched a hand to her freshly washed hair and smiled at his compliment. "You look amazing."

He stopped very close but without touching her. "I like seeing you without your weapons."

"It feels a little odd after so long, but…not in a bad way."

"Do you remember me teaching you to use a bow?"

"Of course. My father bribed you." She chuckled.

"I volunteered. Though I made sure your father didn't realize I was volunteering."

"Why? It meant I was better able to tell when you were trying to sell us less-than-perfect weapons."

He shrugged. "It made the negotiations more interesting. You and your parents are some of the best I've ever bartered with. How could I resist making the process even more challenging? And I wanted to spend more time with you."

"You did? As far back as that?"

He nodded. "And despite the closeness forced on us during

those lessons, you never once reacted to me. I was never sure what to think of that."

She snorted and shook her head. "I was a mess every time you got close. I'd just spent years learning how to deal with that response so I could function around you."

"You laughed a lot, though. I remember that well. I've missed that laughter." He fell silent, his gaze roaming over her face for a moment. Then, quietly, he said, "I'm glad you came."

"How could I resist your invitation?"

"After everything that happened… I wasn't sure you'd trust your safe passage."

"Ulric." She reached out and cupped his cheek. When she did, she felt all his muscles relax and his breath whooshed out audibly. "I told you, I trust you." She studied his face, watching his emotions play out in his eyes. "You were willing to kill your brother to protect me," she murmured. "How could I not trust you after that?"

He let out another deep breath and wrapped his arms around her waist. "I can't remember the last time I saw you in a skirt. You look very sexy."

She felt sexy under his warm gaze. "Your clearing is full of honeysuckle. I love that smell."

"I know. That's why I had it planted here."

"For me?"

"I hoped you'd come here someday."

His simple statement made her smile and the last of her own tension eased away. "I've missed you. I…I wasn't sure how long it would be before I could see you again."

"I've been in discussions with the court. Things are going to improve. Soon."

"Yes."

"I don't want you working as an assassin anymore," he blurted out, then looked annoyed by his own comment. "I had intended to work around to that, to be a little more subtle and charming when I posed the idea."

She chuckled. "That sounded more like an order." She leaned into him, settling her hands on his shoulders. "I'm the best archer in the city. In no small part, thanks to you."

"And you've nearly died twice just in the last few weeks. You've done your duty. Assassinated traitor elves, killed minions and even a Sorcerer early in the war. That's enough." His grip tightened and urgency colored his tone.

"I understand your worry, Ulric. I do. But you have to understand, I still have to contribute to the war effort. It's not over yet. The Sorcerers still pose a very significant threat."

"There must be something else you can do, some other way to serve your people and still stay safely behind the front line. I don't want to lose you after we've come this far."

Her heart started to pound hard against her ribs. "I love you too," she said. "But as it happens, the council has already assigned me my next mission."

"Damn it, Layla, you can't—"

She put a finger over his lips to stop his tirade. "I'm to head the trade negotiations for Glengowyn weapons with the elf delegates. I'll be facilitating the exchange and movement of weapons into the city."

His mouth actually popped open. "Why…? You won't be on the front anymore?"

She shook her head. "The council has decided my experience in working with weapons and trading with the elves is more valuable than my skill with a bow. And since my parents aren't in a position to head up the trade, I'm responsible for the entire thing."

"That's a big job," he said quite seriously.

But she could see the smile edging his lips. "Don't look so smug. I didn't do this for you. I did it for my people."

"I don't care why. I only care that you'll be out of danger."

"Well, not completely. The Sorcerers may try to prevent or interrupt trade."

"I'll make sure they fail."

She raised a brow. "*We'll* make sure they fail."

"We?" He nodded. "I can live with 'we'."

He leaned down and brushed his lips across hers. But his comment brought up the other problem facing them. His lifespan was going to be significantly longer than hers.

"At least we'll have a few years."

When he pulled back, she realized she'd spoken aloud. "I just mean, even if the war ends tomorrow, you're going to live so much longer than I will…" She trailed off as a funny look crossed his face. "What?"

"I have something to tell you, something that I will be trusting you to keep secret."

"What—?"

He pulled her farther inside. "First, let's get comfortable."

He took her hand and tugged her through his home, but she barely noticed the splendor around her.

She was too anxious about what he had to say.

He led her to a large, open room, the painted ceiling soaring high above where vines twined through slits in the roof to weave through the mural adding an extra dimension. Low couches covered with dark blue and purple cushions surrounded a fire burning in a large, open pit in the middle of the space. Thick rugs covered the stone floors, and columns and stained glass made up the walls. During the day, this room would be alight with color. Tonight, everything glowed in rosy overtones from the fire.

Ulric eased her down onto one of the couches, turning to face her while holding her hands in his.

"There's more to the *Shaerta* than humans know."

She was glad he got right to the point. She nodded for him to continue when he paused.

"Beyond the addictive nature for humans, and the…benefits to sex, there is an additional chemical reaction possible. It only happens between long-term lovers."

"But elves don't take long-term lovers among humans. At least, I mean, outside of us."

"And this is another of the reasons they don't."

"Am I going to die faster because of my exposure to elf-fire?"

"What? No. What made you assume that?"

"Well, why else avoid this effect by avoiding a human lover?"

"No, the effect is just the opposite."

She frowned.

"Your life will be extended. To match mine."

"What?"

"We'll have to make love a lot, to maintain the chemical changes."

She almost laughed. "That will be a difficult task."

His serious expression cracked a bit and a small smile slipped through. "After centuries together, you may not be so eager for all that sex."

"I'm willing to find out."

"You don't fully understand the implications, Layla. You'll outlive every human you know. We'll have to be together regularly, and that kind of closeness can test even the strongest loves. Very few human/elf relationships have lasted more than a single human lifetime before the lovers give up on each other."

"And what happens to the humans then?"

"They return to aging at their normal rate, but by that time everyone they've known is old or passed on. It's a difficult existence."

"So what are you saying? That we shouldn't try because we might not make it?"

"No!" His grip tightened on her hands as if he expected her to pull away. "No, not… I just want you to understand what you're getting into. I love you. I will love you for the rest of my life. I've lived long enough to know this. But you're so young. You need to understand. If we continue on, the elf-fire will cause this chemical change in you and it will be more than addicting. There are physical consequences to an abrupt stop."

"Like what?"

"The humans who've carried on long-term affairs with elves, when those affairs end, their bodies deteriorate and many of their minds have broken."

She straightened. "So if you leave me, I risk…insanity, physical illness?"

"I won't leave you. Ever. But if you decide to go… There's more."

More? She wasn't sure how much more she could take.

"The effects are actually worse on couples who aren't truly in love. Those who are in love, honest love, their lives together can be successful. Those are the couples we write songs about. They're legends. And they are rare. Most elves are frankly not willing to take the risk."

She stared at him for a long moment before speaking. "You're saying that if I don't really love you, if what I feel isn't…honest, then I stand to suffer for it later on."

"Yes."

She felt the tremble in his hands and watched his breath come more rapidly as she continued to stare at him. There was nothing in his expression to give away his thoughts, but she could feel his tension easily enough. She blinked as she realized he was worried about the strength of *her* feelings. He was willing to risk a long-term relationship with her, the kind of relationship most elves weren't willing to take a chance on. He believed his love was true and would last forever. He was worried hers wasn't. How little he knew.

She smiled. When he frowned, her smile turned to an outright grin. "Ulric." She leaned forward and kissed him. "I don't think we have anything to worry about."

"But…"

"Trust me," she said against his mouth. "People will write songs about our love. I promise. I've loved you my whole life. That's not about to change, even if I live as long as an elf."

He chuckled against her lips, then sealed his mouth to hers, kissing her deeply. She could already feel the elf-fire rising, washing over her, taking her into her new life.

"I love you, Ulric. Forever."

"Forever," he repeated. And eased her back into the couch. "But I think we need to make sure. We have a lot of lovemaking to do."

She laughed even as she arched up so he could pull her tunic off over her head. His lips closed on hers again, swallowing her chuckle. She wrapped herself around him and sighed, looking forward to the future more than she ever had before, a long, long future with the man she loved.

Fire & Tears
Book Two

DARKNESS SINGED

Author Kat Simons writing as

ISABO KELLY

DARKNESS SINGED

FIRE AND TEARS BOOK TWO

DARK HISTORY CONFRONTED

Nuala of Glengowyn hasn't left the elven kingdom in over a century, but not by choice. Her skills as a weapons master have made her a prisoner of her people, held apart, protected in the extreme. Until Sorcerers attack the neighboring human city. When she's sent to help the humans, however, Nuala is still far from free. Because she's forced to travel with a bodyguard, the most fearsome warrior among her people—and the only man Nuala has ever loved.

Einar is known as a battle-crazed destroyer, so feared among elves he's called by a single name: Darkness. And he has only one weakness—Nuala. Their union is forbidden, because melding their magics could destroy Nuala's gifts. But as they journey through the war-torn human city, no royal decree is a match for two hundred years of pent-up desire.

Surviving the war zone won't be enough if they give in to their long denied passion. They'll have to confront their sovereigns and face the ultimate punishment—or prove love makes them stronger.

CHAPTER ONE

Nuala of Glengowyn kept her gaze forward and her shoulders proud but loose, determined to hide the tension twisting her stomach from the soldiers surrounding her. She hadn't been outside Glengowyn in nearly a century, most certainly hadn't been allowed to leave since the war between the Sorcerers and the humans of Sinnale began. This trip, necessary though it was, would not have been her choice for her first excursion back into Sinnale.

She rode near the center of the military escort—both human and elven—her bow and quiver bumping gently against her back, comforting in their familiarity. The less comfortable knives in the scabbards strapped to her waist were a steady reminder of the danger. Even the glowering, deadly elf riding beside her couldn't calm her anxiety.

But she'd be damned if she let Einar see her fear.

Lifting her chin to steady herself, she studied the grassy plains bracketing the road from Glengowyn to Sinnale. They'd left the safety of the forest not long ago, and she'd felt exposed and vulnerable ever since. The human city was in view, less than half a mile away, the buildings and houses rising and falling like a clunky, awkward mountain range against the deep blue sky. Beyond and to the west of the city, the real mountains of the Arei-atun Range rose up like purple and gray sentinels. The contrast between nature and the manmade structures was stark and sobering.

"You're hiding your tension well, my lady," the towering man beside her said quietly, for her ears only. "But your mare is beginning to react to your anxiety."

Nuala scowled at Einar then focused on her mount for several moments, working at relaxing her body, her grip on the reins, her knees against the horse's sides. She felt the large gray relax as well and only then realized how tightly the mare had been holding herself. If not for Einar's comment, the gray would have started fidgeting openly soon, revealing just how scared her rider was. The fact that Einar had noticed Nuala's unease so easily robbed any feelings of gratitude she might have had for his discreet help, though.

But she was nothing if not well trained to be polite. "Thank you. I will make an effort to control my reactions better."

"You have always been in full control of your reactions, my lady. To everything."

He didn't look at her as he spoke, his gaze sweeping their surroundings, ever watchful. But she heard the bite in the comment, the subtle jab most wouldn't have noticed. She refused to respond, not entirely sure she could censor herself in that moment. Not when she expected a physical attack with every breath. And most definitely not with *him*.

She kept her own gaze on the high grass beside the road so she wouldn't have to face Einar and risk him seeing her inner turmoil. He was the only man, the only person, who had ever been able to read her with any level of accuracy. Even her cousins,

Ulric and Althir, who'd looked after her after her parents were killed in the first goblin war, could never read her moods or thoughts.

Einar was an entirely different story.

She acknowledged, reluctantly, that the danger posed by the Sorcerers and the war weren't the only reasons for her anxiety. When the Darkness of Glengowyn, personal bodyguard to the elf king and queen, had been assigned as her bodyguard, Nuala very nearly backed out.

But to do so would have revealed too much. To everyone. Including *him*.

"You will reach the city safely," Einar murmured. "I swear it."

She continued to stare at the grass so he wouldn't see her expression, though she was sure he wasn't looking at her as he spoke. His words made her throat squeeze tight. "I know you'll do what you can," she returned quietly. "But no caravan reaches Sinnale without being attacked. This will be no different."

"I'm not afraid of the Sorcerers' minions."

"Of course *you're* not." As soon as she spoke, she wished she could take it back. Too much. Those few words revealed too much. And Einar would know. He would understand everything if she wasn't very careful.

She thought maybe he understood too well already.

"You've no need to fear them either."

"I'm not the warrior here. I make the weapons. I don't go into battle with them."

"And I have no intention of risking you in battle now."

A traitorous part of her heart lifted at that. "When the minions attack, you'll have no choice."

He actually turned to look at her and because she could feel his stare on the side of her face, she met his gaze. Black as the deepest, moonless night.

"You think I will let those abominations near you? I have sworn to protect you as I would the king and queen. You doubt me?"

She realized he was actually offended. Most wouldn't have seen it. He hid his emotions better even than she did. Most of the elves of Glengowyn thought he didn't have any. But she'd always seen beyond his façade. The sword cut both ways between them.

"I don't doubt your ability to protect me, Einar. But if the traitors have told the Sorcerers about me, they'll be waiting for this particular caravan. You may not have the choice to keep me out of the fight."

"You're not trained for combat. Do not engage the enemy. Stay beside me, and I will see you safe."

She shook her head and looked away. He was the most deadly elf in all of Glengowyn. But he wasn't invincible. No matter what the others thought.

The one thing in her favor was that, outside of the traitor elves, no one from Sinnale had seen her in the last two human generations. None of the minions would recognize her—if they still retained any memories of their human lives after the Sorcerers were done with them. And she doubted any of the traitors would dirty their hands in an actual caravan attack. The Sorcerers never left the city, and none of them would know her on sight anyway.

The attack, *when* it came, would likely be no different from any other. The heavy guard surrounding her and the wagons of her arrows, both her normal enchanted arrows and the special weapons the Sinnale were only now being allowed to trade for, should have no trouble repelling the minions.

But as she studied the long, waving sheets of golden-green grass along the roadside, a chill skittered along her shoulders and her mare danced a step or two beneath her before she reined her in. Nuala's stomach tightened.

She hadn't been allowed to take risks of any kind since the end of the second goblin war, not since she'd developed the weapon she was now delivering to Sinnale, the weapon that had helped the elves win that war. Once the conflict was over, her particular magic, and her skill in wielding it, had been considered too valuable to endanger.

The sudden rake of terror along her spine could have had something to do with her lack of recent experience with tension and fear. Nothing in the grass signaled a change. The city's outlier buildings grew closer with each clomp of the horses' hooves, close enough now she could see some of the damage to the structures at the edge of Noman's Land, not far from where they would enter the city.

Still, she couldn't shake the sensation of being watched.

A quick glance at Einar, then the other warriors, assured her they were keeping their focus on the surroundings. No one paid her any particular attention. Not for lack of curiosity, she was sure, but because the Darkness of Glengowyn had ordered them to ignore her. Staring would not only distract them from the possible dangers, it would single her out as someone significant. The soldiers were following that order perfectly. She was outwardly no different from any other mounted elf in the caravan.

She studied the grass again, frowning in concentration as she searched the shifting waves.

That focus saved her life.

CHAPTER TWO

An arrow flashed silver in the glinting sunshine, so fast and true, Nuala might have been impressed if not for the fact that the arrow was heading for her. She spurred her mare forward, ducking low to the gray's neck, and still felt the arrow whisper just above her spine. She screamed a warning at the same instant, praying to the Goddess that Einar wasn't hit by the deadly missile meant for her. She'd never survive that.

Almost before she felt the weapon whistle past, more missiles flew into their ranks. And a moment later, a horde of minions rose from the grass, swords high, silent as the wind as they attacked.

Then Einar raced up beside her, shouting, "Ride! To the city."

She didn't pause to think, just spurred the gray forward. Fortunately, the animal was war trained and didn't panic. She charged over the rutted road, closing in on safety, without any reaction to the sounds of clashing metal and the cries of the wounded and dying.

Keeping her head low, Nuala glanced over her shoulder, confirming Einar kept pace with her. They moved so fast through the middle of their own people, the minions had no chance to reach them—another part of Einar's plan. But the column of protection wouldn't take them all the way to Sinnale. Too soon, they raced beyond the fighting soldiers and into the open to cover the remaining three hundred yards.

The appearance of three minions in their path startled her enough she screamed. Einar changed directions, forcing her and her mare parallel to the city without slowing their run. Behind her, she heard a shout, and another glance back confirmed a dozen minions followed.

"Where did they come from?" she yelled.

"Later." Einar searched the edge of the city. "We need the cover of the buildings." He angled his horse back toward Sinnale, and she followed his lead.

This time when something blocked their path neither reacted fast enough to change directions. Her gray reared. Nuala tightened her thighs, keeping her seat, but the stench of death emanating from the Sorcerer made her gag. Her mare danced under her, faced with a horror beyond her training. Einar pulled his sword and pushed his own mount in front of Nuala's to guard her from the new threat.

The Sorcerer smiled, glanced beyond them. And vanished.

In his place, three of the traitor elves closed in.

Nuala had no time to absorb the shock of this new development. The minions following them were too close. Einar could handle the elves. She shifted her mount to face their rear, dropped the reins, and slid her bow over her head. The gray knew what to do in battle, and Nuala could guide her with her legs, leaving her hands free to use her weapon. She covered Einar's back, firing arrow after arrow as the minions came within range. Of the dozen, eight fell with mortal or near-mortal wounds. Two more were injured enough to slow them down. Only two made it through her barrage.

She tried to keep her mount, using the strong wood of her

weapon to bat at the minions while her horse reared and thrashed. The mare held the two attackers off, but when the wounded minions joined the fight, Nuala knew she and the mare were outnumbered. Her greatest fear in that moment was that the minions would get around her and get to Einar.

She had two arrows left in her quiver, but at close range, the weapon was less useful. As her horse whipped around sharply and kicked at one of the attackers, Nuala grabbed the mare's mane in one hand for balance and dropped the bow over her head, across her back. She reached for the reins, but they'd slipped beyond easy grasp and she overbalanced trying to get them. When her gray spun and jumped sideways at the same time to avoid the swing of a sword, Nuala's stomach clenched as she was tossed to the ground.

She hit hard on her left side, the jolt knocking the wind from her. Over the sounds of clashing metal and screaming horses, she heard Einar call her name. Three of the human slaves stalked toward her as the fourth turned toward Einar and the traitors trying to subdue him. With a wheezing gasp, she stumbled to her feet, barely able to suck in a breath.

Her left arm hurt but didn't feel broken. And when she drew both knives from their scabbards at her waist, her left hand worked enough to hold the hilt firmly. She wasn't a trained warrior, hadn't been allowed to train, but that hadn't stopped her from learning a few things over the years. Thanks to Ulric and Althir's secret lessons.

She waited and watched the three minions as they approached. One smiled at her. The others remained strangely passive, as if the fight wasn't something happening to them at all. One of the expressionless men limped badly, and she realized her gray had got in a clean kick, damaging his leg. He dragged the wounded limb, seemingly unaware of the injury.

Nuala swallowed and raised her knives.

"Stop." A deep voice rose up behind the three attackers.

A familiar voice. But not the one she'd hoped to hear.

One of the traitors passed between the minions, his smirk both smug and confident. "I'll handle the weapons master. Help the others with her guard."

She didn't dare take her eyes off the traitor as he neared, even to check on Einar. The fact that the others were being sent to the fight against him meant he was alive. She could hear the sounds of swords clashing, the screams of pain that weren't Einar's. Even three more minions wouldn't be enough.

"He'll kill them all, Byral," she said as the traitor approached. "You know he will."

"But elves can't kill other elves." Byral stalked her, his gait smooth and graceful. Blood splattered his dark gray tunic. But he didn't look injured.

To kill another elf was a taboo among her kind, so ingrained in their society most elves believed it was physically impossible for one elf to kill another.

Only recently had she been made aware of the truth. But this traitor didn't need to know that. "The minions will be slaughtered. Einar will disable the other two traitors."

Byral's eyes shifted slightly, their deep, intense blue clouding just a little. "Surprising," he said with a slight tilt of his head. "I didn't think the Darkness ever left the king's and queen's sides. But..." He shrugged. "I suppose for you, they would take the risk."

"Why?"

She didn't have to elaborate. Byral knew what she was asking. Rather than answer, he angled around her, circling, looking for an opening in her weak defenses.

"They won't harm you," he said. "The Sorcerers. They can offer you a lot."

"I'm no traitor." He was close enough that the stench of death magic corrupting him filled her nostrils. "They've been teaching you?" She was surprised by that. The Sorcerers were jealous of their powers, despite what they'd told the traitors. She'd been led to believe they hadn't shared any of their magic with the elves.

"Only me." His smirk returned. "I promised them you in return."

Nuala's stomach clenched and her heartbeat jumped. She didn't show the reaction outwardly but fear clogged her throat. Only an act of will kept her from panting as panic crept in around her control. "I won't go quietly. And you can't kill me."

"But I can wound you enough to make you cooperate."

Rather than respond, she focused on her grip on the two knives, making sure she was prepared. When Byral lunged suddenly and with a speed she hadn't anticipated, she reacted without thought. One wide step shifted her out of his reach and gave her an opening to slide her knife across his biceps. He snarled and whipped back to face her, diving into another attack before she had time to feel satisfied with her strike.

This time, she stumbled and fumbled, swinging her knives awkwardly as she tried to put space between them. He didn't raise his sword except to bat away her flailing weapons. He wanted her alive, even if he knew he could kill her—knowledge she wasn't sure he possessed.

She tripped over the grass tangling around her boots and dropped to one knee, losing a knife in the barely controlled fall. Byral chuckled. Behind him, Einar roared her name again. The fact that he was alive dampened her fear. She held Byral's gaze as he loomed over her. With a sniff of disgust, he grabbed her arm and jerked her to her feet.

"They shouldn't have allowed you out of Glengowyn. But I profit from their mistake."

"No."

She saw the slight flicker in his eyes, the beginnings of suspicion, the instant before she plunged her knife into his heart, burying the weapon to the hilt. His blue eyes widened, his mouth dropped open and his grasp on her arm fell away. He looked at the knife in his chest then met her gaze, his mouth moving in a silent denial.

"You should have known better," she murmured. "The *Or'roan* takes you now. Forever death."

The *Or'roan*, a curse only the king and queen could inflict on the elves, ended their existence forever—no afterlife, no rebirth into future lives, no hope for any future existence. The end of all they'd ever been and all they would be was greatly feared by every elf. And all but one of the traitors was currently under the *Or'roan*.

Terror transformed Byral's once starkly handsome face into a distorted mask. "No," he forced out with his last breath. He never lost the grip on his sword, even when he collapsed.

She swallowed down the bile in her throat, retrieved the knife she'd lost in the grass when she'd tripped, and forced herself to focus on Einar and his fight. She would deal with the fact that she'd just done the unthinkable, the impossible, later.

The minions hadn't stood a chance against the Darkness. They lay in silent heaps around the swirling rage that was Einar in battle. The two remaining elves were both bloodied and retreating under the hail of Einar's attack. The flow of the fight moved them closer to the city, and Nuala realized suddenly that the elves' retreat was strategic. She didn't dare call out to warn Einar for fear of distracting him. But she knew with certainty the traitors were drawing him into a trap.

The Sorcerer.

She scanned the area, noting with an ache that would hurt more when she had time that Einar's horse was among the wounded, its dark sides no longer rising and falling. Her mare was nowhere in sight, and she could only assume the animal had been smart enough to flee. Most of the Glengowyn steeds would fight to the death. But Nuala couldn't face the thought of another life lost so was glad the animal's training had failed.

She worked her way toward Einar, watching carefully to make sure the traitors didn't notice her. But the Darkness was no ordinary elf and the traitors didn't dare look away. In the distance, she could hear the sounds of battle from the caravan. She and Einar had gone too far east for her to find help from that direction, though. The edge of the city was near enough for them to reach at a sprint, but she had no idea what dangers lurked in those streets. And the forest was too far away for them to make a run for it on foot.

Somewhere out there, the Sorcerer who'd stopped their escape was waiting. She couldn't see or sense him. But she knew he was there. Somewhere.

She got close enough to Einar to guard his back even as the traitors continued to lure them closer to the city's outer buildings. The two elves spread out, forcing Einar to face one or the other, an attempt to outflank him.

Refusing to think about her actions, Nuala flipped the knife so she held the tip in her fingers. With a flick of her wrist, she sent her last weapon flying. It struck the traitor on Einar's left, burying deep into the space between his shoulder and chest. Not a deadly hit. Her aim wasn't that good. But the injury was enough to make him drop his sword.

He looked at the knife with the same dumbfounded shock as Byral had, facing her with wide eyes an instant before Einar drove a sword through his throat.

The final elf shouted something she didn't catch and fled toward the city. She reached out to take Einar's arm, afraid he'd try to follow the retreating man, but Einar stood solid and immovable, the blood on his sword dripping into the soil. The stench of death and blood clogged her throat, bringing back memories long buried.

"We need cover," Einar said as he glanced toward the caravan fight, then back at the city. "Forest is too far."

Prickles of tension raced along her arms. "The Sorcerer is there." She nodded at the city even as she continued to scan their surroundings. They stood out in the open, horribly exposed and vulnerable. With each breath, she anticipated another attack.

"He's not," Einar stated.

Not bothering to explain, he grabbed her hand and raced toward the dubious cover of the outlier buildings.

CHAPTER THREE

The transition from rough grass to cobbled streets jolted through Nuala's calves as they barreled between two scarred brick structures and into the city proper. When they weren't followed, when no magical attack came, she actually felt relief wash through her.

But when she would have slowed to a trot, Einar tightened his hold on her hand and continued to pull her along at a fast run. He turned corners, raced down alleys and small streets, hurried along the edge of open courtyards, keeping her close to the looming shadows of the surrounding buildings as they went.

After so long, she barely recognized the city. Empty, quiet, the stench of things she remembered from another war permeating the air. The bright sun seemed somehow diminished, cooled and weakened by the pervasive gloom that hung over the streets.

Einar finally slowed to a trot and then a fast walk.

"Where are we?" she asked, her heart thumping from both the run and her own fear.

"Noman's Land."

"What happened to the Sorcerer? Why didn't he attack?"

"He was never real."

She frowned, wanting to ask more questions, but Einar didn't give her a chance.

"We need to get inside."

"Why don't we just head toward Sinnale-held territory?"

"We need time. And a plan." He pushed her back against a brick façade and held her in place for several long moments.

She listened intently, waiting for…something. The area was eerily silent, only the faint creak of wood and the barest brush of moving air. No rustling leaves. No bird song. No quiet hum of the forest. Nuala had never felt so disconnected and displaced.

Einar remained motionless for what seemed like a very long time. Then he ushered her across the empty street and straight into a relatively intact building. The small, three-story structure had most of its windows and shutters in place, and the front door was solid, if unlocked.

"Is this safe?" she said, so quietly human ears would never detect the sound.

"Abandoned."

When he pushed her into the cool darkness, Nuala took a moment to let her eyes adjust and her heart rate slow.

"Are you hurt?" Einar asked from his position near the door. He was studying the street, not looking at her.

That lack of attention was as much of a relief as the relative safety of being inside. "No," she said to keep him from facing her for a few more moments. "Are you?"

He didn't answer. She swept his big body with a searching gaze, frowning as she looked for wounds. There was a superficial cut on his left biceps, visible through his ripped shirt sleeve, and a tear in his leather trousers, just across the thick muscle of his thigh. But she couldn't see anything that looked serious.

Satisfied, she turned in a small circle to survey their hiding spot.

They stood in what had been the foyer to a smart, elegant townhouse. Not that the elegance remained. But at one time, she was sure someone of wealth and significance had called this place home. The walls were hung with faded, dirty silk that might have been a pale color sometime in its past. No furniture remained, but stairs to the left led to the upper floors and several closed doors flanked the open entryway. Spaces that had probably contained pictures or mirrors or some other decoration left lighter rectangles in the grime covering the silk wall drapings. The floor was bare wood but inlaid in a beautiful pattern, which would look stunning after a clean and polish.

An ache of loss settled around her chest. Had the owners of this once-beautiful home been killed? Sacrificed to the Sorcerers' spells? Turned minion? Did a human live who might one day reclaim this place?

Caught up in her sense of sorrow, she jumped when she felt Einar's hand on her shoulder. Without turning to face him, she said, "I hate war. I always have."

"I know."

His understanding only made her throat tighten further.

"We can rest here." Einar's deep voice was quiet in the stillness. "But not for long. This is too close to the Sorcerers' territory."

"We're that far east?"

"We entered the city in their territory."

She blinked. She hadn't realized. "How did you know where to go? Are you sure we're outside their borders?"

The Sorcerers' borders were guarded with deadly, nasty spells. They'd been lucky not to trigger any. Or else Einar had talents he'd never revealed to her.

"We're safe for now. I'm certain we're in Noman's Land."

She released a pent-up breath. "And after we've rested?" She finally found the courage to face him. They didn't have time for her to fall apart. Not yet.

"Then we make our way to the Sinnale. And hope they don't kill us on sight."

"Why would they?"

He dropped his chin to meet her gaze. "Unknown elves crossing over from Noman's Land? Only traitor elves should be coming from this direction."

"But someone in the caravan must have made the city limits. They'll tell the humans what's happened."

Einar didn't look convinced. "If they realize we survived the attack. But there are very, very few in this city who will recognize me. And no human will know you on sight, even those who survived the caravan attack."

The king had put a small glamour spell on her, just enough to keep humans from remembering her too well once she was no longer in their company—a precaution that now seemed more of a hindrance.

"We can't assume a friendly reception," Einar finished.

"Should we try to return to Glengowyn? When the sun sets?"

His frown deepened. "One traitor survived the attack. He'll tell the Sorcerers we're alive and in the city. They'll assume we'll try to either return to Glengowyn or make the Sinnale border tonight."

"You think they'll attempt to take us again?"

He met her gaze. "They will come for you again. Yes."

She didn't miss his pointed omission. "You think they'll kill you?"

"They'll try."

The very thought of Einar being killed left a hollow ache in the pit of her stomach. She might not admit to him how she felt, but her feelings for the Darkness of Glengowyn had remained constant for more than two hundred years. Even though she couldn't have him for her own, she'd had the comfort of knowing he was on this plane, nearby, close enough to see and touch, smell and hear. He'd been a part of her life for as long as she could remember. He'd been her heart's desire for so long now she couldn't even begin to image her world without him in it.

To fight back the devastation even the thought of his death brought her, she lifted her chin and said, "You're no easy kill, Darkness. They'll be cautious."

"But you're valuable enough to risk my wrath."

Her heart tripped a little when he said "my" and not "the wrath of Glengowyn". But she realized he hadn't meant the comment as anything personal. He protected her because the king and queen asked it of him. Nothing more.

"What do you suggest?" She had to keep her focus on the situation. To think too much about Einar robbed her of her sense and reason.

"We keep cover here for the night. I'll attempt to get a message to the Sinnale. And the king. You'll be safer if they know to expect us. They may even be able to send aid."

"You don't think the minions will be sent to hunt us down here?"

"Both sides patrol Noman's Land. We'll be in danger from humans and minions."

"That's not really an answer to my question."

He held her gaze without blinking as he said, "They'll hunt for us here."

"We have allies in the Sinnale. I still think we should work our way toward their border."

"Not until I know our way will be safe. You're too valuable."

She snorted at his last statement and spun away. Goddess, how she hated being reminded every day, every hour of just how *valuable* she was to everyone else. Everyone but him.

She forced back that thought. It wasn't fair to him. But a thread of bitterness crept into her voice when she said, "And how will you ensure I'm protected now?"

There was no emotion in his tone when he answered. "The owls."

She nodded in understanding. He had a special affinity with the owls that carried messages for the elves. They did so only because Einar asked. The birds weren't trained carriers, not the way such creatures might have been trained in the past. Owls assisted the Glengowyn elves because Einar requested their assistance. The clever beings wouldn't continue in that job if Einar died. Something most elves had probably forgotten.

Like they'd forgotten elves were physically capable of killing other elves.

That thought reminded her vividly of the life she'd taken. She suspected Einar had killed other elves before—though most would have been unaware of the acts—but she'd been subject to the taboo her entire life. She could hardly believe she'd really done it, that she'd been able to.

That she didn't regret the act as she'd assumed she would.

Those thoughts led her down a path she didn't have time for. "So," she said, facing him. "We wait here for a short time? Or for the night? Will you request an owl come here?"

He stared at the floor, his brow furrowed. "I don't like to ask them to come to Noman's Land. But we have no choice."

"We can move closer to the edge of the city, so they won't have to fly too far into danger."

"The Sorcerers will be watching the city border closest, assuming I'll try to return you to Glengowyn."

"You're sure?"

"It's what I would tell them if I were one of the traitors. It's what most would do in this situation, given your value. So we'll stay here for a few hours, watch to see if we've been found. Once it's full dark, we'll find a new location."

"Toward the Sinnale?"

He dipped his chin in a sharp affirmative. "I'll have an owl come to me in our next location, if it's safe."

She stared at him for a few more minutes, caught by his intensity. To escape, she glanced down at his injured arm. "I can wrap that for you." She gestured to the wound.

He gave it a cursory glance. "It's only a scratch."

"But neither of us can afford to have you weakened." She spun in a slow circle, then started opening doors. When she found a room that contained a couch, she led him inside. "Sit," she ordered.

Without supplies, her only option for binding the wound was the hem of her riding robe. "Your knife." She held out a hand without looking at him and pulled up the long length of material.

"It's not necessary."

"Don't argue." She wiggled her fingers, still focused on the material in her hand. His presence threw her off balance and looking directly at him made it worse. They hadn't spent this much time together, alone and in close proximity, since…

She didn't want to think about the last time.

After the knife hilt settled gently into her palm, she sliced a few lengths of silk along the split front hem of the robe. It would leave a wider V in the front, but since they had to travel quickly, she was considering cutting off the length completely anyway. Once the sun set, the early autumn nights were too cold to get rid of the over-robe altogether. And it was designed to allow easy, free movement, with slits in front and back so she could sit astride her horse without the long material getting in the way. It had stayed out of her way during the earlier fight too. But those lengths of material could be put to better use. And the less she had to worry about right now, the better.

Once she had sufficient improvised bandages, she turned to

Einar. "Take your tunic off," she said, her voice as firm and emotionless as she could make it.

She tried not to be affected as he stood, removed his scabbard belt, then slipped his short vest off and dragged his tunic up over his head. Unfortunately, she couldn't hold back her quickly drawn breath when the magnificent musculature of his chest was revealed in full.

This wasn't the first time she'd seen him bare-chested, but the sight never ceased to stir her. When she looked up, she found him staring at her, his dark eyes nearly black in the dim light leaking in through grimy windows. She swallowed and focused on his arm. Her heartbeat sped as she drew near enough to feel the heat of his skin and smell the tangy combination of his natural spicy musk mixed with the sweat of battle. With Einar, that combination had always overwhelmed her better judgment, targeting her most desperate desires. Only with him.

Yet another reason she'd spent so many years avoiding him.

Though her pulse pounded in her ears, she concentrated on making her hands steady, her touch gentle. She used one length of material to gently blot the worst of the blood away. Some still seeped slowly from the injury, but not enough to be dangerous. Once she'd gotten the area as clean as possible with a dry cloth, she used another length to tightly bind the wound.

His muscles flexed under her touch, which didn't help. "Relax," she ordered, her voice irritatingly husky.

He let out a long, slow exhale that brushed over the top of her head, and his biceps relaxed. She noticed at a glance, however, that his stomach muscles were tightly clenched. When she risked a peek at his face, his jaw was also tight, and he stared at the wall across from where they stood.

She turned back to her work, knowing she shouldn't have risked this kind of proximity for this long. Einar had more power over her body and heart than any other elf. A fact they were both growing more aware of with each passing moment.

When she'd tied off the bandage, satisfied it would do for now, she stepped back and gestured at his leg without actually looking down. "Are you cut or was it just your trousers?"

"It's nothing."

"Nothing as in no blood, or nothing as in you don't wish me to bandage the wound?"

His gaze jumped from the wall to her and she took another involuntary step back. Heat, promise, need and something she didn't want to admit seeing blazed out at her, an arrow right into her heart.

"You made it clear," he said quietly, "that your magic was not something you could sacrifice. We should not remain this close. And I should *not* take off any more clothing around you."

Her throat was too dry to even swallow. She could feel it, as she was certain he could—the *Shaerta*. Humans called it elf-fire. And sometimes elf-tears because it was addictive to them. Between elves, it was strong but didn't cause permanent damage with exposure. What *would* happen if they heeded its call, if they allowed themselves to truly bond, was a melding of their magics. The results were unpredictable. She wouldn't know until it was too late what form her abilities would take after a bonding.

Queen Rohannah had made it very clear that Nuala's talents were too valuable to risk.

"You agreed," she said. "Without any argument, as I recall."

She heard the bitterness in her own voice and was sorry for it. She'd been the one to say they should separate, knowing he would choose his loyalty to the sovereigns over her. She hadn't wanted to hear him say it aloud. So she'd been the one to instigate the break. She couldn't blame him for doing exactly what she'd expected, what she'd *known* he would do.

Even though she'd wanted him to argue. Even though she'd wanted him to fight for her, to ignore his loyalty to the king and queen, to ignore everything in order to have her.

Long-festering pain lanced her, her chest tightening under the weight of it. Even as the *Shaerta* rose between them, the longing and need for him so strong she could barely keep from moving into his arms, the hurt of their break brought tears to her eyes.

Appalled by the fact that he probably saw the shimmering wetness, she turned away. She tossed her remaining strips of material toward the couch. "Bind your leg. Bleeding to weakness out of stubbornness won't help either one of us."

She left the sitting room to pace in the large foyer, carefully avoiding looking back at Einar.

CHAPTER FOUR

$\mathcal{A}$s Nuala waited on Einar, she checked her own body for injuries she might not have noticed. Her arm ached a little and a large bruise covered her upper biceps and shoulder, but otherwise, no cuts or broken bones.

Her stomach growled as she returned to pacing.

"You're hungry," Einar said.

Surprised by his voice, she spun to face him. He was fully dressed again, his sword strapped back into place. And through the tear in his trousers she could see some of the green-blue silk of a bandage.

"A little," she answered. "What supplies I had fled with my mare."

"I've nothing either, I'm afraid." He glanced at the front door, his scowl forming deep creases in his forehead. "I should have grabbed my saddle pack before we made for the city."

"We didn't know how much time we had or who might be nearby." She might not be able to deal with him on an emotional level. But he was the fiercest warrior in Glengowyn. And he'd helped save her life. She wouldn't allow him to berate his actions in the heat of battle.

She'd never allowed that.

His lips lifted, as if he was remembering the same fact.

And again, Nuala found herself short of breath. Einar was gorgeous when serious, but his smile, rare as it was, left her helpless against his male beauty.

His expression remained soft, the bare smile not faltering as they stared at each other.

Then her stomach growled again. The sound was loud in the quiet foyer and without meaning to, Nuala laughed. Surprised by her own outburst, she covered her mouth. "Sorry," she mumbled around her hand. "I know we need to be quiet."

"In that case, we should feed you or the whole of Sinnale will hear your hunger."

She snorted again into her hand, trying to stifle her amusement. But he smiled a little more at her reaction.

In an attempt to return to the seriousness of the situation, she said, "I can do without for a while. We won't be hiding for long. And besides, where would we find food in Noman's Land?"

"Some humans continue to squat in the buildings closer to Sinnale territory," he said.

But he frowned and she knew he'd considered the same thing she had.

"We won't be any more welcome by them than the border guards because we're unknown elves."

He nodded. "I can go out and scavenge."

"No." Fear tightened her throat. "I don't think we should separate." Though being around Einar was a kind of torture, letting him go into danger on his own was unacceptable. She didn't care if he was the great and terrible Darkness of Glengowyn. If he got hurt, or worse killed, trying to find her food, she'd never survive it.

He was silent for a long moment. Then, "When I call an owl, I'll see if he might bring us some food."

"So long as it's not a dead rodent." She shivered, only half teasing.

"As you wish," he said so seriously, she burbled out another repressed laugh.

"Until then," he said, glancing at the front door, "rest. Take the sitting room. Try to sleep if you can. It will be a long night."

"And you?"

"I'll wake you in a few hours. You can watch while I rest."

She was afraid he wouldn't sleep, that he wouldn't bother to wake her. He'd been known to remain awake for days in battle and he would consider this a similar enough situation. "Promise me you'll try to sleep, not just rest," she said, even though she knew it was futile.

"I would never promise you anything I might not be able to deliver." His voice dropped to a quiet, deep octave.

The sound sent tremors of tingling sensation through her stomach and down to her core. Again, she wanted to step into him, forgo her duty to Glengowyn, risk her magic, risk everything she was to have him. To lay him on the couch and fuck him until the world ended around them.

Instead, she disappeared into the sitting room. She doubted she'd be able to sleep, but being near him eroded her will, and their situation was too precarious to risk giving in to the *Shaerta*. Or her years of yearning and love.

To Nuala's surprise, she did nap for a bit, blissfully without dreams. When Einar woke her, it was twilight dark. "You let me sleep too long," she accused.

"We can't leave until it's full dark. I'll have time to rest."

She sat up on the couch, a move that brought her level with his groin. Still half asleep, she allowed herself to stare as memories of his thick, perfect cock tormented her. Oh the pleasures they could give each other.

His growl startled her out of her erotic thoughts.

"Don't promise what you have no intention of seeing through," he muttered.

"Don't I?" She was asking herself as much as him. They'd managed to avoid each other's company for two centuries, despite living in the same city. She'd only glimpsed him on the rare occasions she was called to Court, and then there were so many others around, they were safe from this attraction between them.

Now, with no buffers, no royal leaders watching their every move, she was no longer sure she wanted to resist him. Denying herself his love all these years had slowly killed something in her. That something seemed to be stirring back to life. And she wasn't entirely sure she wanted to sacrifice that part of herself again.

Why had the queen and king sent him to guard her? They must have known. Did they really think the centuries would dim her desire for Einar? Why did they tempt them this way if they valued her magic as it was?

She rose. "I'm sorry. That wasn't kind of me. With you…" She waved a hand vaguely in the air, not sure how to explain.

"It's the same for me. With you."

None of the exhaustion he must feel showed in his face, but knowledge that he had to be tired after the fight and the injuries forced her away from their personal desires.

"I'll keep watch. *Try* to sleep." She gave him a level look, which brought out his slight smile, and she gave up. Shaking her head, she picked up her quiver and bow from beside the couch and draped them over her head to rest along her back, then headed toward the doorway and the window at the front door where she could keep an eye on the street.

Before she left the sitting room, though, Einar called her back. "Take my knife. Just in case. Though if you see anyone, let me know immediately."

"I will." She stared down at the knife, thoughts of the elf she'd actually killed rising up.

"I…didn't realize you'd learned to throw knives," he said into the silence.

"I'm not as good as I should be." She shrugged. "Ulric insisted I learn. My talent with bow and arrow notwithstanding, he said I needed a second way to defend myself. Just in case."

"Your cousin is a good man. I'm glad he was able to teach you."

She slipped the borrowed weapon into her belt sheath. "I'll wake you once it's been full dark for a bit. Thank you for the knife."

She was at the doorway when his voice made her pause again.

"He deserved to die, Nuala. Don't regret killing the traitor."

Without turning, she said, "I don't. But the fact that I could, that I had to, makes me…sad."

She left without saying more. This was not the time to discuss her regrets. There were too many anyway.

NUALA CAUGHT SIGHT OF THE SMALL GROUP OF MINIONS WHILE they were a block away. Torn between watching their progress and waking Einar, she decided she had time to wake him.

Slipping on silent feet into the small sitting room, she knelt beside Einar and would have smiled if not for the approaching enemy. He was asleep.

With a soft touch on his shoulder and a finger over his mouth, she murmured his name.

He opened his eyes instantly, coming to full wakefulness

without any of the lag time she usually required. Moving her finger from his mouth, she whispered, "Minions approaching from the southeast."

He flowed to his feet, grabbing his sword from where it lay on the floor beneath the couch. Nuala stepped back to give him room then followed him to the windows. The room didn't have any curtains, but it was completely dark inside now. Still, he kept to the wall, deep in the shadows. She used his larger body to conceal herself.

"There," she said when she spotted an individual minion coming into view. They were only a few doors away, but it was obvious they were searching the buildings.

"How did they find us?" she asked.

"How large was the party?"

She shrugged. "There were five when I first saw them."

"Small groups, then. The Sorcerers have probably sent an army of minions into Noman's Land looking for us. Small groups can cover a lot of territory."

"What about the humans patrolling the area?"

"As dangerous to us as the minions right now."

"But won't they…complicate the search?"

Her heart pounding, she watched as two minions entered the building across the street and two doors away.

"Maybe," Einar answered, his voice barely audible he spoke so quietly, "but that won't help us now. We need to get to the roof."

"Is there time?"

He held still for one more heartbeat, then grabbed her hand and tugged, moving swiftly and silently back through the room to the entryway. Without pause, he led her up the stairs, circling around and climbing until they reached the top floor. Once there, they had to search for some way they might access the roof.

Cursing silently, Nuala studied the ceiling down one length of the hall while Einar searched the opposite side of the corridor. When she heard the front door open, she spun to face Einar. He was already moving toward her, faster than most elves could move. He swept an arm around her waist and hurried her to the window at the end of the hall.

He studied it a moment, then opened it as quietly as he could but some noise squeaked out. They froze. The shuffle of feet in the foyer thudded to the stairs.

"*Fateesh*," he cursed and threw the window open, sticking his head out to study their surroundings.

She watched the stairway, his knife in her hand, her entire body tense.

"Onto my back," he ordered in that barely audible whisper.

"What…?"

But he didn't give her time to question his plan. He grabbed her arm just above her elbow and swung her around to his back with a strength that surprised even her. She clung to his neck with one arm, careful not to choke him, slid his knife into one of the scabbards on her belt, then circled her other arm around his chest. She tried wrapping her legs around him high enough to avoid the sword at his side, but the position meant he wouldn't be able to reach his weapon.

In his ear, she said, "Now what?"

He didn't answer. He just climbed into the window frame, crouched so neither of them would bump their heads. Before she could guess at his intention, he leapt, his powerful thighs pushing them off the window ledge and out into the empty air.

CHAPTER FIVE

Nuala's stomach dropped and it took all her will not to squeal in alarm. She clenched Einar tighter, reflexively, her face pressed into his shoulder as terror slammed through her. The jolt of landing nearly forced her hold to relax. His arm came up and braced her lower back, keeping her from falling.

"Are you okay?" he asked.

She looked around. They'd landed on the roof of a neighboring building, one story below the window they'd jumped from, but far enough away she wouldn't have thought the leap possible. "How?"

"Killing isn't my only skill. You know that."

She unfolded her legs and slid to the ground, stepping away from him before she noticed the contact too much. "Now where?"

He took her hand again and pulled her to the opposite side of the flat rooftop, ducking behind a tall brick chimney just before she heard voices from the window they'd leapt from.

"Anything?"

"No elves. Could they make that jump?"

Silence. Then, "Doubt it. Too far even for an elf."

"The others should go into that building anyway."

"I'll tell them."

"I'll finish here."

Nuala waited in silence for at least ten heartbeats after the voices disappeared, then she raised her brows. Einar nodded. They faced the next neighboring building.

"Me first," he said. "You can make this?"

"Yes." She'd cliff-jumped as a youth, just like the other elves. This distance was at the farthest reach of her abilities but she'd done it before. She held her breath as he made the leap, landing easily and gracefully on the next roof. Then she backed up two steps and threw herself into the jump. When she landed beside him, she laughed, muffling the sound with her hand, but completely unable to contain her reaction to the thrill of making that distance.

He frowned at her. She grinned and shrugged.

"I haven't done that in a while. I forgot how much fun it is."

His frown remained in place but his expression seemed to ease a little. Or at least she thought it did. With the only illumination coming from the two-thirds first moon, it was hard to tell.

Without a word, he led her across the roof to yet another building. After studying the street below, he nodded and they jumped again. She stumbled a little on this landing, the adrenaline of their escape starting to shiver her muscles. The next building down the street was three stories higher than the one they were on, so they turned to the back of the roof and crossed a foot-wide gap to yet another building.

"We'll have to go back to the street," Einar said, searching the surrounding buildings. Two were too high, the other was on the opposite side of the street and still too high for them to jump.

Her stomach danced with fear now that the excitement of building jumping was over.

This roof had an obvious door leading back inside, but Einar paused to study the streets below first. After several tense moments, he joined her at the door, leading her down the stairwell to the ground floor. Nuala barely noticed the building around them. She had a vague impression of square galleries and a multitude of doors, but her full focus was on trailing Einar down the dark stairs, afraid she'd miss her footing if she didn't pay attention.

At the front entrance, Einar paused again, studying the street through the windows beside the door. She had to force air in and out of her lungs. Finally, he eased open the door, which moved on surprisingly silent hinges, and they slipped into the street, sticking close to the building walls.

Sounds from in front of them, the direction they wanted to go, forced them to back-peddle into the alley next to the building, opposite their planned escape route. Einar blocked her view, putting his large frame in front of hers as they pressed close to the alley wall and listened.

The heavy fall of booted feet clicked across the cobbled streets. Listening carefully, she thought she heard two, maybe three different individuals. But since they didn't speak, she couldn't be sure. She and Einar waited for a long while, listening to those boot steps. The sounds faded in and out but there was always at least one person on the road at any given time, making it impossible for her and Einar to go that direction.

She studied the opposite end of the alleyway in frustration. It was a dead end, and at any rate, led them back toward the original group of minions they'd just escaped.

The feel of Einar's breath at her ear made her jump.

"More minions," he said. "Heading away. When I move, don't hesitate."

She squeezed his arm in understanding and turned her focus on his shoulder, braced to run when he did.

As she waited, a sound carried to her across the wind and

Einar's back stiffened. She strained to catch more of the noise. Shouts. The clashing of metal. The sharp *swack* of a bowstring releasing. Her heartbeat accelerated.

"A fight, only a street or two over," she murmured. "Sinnale soldiers must have found one of the minion groups."

He nodded in agreement, though he never took his attention from the minions in the street ahead of them. He raised a hand, a silent warning to prepare, and then sprinted across the road. She followed, racing a step behind him. When they made the next alley, he paused and lifted his head, listening.

She could hear it too, more joining the fight. A full-blown skirmish was underway.

"The others are joining the fight," Einar said. "More minions will make their way toward it."

"What do we do? Should we help? Or…"

He shook his head before she could finish. "Sinnale will assume we're traitor elves. Minions will try to kill or capture us. We need to avoid the fight, find another hiding spot."

"The minions will just continue searching. Where can we be safe?"

As he considered their options, they watched another small group of minions race by, heading toward the growing conflict.

"Opposite the fight and toward Sinnale territory," Einar finally said. "As we originally planned. This skirmish is deep in Noman's Land. The Sinnale soldiers are probably all over the area hunting the minions. Neither side will have time to look for two missing elves for hours, maybe not for the rest of the night if the Sinnale win these fights and drive the minions back to Sorcerer territory."

"We'll have to avoid human patrols too," she pointed out.

"They aren't looking for us. We can hide from them. We just need an empty building, no human squatters."

Carefully, and sticking close to the buildings, they made their way through the deserted, ramshackle part of the city that was the buffer between the two warring parties. The occasional gaslamp provided small pools of light, but most of them were dark. And the closer they got to the Sinnale border, the fewer patches of light there were.

Twice they ducked into dark recesses to avoid human patrols. Once they nearly walked out into the path of a minion group. And once they had to change direction to avoid another skirmish. First moon was high overhead by the time they found an empty building that Einar deemed a suitable hiding spot.

Inside, they quietly searched the three levels of the small building, checking for the presence of others likely to return. Every room and corridor was covered in dust that looked undisturbed for months, maybe years. Einar checked the roof as well, assessing possible escape routes. When he was satisfied they were as safe as they could be for the night, he motioned her back inside.

"I'll call an owl. But you'll be more comfortable downstairs."

"I won't be comfortable until we make contact with someone who can help us," she said.

"Still. It's cold tonight. I don't want you to take a chill." He gestured to her torn riding robe. "You've been running and tense. When the sweat cools, you'll notice the cold out here."

"So will you," she said. Then smiled. "And are you trying to tell me I stink of sweat?"

His mouth crooked up at one side, just barely. "You always smell lovely. Go inside. I'll join you shortly."

Giving in, she took the roof stairs to the third floor to scout a suitable room to rest in. They were fortunate that the windows in this building were mostly intact, at least on this floor. Several of the rooms had furniture, though most of it was too filthy to make for comfortable sitting. She found two rooms with beds and one of those beds appeared relatively clean, though it was bare. She studied that room and realized it wasn't as dirty in general as the other rooms, the dust only just starting to accumulate again.

Someone had used that space, not long ago. But there were no signs of it being readied for a return visitor. When she checked the ceramic heater in the corner, there was no kindling or flint and steel to start a fire with. Someone planning on using this room again would have left something behind to start a fire. Or left some clean linens for the bed. She opened the single oak trunk in the room, but it was empty. No, there didn't seem to be signs that whoever had used this room might return. She and Einar should be safe enough here.

With a little sigh, she flipped the mattress over, exposing a dust-free side that was in decent shape, better than she'd expected. Then she sat and waited for Einar.

He didn't leave her alone for long. He filled the doorway when he did join her, his large, muscled frame a paler darkness. Ambient light from both the waning moon and a single working gaslamp gave the room some illumination, but not enough to see his facial expression clearly as he hovered in the shadows.

"Did an owl come?"

He made a noise that sounded like a short, broken laugh. "Of course. They're always happy to answer my requests."

"How do you send messages without anything to write with?" She knew he could do this. He'd done it before. But she'd never asked how he managed. For every other elf, the owls would deliver written notes. Only Einar could deliver a verbal one.

He came into the room, hesitating a few feet from the bed. There was nowhere else to sit, and his hovering rubbed irritatingly against her nerves.

"Sit down, Einar. I won't attack you. We can be in each other's company for a few minutes without succumbing to the *Shaerta*."

Still reluctant, he finally settled on the opposite end of the bed.

"Now. How do you send verbal messages with the owls? I've always wondered and been afraid to ask."

He tilted his head to one side. "You afraid? I find that hard to believe."

"You're avoiding the question."

"The owls can deliver my verbal messages to the king. He's the only other elf who can understand, though he does so in a different manner than I do. He…sees the messages, almost like pictures, from the owl's mind."

"And you? Can you receive verbal messages?" Before he could answer, she let out a half laugh. "But of course you wouldn't know, as the owls won't carry verbal messages from other elves."

"They bring me news that was spoken within their hearing."

She focused on him more fully. "What?"

"While collecting written messages, if they glean information they feel I should know, they tell me. I understand their…language is the only way to describe it. When they speak, I know what they're saying."

"Unlike the king."

"Different from the king."

"What did you ask His Majesty to do?"

"To inform your cousin that we need safe passage from Noman's Land. Once he has a safe way for us to enter Sinnale territory, he can relay that information through the king via the owls."

She released a small breath and smiled. "Ulric. Very clever. Trusted by the humans now. And will recognize us both on sight."

"He'll arrange the proper security so the Sorcerers don't try to infiltrate their territory by pretending to be you and me."

"I hadn't thought of that." She straightened her shoulders. "A further complication to us just waltzing into Sinnale territory."

"Yes."

"Do they have something or someone who can see through illusion spells?"

"Likely Ulric will impose on the queen. She's the only one of sufficient skill to ensure we're who we say we are."

"Won't that be dangerous for her? If the Sorcerers came after me, surely they'll want the queen when they get word of her coming into Sinnale."

Though the king and queen had both entered the city on several occasions while the elves were technically neutral in the war, they had remained safe in Glengowyn once their support of the Sinnale was made official.

Since Einar was the bodyguard to the royal couple, she was certain he would find the plan too risky. He surprised her by smiling. A full-blown, all-out grin.

"Her Majesty has ways of getting around that most elves are unaware of. She's very purposefully kept a few of her skills a secret. Getting in and out of Sinnale is not as difficult for her as it is for most."

Nuala widened her eyes in surprise. The king and queen had reigned for centuries, so long she'd thought all their magics must have been revealed. Apparently, she was wrong.

"So. We'll see the queen when we finally reach safety."

"I would assume so."

She took in the implications of that for a long moment.

"What are you thinking?" he asked, his voice quiet.

How to tell him? They'd been avoiding this for two hundred years.

Instead of a direct approach, she said, "Why do you think they risk…us on this mission? Together?"

"You're highly valuable to Glengowyn. Who else would they trust with your safety?"

"Ulric."

He dipped his head to the side, a half nod, half shrug. "He would have made an excellent guard. But he's too well known among the Sorcerers now. It was felt his presence would call too much attention to your...importance."

"Many of the traitor elves know you too. Even if they didn't recognize me, seeing the Darkness of Glengowyn would reveal my *importance*." She wanted to sneer the word but kept that reaction to herself. She accepted her position in Glengowyn society, but centuries of the overprotective efforts of the royal couple had left her weary.

She watched Einar carefully as he faced the wall. The soft rise and fall of his chest drew her gaze to the thick muscles. She remembered well how those muscles felt under her hands, pressing against her naked breasts. The weight of him as he covered her. His scent filled her. Mixed with dust and sweat was that distinct spicy musk that was Einar's alone. She'd never met elf or human whose scent called to her the way his did. Unable to resist, she took another deep breath.

Her movements attracted his gaze. Even with him sitting so close, she couldn't read anything in his dark eyes. But she felt the *Shaerta* tickling her skin. His reaction or hers, she couldn't tell. Maybe both. The fire was rising, though. And too much longer on this bed, in this quiet, isolated room, would leave her defenseless to him.

"No one knew I would join the group," he said into the silence. "Only the king, queen and Ulric. The traitors wouldn't have expected me to leave the sovereigns' side. That gave us an advantage. And while many elves think they know what I look like, most have never looked close enough to recognize me out of context."

She wondered if that was true. Byral hadn't recognized him and Byral had been to Court at least a few times. Maybe fear of the

Darkness really did keep the others from looking too closely. She couldn't imagine *not* looking at Einar or knowing every detail of his face. The brush of short hair against his collar and the sharp points of his ears just peeking past the dark, thick waves, the ever-so-slight tilt of his eyes, the firm set of his mouth and solid angle of his jaw. Every detail etched into her heart for centuries.

She blinked and dragged her thoughts back to the conversation. "The traitors did expect me, though," she said. "They knew I was there. They came for me specifically. It wouldn't have mattered if Ulric was with me or not."

"We know that now. They've probably been watching all the caravans, waiting for you to appear. When the plans were made, however, it was thought best to draw as little attention to you as possible while providing you with the highest level of security."

"You."

"Me."

"Did they..." She swallowed as she found herself leaning toward him without meaning to. "Didn't they worry about the *Shaerta*?"

He held perfectly still, not moving closer. Her own weakening will kept her edging across the bed, very slightly, toward him.

"They trusted you to uphold their decree."

"Not you?" That surprised her. He'd been as disciplined at avoiding her as she'd been at avoiding him. Maybe more so. He'd never once shown signs of the weakness she often felt when it came to him.

He didn't answer. Instead, he stood and paced to the opposite side of the room. Then he headed for the door. "I need to check on the skirmishes. I'll be back soon."

He left without a backward glance. Nuala sighed. She removed her bow and quiver and set them beside her on the bed, then leaned on the headboard. Again his willpower managed to stay strong where hers faltered.

But what did she expect? They'd see the queen soon enough. Giving in to the *Shaerta* wasn't an option. While they might be able to get away with a single encounter after all these years, she knew one night with Einar would never be enough. Succumbing to her desires once would make it impossible for her to deny them anymore. Making love to Einar again would ruin her.

And yet, somehow that ruin no longer seemed so bad.

With a groan, she stretched out on the bed to await his return, trying to remind herself why she'd heeded the queen and king's edict in the first place. To ignore their order would lead to banishment for both her and Einar. After so long, that punishment didn't scare her as much. But Einar… She couldn't do that to him. She was sure he wouldn't risk it. Why else had he left the room? He was right. She knew he was. Her value was significant. Banishment would be disastrous for everyone.

But oh how she wanted him to throw caution to the wind, stalk into the room, strip her naked, and fuck her like nothing else in the world mattered.

A dream, she knew. But a pleasant one that carried her into a light doze as she waited.

CHAPTER SIX

$\mathcal{E}$inar woke her with a gentle touch on her shoulder. Dawn light peeked in through the single window, just enough to see his face clearly.

"Danger?" she asked, half sitting.

"No. We're safe. The fighting moved through Noman's Land most of the night, but the skirmishes shifted toward the Sorcerers' territory and away from us."

"How…?"

He lifted his lips, an almost smile. "The owls."

"Ah. Of course. So…" She sat up completely and looked around the room. Einar straightened and took a few steps back from the bed. "So now what?" she asked. "We wait here?"

"We'll need food and water soon. But for the day, this location should be safe enough."

"I can go without food and water for a bit longer if necessary."

His expression took on a faraway, thoughtful look. "I know. I remember."

She remembered too. The last goblin war had been even harder on them all than the first. In the heat of battle, as she worked frantically to provide enough of her special arrows, she'd often gone for days with only a minimum of food and water. Usually what she got came from Einar's own hands.

"We'll be stronger for any fighting or fleeing if we eat," he said finally.

"There won't be much to find. Not here."

"I've already taken care of it."

"The owls again?"

He dipped his head once in affirmation.

"Very handy, those birds. When they do as you ask."

"It's because I ask nicely."

She snorted. "Of course."

Stretching her arms forward, she loosened her back and shoulder muscles. Then she went to look out the window, carefully standing to one side so she couldn't be spotted from the street.

"No patrols yet this morning?" She kept her face turned away from him as she studied the chunk of city she could see.

"No patrols. From either side. After the fighting, things will likely be quiet for a few hours, at least. Especially since the humans won."

"Did they? I'm glad."

"They drove the minions back behind their own lines. The minions weren't prepared for a full battle."

"And the Sinnale are stronger now. With our help."

Nothing moved on the cobbles below. Not even bits of rubbish blew down the empty alleys and courtyards. The morning air was still and quiet, casting a pink glow that softened the battered buildings and hid the neglect and damage. In that light, she could almost see the city as it had been before the war, a century ago when she'd last been here.

"I'm sorry I can't provide enough water for washing," Einar

murmured. "The owls couldn't risk bringing in items too large. Or too many of them flying to the same place. That would give us away."

"It's not a problem. I realize I probably stink." She grinned over her shoulder. "But I can stand it for another day if you can."

The thought of the owls being tracked had her turning to face him fully. "Will they be able to get any supplies to us without attracting attention? Especially in the daytime when they shouldn't really be about except for passing messages. Some lookout somewhere will spot them."

"They can fly low when needs be, avoiding too much attention. But only if there are no more than two or three. More would attract notice."

"Again, I can go without food or water. I wouldn't want to see one of them hurt."

He tilted his head to one side. "I wouldn't risk them unnecessarily."

"I know. I meant… Maybe my comfort isn't necessary enough for their risk."

"Your comfort isn't my concern. Your strength and ability to escape danger is."

How could she argue with that? She looked out the window again, not sure what else to say. Searching for a topic, she recalled one of the questions she'd never broached yesterday. "I forgot until now, but…the Sorcerer who was part of the caravan attack? You said he was never real. What did you mean? I could smell the death stench surrounding him. Even the horses reacted to him."

"He was a…*projection* the king calls it. Difficult and draining magic when so much detail is incorporated. But useful. They send their essence, their spirit, away from their bodies to whatever location they choose, but they aren't there in a form that can be attacked or killed. Their bodies remain safe, probably inside the citadel or their own strongholds. Somewhere within range of the projection location. Ulric noticed them using this technique during the most recent battles with the Sinnale. The Sorcerers can direct efforts and watch the movements of the humans without having to endanger themselves by being physically present during the fight."

"Can these projections cast spells?"

"No. They're limited to observation. That's how I knew the Sorcerer at the caravan attack wasn't real."

Ah. Now she understood. "He would have used magic to stop our escape if he'd been real."

She glanced back at Einar in time to see him nod.

"You said the magic for projection was draining?"

"Very costly to their power stores."

"Then they are weakening by using this spell?"

"Or using up more of their captives toward their magic."

Her shoulders jerked in a shiver she couldn't control. The poor humans. It was no wonder Ulric had been so vocal about bringing Glengowyn into this war. The woman he loved could have been taken and used that way. Nuala couldn't imagine much worse than knowing Einar had been tortured and killed to feed the evil of death magic. Realizing that it could still happen if they didn't reach Sinnale territory safely closed her throat.

She turned back to the window so he wouldn't see her sudden jolt of fear.

As she studied the city and tried not to feel the pull toward Einar that was beyond her control, she began plucking pins from her hair. The tight, battle-ready bun at the base of her head had finally come loose, and the escaped tendrils were itching her neck. She didn't wear her hair this tightly bound often, so her scalp was sore. She set the pins on the windowsill and unwound the bun, leaving the golden-brown braid to fall down her back. She didn't have a brush, and wouldn't have water to rise out the sweat and dust, but even a finger comb would relieve some of the pressure on her scalp.

Removing a final stray pin, she set it with the others, rubbed her fingers across her head, then reached for the strap of leather holding the end of her braid. She jumped when she felt Einar's hands on her shoulders.

The sensation, both familiar and new after all this time, sent a tremor of heat through her belly. With only that brief contact, she could already feel the *Shaerta* rising. Her nerves danced. She drew in a deep breath, absorbing Einar's scent, and the heat in her stomach spread through her abdomen to her core.

Turning to face him just then would destroy what little resistance she had, so she kept her body motionless, her gaze on the street.

He skimmed his hands down the length of her arms, leaving a hot chill along her skin and forcing her hands down to her sides. Then he leaned in and said against her ear, "Allow me."

She wanted to melt into him but couldn't manage any movement, closer or away. He released her wrists and shifted to her braid, untying the leather strap, then slowly separating the strands.

Heart pounding, Nuala closed her eyes, the wash of sensation from having his hands on her overwhelming and perfect. She concentrated on the play of his fingers up her braid, the gentle run of his palms over and through the strands, the heavy fall of weight when her hair was fully freed of its confines, and the merciless thrill of him brushing her hair, his fingers threading over her scalp, pulling the thick locks away from her face. She tilted her head back at his urging, giving him access to better massage her temples. Without realizing she would, she groaned.

"I've missed this," he said, his voice low and deep. "The feel of your hair, your skin."

"I've missed you too," she admitted, despite her best intentions. "I've felt…half of myself for a long time now."

His grip tightened at her admission. Then he released her, and Nuala wanted to cry, knowing he would continue to resist where she could not.

An instant later, she was facing him, his hands tight on her shoulders. His dark eyes sparked in the early morning light, his expression more animated, more desperate than anything she'd ever seen him reveal. Before she could absorb the full impact, his mouth was on hers, firm, strong and so heartbreakingly gentle her entire body relaxed into him.

Einar. After all this time. To taste him again was beyond exquisite, beyond joy. She had no way to put into words the sensation that enveloped her except that it felt like her world finally settled into place and became real.

He cupped her cheeks in his hands, holding her near as his kiss deepened. Still controlled, still luxurious, as if they had all the time in the world for just this kiss. Gripping his waist, she followed him into that place, her tongue brushing and swirling around his, a delicate duel no one would suspect the Darkness capable of. Most thought him hard, emotionless, cold.

She knew better. He was all heat and warmth and emotion. With her, he was passion. And she was free.

Their kiss heated slowly, perfectly. Destroying her and renewing her with each play of lips against lips. He slipped his hands from her face to her waist, snugging her tightly to his body. The press of her breasts against the thick expanse of muscles along his chest weakened her knees. The feel of his cock already hard against her abdomen thrilled her on a deep level. And suddenly all she wanted was the heat of his skin, naked against hers, so she could explore this body she'd been denied for too long.

The *Shaerta* raged through her, heightening her every sense.

That underlying musky scent that was Einar filled her head. The touch of his hands, strong on her waist, branded her. The heat of his cock warmed her through her clothes as if there was no barrier between them. And still his kiss was deliberately languorous, deliciously tempting.

Tension flexed his muscles, a tightness echoing her building passion, yet she couldn't rush this reunion any more than he could.

So long, so much time wasted. The reason for their separation no longer seemed to make sense. Not when they had this. Not when she loved him so very much.

Without allowing any space between them, Einar edged her back toward the bed. She followed his lead, step by step, floating over the dust-covered wood in moments and hours. Her legs touched the mattress and she dropped back, dragging him with her. The drop made them bounce, and despite everything, Nuala giggled.

Einar lifted enough to look down at her, his expression beautifully open. A small smile tugged at his lips, the stone mask he normally wore gone to reveal a tenderness only she was allowed to see.

Reaching up, she cupped his cheek, too touched for words, too happy for regrets.

They would deal with the aftermath of this day soon enough. Now, having him inside her was as vital to her as water and air. More powerful than magic.

With the *Shaerta* riding her, she embraced the consequences, tugging his mouth back to hers.

CHAPTER SEVEN

he first touch of his warm palms on her breasts, even through her clothing, was enough to turn tenderness to desperation. Nuala arched against him, moaning into his mouth. And his grip tightened. Her skin was incredibly sensitive, so that when he found her nipples through her shirt, the tug and pinch was almost painful. She wouldn't have changed a second of that sensation.

But she wanted his hands on her bare skin. Pushing him off, she sat up.

"Nuala?"

The uncertainty in his voice squeezed at her heart. She leaned close again to kiss him, running her hand down his stomach to the thick bulge pressing against his trousers.

"I have no intention of leaving without getting my hands and my mouth on your cock," she said. "I want every inch of you, naked and at my mercy. But I don't want to enjoy you with my clothes on."

Her admission brought more heat to his dark eyes, so black now they were almost frightening. "I can help with removing your clothing," he said.

Rubbing his cock through his trousers, she shook her head. "You have more important things to do."

He raised his brows.

"Take off your own."

She slid away before he tried to change her mind. Watching him, she unbuckled her belt with Einar's knife in one scabbard and set it gently on the floor. Then she undid the ties closing the front of her robe as he sat up and slipped off his vest and tunic. She allowed herself the freedom to fully appreciate that beautiful chest of his, finally and after so long.

Licking her lips, she dropped her robe and started unlacing the front of her blouse. The heat of his gaze was like a physical touch, a touch she couldn't deny. She opened her shirt, letting the soft material fall down her arms to pool on top of her robe, then quickly pulled off the fitted vest that kept her breasts contained.

He groaned, his gaze locked on her chest as she cupped her breasts and pinched her nipples into hardness.

"You've too much on," she reminded him as she continued to play with herself, knowing how it affected him.

Without taking his gaze from her, he shifted to the edge of the bed to tug off his boots. Rubbing one hand down her abdomen to the top of her riding trousers, she watched him watching her, knowing he wanted to put his hands on her more than he wanted to breathe. Knowing because she felt the same. He stood and shucked off his trousers and underpants, barely paying attention to his own actions.

Because he was doing exactly what she asked, she opened the buttons on her trousers. Then bent to remove her boots. The forward motion made her breasts sway, and cool air caressed her skin, emphasizing how hot she felt, how deliciously sensitive and ready.

With her boots tossed aside, she straightened and edged her pants down her hips, wiggling a little to free the material. Einar's nostrils flared. He was standing now, as if he hadn't been able to move once he'd stripped. As he watched her reveal the rest of her body, he took his thick erection into his palm and stroked slowly, almost absentmindedly, like he couldn't help himself.

Hunger like she'd never felt swept through her. She wanted her hand on him, her mouth. But she was mesmerized watching him stroke himself. She found herself following his example, letting her fingers dip into her wet curls, stroke through the slick folds of her sex. A shiver took her as she cupped one breast with her free hand.

"I've spent too many nights touching myself and thinking of you," she whispered into the silence, which was punctuated only by their ragged breathing.

"Nuala," he moaned and his fingers flexed around his cock.

"Now, with you watching, I feel whole again. Because I know your hands will be here—" she slid her fingers deeper into her heat, "—taking me, feeling how much I want you."

"You have driven me wild from the first moment we met, Nuala. An insanity I can't regret now."

She smiled and finally allowed herself close to him again. He grabbed the hand she'd used on herself and brought her still-damp fingers to his mouth, sucking the moisture off gently. Her heart thundered, and her knees trembled. Goddess, but he was magnificent. And for this moment, he was hers completely.

Dropping to his knees in front of her, he kissed the skin above her curls, low on her abdomen. Every muscle in her body tightened in reaction, in anticipation. To her relief, he didn't tease her. He mouth dipped lower, over her heat, his tongue licking through her folds and pressing eagerly against her clitoris. She cried out, so sensitive she knew she would come quickly. She didn't care. She would come as often today as he'd allow her. Her fingers shook as she buried them in his short, thick hair and let her head fall back and her eyes close.

He licked and sucked her swollen flesh until she trembled all over, her legs barely holding her upright. The building pressure swelled, consumed, engulfed her until only his mouth on her anchored her to reality. Then the pressure broke and she cried out, despite knowing she should remain quiet. The sound came without thought or permission, a primitive reaction to a release so hard and thorough her knees finally did give out.

Einar caught her before she collapsed, his arms circling around her hips. When she opened her eyes and looked down, he was staring at her, his gaze full of satisfaction.

"I've missed watching you come," he said, his voice deep. "I've never seen anything more beautiful in my long life."

She smiled. "I hope you intend to watch me come a few more times before we're done."

"As often as you can stand," he promised. Then he rose to his feet, his big body enveloping hers as he kissed her again, his hands tight on her waist.

She wrapped her arms around his neck and allowed him to lift her, turning her back to the bed. So much she wanted to do to him. So much she needed from him. As they tumbled to the mattress again, she reached for his cock, delighting in the heat and hardness of him.

His mouth devoured hers now, a man desperate and quickly losing control. She was the only one who'd ever been allowed to see him this way, so unguarded. So close to the edge of a different kind of madness. The privilege of it took her breath away.

Rolling him onto his back, she sprawled across his body, savoring the feel of his naked flesh against hers, so long remembered, so familiar and beloved. The *Shaerta* made every scrape of his chest hair over her breasts, every slide of damp skin against skin, more electric, harder to take and yet impossible to move away from. Overwhelming.

She'd experienced the effect of the hormone with a few other men in her life. But with Einar it was always different—leaving her both desperate and somehow calm when he finally touched her. As if they had from now until time ended to touch, to feel, to pleasure and enjoy each other. It drove her, until she needed to take now, to have him in her, hard and fast and gentle and slow all at once. Pain and pleasure, words too small to describe how she felt with his hands on her, his mouth tasting her.

Remembering this now, feeling it all again, Nuala accepted that she was lost. She would never be able to give this up, to give him up again. Her magic be damned. His duty be damned. This, this heat and need between them, this was a magic all its own, and it would no longer be denied.

Einar's lips slid along her jaw, down to her neck as he tugged her farther up his body. She might have resisted, except she was too needy, too weak to refuse him whatever he wanted from her. When his lips closed hot around her nipple and his teeth scraped the peak, she bucked in response. He held her in place with one hand on her ass as he suckled her breasts, one at a time. The tug started yet another build low in her abdomen, and she ground her hips against his solid stomach muscles in search of relief.

He rose to a sitting position, which let her drop into his lap, his cock nestled between their bodies, and she continued to rub and grind against him. It would never be enough. She needed him inside her. But she was so lost to sensation, she couldn't even demand he fuck her, couldn't speak or control her body enough to take what she wanted. She was helpless to his onslaught, to his pace, his direction.

And somehow, that was perfect.

When he lifted her hips off his lap, she followed, giving him everything she had. The feel of his thickness pushing at her heat became the center of her existence. She tried to drop back to his lap and take him inside her in one swift move, but he held her tight, sliding her down in agonizingly slow increments. She whimpered, unable to help the soft needy sounds as she circled her hips, trying to take him in faster.

Finally, finally he relaxed his grip and she slammed down, filled and stretched and oh-so-much happier. But the satisfaction of having him fully inside her lasted a heartbeat. Then she had to move.

Despite the wash of need and love filling her soul, she rode him slowly, her hips undulating in a rhythm designed to please them both. In this position, she could watch his expression closely, and the intimacy cemented her fall. She was his. She had been from the very beginning of their relationship. And she let him see that now, after all these years, nothing had changed for her.

She loved him. Beyond reason and sense.

He cupped her cheek in one hand while his other stayed firmly on her hip. The emotions in his eyes engulfed her. Kissing him was like oxygen after that, vital to her existence. She continued her steady rhythm, teasing and taking until her body trembled. Then he retook control.

Rolling her onto her back, he built the speed of their coupling slowly at first, increasing the tension tightening her core. Then harder and faster. She clung to him as everything spun away and her reactions took over.

This time, when the release took her, she muffled her cry against his chest, biting down to keep silent. A moment later, she felt him follow her, his body tightening as he came for her.

A pleasure and satisfaction unlike anything she'd known with anyone else lapped over her, leaving her content and savoring a moment she'd remember always.

He hugged her close for a long while after, their breathing slowing together. When he slipped to the side, he gathered her to him, leaving no space between their bodies. His heat seeped into Nuala, keeping her warm despite the chill in the room and the sweat cooling on her body.

In the silence, she wanted to pretend this could last. They could be together with no repercussions. But even her love and contentment didn't allow her the delusion. There would be consequences to this perfection.

She opened her mouth to start a conversation she didn't really want to have, but stopped when her stomach growled so loudly it echoed in the quiet.

The sound was so unexpected she started to giggle. When she felt Einar's chest bumping her cheek as he tried to suppress his own amusement, she laughed harder. A moment later, he lost control and his deep, uncontrolled chuckle joined hers. He so rarely laughed that the sound enchanted her.

She looked up into his face and smiled. Serious conversations could wait a little longer.

"I guess that means I'm hungry."

"Running across the rooftops then monumentally fabulous sex does tend to do that."

"You experience both together often?"

"Only with you."

She reached up for a kiss.

"The owls should have delivered some food by now. I'll go check." His hand stroked up the length of her bare back. "I want to tell you to stay naked. But…"

His hesitance surprised her. "But?"

"If someone enters the building while I'm on the roof, I don't want you to be vulnerable."

She cupped his cheek. "I'm not vulnerable without clothes.

Except with you. But if it will make you more comfortable, I'll dress while you're gone and strip immediately after you return."

That earned her another of his glorious smiles, this one sexy and deliciously wicked. "I do prefer keeping the sight of your beautiful body to myself. I'll be quick."

He was out of bed and dressing so fast, she giggled again. As he hurried out the door to the roof, she tugged on her trousers and shirt, not bothering with the niceties of undergarments or her riding robe. She wouldn't be keeping these clothes on long enough for that.

She did, however, uncover her scabbard belt from the pile of clothes and remove Einar's knife. She only noticed then that he'd moved her bow and quiver to lean against the wall near the head of the bed. She'd been so caught up in their passion, she'd forgotten she'd left them on the mattress.

After a brief hunt in the room next door, she uncovered an empty, thankfully intact chamber pot and took advantage of the find. Then she went to stand by the window in their room and study the street carefully while she waited for Einar to return. As before, everything was silent, giving the area an abandoned feel.

Likely, this part of Noman's Land *was* abandoned. Or any squatters were hiding and asleep. She'd never stopped to consider if the Sorcerers attacked during the day or kept their movements restricted to the night. There was no reason they wouldn't be about during the day, not that she could think of, but the utter silence of the morning hinted that everyone had huddled back behind their lines to wait for…something.

She didn't look away from the street when she heard Einar return, giving the area a final sweep, just in case. Silence and stillness reigned.

"I didn't see anything from the roof either," he said quietly. "We have more time. To rest."

She faced him. "I hope you intend to do more than just rest with me."

He lifted three small sacks. "I also intend to feed you."

Sidling toward him, she set the knife onto a locker beside the bed and without pausing opened her shirt and let it slip off her arms to the floor. His gaze dropped to her breasts as her nipples puckered in the cool air.

"Only food?" she asked as she tugged her trousers off with equal speed and lack of ceremony. The increasing rise and fall of his chest as his breathing sped made her shiver.

"Not just the food," he confirmed to her satisfaction. When he met her gaze, both amusement and heat flickered in his dark eyes. "But you need to eat and drink before any other activities."

"Hmmm. Maybe."

Though the water did sound very good at the moment, the feel of Einar's chest against her palms seemed more important. The *Shaerta* continued to spark and fizzle in her blood. They hadn't been apart long enough for it to ease. And it drove her beyond other bodily needs.

But when he drew out a water sack, thirst did reassert itself, and she gulped down a heavy few swallows gratefully. He made sure she was drinking before uncorking a second sack for himself. Watching the way his throat worked as he swallowed amplified the building heat between her legs.

Though she knew she couldn't afford to waste drinking water on cleaning herself fully, she retrieved one of the remaining strips of silk she'd cut for bandages from her robe and poured just enough water onto it to wash her most intimate parts.

Einar watched, still as a statue, while she caressed the damp silk over her swollen flesh, between her legs. His focused attention started her heart beating rapidly, and the excitement already a low hum in her veins thrummed.

"You're more beautiful than anything I've ever seen," he said, his gaze locked on her gentle movements.

She wanted to tell him she loved him too. But she held back, knowing that declaration would require a serious conversation. And in that moment, she didn't want talk.

"You're overdressed," she commented as she set the strip of silk aside and reached for the remaining two burlap sacks, each holding enough food to see them through the day.

She investigated their food while watching him strip from the corner of her eye. He was already hard, much to her pleasure. The sight kept her breathing erratic, even when her stomach rumbled again as the scent of strong cheese rose up to her.

The owls had brought them a round of Glengowyn cheese, two small loaves of bread and some dried fruit and nuts. Lightweight but substantial enough to keep up their energy for the night ahead.

Though, given the energy they'd just used, and were about to use again, they probably could have done with another round of cheese.

Despite his obvious desire and the gentle bump of his erection against her hip, he did make sure she ate some of the food first, popping a small bite of cheese between her lips while she was too distracted by his nearness to think.

She chuckled and allowed him to feed her, savoring the care, the attention. While her people coddled her because of her magic, no one but Einar ever thought to really take care of her in so fundamental and loving a way.

During the second goblin war, he'd done the same, ensuring she ate and drank, watching until he was satisfied she'd consumed enough to continue working. And her awe, the power of the gesture, came from the fact that he didn't pay any attention to who witnessed his care for her. He didn't try to hide how he looked out for her.

The most deadly and dangerous elf of Glengowyn, the warrior singlehandedly responsible for the deaths of hundreds, maybe thousands of enemies, so feared even his fellow soldiers stepped carefully around him, took the time to care for her and only her. The contrast and his lack of concern for what others thought of his actions were the tipping points for her, the moments that sent her from desire into a deep love she'd never been able to overcome.

After making sure she ate enough cheese and bread to keep her stomach from growling again, she insisted Einar eat as well. It didn't escape her that he didn't eat while he focused on her. So she returned the attention, making him sit on the bed as she handed over chunks of cheese and dried fruit. Only when she was satisfied he'd had enough to curb his own hunger did she allow him to set the remaining food aside and take her into his arms.

His kiss was hard, with an edge of desperation, as he pressed her back into the mattress. As if the short time they'd been apart had seemed longer. He cupped her breasts in both hands and she arched beneath him, moaning into his mouth when he pinched her nipples into hard little peaks. He wasn't rough, but he wasn't delicate with her either. And the strength of his callused fingers rubbing over her skin drove her wild.

She reached for his cock, but he grabbed her wrists and stretched them up over her head, pinning her with one large hand while the other returned to her breast.

He kissed his way along her jaw to her ear and murmured, "You can touch soon. But I need my fill first." Then he gently bit her lobe.

She shivered in reaction. Her ears were actually quite sensitive —most elves' were—but Einar knew exactly how much pressure, how much pain to inflict to bring her the most satisfaction. Using his teeth, he tugged her lobe just enough to make her gasp, then nibbled his way down her throat, savoring her skin.

Almost without meaning to, she jerked her hands against his hold, the desire to return his caresses, to run her nails across his skin was so strong. He held her in place easily, and his strength, his control of her body might have been intimidating from any other man. But with Einar, she felt safe and loved, even as he drove her to mindless desperation.

His mouth slipped across her collarbone and then his lips replaced his fingers on her breast, sucking the sensitive skin hard. Her hips bucked, rubbing his erection. He growled but didn't release her nipple or her wrists.

Nuala's skin sparked with sensation as he shifted to her other breast. She watched him as he licked her nipple in a slow circle, his focus on her body so complete it was breath-stealing. The wet slide of his tongue, the suck and tug of his teeth made the muscles of her stomach quiver. She wanted his mouth lower, yet she didn't want him to stop his current torture, so she bit her lip and closed her eyes, concentrating on the feel, the sensations dancing over her.

He released her wrists only when he dipped lower. She started to lift her arms, but he ordered, "Don't move."

She complied even though she was desperate to touch him. Then he kissed across her waist, along her sides, and she clenched her jaw to keep from screaming. Her skin was beyond sensitive now, and again she rode the edge of pleasure just a hair short of pain. It took what little restraint she had to keep her arms in place above her head, but letting him take whatever he wanted from her, as he wanted it, was a heady sensation she found intoxicating.

She watched him when she could keep her eyes open, trembling as his lips glided across her hip bone, his tongue licking into the crease between her thigh and pelvis. She couldn't control the way her body writhed under his touch, but he held her hips and kept her in place for the torture.

His breath was warm over her damp curls, turning her ragged

breaths to pants as anticipation tightened her muscles. She felt stretched and too hot. So that when his mouth finally closed, hard and demanding over her wetness, she barely held a scream back.

He licked through her folds and dipped his tongue deep into her, mimicking the slide of his cock. She dug her fingers into the mattress above her head to keep from reaching for him. The play of his lips and tongue, working her skin, circling and sucking her clit while she was unable to touch him forced her full focus on his attentions.

Every part of her drew down to a tight center, aided by the brush of cool air over her puckered nipples, the tight grip of his fingers on her ass as he lifted her hips to better his access. She was completely open to him, at his mercy, and knowing he wanted her there drove her past restraint.

She came against his mouth, her hips bucking, her body jerking out of her control. When he continued to lick her, she did cry out, too sensitive to remain quiet.

With the *Shaerta*, her body felt like an exposed nerve. She was overly sensitive and afraid she couldn't take much more. And yet she did. He forced her into another, almost painful climax, this one deep and resonant.

He didn't give her time to come down from her orgasm before he replaced his mouth with his cock, rubbing the tip of his erection through her folds, teasing, taunting. He stared at the place where their bodies came together, and she followed his gaze, unable to look away as he held himself at her entrance without actually sliding in. She wanted to beg, plead for more, but she couldn't find her voice.

His expression and focus were fierce, and all for her. That more than anything allowed her to take his torture. But she couldn't stop her hips from jerking in a vain attempt to force him closer.

When he finally pressed the heavy, thick tip of his erection just inside her, she jerked again. He looked up, his eyes dark as he held her gaze.

"Mine," he growled, his voice a harsh pant.

"Yes," she answered, though only a hint of sound got through her clenched teeth.

He eased inside her another inch. The slow entrance kept all her attention on her own body and what he was doing to her. She couldn't get away, couldn't distract herself with any other sensations. He forced her to feel each inch of his cock, the stretch of her passage, the friction of his velvet-hard skin pushing deeper. Never had she been so aware of every jump and sizzle of her nerves, every brush of air, each pulse of her heartbeat. So that when he finally filled her fully, she was almost ready to come again.

He set a steady, deliberate rhythm, pulling almost out before sliding back in. He didn't move fast, he didn't fuck her hard, he kept to a relentless pace that drew out more sensation than if he'd slammed into her. And her orgasm this time was so deep, so complete, so long, she lost all sense of the world around her, of everything but Einar.

By the time she came back to herself, his mouth was on hers, his kiss both sweet and desperate as he finally increased his rhythm, pounding hard to an orgasm she felt along every inch or her own body. He pumped into her several strokes after he came, as if he was no more in control of his body than she was of hers.

She took advantage of his release to finally lower her arms, bringing her hands to his face, holding him there as she savored the brush and play of his tongue with hers. Finally, he lifted onto his forearms and looked down at her. The love, the intensity in his expression was worth everything to her.

Whatever the future held for them, she would hold this moment and his love close to her soul forever.

They spent the rest of the morning in soft caresses, eager kisses, heat and powerful need. Nuala indulged all the desires she'd kept locked tight in her heart for the long centuries, sucking, licking, tasting, fucking, savoring every inch, every ounce of his body. They barely spoke, and while she didn't know why he remained quiet, she knew for her part, she didn't want to risk breaking the spell, allowing reality to intrude on this ideal time. To speak would be to admit her love, to admit things had changed and there was no going back.

So silently she loved him, pleasured him and allowed him to be her world for the few hours they had, the only time they might ever have once news of their fall reached the king and queen.

She buried that fear deep, hiding from it while she anchored herself to the present and her love for Einar.

CHAPTER EIGHT

 uala rolled into Einar's arms after a light doze, feeling rested and sated in her soul. He stared down at her, his dark eyes thoughtful, his expression quiet.

And now what? she thought. She loved him. They'd defied their king and queen. Already she could feel the threads connecting them binding tighter. They couldn't stop the process now. The *Shaerta* was too strong between them. A reaction only possible when two were in love. She'd managed to step away from this love once. Now, that was no longer possible.

"We'll be banished," she said, surprised how matter-of-fact her tone was, how easy it was to say aloud after avoiding those very words for the last few hours.

He nodded.

"Will they...?" She swallowed. "Will they impose the *Or'roan?*"

She was no different from the other elves. The thought of ending forever, of joining the traitor she'd killed in black nothingness, terrified her. Never to move on to the next plane or see another life… Horrifying prospect. It was why the punishment was so powerful among her people. They all feared it. Which was one of the many reasons the sovereigns had imposed the *Or'roan* on the traitors.

And by loving the Darkness and risking her magic, she'd put both herself and Einar in the same position as the traitors.

"They may," he said after a quiet moment. "Mainly as a statement to others who might dare to defy them. It depends on how angry they are with us."

"We've never been sure how this would affect my magic. Maybe it won't be so bad? Maybe they won't have to punish us, after all."

Desperate dreams, she knew. The queen had made her position on this clear when she'd ordered Nuala to stay away from Einar, to never bond with him. There would be no mercy.

His firm mouth tilted up at one corner. "We'll be banished. But maybe they'll resist cursing us. Either way, you're worth it to me."

Her throat tightened with emotions she tried to suppress. Though why she felt the need to hold anything back with Einar, she wasn't sure. "As long as I'm with you, even if we can't travel to the afterworld together, I'll be happy."

He gathered her close and kissed her.

At sundown, they dressed and returned to the roof, hiding behind the parapet as they studied the streets. Noman's Land had been quiet all day, something that surprised Nuala. She'd expected at least a human patrol after the night of fighting. But the streets remained eerily silent. Not even random squatters or sentries made themselves known.

They waited for a carrier owl until well after full dark, silently keeping vigil. She wanted to talk more, to make sure he was prepared for the consequences of what they'd spent the day doing. Could he really just abandon all he'd ever stood for—Glengowyn, protecting the sovereigns, defending his people? All of that... for her?

And there were his inner demons, the topic they'd avoided all this time. The brutal killer he became in battle. Some called him a berserker. She knew that wasn't the right description. He wasn't overwhelmed by bloodlust, killing indiscriminately. What happened to Einar was scarier, colder, more methodical. A type of battle madness never seen before among the elves.

There was no name for it. But the berserker title added weight to his position as bodyguard to the royal couple, so he didn't try to deny the rumor. Neither did he comment on the suspicion that he was the only elf capable of killing other elves. She knew better than that too—from her own experience now. But again, the whispers added to his legend. Something she was sure the queen and king encouraged.

Beyond the legend and rumors surrounding the Darkness, though, there *was* a violence in Einar, just under the skin. Whatever it was that made him so terrifying a warrior. Would he be able to bank that part of himself for a quiet, isolated life with her?

Banishment would mean they wouldn't be welcomed in any elf city on the planet. And any human city that traded with elves would shun them as well. Their only possible choice would be isolation somewhere out of the way of everyone. But could he survive that?

Could she?

She'd told him the truth. So long as they were together, she could survive anything and be happy. She knew he loved her, even without words. But would he feel the same way after a century of solitude?

The barest of movements from Einar brought her to full alert. Barely visible in the light from the two-thirds first moon and the single gaslamp working on that block, she made out the white ghost of a messenger owl, gently gliding toward them. Einar remained seated but raised his arm to provide a perch for the bird.

She opened her mouth to protest. He wasn't wearing protective leathers. The bird's claws would slice his arm. But a moment later, the owl alighted and somehow avoided digging its talons into Einar's vulnerable skin.

"How…?" she murmured.

He smiled but his gaze was focused on the bird. "My arm seems to be resistant to injury. Part of the way my magic works."

"Amazing." She watched him with the owl, taking advantage of a rare opportunity to witness him with the creatures he was so tied to, his unique magic.

Some thought his fighting skills were enhanced by magic also. Einar had never confirmed or denied that. The king and queen probably knew. The queen had a skill for identifying talents. But the owls, that was definitely a kind of magic. Watching him this closely with them was fascinating.

After a long silence, Einar finally opened his mouth and a soft whispery sound came out. Not at all what she was anticipating. She'd half expected him to screech like the owls. His whisper was mixed with very faint whistles. And then the owl launched upward, its powerful wings fanning her face with cool air as it gained height and angled back toward Glengowyn.

"So," she said. "Do we have safe passage?"

He nodded but his gaze remained on the retreating owl. "Ulric and the queen will meet us at a sentry point at the border at dawn."

"Dawn? Why not now?"

"No explanation was given. We'll have to make our way toward the meeting point well before dawn to make the appointed time, but we have to stay hidden for most of the night."

"How will we know where to go? Is it a location you're familiar with? Can you be sure it won't take us most of the night to get there?"

"The owl provided an aerial map of the area so I can find the sentry point. And he flew the most direct route so I could judge the required time. That route wouldn't take us long, but I doubt we'll be able to travel easily. The owl spotted at least one minion patrol near that area. There will be more."

"Then we won't be able to wait here?"

"Probably not. They'll be looking for us again."

She stared out over the streets, surprised the idea of leaving this little island of quiet made her sad. It wasn't exactly luxurious accommodations. But it had kept them safe through the day and given them a place to be together again. Leaving meant facing reality and consequences.

Einar gripped her chin and turned her face back toward his. He was closer now, his gaze direct when he said, "We'll face what we must together. I won't let the Sorcerers have you."

"And what of the queen?"

"She won't take you away from me either. Not again."

Her breath shivered out of her, but she firmed her shoulders and pushed back the worry. "When should we leave?"

He studied the street below, and she watched the side of his face as he thought and considered. Finally, he nodded as if confirming something to himself.

"We'll leave now, go slowly and carefully. I don't want to get caught far away from the meeting point at dawn because we were forced by minion activity to move in the opposite direction."

"What if there's no safe place nearby to wait?"

"We'll find something." He looked back at her. "You only have two arrows left. Keep my knife with you and don't hesitate to use it, on minion or elf."

She swallowed. "It wasn't as difficult as I thought it would be, killing the traitor yesterday."

"No. It isn't. Some deaths are easy to mete out."

"But I'm not you."

He touched her cheek with the tips of his fingers before dropping his hand. "And I'm very grateful for that. You are, however, noble and just. Your actions come from that part of you. Not the place where my abilities come from."

Because he'd broached the subject, she asked, "Will banishment…make things…difficult for you? In that regard."

Tilting his head, he frowned as if she'd asked him something nonsensical. "I would welcome a reprieve from the Darkness."

"But for how long?"

"To be with you? Forever."

Her throat tightened again. In that moment, with the *Shaerta* still a tangible thing between them, he could speak of forever and no regrets. He could be sure the violence that made him who he was would just go away. But, for his sake, she couldn't afford the luxury of that assurance. She didn't push him further though. They had to survive the night.

And face the queen.

THEY COLLECTED THE REMAINING FRUIT FROM THEIR FOOD STORES and the little bit of water in their sacks, strapped on their weapons and left their sanctuary as carefully and quietly as they'd entered it that morning.

A cold breeze hummed through the city, kicking up dust and debris from the cobbles. She tugged the remains of her riding robe tighter around her and followed Einar through the shadows, keeping her attention on the streets and alleys at their back while Einar focused on what was ahead.

They traveled slowly, sticking to the deepest dark pools at the sides of buildings and in narrow passageways. Most of Noman's Land remained black, with only the occasional gaslamp to provide any light, so staying to the shadows was easy enough. As they skirted one of the rare lit lamps, Nuala couldn't help but wonder who was lighting them, the humans or the Sorcerers.

The first sounds of booted feet sent them down a side road, into a blackness between buildings she had trouble navigating. She kept a hand on Einar's lower back so she wouldn't lose him and allowed him to lead her to a more open street a block away.

While waiting to make sure their way would be clear, he leaned in and said, "That sounded like humans. But farther away, I heard carriage wheels."

That made her frown. His hearing was significantly better than hers, despite how acute hers was, but that wasn't what bothered her. Why a carriage in Noman's Land? What were they moving that couldn't just walk? And who was moving the mysterious something? A carriage was too easy to hear, too easy for two lone elves to hide from. It made no sense to bring something so awkward and noisy into a search, if the carriage belonged to the Sorcerers, not when there were more than enough minions to scour the streets on foot. And she couldn't think of a single reason the Sinnale might send a valuable carriage into Noman's Land.

"Stay alert," Einar said, then led her across the open street to yet another set of quiet shadows circling what had once been a greenery-filled square.

They edged through the blocks so slowly, so carefully, it felt as if the journey that should have taken a short time took half the night. Nuala's muscles remained tense as she kept alert for movement and sound. Maintaining that kind of vigil wore on her, and exhaustion crept through her body with the passing minutes.

As they waited, yet again, while Einar assured himself of their way, she rubbed her shoulders in an attempt to release some of the tension and pressure. She'd be no good in a fight if her body was already too tired to react because she'd gotten tight from containing her fear.

The goblin war had been… Not easier. Still tense, still exhausting. But the constant action and battles had kept her too busy to spend much time thinking and worrying. There were only a few quiet moments, a few brief respites during which to consider the fear in her gut. And Einar had always distracted her with conversation during those quiet times. This was different. Though they were moving, the tension of hiding and remaining silent while others hunted for them didn't keep her from thinking and considering the worst.

She would not allow the Sorcerers to take her. Or to kill Einar, if she could help it. Unfortunately, she was woefully undertrained for a fight, and she kept imagining Einar's death. Even the thought clogged her throat and brought tears to her eyes. To actually see such a thing…

Rolling her shoulders, she pulled in a deep silent breath, held it, then let it out slowly through her nose, releasing the building panic. So far, they'd avoided the various patrols—both human and minion. They were nearing the rendezvous point. Safety was in sight. They'd both survive this.

Einar held their position for longer than at any other part of their journey, his body so still she reached out to touch his back just to assure herself he was breathing.

Leaning in close, she said, "What's wrong?"

He held up a hand for silence. After another torturous few moments passed, he turned and spoke into her ear, his voice barely audible. "Minions have surrounded the area near the meeting point. Several contingents. Something has given the location away."

"Where?" she mouthed, knowing he would hear without her having to make more than the barest of sounds.

"In the buildings. On the rooftops. I've spotted them in at least three different locations, so far. The center of their positions is the sector of Sinnale border where Ulric is supposed to meet us."

"Will the humans come if there are so many minions waiting?"

He didn't immediately answer, and his silence made her already jumping heartbeat speed.

"They may be there already," he finally said. "That could be why so many minions have gathered. But we're not close enough for me to see."

"They'll wait for us. They won't start fighting yet."

"There's some time before dawn. We're not safe here, but I can hear minions moving in behind us."

His comment startled her. She directed her attention back to the area they'd already passed through, and now she could hear the faint sound of marching, several blocks away but moving swiftly in this direction.

They were surrounded.

CHAPTER NINE

ow what?" Nuala said, leaning closer to Einar as the tension that had carried her through the streets turned to full-fledged fear.

He stared up at the sky as if in thought, and because she trusted him, she didn't interrupt. But the sound of approaching footsteps sent her pulse racing. She slipped her bow over her head, readied one of her two remaining arrows, and faced the path behind them, watching their backs.

An intolerable few moments passed in silence and anticipation of attack, reminding her of their ride in to Sinnale and the knowledge that they *would* be attacked at some point in their journey. Then Einar sucked in a deep gulp of air.

"We'll have help in a moment," he said against her ear.

She frowned up at him, about to ask what help, when slight movement from the corner of her eye made her pause. She looked toward the sky. Past some of the lower rooftops, she caught flashes of white, gliding silently in their direction. It took her a beat to realize what she was seeing. Owls. A lot of them, approaching in a fast, silent mass from the direction of Glengowyn.

She gripped Einar's arm. "They'll be hurt."

"Watch. And follow my direction."

She kept her gaze on the approaching birds, the readied bow and arrow in hand. The mass swished overhead, silent except for the beat of their wings. In that pass, a few shouts rose from the surrounding buildings, and Nuala spotted a number of minions pointing toward the sky. To her horror, she watched as one drew back the string on his bow. But before he could fire, something dark dropped from the sky, hitting him on the very top of his head. The man collapsed without even a shout to indicate he was hurt.

Nuala looked up to see even more owls, circling above the area. One by one, they dropped low, released something from their talons, then climbed quickly back to join the others. More shouts rose from around them, echoing through the streets. Arrows launched into the sky, but the owls kept high and beyond their reach. And then another volley of arrows filled the air, this one aimed at the rooftops, toward the minions.

Chaos erupted then. Arrows flew. The sound of swords clashing rang. Minions poured out of the surrounding buildings as human soldiers charged into the streets. A full-blown assault filled the early hour before dawn with noise and madness.

"This helps us?" she asked Einar as she glanced back toward the owls. The mass of white circled farther away, near enough to return if needed but well beyond the reach of the combatants' weapons.

"We can move through chaos. Without this, we were dead."

She hoped he was right. But when he stepped out from their cover and into the street, toward the fighting, she didn't hesitate to follow. His sword in one hand, he edged her through the conflict, easing them toward the border. She kept her bow readied but angled down. With only two arrows and a knife, she had to be careful how she used her weaponry.

A minion spotted them and turned to attack, only to be cut down by a human soldier before she could speak. The human stared at them a moment, and then was distracted by more minions.

"We're in as much trouble from the humans out here, aren't we?" she shouted to be heard above the cacophony.

"Yes. We need to find Ulric."

Their path was blocked by three minions, all of them with a blank, dead look on their faces. The lack of emotion didn't take away from the wicked-looking edges on their blades. They attacked en masse, and Einar met them, sword raised. Nuala put her back to a wall and kept an eye on the fighting behind them, ready to use those last two arrows.

She jumped when a hand grabbed her wrist, but recognition of that touch sank in before she even faced Einar. He tugged her farther up the street, passing the three minions he'd killed so quickly.

They ducked into doorways to let individual fights slide past and edged around what they could. When minions attacked them directly, Einar dispatched them. Only one or two humans made an attempt to reach them, but each time they were turned away by minions. Since Nuala didn't want to risk having to kill a Sinnale, she was grateful the battle chaos prevented any humans from getting to them.

As they neared the border, the fighting grew thicker, heavier. The volley of arrows more dangerous. They kept to cover, but several missiles clattered near their feet. Nuala clenched her jaw tight to keep from screeching in surprise. The battle grew too thick to navigate, and Einar was forced to engage more enemies, beating a swath through the swarms of bodies.

She covered his back, keeping close enough to follow but far enough away to prevent hindering him. She used her last two arrows efficiently to end a charge by three minions. Then she turned to the knife, slicing a threat when anyone got too close. But Einar was a force in battle, unlike anything most of these humans had seen. And it was all they could do to avoid his blade.

Unfortunately, the current of the fighting pulled him too far away, and suddenly she was alone and surrounded by dead-eyed minions. The stench of rot that clung to them wafted toward her. At the edge of the circle, humans continued to pick their former city mates off one by one, but the four that focused on Nuala approached without pause.

She raised the knife, preparing to defend herself. Above the screams and clashes of metal, she heard her name bellowed. Beyond the approaching four, she saw bodies actually flying through the air to slam into brick walls. Einar. Becoming the warrior so feared by elves and goblins.

The four closing in on her didn't realize the Darkness was coming for them.

Two of them vanished so quickly from in front of her she didn't even see Einar take them. One moment they were there, the next they were gone. The remaining two continued forward as if they didn't notice the others had disappeared. The nearer they got, the stronger that faint hint of decay that emanated from them grew. The scent had surrounded her as they'd worked through the crowds, but now she seemed to home in on it, a primal part of her recognizing the meaning and gagging at the thought of the twisted magics that caused that smell.

From the surrounding madness, Einar appeared. He plucked up one of the remaining two attackers and launched him into the nearest group of fighters, sending all of them into a crumpled heap of bodies—Sinnale and minion alike.

Nuala gasped. She hadn't seen Einar like this in centuries. And then only once, because she'd been so carefully kept back behind the front lines. A small group of goblins had tried to infiltrate their camp, purely by chance stumbling across her tent. The elf warrior who came to her rescue was like nothing Nuala had ever seen. Cold, focused madness, speed and a kind of anger that cut down all in its path.

When the goblins had been slaughtered, singlehandedly, and Einar stood barely breathing heavily in the aftermath with blood dripping from his sword and body, his reputation as the Darkness was sealed for all time. Those who'd witnessed the destruction he'd wrought would never forget that sight.

Nuala never had. Seeing him in that same state of cold rage now spiked her pulse and sent a new kind of fear through her. Fear for him and what this might do to him. She knew this would cost him, cost his soul. She was probably the only one who did. And yet she was awed by the sight, the beauty of something so deadly, so powerful…protecting her.

The fourth minion was a bloody splotch on a nearby building before he fully turned to face the danger. Einar roared and those near him fled, both human and minion. The sound even made the hairs on Nuala's nape rise. Though the fighting continued, it moved away from them, leaving them in a circle of calm emptiness.

He faced her and she watched him physically work to control himself, to return to a more natural state. His eyes were black. Blood ran in rivulets across his face and body. The thought that some of that might be his sent her to his side. No other elf would approach him like this. But she knew he'd never hurt her.

"Are you wounded?" she asked, examining him with her eyes and hands without waiting for his answer.

"Nothing of consequence."

"This is mostly their blood then." She confirmed that with her cursory exam. "Good."

Her comment seemed to surprise him, though she wasn't sure why, and the last of the battle madness eased from his eyes.

"You aren't hurt?" he said, his voice rough.

"Of course not. You didn't give them time to get close. Thank you. I'm not that good with the knife." She touched his cheek. "I'm sorry for this, though."

Before he could answer, a scream of attack rose up to invade their circle of solitude. Einar spun to face the threat, pushing her behind him. But before the minion closed, an arrow thwacked into his chest, directly through his heart. He hit the ground face first, sword still raised above his head. The fall broke the arrow and the puff of a dying spell reached out to tap at Nuala's magic.

An elf arrow. She looked toward the alley from which the arrow had flown just as another elf approached them from farther up the street. Not a traitor this time, though. Nuala's shoulders relaxed.

"Ulric."

Her cousin greeted them with a sharp nod, and he and Einar grasped wrists in a soldier's solute.

"You're well, both of you? Injuries?"

"Nothing significant. We must get her to the safety of the border." Einar wasted no time with pleasantries.

From the alleyway Nuala had been half watching, a Sinnale woman approached, her bow in hand but without an arrow nocked in place. She was a striking woman, with short brown hair, sharp features and deep brown eyes.

Einar looked at her in surprise then said to Ulric, "You allowed her into battle? I thought…"

Ulric rolled his eyes and the woman smirked. "I had very little say in keeping her away. Stubborn woman."

The woman introduced herself to Nuala. "I'm Layla Brightarrow. It's truly a pleasure to meet you in person, Nuala of Glengowyn. Your cousin has sung your praises."

"Ulric's mate." Nuala understood the surprise. Ulric was so protective of his mate, Nuala hadn't even met her yet, though the woman had been to Glengowyn several times to negotiate for weapons. Obviously, Nuala had drawn the wrong conclusions—she'd assumed by Ulric's protectiveness that Layla wasn't much of a soldier. But this thin, tall woman held the bow like it was part of her. And she didn't look at all shaken by the chaos.

"I understood you'd given up fighting," Nuala said to cover her surprise, "in favor of weapons trade."

Layla glanced at Ulric and shrugged. "I have. I can do without this death and killing. But you represent our chance to end this war once and for all. I'd hardly stay safe while you were in danger."

The human's declaration made Nuala feel both pleased and little hurt, though she wasn't sure why the hurt.

"Besides," Layla finished with another half-smile, "I couldn't wait to meet a relative of Ulric's that he actually likes."

Ulric scowled and sniffed as if this was a subject he'd rather not discuss. Nuala couldn't blame him. They'd both been baffled and hurt by Althir's turning traitor to join the Sorcerers. She still had trouble believing it of him. Althir was many things—vain, too charming, arrogant, rude, impossible and jealous of Ulric—but she'd have sworn he was loyal to Glengowyn above all else.

Einar brought the small group back to the issue at hand. "We need to make for the border. The queen…"

"Has already confirmed who you are. Though after…" Ulric waved his hand at the smashed and bloody heaps of bodies Einar had left in his wake. "After witnessing the Darkness in action again, there could hardly be doubt."

"The queen is here?" Nuala asked, a tickle of dread curling in her stomach.

"She returned to Glengowyn just after the battle got underway."

"Then how?" Nuala glanced between herself and Einar. How

could the queen have confirmed their identity for Ulric before even seeing them?

"The owls," Einar answered, surprising her.

"Ah." Between the presence of the owls earlier to confirm Einar was near and witnessing the release of the Darkness just now, it would be hard for Ulric to doubt him. And if Einar claimed she was Nuala, no one would argue the point. Though her cousin might have been fooled by a Sorcerer's spell, Einar would never be when it came to her. The queen would know that.

"The queen also sent out a *reaching* to make sure there were no glamour spells in the center of the owls' attack," Ulric continued. "She sensed only you and Nuala."

So the queen had been comfortable confirming their identity, sight unseen. Part of Nuala was more than a little relieved. But an edge of anxiety, waiting for the confrontation with the sovereigns to finally come, kept her from relaxing.

The sounds of conflict, though farther way, were starting to quiet.

"Come," Ulric said. "The border is just beyond that block. There's a line of soldiers waiting to defend our backs. But..." He glanced off toward the sound of retreating battle. "But I think we've beaten them back for the night. The sight of you in all your battle anger probably terrified even the minions."

Einar didn't comment. He just took Nuala's arm and followed Ulric and Layla to the border. He didn't return his sword to his scabbard, and she didn't put away her knife, until they were well behind the safety of the Sinnale line. And even then, when Layla dropped her bow over her head to lie across her back, Nuala waited for Einar to ease his guard before she allowed herself to do the same.

As morning light spilled into the city streets, the exhaustion of the last few days finally took its toll. She leaned against Einar as they walked farther into safe territory. He wrapped an arm around her shoulders, keeping her close.

Soft pink sunlight colored the air and painted the bricks and cobbles, making everything look cleaner, fresher than it would in bright sun. Nuala loved sunrise. There was a stillness, a quiet to it that usually settled her mind.

But even exhausted, even passing alive and well through her favorite time of day, a low level of tension tightened Nuala's stomach.

They'd avoided having to face the queen and reveal their fall. For now. But it loomed ahead of them. They wouldn't be able to break the bonding between them now. Nor could they hide it from the queen and king. And while she found a small sense of peace having survived the night, with Einar strong at her side, she knew they were far from done with their final fight.

CHAPTER TEN

After brief introductions to some of the Sinnale council members, including Layla's parents, Nuala and Einar were shown rooms in which to rest and bathe, and promised to be directed to the armory later that afternoon. Nuala had work to do now that she was safely within Sinnale-held territory—at the very center of their defenses. But her magic took energy and she needed rest and food first.

Though they were given separate rooms, Einar knocked on her door not long after Ulric left to get their breakfast. She'd just finished washing off the dirt, sweat and blood of the last two days, and had slipped into a clean tunic and a loose skirt.

When she let him in, he didn't say anything at first, just paced around her room. He'd taken the time to clean up as well, washing away the dried blood that had caused the council members to hesitate and back away from him when Ulric presented him. She had no doubt that all the legends of the Darkness of Glengowyn were running through their heads as they bowed to him. Einar, for his part, remained quiet, distant and respectful, never showing any emotion one way or the other.

She watched him stalk around her room and wondered if their reactions bothered him or if he preferred for people to think him that bloodthirsty and cold. He looked noble and controlled now, in clean trousers, tunic and vest. His short hair was damp, and whatever soap they'd provided for him surrounded him in a clean, earthy scent. She noticed, though, that he hadn't let down his guard in the safer surroundings. He'd strapped his sword around his waist before joining her.

Her room, small but very clean, looked smaller still with him in it. But the space was comfortable after their previous surroundings. The washbasin had been filled with fresh water. Clean, lightly scented towels were stacked under the basin stand. A blue ceramic heater in one corner was stocked with kindling, flint and wood, should she get cold. The bed was high and comfortably made up with thick blankets and several pillows. A small wooden wardrobe sat in the corner opposite the heater. Inside, she'd found several changes of clothes, all freshly laundered, some of them her own from the supply wagons that had traveled with her party from Glengowyn. The tunic and skirt she'd been able to don after bathing were her own, and having her own clothing was a comfort.

Given that the city had been at war for two years, Nuala suspected her room was one of their best and was grateful for the Sinnale's thoughtfulness.

Einar stopped pacing at the first of two large windows that spilled morning light into the room. He studied the street below, the outside walls of the building and the lock above the double panes before moving to the next window.

Checking on her security, she thought. Even here in allied territory.

"I'm sure we're safe," she commented, though she didn't stop him from doing what he thought best. He was here as her bodyguard after all. Though there was more between them—and his actions—than that. No one would begrudge him his precautions.

When he'd finished his study of the windows, he opened the wardrobe and nodded approvingly at the clothing. "I'm glad some of the wagons made it through the attack."

That had been one of his first questions to Ulric once they were inside Sinnale borders. She and Einar had both been relieved to hear the casualties of that attack had been minimal. Once she'd escaped, the fighting had ended quickly. Because of that, the supplies of arrows—both her standard; the fire-tips, which were only now being traded with the Sinnale; and Nuala's particular special arrows, also only now being allowed into Sinnale hands—had arrived safely and were waiting for her to set.

"The elves of your guard are still here," he continued. "You'll have a proper escort back to Glengowyn."

The thought of going home sent her stomach dancing with nerves. She wanted to say something about that fear, but Einar's mood seemed so pensive she decided it best to wait for him to say what he was here to say.

He finally stopped moving and settled his hands on his hips, his head bowed forward. Then he straightened. "You need rest and food. We can talk later."

"Einar..." She stopped him as he made for the door. "What's wrong?"

He held perfectly still with his back to her for a moment. Then he turned and closed the space between them in two steps. Before she could gasp, he had her face between his palms and he was kissing her, desperately, hard, like they'd been separated again for a century. She wrapped herself around him, matching the kiss, matching the passion. She couldn't stop. Though she didn't fully understand what drove him, in that moment, she didn't care.

He lifted his mouth too soon and stared down at her. "I would do anything for you. Remember that."

She sucked in a sharp breath at the intensity in his gaze.

"I will let you go if you don't want to face banishment."

The statement startled her and she stepped back quickly as if she'd been slapped. He let her. "What are you talking about? I thought I made myself clear on this subject."

"Passion in the moment."

"How dare you?" she hissed. "After everything, how dare you presume my feelings for you are that fleeting."

"When the queen and king demanded we separate, you broke with me." He firmed his shoulders and there was no longer emotion in his expression. "You chose then."

"I chose? I knew what you would choose and simply beat you to the break."

He frowned. "You have no idea what I wanted. You never asked."

"You were the king and queen's personal guard. You have always been about duty above anything else. Your loyalty was beyond question. Of course you would choose them over me. How could I think otherwise?"

He crossed the space between them in a single step and took her shoulders in his hands, bringing his face close to hers. "Listen to this well, Nuala. I was prepared to choose banishment. I came to you that day to tell you I wanted you above everything. And *you* set *me* aside. In the name of duty."

She shook her head, denying words she couldn't believe.

"I told the queen, before I came to you, that I would not be separated from you if you wanted me. She threatened banishment, the *Or'roan*. And I chose you."

"Why didn't you tell me?" she wailed.

Two centuries. Two centuries of pain and loss and longing. Two centuries of denying this love between them. Because she *thought* he would choose his sovereigns over her.

"You made your choice."

"Only because I thought I knew what you'd say, and I didn't…" Her throat closed up as centuries of suppressed tears built and threatened to flow. "I couldn't hear you say you didn't love me enough to stay," she finally whispered. And the tears fell.

Between her exhaustion, the recent battles, the bonding with Einar, Nuala was overwhelmed and exposed. She couldn't hide from him. She couldn't control the emotions rolling through her. Regret and fear tangled with love and need, desperation and loss all one giant hand closing around her heart and squeezing.

Einar released a sigh that took all the tension from his shoulders and his grip on her arms. He hugged her close, tucking her head beneath his chin, and held her as tightly as she clung to him.

When the emotional storm started to ease, Einar skimmed one hand up and down her back, the gentle stroke a comfort.

"I've always loved you," she said. She'd held those words inside for so long, even during their initial mating, it felt cathartic to finally allow them out and hear them aloud.

"You've never told me before," he murmured into her hair.

"Neither have you," she challenged. But she knew he loved her. It was there in the *Shaerta* when they made love.

His chest rose and fell with a deep breath. "I've loved you much longer than you could know. Well before our first mating. Before the war."

She leaned back to look up at him. "Before the war? We barely spoke before then."

"I knew."

"Knew?"

"We would bond. I could feel it in my soul. If we mated, we'd bond. Our magics would mix. I knew that would…complicate things. And you would break my heart. But I couldn't stop loving you."

She wanted to cry again, but her tears had dried up. "What changed?"

"You didn't run away when you saw what I could be. You weren't afraid, after that night in the camp when the goblins snuck in. You were the only one who didn't change toward me."

"Ulric didn't. The soldiers in your regiment didn't."

"Ulric was my commander. He'd seen me in battle and knew what I was capable of. He'd already seen my worst. You don't really remember our friendship before that war, do you?"

"No."

"He was already an admired soldier from the first war. I respected him and looked up to him. I wanted to fight under his command. But until we went into battle, even I didn't know what I was capable of. He… Well, he wasn't as easy with me after that. There was respect. But no longer the camaraderie he had with the others under his command. None of the other soldiers were comfortable with me either."

He cupped her cheek in one large hand, his thumb lightly caressing her cheekbone. "But you… You worried about *me* after seeing what I became when I let myself. You came to me immediately. Washed away the blood. Checked for wounds. The same as today. You didn't shy back. You weren't afraid."

"I could never be afraid of you. Not that way."

"What way then?"

"Oh, Einar. The damage you could do to my heart terrifies me. I'm afraid of that. But I don't worry, even in the heat of battle, that you would lash out at me."

She watched his throat work as he swallowed hard. "I would do anything for you, Nuala. You know that? I would happily go into banishment, take on the *Or'roan*… I would even give you up again if that made you happier."

"Stop. Don't ever say that to me again. Not ever."

"It's not too late—"

"Enough, I said. It is too late. It was too late centuries ago. We just weren't ready to accept. I didn't trust your feelings, and you didn't trust mine. But this time… This time the bond is tightening. You can feel it too. There's no going back now. I wouldn't want to even if we could."

"Your magic?"

She looked away. "I don't know. I'll know when I try. I haven't felt different, so it's possible we haven't melded completely yet."

He stepped away from her so suddenly, she rocked backward. "I'll leave then. If we can keep the balance for a little while longer, so you can finish this last trade, maybe the king and queen will be merciful. Banishment but no curse."

She was exhausted, emotionally wrung out, and in need of food and sleep before working her magic later. He was right, it would be better if he left. If for no other reason than she'd actually sleep. But she didn't want him to go. They'd been through too much in such a short period of time. All she wanted was the comfort of his big body next to her.

"Don't," she said, flattening her hands on his chest. "Not yet. I know I need to rest, but… At least keep me company while we eat. I don't want to be alone yet."

His entire body loosened as tension dropped away and he tugged her back into his arms. "I never could refuse you anything."

She snorted, snuggling her cheek against his chest. "You refused to teach me how to fight, as I recall."

"Ah. That was an order from King Varim. He didn't think you'd need it and was afraid it would take too much time away from working your magic."

"Ulric and Althir still taught me to throw a knife."

"Ulric is a favorite of the sovereigns. He could get away with more than I could. At least where you were concerned. And Althir…Althir could charm his way out of a *dargem* pit."

She shivered at the mention of the deadly creatures that called the Unseen Plain their home. They were the stuff of elven nightmares, grotesque and lethal. Since she didn't want to have nightmares when she finally slept, she concentrated on the first part of his comment.

"You're a favorite with the sovereigns too. Queen Rohannah made that clear when she ordered me to stay away from you. She didn't want to lose you any more than she wanted to endanger my magic."

"I'm…a good threat. Having me behind them ensures no one risks their wrath."

Nuala pursed her lips. "Hmm. I'm not sure that's the only reason the queen favors you."

She felt his silent chuckle in the sudden movement of his chest against her cheek. Looking up, she scowled. "Why are you laughing?"

"I'm surprised. Is that jealousy I hear?"

Her scowl deepened. "Don't you dare tease me. The queen is beautiful and powerful, and she gets what she wants. And you're always around her. How could she not want you?"

He leaned down and kissed her frowning mouth, the humor in his eyes mixing with tenderness.

"As I've said, my heart has been yours for a very long time now. Even the queen couldn't change that." He set his nose close to hers, forcing her to look him in the eyes. "And she never tried. She recognized a lost cause when she saw one."

Wrinkling her nose, trying to ignore the heat in her cheeks, she shrugged. "Fine."

"And you?"

"Me what?"

"There have been men since me who've wanted you. Powerful elves."

"Oh, I was never one to worry about. After the war, the queen and king made it perfectly clear to all that I was off limits. Too valuable to risk." She couldn't stop herself from sneering that last. Her *value* had kept her from the man she loved for so long, resentment was a ready companion.

"So…" Einar drawled, tilting his head to the side. "There would have been others, if not for their order?"

She raised her brows at the sudden deepening of his voice. Her turn to smile. "You know better than that."

"Do I?"

"You should by now." She snuggled close to him, running her hands over his shoulders and down his chest, loving the feel of his heartbeat picking up under her palms. "I only ever wanted you. I still want you. More than I want food or sleep."

She rose onto her toes and kissed him, hard, sure. Letting him know just how much she did want him. Silly man, thinking she could ever bed another after being with him. He hesitated to return her kiss, and she knew why. But she took his pause as a challenge rather than a warning. She nibbled her way along his jaw, then kissed the strong column of his throat, licking her way across freshly cleaned skin.

"Nuala…"

His groan made her smile. She slid her hands up under his shirt, flattening her palms on the solid muscles of his lower abdomen. Low enough to hint and tease, promising without delivering. Yet.

He gripped her wrists but didn't do more, and she knew he would give in. He could no more resist her than she could him. There was power in that knowledge, power magnified by her love for him. She continued to kiss her way down his throat, to the hollow at the base of his neck. His shirt was in the way, so she nuzzled it aside, leaving her hands braced exactly where they were. His muscles were tight everywhere now, and the tension in his grip was thrilling.

"The food will be here soon," he said, his voice very deep.

"Yes," she agreed without stopping her exploration of him with her mouth.

She let her fingernails dig ever so slightly into his skin, and his body jerked in response. Releasing her wrists, he shifted his hands to her ass and pulled her tight to his erection.

"This should stop," he muttered, but his fingers kneaded her flesh and he ground his hips against hers, belying his words.

"Are you sure you want me to stop?" she said into his neck, before biting down lightly on the skin between his throat and shoulder.

"Goddess, no."

The sheer desperation in his voice made her chuckle. "Then I think I'll continue."

Finally moving her hands from where they were trapped between their bodies, she slipped her palms higher, caressing his skin softly with her nails. The movement pushed his shirt higher, giving her access to all the hard planes of muscle. She dropped to her knees in front of him, despite his warning growl and his attempt to keep her in place. The heat of his skin was a lure she refused to resist. Placing her lips gently on his abdomen, she reveled in the trembling of muscle she felt.

She trailed her tongue down the center of his stomach, stopping only when she reached the top of his trousers. Then she pushed the material down ever so slightly and licked.

The sound he made in response was part moan, part shout, but muffled as if he didn't want to make too much noise. The response pleased her. She nuzzled her cheek against his erection, still unfortunately confined by his trousers.

"This can't be very comfortable. Wouldn't you be happier without these?" She tugged gently at the top of his trousers to make her point.

"Yes."

The gravel of his voice sent a spike of heat to her core. But before she could make good on removing his trousers, someone knocked at the door. With a soft grunt of regret, she nuzzled his erection again, then stood.

Grinning, she pointed to the bed. "Maybe you should sit down and make that beautifully hard cock less obvious. We wouldn't want to scare anyone."

His dark expression only made her grin more.

When he was seated, uncomfortably, on the edge of the mattress, she opened the door and let in a human woman carrying a large tray. She startled when she saw Einar in the room.

"Oh, I'm sorry, my lord. I left your meal in your room. Will I bring it here?"

He nodded, quick and sharp, without unclenching his jaw.

Setting her tray down on the small table next to the bed, the woman hurried off, glancing nervously at the large warrior elf scowling from his place on the bed.

When she was gone, Nuala said, "You're scaring her, you know. You might want to try a less…threatening expression."

He snorted but still didn't speak. When the girl returned, she looked around for a place to put the second tray, her gaze continuing to jump nervously toward Einar.

"Here," Nuala said, feeling sorry for the poor woman. She took the tray. "Don't let him scare you. He's just…in a mood."

The woman tried to smile, but when she glanced at Einar again, her faint smile dropped. "If there will be nothing else?"

"No. Thank you very much for the food."

The human dipped into a slight curtsy and fled, closing the door solidly behind her.

"Einar. That wasn't very nice."

She turned to scold him and found him standing in front of her. Silently, he took the tray, set it to one side on the floor, and yanked her back into his arms.

"You want nice," he said in that same gravelly voice. "I'll give you nice."

His threat sent a shiver of excitement across her skin, and she sank against him as he finally captured her mouth in a hard, demanding kiss.

CHAPTER ELEVEN

Nuala barely had time to catch her breath before Einar had her stripped naked and sprawled across the bed. The *Shaerta* roared through her, making her skin so sensitive, his every touch was an exquisite balance between pleasure and pain. Before she could gain the upper hand again, he settled between her legs and licked into her wet, hot folds, sending her body into a spiral of desperation.

Knowing there were other people in the building, near enough to hear her, she kept her screams of pleasure locked behind clenched teeth. Then Einar's revenge swept her up into a fast, hard orgasm so overwhelming it stole her voice.

He tried to take advantage of her loss of control, to keep her in the throes of his revenge. But she wanted too much from him to allow that. Despite his superior size, she surprised him by flipping him onto his back. Her needs rode her hard, making her rough as she opened his belt and wrenched his trousers apart, forcing them down his hips. She didn't even bother to fully strip him, just leaned over his throbbing cock and took him into her mouth.

Einar's back arched off the bed and he dropped his hands to her head, burying his fingers in the thick mass of her hair. The long locks fell in waves around her, covering his hips, creating a curtain that added intimacy as she licked and sucked him.

Controlling his body, this warrior so feared by everyone else, gave her as much pleasure as his mouth had just given her. She couldn't stop, even when she knew he was close to losing control. And she didn't want to. His pants and moans, the near painful grip of his hands, sent her own body tightening again, climbing toward another orgasm without him even having to touch her.

His scent rose up to surround her, mixing with the already potent *Shaerta* to drive her beyond thought. Pleasure, need, taking and giving. Nothing else mattered in that moment. Only the hard length of him between her lips, the desperate sounds he made from between clenched teeth, the rasps of their panting mingling in the quiet room.

Driven beyond madness by her desires, she straddled one of his legs and rubbed herself along the smooth leather of his trousers, even as she continued to savor the taste of his cock. The sensation of cool, smooth material against her hot, wet clit pushed her to the very edge of her control. And when she felt Einar pulse in her mouth, when he ground out her name and came with a suppressed roar, she followed. The spiraling pleasure jerked through her body as she continued to suck the last of Einar's orgasm from him.

Panting and gloriously, if momentarily, satisfied, Nuala released him from her lips and nuzzled his hip with her cheek.

His eyes were so dark they were nearly black, and the love and desire there squeezed around her heart. He still had one hand in her hair, caressing her scalp gently, and she wanted to purr like one of the cats she remembered from her last visit to Sinnale.

"You'll eat now," he growled down at her, his voice so harsh another might have thought him angry.

She raised her brows and smiled, glancing at his semi-erect cock.

"The food," he clarified. And she laughed.

"You'll eat—the food—too. It's been a long night. Then I do need to sleep. But—" she held up a hand when he started to speak, "—I want you to stay with me, sleep here with me."

He still looked like he wanted to protest. "The bonding…we made things worse just now."

"And I want you here too much to care if we continue to make things worse." She crawled up his body and settled beside him, leaning over to hold his gaze so he couldn't doubt her words. "It's too late, Einar. And I don't care. For you, for us, I will take the worst punishment the queen and king will hand out."

"You're not scared of the *Or'roan*?"

"Oh, I'm scared of that. I don't want to meet a permanent end to my soul. Mostly because it means I'll only have this lifetime with you. And I want more. I don't want to risk your afterlife, your lifetimes either. If you walked away from me to avoid the *Or'roan*, I'd let you go."

"Never," he hissed, his arms tightening around her hard and fast.

She released a little breath, only just then realizing a small part of her had worried he'd make the choice to abandon what they had if she offered him the out.

"Then you should know I will always choose this life with you," she said, "no matter how long we have, whether we can travel into the next realm together or not. I can't continue without you anymore. I don't want to."

"I don't want to either." He kissed her, a soft promise. When he straightened, though, his brow was creased and his mouth tightened. "I can feel a difference," he said quietly. "In my magic. Already I can feel a difference."

She let her attention turn inward, toward that place at her very center where her essence and magic mixed to make her who she was. She concentrated on the swirls of energy, the ebbs and flows. And realized she too felt different.

There were changes happening. She wouldn't be able to tell how those changes would manifest in her magic until she tried to work it. But she and Einar were linked now, their bonding almost fully complete. And with that came a melding of powers and talents, leaving in its wake something new and untried.

She refocused on him. "As I said. Too late. So now there's no reason for you to leave. Stay with me. I'll sleep better knowing you're next to me."

He kissed her again before saying, "I don't want to be anywhere else ever again."

Ulric and Layla came personally to show Nuala to the armory and the room set up for her work. Einar insisted on escorting her despite the fact that she was safe with her cousin.

She allowed Einar and Layla, busy discussing the tensile strength of the steel used in various elf swords, to move ahead so she could have a private word with Ulric as they walked.

"Your brother?" she said in their own language, in case Ulric didn't want his feelings on the subject known to the Sinnale.

The expression on Ulric's face was not friendly. His blue eyes narrowed and a set of deep lines furrowed his brow. "The humans have agreed to hold Althir in a comfortable prison for the time being. I think they give him too much luxury."

"He is your brother."

"His selfishness almost got Layla killed. *He* almost killed Layla. Though he claims he didn't know it was her when he fired." This last he muttered quietly, reluctantly, as if part of him believed Althir and resented doing so.

"Ah." She understood, better than Ulric knew. The brothers had never been particularly close, so Althir having anything to do with harming the woman Ulric loved would likely override his brotherly feelings. The fact that Althir could have killed Layla, whether he meant to or not… Nuala wasn't particularly surprised Ulric was so angry. She could imagine the feeling too well when it came to Einar. Still…

Ulric and Althir's relationship was unique. Most elf siblings weren't born so close together—they were usually separated by centuries rather than decades like her cousins. She'd always thought it a shame they couldn't get along better. They were much more alike than either would care to admit.

Not the least being their loyalty to the king and queen. She often thought Althir's jealousy of Ulric came from that loyalty and the favor the sovereigns paid the older brother. And while his turning traitor had shocked her deeply, a part of her wondered if Althir had done that because the sovereigns didn't acknowledge him the way they did Ulric.

"But he's helping the humans now," she said. "You begrudge him some comfort? He's provided information that will eventually help end the war."

Ulric didn't answer for several minutes. She'd decided he wouldn't when he finally said, "I can't trust him ever again. I would have killed him for the threat he was to Layla. There's been too much damage between us for me to think kindly on Althir."

She sighed. A shame, but not unexpected. "Should I… Should I visit him while I'm here?"

"He's not allowed visitors from Glengowyn yet. On order of the king and queen. They worry he'll…corrupt other elves. His charm…"

Althir's magics were tied up in his charm, and he could be very persuasive if he chose to be. Some in Glengowyn whispered Althir was the first to defect, the one who lured the other traitors to the Sorcerers. She had her doubts about that rumor, but it made the sovereigns' order regarding visitors reasonable.

"You visit him, though?" she asked.

"I don't. But not because of the order."

"Then why?"

"I'm still tempted to kill him."

"I had to kill an elf." She blurted the sentence before she realized she would. "One of the traitors who helped in the attack on the caravan. I… I'm not sure I would have if you hadn't confirmed that I could."

"I'm sorry." He sighed. "Maybe I shouldn't have told you."

"No. That's not what I mean. He would have handed me over to the Sorcerers. To be used and drained and eventually killed. I don't regret killing him. In fact, I felt very little about having done it. I wouldn't have known it possible without you, though, and so I might not have tried. You helped save my life by telling me." She shrugged and glanced at him from the corner of her eye. "I guess I'm trying to say thank you for being honest with me."

"Always, cousin. Always." He walked beside her a few more paces before saying, very softly, "I will hate to see you banished."

She pursed her lips. "It's obvious now?"

"That you've bonded with Einar? Yes. They won't be happy when they find out."

"I know. We're prepared."

"I wish I could save you from that as well."

She gave him a small, sad smile. "No one could. But we'll be okay."

"This will affect the magics for the arrows."

He wasn't asking. He knew as well as she did that it would. "I'll keep you aware of what happens. I won't endanger the Sinnale with inadequate weaponry."

He took her hand and squeezed, a gesture that said more than his words could.

"You've lost a brother and a cousin in a war never meant for us," she said quietly.

"I didn't lose my cousin to the war. I lost her to love. And I can't fault her that." He met her gaze. "I am happy for you. You and Einar…you share something deep. I haven't seen you this content in centuries. And that, at least, pleases me."

This time her smile was genuine and big. "Thank you."

They reached the armory then and switched back to speaking in the Sinnale language for Layla's sake.

She held open a thick wooden door for them, gesturing them into a large room filled with strung bows, swords of various sizes, a few vests of chainmail and helmets, a plethora of knives ranging from daggers to throwing darts, a pile of what Nuala guessed were the makings for explosives, and racks of elf arrows—both the regular arrows typically traded with the Sinnale, and the fire-tips which were only now being allowed into Sinnale hands.

The fire-tips had arrowheads that burned as hot as lava after their release, deadly and dangerous. While they could slice through most barriers, including magical ones, they could also ignite major fires if not used carefully. Until recently, the king and queen hadn't wanted that power in the hands of their neighbors.

Several elves created the fire-tips so Nuala was rarely tasked to make many. The king and queen had her concentrate on ordinary arrows—hers were some of the best and so traded well with the Sinnale before the war—and making her special arrows.

The material for which currently sat at the center of the room. A large stack of the pre-fletched, hollowed shafts waited for her to finish them. Several boxes of additional material were piled next to the stack—shrapnel to fill the shafts, arrowheads and leather wraps specifically designed for her specialty.

Without her magic, her spell to set the arrows, they would never fly. Too heavy and off balance when filled with small sharp shards of metal, the arrows should have been useless. But once set with her spell, they became a dangerous bomb, exploding and unleashing chaos wherever they landed. These arrows had helped her people win the last goblin war. The Sinnale were counting on them to put an end to their own war.

If she could get them to work now that her magic had mixed with Einar's.

"Do you have everything you need?" Layla asked as Nuala studied her work area.

There was a comfortable-looking bench for her to sit at, all the tools she needed to hand. And a small, empty table to one side of the bench.

"Everything looks good. The table?"

"For water, meals. Whatever you might need."

"She won't eat while working," Einar said. "But make sure there's water for her."

Layla left to get the water. Nuala stared at Einar for several moments, knowing he was thinking the same thing she was—could she do what was necessary anymore? Could she work the spell, the special magic only she'd ever been able to wield, and turn these arrows into bombs?

Ulric clapped Einar on the back of the shoulder, breaking into their silence. "Come. We'll leave my cousin to her work and you and I can discuss some security issues."

Though he went reluctantly, Einar allowed Ulric to lead him out. A moment later, a pitcher of fresh water and a glass were delivered and left on the table. Then Nuala was alone.

CHAPTER TWELVE

$\mathcal{N}$uala stared at the hollowed-out arrow shafts, and for the first time since discovering this spell, knew real trepidation. She settled herself on the bench, took up the first hollow shaft and dropped in some shrapnel, filling it completely from the closed base where it had already been properly fletched, all the way to the tip where she inserted the point.

As she wrapped securing leather around the arrowhead, she closed her eyes and began the spell, sending power through her body, molding it into the song of enchantment and death that was the weapon. A quiet, mumbling swing of words fell from her lips to swirl around the arrow, infusing and setting it.

But as she worked, the song felt…different. A word, here or there, came out wrong and yet fit perfectly into what she was singing. The tone of certain notes changed, by a flat or sharp, a whole octave deeper or higher. Yet the rhythm felt powerful, the pour of magic through her body flowed easily. It didn't fight the changes in the spell. In fact, the new twists of magic she accessed grew stronger as she chanted, hinting at the final shape without revealing it, bringing a certainty of purpose and strength both different and familiar.

She could almost feel the influence of Einar's magic mingling with her own, turning into its own creation. That it mixed so easily, so well, so perfectly was both surprising and somehow expected. Yet, even as she sang, as she formed the spell and poured power into it, she had no idea what she was really creating. Still a weapon. Maybe even more powerful than her previous spell. But with a difference she couldn't understand. Something more…personal. Something more precise…

When her music faded and she returned from the sensory realms of working the magic back to a more physical state, she stared down at the finished arrow in her hands. A faint golden glow faded as she watched. And then the arrow looked like any other.

What had she done? What would this new creation do?

She set the enigma aside, selected a second arrow shaft and attempted to set it with the original spell. This time, her power flowed in the old ways, lacking the changeable influence of Einar's magic. And when she was done, she'd created one of the original weapons she was here to set. Again she went to the arrow shafts, again the magic bowed to the original intention of the spell. But after another five arrows, the magic bent again. And Nuala made another of the strange anomalous arrows.

Late into the night she worked, remembering to drink only when she felt faint. Her body faded away with each spell-casting, so that she only noticed discomfort for brief minutes between the magics. In those moments, she felt the growing exhaustion that would eventually force her to stop and sleep. But she ignored both the physical and magical depletion to continue working.

When she could no longer concentrate enough to properly form either of the spells, she took stock of her work.

To one side lay almost a hundred of the new type of arrows. To the other, three times that many of her originally spelled weapons. She let out a breath and selected one of the new, studying it, feeling the magic within. She closed her eyes and opened her sense, trying to discern how the new arrow might work, but the solution eluded her. With her original arrows, she'd known as she made them what they would become. This time, the outcome was a mystery.

How could she give these to the Sinnale when she didn't even know what they did? Would they even fly with all the shrapnel inside them, given the changes in the spell? So many uncertainties. And no opportunity to test any possible theory. The human council expected what they'd ordered, what they'd fairly traded for.

Now what?

She set the arrow back in its pile and gulped down the remaining water, not surprised to find her throat so dry it had tightened up. She moved to the cot Layla had provided in one dark corner of the room, curled onto her side, and was asleep instantly.

Though there were windows in the room, she found it impossible to tell how long she'd slept after she returned to consciousness. It was still dark out, so she could have slept for a quarter hour, several hours, even a full day into the next night. Sitting up, she noticed a basin of clean washing water had been brought into the room. The water pitcher was filled again. And there was a small plate of cheese and nuts on the table beside the water.

The idea of food made her stomach roll in disgust, but the water sounded like joy. Once she'd sated her thirst, took care of bodily functions, and paced a few times around the room to loosen up muscles, she returned to setting arrows.

When exhaustion took her again, it was full sunlight, though she still wasn't sure what time. No timer chimes sounded through the city. No time device of any kind was left in the large room. As she worked, time lost meaning anyway, and she stopped only long enough to nap again, then returned to the arrows.

The sun was down, the room shadowed in the corners where the light from the hanging gaslamp refused to go, by the time she'd worked her way through most of the empty arrow shafts.

Einar quietly entered the room sometime during her working. But he remained as unobtrusive and invisible as only a well-trained bodyguard could. Even Nuala only barely noted his presence, and she was overly aware of him.

She let the last song fade away and placed the arrow she'd been working on the pile with the new arrows. The two piles had remained a three-to-one ratio of traditional to new. And she still had no idea what the newest arrows did.

The rest of the water in the pitcher wetted her dry throat before she finally turned to face Einar.

He didn't even have to question her aloud. She could see his concern and curiosity in the slight raise of his brows.

"These—" she pointed to the larger of the two piles, "—are the arrows I'm here to produce. These others are new."

"What do the new ones do?"

"I have no idea," she admitted. "They're different, a product of our melding. But… I have no idea what they're capable of."

He stared at the smaller pile. "What will you tell Ulric, the human council?"

She stood and stretched, letting her spine pop as she worked out the kinks of sitting for so long. "Ulric… Ulric knows we've bonded. He can sense the change."

Einar nodded.

"I'm hoping to persuade him to let me test one or two of these before allowing the humans to use any of them. I don't want to be responsible for any Sinnale deaths because the weapon backfires."

"Reasonable. And you've managed to produce the arrows they

traded for—at least a good number of them came out correctly. That bodes well."

"Maybe." Though she wasn't sure what to make of this mixing of abilities from one moment to the next. "I hope it will be enough to satisfy them until we can figure out what these others do."

"Ulric will make sure it is. Now, you need food."

She blinked. Her mind had been on the rhythm and words of the new spell as she tried to analyze them for a possible explanation. Einar's reminder that she needed to eat made her stomach growl.

"I guess I do need food." She chuckled and left the arrows to join him in his position next to the door. "How long have you been keeping vigil there?"

"Inside the room? Not long. I didn't want to distract you."

His expression remained neutral, but she didn't miss his careful phrasing. "Inside the room not long. How long did you watch over me from outside the room?"

"I've been here all along. I couldn't leave you alone and vulnerable in a strange place. Even if we are surrounded by allies."

He spoke as if she should have known better and her question baffled him. She should have known better. How else would Einar think?

"Come, Ulric has food prepared and waiting in a more comfortable setting."

Without touching her, he led her back down the corridor. The lack of physical contact was exactly what she needed. After working so much magic, her skin was always overly sensitive, and a simple touch often hurt. Einar had always understood this, better than anyone else.

As she thought back on their years of friendship and loving, she realized he always did what was right and best for her—or at least what he thought was best.

The room he led her to was small but comfortably set with a

long table and benches. The table itself was covered with more cheese, dried fruits and some fresh bread.

Layla looked up from setting out plates and greeted them with a smile. "I hope it will be enough. The war has been difficult on our food stores, but we've been doing better lately. We don't have much fresh meat, but there is some dried meat available if you require it."

Nuala waved that off. "I don't need meat. And simple foods are best."

They settled around the table and everyone quietly filled a plate. Einar watched her take her first few bites before taking any himself.

"I'm sorry there's no wine," Layla said into the silence. "There's very little left in the city. And it will be several years before we can start producing again."

"Water is better for me now." Nuala sighed. "But I will miss Sinnale wine. I have for the last few years. Your grapes always seem to produce more interesting flavors than ours."

Layla smiled. "One of the things my parents got the best use out of when trading for weapons. Sinnale wine."

She stared at Nuala for several moments and Nuala held her gaze, wondering at the considering look. She was used to a distant kind of reverence from her own people. And in years past, humans had dealt with her with a kind of awe. But many humans approached the Glengowyn elves that way. She was one of many to them, not considered unique the way she was among her own people.

Now, though, Layla and a handful of other humans knew she was special. Different. She had a feeling she was about to find out how that knowledge would affect their attitudes toward her going forward.

Layla's question, when she finally spoke, surprised Nuala, however.

"Why did you have to come here? That was never made clear in the negotiations with the queen. And despite being willing to trade your special arrows with us to help end the war, she was vague when it came to you."

Nuala shrugged and swallowed her food. "The queen and king are both very protective of me."

"Yes. Which is why I'm surprised they would send you into a war zone."

"Oh, this isn't the first time I've been in a war zone. I developed these arrows for the second goblin war."

"They helped us end that war relatively quickly," Ulric added.

"Not quickly enough," she said, looking at her cousin.

He held her gaze, his expression full of understanding. No one who'd been part of those battles had escaped without scars.

"But to answer your question…" She faced Layla again. "I have to…set the arrows close to the point at which they'll be used. They travel in quivers fine over short distances and so long as there aren't too many in a single quiver. They can be packed with our other spelled arrows for even more secure travel—though I would recommend keeping the fire-tips and my arrows separate. But they can't be stacked in large numbers and carted over long distances, already assembled and spelled. The movement, time and quantity together triggers the spell."

"They explode without being fired," Ulric said. "We learned that the hard way."

Nuala glanced down at her plate. That was one of her scars from the war, a mistake that had cost several strong warrior elves their lives. Einar shifted minutely closer to her, still not touching—not enough time had elapsed for her skin and nerves to have settled— but enough to make his comforting presence felt. She released the tension with a breath and looked up.

"After the…accident. We knew the arrows had to be transported in individual parts, and I'd have to be camped near the battles to be able to set them."

"So, you went into the war," Layla said.

"I went into the war." Nuala blinked back more memories. "And after, the queen in particular but both the sovereigns knew that not only were these weapons something too dangerous to share with outsiders, they were too unstable to trade easily. They also never wanted to risk me being kidnapped or held captive by someone we traded with after I was sent in to set the arrows."

"That's why Nuala hasn't come into Sinnale in a century," Ulric said. "Their protectiveness of her has gotten worse over the years."

Einar grunted, a surprising sound that drew all their gazes. He didn't look up from his plate, just ignored their attention, so they returned to their conversation.

"So," Layla said, "once the traitor elves defected and it became clear this war was coming to Glengowyn if they did nothing, like it or not, they decided to risk you by trading these arrows with us."

"In their way." She dipped her head toward Einar. "They sent me with their most feared personal bodyguard. They did try to minimize the risk."

"The traitors knew who you were though. They guessed you'd come eventually."

Einar grunted again. This time he did speak. "They were likely watching for her, keeping at least one or two of the traitors with each group of minions sent to attack the caravans."

Nuala pursed her lips. "There was no way around my coming here. For your people to have these arrows, to end this war faster, it was necessary for me to come."

"I'm glad they allowed it," Layla said. "We're stronger now, with the reintroduction of the elven weaponry. But the war is dragging on. The Sorcerers continue to capture our people and use them or turn them into minions. We need to drive them out."

"The information Althir provides?"

"Very helpful. We've been able to engage them beyond their own border for the first time since the border was set. We know where their vulnerable spots are, even the location of their individual strongholds outside the main citadel, all the places we'll have to destroy to drive them out. But we haven't been able to break through their defenses thoroughly enough to move far enough into their territory to end things."

Nuala caught Ulric's gaze as she said, "Some of the arrows… didn't turn out as they should have. It happens sometimes." She lied and made sure Ulric knew it. "I'll need to run a few tests on the different ones before they're allowed into a battle. In the meantime, the ones provided combined with our ordinary arrows and the fire-tips should be sufficient to aid in an offensive."

Ulric nodded in understanding, his gaze darting to Einar and then to Layla. Layla didn't comment but her eyes narrowed.

She was smart, Ulric's mate. She knew something wasn't exactly right with what Nuala had said, but she kept that knowledge to herself and outwardly accepted the story.

"I'll be sure the arms marshal knows which arrows are not ready to be used," she said.

Nuala felt tension she'd only barely been aware of uncurl. Until she could figure out what the new arrows did, she did not want to risk another accident. She'd never forgive herself if some of the Sinnale were killed because of her, the way her own people had died before she knew more about her shrapnel arrows. She would not make that mistake again.

CHAPTER THIRTEEN

he Sinnale had already started planning another offensive before Nuala and her arrows entered the city, with the new weapons at the core of their plans. Once Nuala and Einar had arrived, the human council finalized their strategy and began organizing their people.

Nuala spent the next day and a half in the armory. While trying to unravel the purpose of the new arrows, she also ensured they weren't inadvertently added to the weaponry the humans planned to use for the coming battle. Unfortunately, the ultimate results of the spell continued to elude her.

"This has never happened before," she complained to Einar after the first day. "How can I not know what magic I've wrought?"

"You've never dealt with blended magics before," he assured her, remaining a calming presence beside her the entire time. "You'll understand soon."

But when another half day passed with her at a loss, Einar insisted she leave the armory to rest. "Ulric will make sure none of these make it into the battle preparations. You won't find answers if you're too exhausted to think."

She didn't want to stop but knew he was right. If she didn't sleep properly, she might even miss the answer right in front of her.

They hadn't had much time alone since she started her work in the armory. Between the exertions of her magic and the time spent trying to unravel the spell she'd placed on the new arrows, she'd never stopped to wonder how their bonding had affected his magic. Or him.

Without argument or even the need for words, he followed her into her room. As soon as she shut the door, he gathered her close and kissed her. The kiss was gentle, not demanding, but she felt his longing in the tightness of his muscles. She sighed into the sensations and gave herself over to his kiss, returning it with equal tenderness.

"I've missed this," he murmured. "Only a few days, and I've missed kissing you. I won't be able to go back to how things were between us."

"Me neither." She eased back enough to look at him directly. "I have no intention of going back, either. But…"

He stiffened. "But?"

"We haven't stopped to consider how this has affected your magic. Until now, everyone's been more concerned with what might happen to my skills. I haven't stopped to think what this might have done to you."

Holding her at his side, he led her to the bed. "I haven't attempted anything yet."

They lay down, fully clothed, and she rested her head on his chest. "Is your…is your battle state part of your magic?" No one knew, at least not that she'd ever spoken with, though she was sure the queen knew, and no one seemed inclined to ask him. She'd never been brave enough to bring up the topic.

He remained silent for a while, and she gave him time, listening to his heart beat steady against her cheek.

Finally, he said, "I've never been sure. I don't feel like I'm tapping magic when I…let go. Unlike the owls. I feel that, the mixing of magic and my essence to make that possible. In battle… All I ever feel is rage. And when I turn the rage loose, I become the Darkness."

"So you'll still be capable of doing what you do in battle?" She realized that gave her a measure of relief she hadn't anticipated. She was quite certain one of the things that kept Einar safe was the fear he inspired. Even the king wouldn't think to challenge him in combat. But if that had changed because of what they'd done, he would be vulnerable.

"That skill at least should be fine," he reassured. "The owls…"

"Has something changed with that?"

"Not that I can put words to. I can still feel the ability to speak with them within me. But something in the calling has changed."

"The calling? Being able to get them to come to you?"

"It hasn't gone away. I can call them. I think. But there's a difference to it. I can't really explain. Maybe a different focus?"

"Different focus. That sort of describes what I'm sensing in the new arrows. No. Not difference so much as *more* focus. There's something…precise about the spell, something specific that wasn't there before."

"Yes. That's a good way to explain it. There's a precision to the feel of the calling now, a specificity that wasn't required before."

"Does it make things more difficult?"

She felt his shrug. "I haven't tried to actually bring an owl to me yet, so I can't say. I'm going on the way the magic feels."

"You should try. Soon."

"It isn't as important as the new arrows. It can wait."

She licked her lips before asking, "Will they stop carrying messages for Glengowyn if you're banished?"

"I don't know that either. When the king first threatened me with banishment if I didn't stay away from you, I asked the owls and they said they wouldn't continue. But...a lot of time has passed since then. And with the change in my magic... I'll have to ask them again."

She didn't think the threat of losing the owls would be enough to earn them forgiveness from their sovereigns, but it was something to consider.

Her head lifted slightly as Einar pulled in a deep breath. "Sleep, Nuala. We can worry about these things another time."

He was right. They would worry about them when they returned to Glengowyn. A small part of her wondered if they should bother going back. Just take themselves into banishment now before the king and queen publicly sent them away. It wouldn't save them from the consequences of their actions. And the sovereigns, if they wanted to, could place the *Or'roan* on her and Einar no matter where they went. But it would be easier not to have to face the censure of the king or the wrath of the queen in person.

She closed her eyes and allowed her tired body the rest it needed, taking comfort in the fact that at least she and Einar would face that future together, no matter what the sovereigns decided.

Nuala watched the final preparations for the offensive strike against the Sorcerers' borders from the rooftop of the council's meeting hall. Gaslamps lit the movements of humans in and out of the hall and through the neighboring streets. A cool breeze ruffled the night, bringing a freshness to the air along with the anticipation of a battle to come.

She'd spent more time with her new arrows, digging through the layers of the spell. And had come to one conclusion.

"They have to be tried," she said to Einar, who stood at her back. "I have to use one to see what it will do."

He didn't pretend not to understand her meaning. "You're not a soldier. You're too valuable to be sent directly into a battle like this. I will go and try the weapon."

"No." She turned and faced him. "It's my spell. My risk. And you won't *know* the difference the way I will when I use one. There's no other place to try them. I can't just fire one randomly at a target like the others. There's…something about that sort of experiment that feels more dangerous than firing one in battle." She raised her hands, palms up. "I wish I could explain better."

"Nuala, I can't allow you to go into this fight. You're not prepared."

"I've been fighting since we left Glengowyn."

"This isn't your war. It's the Sinnale's. Besides, the king and queen—"

"Are about to impose severe punishments on us for our love. They will hardly blame you more if you take me into a fight." She stepped close and cupped his cheeks. His jaw was hard as stone beneath her palms, and he refused to meet her gaze when she looked up at him.

"Einar. This is the only way to test them. I don't dare leave them untested. I can't move them now that they've been set. They're more dangerous like this, so I can't just walk away and relinquish the responsibility of them to the humans. I *have* to solve this. And it has to be done in battle where the only ones hurt will be the enemy."

"I don't want you to do this."

The petulance in his voice forced a half laugh from her. "I don't want to either. I'm more than aware of my deficiencies in a fight.

But I'll stay back from the ground attack, in the rooftops with the other archers."

"That position is not safe from the Sorcerers' spells."

"Safer than being in the middle of swinging swords."

"Not by much."

"You know this has to be done." She rubbed her thumbs across his cheeks, trying to loosen the tight muscles under her fingers.

"I don't like it. So you will follow my direction. I will be by your side every moment."

"I expected nothing less."

"And if I say run, fall back or give you any other warning to leave the field, you will go."

She nodded. "I'm not trying to get myself killed. I just don't want any of our allies killed either." She licked her lips. "And a concession from you."

His brows rose sharply as he dropped his chin back. "A concession from me? I'm the warrior between us."

"Yes and that's the problem. We'll be in the middle of a conflict that isn't yours any more than it's mine. It's for the Sinnale to drive the Sorcerers out. We do our part with weapons. But we're not here to really fight. I don't want you in the middle of things. And I will make it clear to Ulric that you are not taking part as anything but my bodyguard. I'm not taking part except to discover what these new arrows really do in the only way that won't endanger the humans. But beyond that, no. You are not here to be their Darkness."

The night breeze blew through his short hair, rippling the edges around his ears so the points were more prominent than usual. Light from the gaslamps below bathed his features but kept his eyes dark and difficult to read. She didn't flinch away from his silent look, though. He had to understand, his safety was as important to her as hers was to him.

"You are the only one I will be the Darkness for ever again," he said quietly. "My loyalty is with you now. Not Glengowyn. And if you ask me to fight, I will. If you ask me to avoid fighting—except where I must defend you—I will. From this time forward, you're my city, my people, my life."

Her chest ached at the declaration, making it impossible to speak. So she did what she wanted to do anyway. She drew his face close to hers and kissed him, letting just a hint of the *Shaerta* rise to add weight and power to their kiss. Letting him understand she felt exactly the same way.

She only stopped to avoid getting carried away, but she rested her head against his forehead for a long moment. Then she said, "Let's go talk with Ulric."

CHAPTER FOURTEEN

*N*uala watched from a rooftop as the madness of battle raged below in the streets. Minions and Sinnale fought just inside the Sorcerers' border, swords clashing, the sounds of screams, metal on metal, shouts and the *thwack* of launching arrows matched only by the roar of magic.

The Sorcerers remained behind the main front but made themselves known in the drop of fire spells, which melted cobbles and brick and any hapless living thing that got in their way. Bolts of energy slammed into the midst of the chaos along with the fire, creating a cacophony of death. The Sinnale archers focused their efforts on the Sorcerers, making the attacks less consistent and overwhelming than they might have been otherwise.

Nuala even witnessed the death of one Sorcerer who happened to be standing too near when an archer finally used one of her special arrows. The shrapnel carried a spell of its own that punched through magic shields. The Sorcerer in the way of that shrapnel died in bloody shreds.

A cheer rose from the surrounding archers, spurring the Sinnale attack below.

After that, the attacking spells from the Sorcerers were even more sporadic, the focus almost defensive. The archers kept their attention on the rooftops, protecting the street soldiers below. Now that her weapons had been tried successfully, others used them as well, carefully but with a kind of relish that was almost disturbing. If Nuala hadn't known exactly what these people had been through over the last two years, she might have been bothered by their glee.

As the fighting moved deeper into the Sorcerers' territory, Nuala and the other archers followed. Einar, true to his word, stayed with her and out of the mêlée below. She kept her distance from the fighting too, remaining to the rear of the archers as they descended to street level to find another rooftop vantage point.

Down on the ground, she felt infinitely more vulnerable and so stayed close to Einar. Unlike their entrance into the city, however, no one was after them specifically this time and that made their passage somehow easier.

At the next rooftop, Nuala got her opportunity to try her new arrow. She'd only brought three with her, with the intention of using only one. And while she carried more ordinary-spelled arrows in her quiver, they were only to defend herself if it became necessary. To Einar's surprise and approval, she'd also strapped his knife to her hip. Though she had no intention of getting involved in the fighting, battles changed directions fast and there were some situations in which a bow was less useful than a knife.

She spotted the Sorcerer as she rose just above a low parapet to study the street. Nuala had taken a position away from the others, putting herself beyond the focus of most of the Sinnale archers. None of them paid attention to her or seemed to have noticed the robed woman standing two buildings over, studying the battle. Nuala watched the woman, but the Sorcerer merely observed the fighting below. It didn't matter. She was an enemy, and Nuala had her opportunity to test her new creation.

She nudged Einar and he grunted quietly in affirmation.

With a careful eye on the target, Nuala nocked the new arrow into place and drew back her bowstring. But when she released the string, nothing happened. The arrow remained in place, hovering oddly as it held the string stretched without any pressure from her.

Because she didn't want the humans to notice, she quickly replaced her fingers so it would look like she was still aiming. Then she attempted to ease the string back and relax the arrow in its position. Nothing. The thing remained nocked and drawn, ready to fire and yet not going anywhere no matter what she tried.

A tickle of panic set in. She didn't dare turn the point away from a potential target, but she had no idea how to get the bloody thing to launch.

As she pondered her quandary, a shout rose from below. She glanced down long enough to see three of the traitor elves joining the fight, bringing a level of skill with them that the minions couldn't match—and neither could a lot of the Sinnale.

"I didn't think they fought in the battles and skirmishes, not like that," she said to Einar.

"Something must have changed. Perhaps the threat of the humans finally beating the Sorcerers. I doubt they want to be on the losing side after all this."

He sounded almost disinterested. As if the traitors meant very little to him. But she recognized all three of them. And one, many, many years ago, had been a friend. Sareena had grown resentful and mean after the wars, though. More than once she'd taken her bitterness out on Nuala, at first verbally. But twice she'd attempted to physically attack her. Those occasions had resulted in severe punishment from the king and queen, which only made Sareena's anger stronger.

When the attacks had started, Nuala had been hurt and baffled by her former friend's attitude. After the second physical attack, she'd grown angry. Well before Sareena had defected to the Sorcerers, she and Nuala had danced around each other as hostile acquaintances. When Sareena turned traitor, no one, least of all Nuala, was surprised.

Though Nuala kept the point of her arrow toward the Sorcerer, she stared down at Sareena and a deep anger rose, for her once friend, for all the traitors who'd placed their own desires above the safety of both Sinnale and Glengowyn.

"Sareena," Nuala hissed aloud, jutting her chin toward the traitor so Einar would understand her statement. Before she could say more, however, her poised arrow began to tremble. And without Nuala releasing the string, it flew from her bow.

Gasping, Nuala watched, expecting it to fly in the direction it was aimed. Instead, the arrow turned unnaturally, as if guided by an unseen hand, and flew toward the place where the traitor elves fought.

Nuala choked down a shout of dismay. There were Sinnale all around the elves. If that arrow landed among them, it would kill as many allies as enemy. And because she hadn't aimed, she had no idea who it might hit.

"Einar! What have I done?"

He stood beside her with a hand on her shoulder, watching the disaster unfold. But the arrow swerved and shivered through the chaos, actually turning to avoid hitting anyone who got in its way. The passage was impossible and defied all laws of aerodynamics. But the missile wound its way through the throngs of fighters, and to her utter astonishment, slammed directly into Sareena's chest.

The traitor looked down at the arrow, her expression almost comically surprised. Then the missile exploded in a bright flash of white light. Nuala did scream then, knowing others near Sareena would be killed too.

Instead of the mess of carnage, however, a small smoking hole dented the cobbles and the bloody remains of a single elf colored a confined area on the street. Those close to the death—minion, elf and Sinnale alike—stared without moving at the bits and pieces that were all that was left of the traitor elf. Yet no other bodies littered the ground. No one else was hurt.

The pause in fighting only lasted a beat before swords were raised again and the conflict resumed, ebbing over the dead elf and moving on. But Nuala remained frozen, too stunned to react.

After several moments, she felt the gaze of others on her. Looking up, she noticed first that the Sorcerer she'd been hoping to kill was staring at her, dark eyes wide and jaw tight. Nuala barely took note of the woman's expression before she vanished as if never having been there. The suddenness made Nuala gasp.

Einar's hand tightened on her shoulder. She turned to ask if he'd see the Sorcerer vanish, only to realize the other archers on the rooftop were staring at her.

"We should leave," Einar said close to her ear.

She started toward the door leading from the roof. But the commander of the regiment, a short, stocky man in his middle years, approached them, blocking their exit.

"What type of arrow was that? It defied all that's logical. Can we trade for it?"

Nuala hadn't had time to figure out exactly what had happened with her new arrow, nonetheless prepared herself for a request for more. "It's…experimental and not yet ready for trade." She hoped the explanation would satisfy him.

He frowned but didn't argue. "As soon as it's ready, let us know. I'll make sure the council buys as many as we can afford."

Because she didn't know what else to say, she let Einar lead her away. The Sinnale archers turned back to their part in the battle, but she heard murmurs of curiosity and interest even as they continued the fight.

She and Einar reached the street before she spoke. "I said her name, Einar. I said Sareena's name aloud. And the arrow targeted her. I didn't have to fire it. It flew of its own accord." That realization made her clamp a hand over her mouth. "What have I done? I've just used your name aloud. What if the remaining two arrows target you?"

She wanted to throw her quiver away to keep the arrows as far from Einar as she could manage. But she was too stunned to put action to fear.

He took her shoulders in his hands and met her gaze. "Explain to me exactly how everything felt from the moment you nocked the arrow into place."

She breathed carefully and turned her senses back in time to the memories and details.

"Until I put the arrow into the bow, I didn't feel anything from it other than its bespelled nature, what I'd felt from the moment I set it," she started slowly, working past the other distractions of battle to the specific sensations. "Once I placed the arrow against the string and pulled the string back, there was a sense of…readiness. Potential. Similar to the reaction from any elf arrow."

"So until it's brought into firing position, it doesn't feel active?"

She sighed. "Maybe. When I released the string, the potential felt suspended. It was hard to tell, given the noise from the fight, but I swear I heard a low hum of…waiting. I just couldn't tell what it was waiting for."

"The name of a target."

She refocused on Einar. "When you call the owls, do you call a specific animal or just any who happen to be near?"

"Before, I could call either way—in general or specifically.

Now… I'm not sure anymore. Did the arrows ever react when you said a name while in the armory?"

She frowned, her eyes narrowing. "I can't remember saying anyone's name in the armory. I must have, but… I can't be sure."

"You've said names since we followed the battle, though." He looked away for a moment. "I remember hearing you specifically say Ulric's name. I think it's safe to say that until you nock the arrow, the…seeking aspect of the spell doesn't activate."

Her shoulders drooped in relief. "So I haven't turned the remaining two into weapons aimed at you."

"I don't think so." His brow lowered. "Can you destroy these arrows? Safely. Without using them?"

"Undo the spell? I've never tried before, on any of the arrows I create. You think I should destroy these, not let them get out?"

"Not necessarily. I was just considering our options. This is an even more deadly weapon than your previous invention."

"And yet the shrapnel didn't spray out and kill those around Sareena. The destruction was focused and confined."

"An assassin's tool."

Nuala straightened. "A terrifying tool."

He took her hand. "Come. We need to return to Sinnale territory and discuss this more. But I want you away from the conflict."

She glanced back through the walls of the building, as if she could see the fighting. "Will they succeed tonight, do you think? The battle was moving in the Sinnale's favor."

"We can hope. If they drive the Sorcerers out over the next few days, there will be no need for them to request a trade in this newest weapon of yours. And I think that would be best for all."

She had to agree. The full weight of what she had created was starting to sink in, the devastation this one type of arrow could reap if placed in the wrong hands. For once, she actually agreed with her sovereigns' position on not trading her most deadly creations.

As they made their way back to the deserted streets of Noman's Land, Nuala wasn't so sure she even wanted her king and queen to know about this new weapon. If they did, she doubted they would banish her. They could hardly allow her to leave their rule given what she could now create. But would they just allow her and Einar to disobey a royal decree without punishment? Could they and still maintain the allegiance of their subjects?

A new kind of fear rolled through Nuala's gut. Suddenly banishment didn't seem so bad.

CHAPTER FIFTEEN

Once back inside Sinnale territory and safely ensconced in the council's meeting hall, Nuala and Einar made their way to the rooftop again—for both privacy and an experiment. It was time for Einar to call the owls and see how his own magics had been affected by their bond.

She settled silently at his side and waited with more patience than she thought she had left, knowing this was as important as what had happened to her magic. If he could no longer call the owls, one more aspect of his value to the king and queen vanished. Without that value, even though he remained a warrior to be feared, she couldn't be sure of the punishment they might mete out.

She almost shouted when she saw the silent, white blur in the distance, approaching steadily over the rooftops in their direction. Einar put up his arm and the owl landed gracefully. The two stared at each other for a long moment. Nuala wanted badly to speak but was afraid to distract from what was happening.

Eventually, Einar made the same soft sounds she'd heard before when speaking to the owls. There was another moment of silence.

The owl screeched and Einar nodded. Then the bird launched into the air, heading back in the direction of Glengowyn.

"So," Nuala said as soon as the creature was away. "Was that a specific animal you called? Was there a difference in the communication?"

Einar leaned on the low wall circling the roof and crossed his arms over his chest, his mouth pursed in a slight frown. "The process was…different. That was a specific owl. He was actually quite far away when I called. But he came the distance, despite there being more who could have come. Apparently, the others didn't hear."

"So you can't call them generally anymore?"

"No. I can still call them generally. But now, when I'm specific, that specific animal can hear me from a much greater distance than ever before. And find me much easier without other owls passing on my position. Even a specific call before tended to be…passed between the owls. It seems that's no longer necessary."

"And the actual talking? The same or different?"

"Stronger. Clearer. I thought I could understand them perfectly before, but now… There's an added layer of meaning within our communication that was never there before. I understood him better. And he understood me better too."

"This is good!" Nuala gripped his biceps. "Stronger, better, that works in your favor. You have something the king and queen still want."

He looked down at her, his eyes dark. "You've considered that as well?"

She moved closer and he wrapped her in his arms without her having to ask. "I've considered that if they know about my newest arrows, they won't want to send me from Glengowyn. But you… We've disobeyed them. Their decree that we stay apart was no secret. Others know, and our defiance will challenge their leadership. If we bring nothing of value to earn their mercy…" She trailed off, unable to finish the sentence.

But they both knew they'd left themselves vulnerable to the same punishments placed on the traitors. If they continued to be of use to Glengowyn, however, they might just avoid the very worst possible option.

Einar tightened his hold and said aloud what she couldn't. "If they have me killed by the Sinnale, especially under the *Or'roan*, they risk killing you through the bond-link as well," he pointed out.

Though Nuala suspected Einar had been charged once or twice with assassinating another elf—secretly so that there was no evidence, only rumor—the king and queen made a point of upholding the taboo and not actually having their subjects executed by their own hands, or that of any other elf. To kill Einar would require the help of the Sinnale. But after everything the sovereigns were doing for the humans now, Nuala doubted they would object if the matter was put to them right.

"And even if you survived my death, the violent breaking of the bond could destroy this new skill of yours," he added.

"Keeping the skill or destroying it utterly would serve the same purpose—preventing others from having access to these…assassin's tools. They may not care which happens." She snuggled her head under his chin and squeezed her arms around his waist. "We should run. Now. Go as far as we can. They don't need to know about the new arrows. They can assume we took ourselves into banishment because of our bonding. They never need to know."

"And what of the arrows below in the armory? If you can't destroy them, they remain a danger." He lifted her chin with the side of his hand so she was forced to look at him. "And the humans on that rooftop witnessed the power of these arrows. Word will reach Glengowyn. We won't be safe even if we run."

She pressed her lips together to hold back the helplessness

sweeping through her. "What will we do? How can we survive this?"

His large hand cupped her cheek, and he kissed her softly. But he didn't answer her questions.

NUALA SPENT THE REMAINDER OF THAT NIGHT AND MUCH OF THE next day attempting to unravel the assassin spell, to destroy the arrows she'd created. The process was slow and tedious because she didn't want to kill anyone—or herself—in the process.

After some work and concentration, knowing Einar was nearby keeping watch, she managed to find the key to breaking down the spell safely. It was almost more complicated than setting the original spell had been. And it took more energy. But knowing she didn't have to leave such a deadly weapon lying about was a relief worth the energy output.

That night, after she'd managed to undo the spell on a fraction of the arrows, members of the council started to approach her. At first singly, then several of them at a time.

Rumors of the arrow she was "developing" had reached them from the front lines, where the Sinnale were slowly but steadily forcing the Sorcerers to give ground. They questioned how long it would take for the new arrows to be available, what price Glengowyn would require for them, when was the earliest date at which they could anticipate a trade arrangement?

Nuala prevaricated, never answering directly. Only saying the arrows weren't ready yet. And every time she sent the council members away, she returned to destroying more of her creations.

Einar remained a dark presence at her side, hovering and intimidating enough to keep the council from pushing her. But she knew they were working against time. News of this would reach

Glengowyn soon. The council would eventually turn directly to the king and queen for real answers.

In turn, the king and queen would demand answers of their own.

When she reached the point of exhaustion, Einar made sure she slept. He saw to her needs for food and water. He kept watch when she was deep inside her magics. At the back of her mind, he was there, a safe haven in a dangerous new world.

By the second day, only about twenty of the assassin arrows remained. News reached them of the fighting and she knew the Sinnale had retaken an entire section of the city. But the forward progress had been stopped again. The Sorcerers had set new border spells the Sinnale could no longer pinpoint and avoid. And both traitor elves and Sorcerers remained beyond the reach of the shrapnel bomb arrows now, well behind the spells the humans couldn't get around to make the weapons effective.

Another standoff ensued. But the Sorcerers were on the defensive now more than ever. And a sense of satisfaction came with the stories of what was happening.

But also frustration. The council pushed a little harder for more information on her newest arrows. Would they be able to penetrate these new spells the Sorcerers had set up? How much longer before they were ready to use? Over the course of that second day, she was visited no less than five times by various humans. And each time, their interest intensified.

"I can't blame them," she told Einar during one of the breaks he forced her to take.

"Neither can I, now that they see a possible victory in sight," he said. "But I'm reluctant to have anyone know what you can do now. I'd rather you didn't even tell Ulric."

"I won't be able to lie to him if he asks directly," she admitted. "I've never been able to lie to him."

"Have you ever had cause before?"

She met his gaze. "With you. When we first mated. When we broke. I tried to keep all that to myself, but he knew. Even when I didn't say anything aloud."

Einar frowned. "Your cousin is too observant. It made him a brilliant commander during he wars, in conjunction with his talent for strategy. And I know he negotiates well with the humans in trade because of those traits. But it is inconvenient in this case."

She snorted and pointed with her dinner knife to the plate in front of him. "You eat too. You've been keeping vigil constantly since I started dismantling the arrows." She studied his face. "Have you slept at all?"

"You know I can go for long periods without sleep."

"Einar…"

Her warning actually lightened the frown creasing his brows and crinkling his eyes. An almost-smile lifted the corners of his mouth. "I find it…unusual, how you worry about me. I'm not used to it. At least not from anyone but you."

"You know well why I worry."

"And I love you too."

She rolled her eyes and smiled. "That, unfortunately, is part of our problem."

"But the best part," he said, gripping her hand in a tight squeeze. He released her and gestured back to her plate, a not-so-subtle reminder for her to continue her meal. "I have been considering the Sinnale's interest in your weapon, the weapon itself… Has it occurred to you that if they had the names of the individual Sorcerers, it might be possible to kill them without having to engage in all-out offensives anymore?"

"Yes, actually. In the midst of all their questions, I did consider that. But they'd need the Sorcerers' real names. Not what they go by, not what the minions call them. Their true names."

"You're sure?"

"I learned a lot more about the spell during the dismantling. Knowing what the trigger is has given me an insight that's let me understand the workings of the magic better. The arrow that killed Sareena wouldn't have flown without her real name."

"So much has happened…" He paused, studying her for a quiet moment. "Are you sorry about that killing? Once again you've been forced to break the taboo. Are there regrets?"

She tilted her head. She'd been so concerned with the dangerous weapon she'd made she'd barely considered that she'd taken yet another elf's life. That others had witnessed her doing what elves were not supposed to be able to do.

"I hadn't thought about that until now," she admitted. "Not only have I created an assassin's weapon, but the humans saw me kill another elf. They know about the taboo. They think it's impossible for us to kill one another. Now that they've seen that's not the case… I'm not sure what this means."

"I'm more concerned with how you're feeling about it. The humans and what they believe or don't believe holds no real interest for me."

"I don't regret Sareena's death," she said, and knew she told only the truth. "The traitors forfeit their right to my sympathy. And the longer I'm in Sinnale, the more firmly I feel about that. These people have been our allies for centuries, since settling near Glengowyn. I will never understand or forgive the traitors' defection."

"I'm glad to hear it. I would not see you suffer for killing one who would, given the chance, hand you over to the Sorcerers."

"All the killing… Have you ever felt remorse?" she asked.

"No." His tone was flat and matter-of-fact. "I'm not sure I have it in me. It seems to be part of the same aspect of me that becomes…what I become in the heat of battle. Sometimes…" He trailed off and looked away.

She reached across to take hold of his hand this time, snapping his attention back to her. "Sometimes?"

"I suspect it's a…fault in my character that I can't feel regret for the deaths I bring. I should have some emotional reaction to it. Don't you think?"

"Why? You've only ever killed those threatening your people, right? You've never killed for pleasure or fun. You don't kill simply to kill. Where is there any call for regrets?"

He tilted his head as if he'd never considered her points and blinked slowly. "Other warriors, after the wars, talked about the… effect all the death had on them. I never experienced those same scars."

"I actually envy you that."

"So you do regret killing the two traitors?"

"No, no. Not them. But at the start of the war, when my mistake in transporting the shrapnel arrows cost so many elves their lives? I've always felt a great deal of guilt about that. They were senseless, pointless deaths. But the traitors… No. With Sareena, I only felt a rage for her betrayal. When the arrow flew, I was terrified I'd kill the Sinnale surrounding her. *That* I would have regretted. But I just don't seem to feel anything at all for her death."

Einar's frown turned fierce. "I have passed that to you too with our bonding," he growled and stood to pace away from her. "The king was right to order me away from you. I have…infected you with my greatest fault."

"Einar, don't be ridiculous. Even before the bond took hold, I had no regrets about killing Byral. You haven't 'infected' me with anything. Perhaps this is *my* character flaw. I'm not a warrior. Shouldn't I be more affected by killing? Yet I'm not. I say that speaks very poorly of my conscience."

She blinked and he'd crossed the room to loom over her.

"Never say such things. You are the most honorable and

beautiful soul I've ever known." He leaned down, putting his face close to hers. "And I will not have you speaking poorly of yourself."

He was so fierce in his defense of her, she warmed all the way to her core. Taking his face in her hands, she touched her nose to his and said, "I feel the same of you. So stop talking of 'infecting' me, or I will have to get very cross with you."

She kissed him to silence any protest he might make. As she swept her tongue into his mouth to tangle with his, she grew more and more annoyed that he would dare to insult his own character as he had. And then feel he could reprimand her for the same comments!

She took her annoyance out on him, standing to press tight to him and kissing him with a fierce possessiveness she'd never felt for any other man.

His arms tightened around her waist as she felt the *Shaerta* rising. And a thrill of satisfaction roared into her blood.

"You are good," she said between kisses. "And you will never think otherwise while I live."

She trailed hot, openmouthed kisses down his throat, nipping and biting, tasting the salt on his skin. "I love you, Einar. For everything you are."

"And I you." He tightened his hold in a convulsive hug before moving his hands to her ass and grinding her tight against his erection.

The feel of him, hard and solid, was a balm to her fears, regrets and lack of regrets. Though they were still in the armory, though the door was only nominally sealed since they were eating, she wanted him. There and then. To feel the rightness between them, letting the significance of what they had override all the other doubts and complications.

He didn't resist as she backed him up to the wall, only grunted when they hit the solid stone a little harder than she'd intended. But he never loosened his hold on her or stopped kissing her.

He ravaged her mouth, giving her exactly what she needed, what she wanted from him. Hard hands, desperate demands. Her tunic came up over her head with barely a break in their contact. She ripped material as she stripped off his shirt and vest. The heat of his skin enveloped her, making her moan as she rubbed her breasts against him.

She would have easily, happily fucked him against the wall, but he shifted and angled her toward the small cot she'd been using to nap on between magical sessions. Before laying her down, he dropped to his knees and wrenched off her trousers and boots. He licked into her core while still removing her clothing, and the feel of his tongue circling her clit sent a tremor of shockwaves through her body, making her knees quake.

After he stripped her completely, he moved from her sensitive clit back up her body along her stomach, kissing and licking skin now sensitive enough to ache with the pleasure. His teeth closed around her nipple, and he tugged gently before he licked away the brief sting. Then he sucked her nipple into his mouth, the heat and pull causing a fresh wave of wetness between her legs. She moaned, burying her hands in his hair as her hips jerked in reaction.

By the time he reached her mouth, she could taste her own skin, her own juices on his lips, and the flavor mixing with his moved her beyond needy to desperate. Though she attempted to assist him with his trousers, he pushed her hands aside and stripped quickly and efficiently himself. And then they were on the bed with his weight anchoring her to the mattress.

She couldn't have him inside her fast enough, couldn't taste or feel or squeeze enough, as the *Shaerta* drove them harder and harder. He slammed into her in a single thrust, and she arched up under him, stifling a shout. He filled her completely, in every possible way, and she welcomed every beloved inch.

He wasn't gentle. She refused to be tender. She wanted him out of control, wanted to lose control herself. And only with Einar was she safe enough to completely let go.

She bit his shoulder to keep from crying out when her first orgasm hit. He reacted to the feel of her teeth by pounding harder into her, his own groan muffled against her throat. The increased speed and the feel of his coarse hair rubbing her clit sent her into a second orgasm almost immediately, only ever possible with Einar, even under the full influence of the *Shaerta*. She couldn't hold back her shout this time and no longer cared if the entire hall heard them.

Digging her nails into his back, anchoring her heels on the backs of his legs, she clenched and thrust and chased his rhythm, feeling him storming to his own breaking point. And when he hit that edge and threw himself off, she ground against him and came again, her body so awash in sensation all she knew for long moments was the spasms and euphoria of release in Einar's arms.

They ended their dance more slowly than they'd started, panting and clinging to one another, warm in the heat they'd generated. She hugged him tight, refusing to let go, keeping him inside her for as long as possible.

Her brain would have happily shut down, but behind the contentment and sleepiness, the nagging thought remained to follow her into a doze—they couldn't delay facing the king and queen for much longer.

Shortly after they woke up, they received word from Glengowyn via a messenger owl.

Their presence was required at Court.

CHAPTER SIXTEEN

uala stood with her back straight, careful not to touch Einar as they faced their king and queen side by side. They'd been given time to change and ready themselves, but not much longer before the Court guards came to collect them for their audience.

Silence hung heavily over the area. Surrounded by trees dripping with foliage, the Court was open to the air but sheltered from inclement weather by the thickness of the trees and one of the king's spells. The thrones themselves weren't all that grand—simple affairs of wood and soft cushions, set with winking jewels peeking from between the twists and turns of the wood. Neither the king nor queen required a background of grandeur to reflect their power. The very simplicity of the Court highlighted just how spectacular the royal couple was.

Nuala had never been so nervous in her life. She wanted desperately to grasp Einar's hand, for support and comfort. But she didn't dare. She held herself motionless and waited for her sovereigns to begin—she was forbidden by Court etiquette from speaking first but wouldn't have even if she could.

She found it impossible to read either of their facial expressions. Though that wasn't unusual, it was the first time those blank, neutral masks had been directed at her while she knew she was facing punishment.

The queen was stunning, her hair a silken cloak around her shoulders, several shades darker than the lightest blonds in Glengowyn but full of sparkling life like it was a creature all its own. Her face was narrow, her cheekbones sharp, her full lips set in a neutral line, her eyes a piercing violet that was unusual among the Glengowyn elves. She had her long-fingered hands resting at the edge of the armrests on her throne, and the single ring she wore—a bejeweled indication of her position—winked in the glowing bluish-white lights coming from the surrounding trees.

The king was almost innocuous in his appearance, if one didn't take the time to really look at him. He was of average height for an elf, with hip-length brown hair and dark eyes that tilted up just a little at the corners. His jaw was solid and his lips thin and firm. The golden torc around his throat, which announced his position, highlighted the firm musculature of his upper body, at once powerful and understated beneath his heavy silk tunic.

His power emanated from him in an unseen aura, breathtaking in its strength. Simply standing before him had driven many an elf humbly to their knees without the king having to raise a finger or exert any magical force.

Together, the royal couple had ruled Glengowyn since well before Nuala's parents had been born. They had a timeless feel about them that brooked no disobedience.

And here she stood, having disobeyed them because she could no longer deny her love for Einar.

Just as their silence stretched her nerves to the snapping point, the queen spoke.

"We are disappointed, Nuala. Einar. Our position on your relationship was clear."

Nuala ducked her head in a slight bow without taking her eyes off the queen's face. To look away was to open herself up to an unexpected attack.

"Your Majesty," she said, as firmly and humbly as she could manage, "my magic still produces the weapons you wished to protect. Despite our…lapse, you have not lost anything that I can give to Glengowyn."

"We understand that contrary to losing, you have gained," the king said, the deep power of his voice commanding her attention. "The council is asking if we will trade in this 'experimental' weapon of yours."

She swallowed and risked a glance around the hall. Other elves circled the perimeter, members of the Court, important advisors to the sovereigns. This hearing wasn't open to all of Glengowyn, but she wasn't sure how much to say out loud, how much the royal couple would want her to admit in front of the audience.

"My magics have been…affected by the bonding, Your Majesty. A new type of arrow has been created."

"And this arrow does what, exactly?" the queen asked.

Nuala still couldn't read either of their moods from their expressions. The lack of feedback tightened the tension crawling through her gut. She made a point of gesturing to the surrounding Court and asked, "May I explain now? Or would you prefer a private explanation?"

"That deadly?" the king murmured.

"That dangerous," she affirmed as quietly as she could.

For the first time, a slight expression broke through the king's neutrality. His features didn't exactly change, but she thought she detected a hint of approval in his eyes.

"Should we share such a weapon with the Sinnale, do you think?" the queen asked, her demeanor still scarily neutral.

"I would leave that decision to the wisdom of Your Majesties."

"Of course it will be our decision. Would these weapons compromise Glengowyn if we were to share them with the humans?"

Nuala was silent for a long moment. Without explaining what the arrows could do, she wasn't sure how to answer. "These weapons are deadly in any hands. Elf and human alike."

Queen Rohannah tilted her head to one side. "You imply elves could use them…in unforeseen ways?"

"I state outright that these are the most *specifically* dangerous arrows I have ever created."

The queen's eyes narrowed, having caught the emphasis Nuala placed on the word "specifically".

She exchanged a look with her king, then swept her gaze over the Court. Immediately, the area cleared so that only the guards remained. Then she turned her piercing violet gaze on Nuala.

"Explain 'specifically'."

Nuala did, revealing not only what the arrow had done, but that she'd killed another elf with it. She didn't mention that she'd managed to kill a traitor elf when they'd first been attacked, and she didn't bring up the fact that she'd witnessed Einar kill an elf.

It was enough for their small remaining audience to know that a humble weapons maker had been able to kill another elf simply by murmuring that elf's name to an arrow.

"So. An assassin's instrument, then," the king said.

"Just so, Your Majesty," she affirmed.

"Would this arrow destroy a Sorcerer?" the queen asked.

Nuala tilted her head to one side, not surprised the queen had hit on the same possibility she and Einar had discussed earlier.

"We would require their *real* names for that to work," she said. "But I do think it's possible. Gaining a Sorcerer's real name is problematic." More like impossible, but she didn't think it wise to say so in that moment. "But the real name of any being would be enough, based on my analysis of the spell."

"How many of these weapons did you create?" The queen again.

She swallowed, not sure if this news would be greeted with approval or disappointment. "I created, in total, just short of three hundred individual arrows, and I have destroyed all but five."

"Destroyed?" The king's eyebrow lifted slightly, his only visible reaction.

"I dismantled the spell and took the arrows themselves apart."

"Because?"

"I felt them too dangerous to leave with the Sinnale when they weren't aware of their potential."

The king drummed his fingers once on his armrest, and again Nuala thought she saw a hint of something like approval in his eyes.

He and the queen exchanged another long look, silent but intent. Nuala tried to stay calm, but her heartbeat hammered and her skin tingled from the nervous energy consuming her. When the royal couple faced them again, she had to force herself not to hold her breath.

"This news, this accomplishment of yours, will affect what we do with you going forward, Nuala," the queen announced. "Your disobedience, and the disobedience of our own Darkness, cannot go unpunished."

Nuala dipped her knee in a slight bow of acknowledgement.

"Darkness—" the queen turned just her gaze on Einar, "—how has the bonding affected your skills? The owls?"

"Still respond to me, Your Majesty. The way in which we communicate has…heightened, but that ability has not been destroyed."

"And yet, I am not sure it's enough to satisfy," she said. "You were our most trusted guard. And you have publicly gone against our orders. This cannot be allowed to stand. Even though we will lose one of our most dangerous allies."

Einar remained unmoving, taking her words in without comment or gesture, patient as always when standing before his king and queen.

"You two have left us in an untenable position." The queen spoke quietly. "Banishment is no longer an option. Nuala's newest ability is too dangerous to go unmonitored. But punishment is necessary."

Her gaze lifted by the barest of flickers, and a moment later, Nuala and Einar were dragged apart by the rough hands of several guards.

Instinctively, Nuala resisted. "Einar…"

He allowed himself to be pulled away from her, but he kept his attention on her now, rather than the royal couple.

"Darkness," the queen intoned. "Your willful disobedience to this Court requires a severe penalty. But which is best? Banishment, the *Or'roan*… Simple banishment would be unwise, given that Nuala will remain here in Glengowyn under our supervision. I do not think you would stay away."

He didn't say anything.

"The *Or'roan* and banishment together would, likewise, hardly concern you now that you have bonded with Nuala."

While he didn't confirm this statement, Nuala saw in his eyes that the queen spoke truthfully.

"You leave us with one option, Darkness. Banishment to the Unseen Plain—"

"No!" Nuala cried out, unable to stop her protest.

That was worse than even a simple death sentence. A punishment that had never been used in Nuala's lifetime. In fact, she couldn't recall any time in her parents' or grandparents' lifetimes when the punishment had been invoked. Nuala hadn't even considered that her sovereigns might use it now.

It meant more than having Einar killed by a human assassin—to preserve the illusion that elves didn't kill each other. Einar would suffer a horrendous, painful death as the *dargem*, those nightmare-inducing creatures that called the Unseen Plain their home, slowly ate and digested him. They weren't just talking about taking his life. They spoke of inflicting one of the worst tortures possible on him before he died.

The queen ignored her outburst. "And you will be sent under the *Or'roan*. Your disobedience cannot be forgiven. The punishment must be severe."

"Please, Your Majesty, not that," Nuala begged, facing her queen. "Killing Einar now could affect my magic more even than the bonding. Would you lose your most dangerous weapon?"

She settled her violet-eyed gaze on Nuala without even blinking. "We will be losing one of our most dangerous weapons already, Nuala. Because of your selfishness and inability to do what we have ordered."

"Please, Your Majesty, not the Unseen Plain."

"Would you take his place?" she asked very quietly.

"Yes," Nuala said without hesitation. "I would take his place. Even under the *Or'roan*, I would suffer the Unseen Plain if Einar could live."

"No," Einar said, his voice deep and resonant, echoing in its quiet intensity.

The queen raised her brows, the first indication of any sort of emotion. "You have presented us with an interesting option, Nuala.

This arrow you've created might be too dangerous to allow into the world. If you are no longer on this plane, you can no longer create such a threat."

She swallowed but straightened her shoulders. The move did nothing to loosen the grip of the guards holding her arms. "Yes, Your Majesty. You could eliminate a possible threat, make the severity of disobeying your orders an example to the rest of Glengowyn, and retain your Darkness. Simply by allowing me to die in Einar's place."

"No," Einar said again, his voice rising only slightly above a reverberating growl.

The queen continued to ignore him. "You make a very good point. Though we would hate to lose your value to us, Nuala, even you are not above our judgment. This would be a good lesson for the others."

"Yes, Your Majesty."

The queen turned on Einar, considering. "This would be a severe punishment for you too, I believe, Darkness. One that would also resonate with the others. We will strip you of that which you value most as punishment for your treachery." She blinked slowly. "Yes. That is much more severe than even death for you, my warrior. An important lesson for the rest of Glengowyn. No matter your station, there will be consequences for disobeying our rule."

Nuala watched Einar's muscles flex against the hold of the two guards, and in an instant, four more surrounded him, their swords drawn and pointed at various vulnerable parts of his body, even as the first two continued to hold him in place. His expression shifted, and she saw the first stirrings of the madness that took him in battle coming over him.

"Einar," she murmured.

He held her gaze, his entire body tensed, as they awaited the final proclamation.

CHAPTER SEVENTEEN

Nuala once again found herself holding her breath, but she couldn't look away from Einar, even when King Varim spoke.

"Do you offer an alternative, Darkness?" the king asked.

"My life, Your Majesty. My existence. Anything you would take from me. Only that you do not send Nuala to the kind of death she would meet on the Unseen Plain."

Another long silence stretched Nuala's nerves. She jerked against the two guards confining her because she had to do something physical or she might just scream.

Finally, the queen said, "For the sovereignty of this Court and the safety of Glengowyn, there is only one answer. Nuala of Glengowyn, you will be banished to the Unseen Plain at dawn, under the *Or'roan*. Einar, you will be witness to this punishment. Your life, your existence, doomed to continue long after you watch Nuala sent to her end."

Nuala began to tremble and a single tear escaped the corner of her eye. Her knees weakened at the thought of what she was going to face, but she tightened the muscles in her thighs to keep upright. Einar couldn't be allowed to see her fear. She would accept the punishment as stoically as she could manage, because it meant Einar would live.

More than any other regret, though, she regretted that she would never know Einar again. That they had had so very little time together.

"I love you," she mouthed as the guards began to haul her away.

They'd barely moved two steps when the battle madness swept over Einar's face.

"No!" His voice roared through the hall, shaking the leaves on the trees, making even Nuala jump in surprise.

He folded his body in tight, bringing the guards close. Swords began to poke into him, positioned to hurt and draw blood rather than kill. But before more than one could penetrate his skin, he cried out another denial and threw his arms wide. The elves surrounding him went flying in all directions, slamming hard into trees, smashing into limp heaps on the smooth stone covering the ground.

He turned to the guards holding her, his eyes blacker than she'd ever seen, and he shouted another denial. The two elves holding her catapulted backward, ripped from her side by invisible hands to be flattened to the ground at the edge of the clearing, their bodies unmoving.

Nuala barely had time to register what had happened before Einar closed the space between them and swung her behind his back as he faced the royal couple.

"You will not send Nuala to the Unseen Plain," he ground out, his voice so deep it was almost unrecognizable.

He barely sounded like a man anymore, something so vicious and deadly crawled through his tone. The sound raised the hairs on Nuala's arms and made her shiver despite herself. She couldn't see his face well, but the all-consuming rage in his expression before he stepped in front of her had been one of the most awesome and terrifying things she'd ever witnessed. And she'd seen Einar at his battle-crazed worst. Without a weapon in hand, the man before her seemed more deadly even than the *dargem* she would face when banished.

The king raised his brows, his only outward reaction to the sudden and explosive chaos. But the queen... Nuala would have sworn she was seeing things. The queen smiled. A very slight lifting of the corners of her mouth, true, but it was, nonetheless, a smile. Her eyes narrowed and sparked. And Nuala got the distinct and disconcerting feeling the queen was...pleased.

"I wondered what it would take, Darkness. You are so difficult to push to this state. I should have guessed earlier the answer would be so simple. You've only ever had but one weakness."

"I don't understand." Nuala dug her fingers into Einar's arm, fear for what he'd done, what he'd become, a tight band around her chest.

"What I am in battle," he said, his voice sounding more normal, his attention still on the queen, "apparently it is part of my magic."

"So much a part of him, even he couldn't tell," the queen affirmed. "And now... Now, my Darkness, you are a killing machine."

"What does she mean?" Nuala asked, looking up at the side of his face. His jaw was stiff, his expression unmoving.

"I could have killed the guards," he explained. "I did not. But I could have. Without using a weapon other than my own rage."

She looked at the fallen guards then back up at him. "You can... explode your rage now, like my shrapnel arrows? Because of the bonding?"

He jerked his head in a single nod.

"But..."

"The melding of your magics," the queen said. "His ability to communicate with the owls is not the only thing that was strengthened." She stared at Einar, again with that pleased, small smile. "He can now level armies without having to remove his sword from its scabbard."

"Very useful," the king said, finally commenting aloud. "Very useful, I should think."

The queen leaned back in her throne, looking for all the world as if she was quite satisfied with this outcome.

"I still don't understand," Nuala said. "What does this mean?"

Even as she asked, the Court began to fill. Not with elves but with owls. They perched on the surrounding trees, flittering but silent witnesses. As Nuala looked around at the descending birds, she realized that, outside of the king, queen, herself, Einar and the unconscious bodies of the guards Einar had attacked, there were no other elves in the Court. The remaining guards had vanished.

She looked back to the queen, who was fully smirking now as she considered the owls.

"Silly girl," she said to Nuala. "Do you think we would have placed you and Einar in such close proximity, after all this time, if we did not have a plan?"

Einar straightened and some of the defensiveness went out of his body. "You intended for us to bond. Why?"

"Beyond growing tired of watching you two mope around this city for the last two centuries?" She snorted, an unusual show of irritated humor. "Let's just say that the possibilities of your bonding were revealed to me. And the time for the change was now."

The queen had mysterious ways of gathering information, sometimes even gaining knowledge of things that had not yet happened. She didn't exercise the skill often, or so Nuala had thought. And the way in which she gathered the information was a mystery. Nuala wasn't even sure if the king knew what the queen did to gain this future sight. But it wasn't a flawless skill.

"You took a great risk," she said as Einar finally allowed her to step out from behind the protection of his body.

"Yes, she did," the king growled. "But the gamble has been well worth the risk, I think."

"Just so, my love," the queen said. "Just so."

"You knew I would create a new arrow?"

"That part was more…nebulous. We knew something powerful would come through you in the bonding."

And suddenly Nuala understood. "But you knew the bonding would affect Einar's fighting ability. That it was part of his magic, even though he didn't realize it. And the blending of our two magics would strengthen his deadliness. You knew what he would become."

The queen could read magic in others, detect spells and see through to the core of an elf. These were traits well known throughout Glengowyn and skills she utilized often. Nuala should have guessed her ability to see the magic inside them all would also affect the knowledge she gained through her future sight.

"And because of my gamble," the queen said, "you have been allowed your love. But there are conditions." Suddenly her satisfied expression fell away and was replaced by the terrifying seriousness she'd worn earlier.

"You have both become more valuable to us," the queen continued. "And at the same time have brought with you skills that are so dangerous, they cannot be allowed free reign."

"You will pledge your loyalty and these new skills to us and Glengowyn," the king said. "For our use alone. On pain of forever death by public and painful means if you should disobey."

"We will make it plain to the city that your bonding was intended. That we saw the magics that would be created." The queen took up the telling. "And you will not contradict us. You will, in fact, say that you were given permission to renew your relationship. No one will disagree with you."

Nuala looked up as the owls fluttered their wings in the treetops. She'd almost forgotten them in her shock.

"We will direct the use of your new skills," the king said, yanking Nuala's attention back down to him. "And you will obey us in our orders going forward."

"In exchange," the queen said, "you have your lives, your bonding and your futures. A fair exchange, I think."

This last she murmured, and Nuala heard the warning just beneath the simple statement.

"Your Majesties," she said, dropping to one knee and bowing her head. "I will give you everything you ask and pledge my loyalty forward, in exchange for the prize of being able to keep Einar."

For a long moment, Einar remained standing, staring at his king and queen. Finally, he too knelt down, though he didn't bow his head. "For the love of Nuala, I will continue to serve you faithfully as my sovereigns. From now until I move to the next plane."

The king nodded in satisfaction. The queen merely blinked her approval.

"Now," the king said after the formalities had been seen to. "Nuala. I would like to discuss this new arrow of yours. And how it might best be used to rid our region of the Sorcerers."

THE SUN THREW SPECKS OF PINK AND ORANGE LIGHT ACROSS THE forest floor as Einar escorted Nuala back to her small home at the very center of the city. He kept his arm around her, holding her close as they strolled down the quiet stone paths leading to her front door.

"I'm not entirely sure how I feel now," she said, her voice low in deference to the quiet time of day. The beauty of it, the fact that they were alive and together was almost more than her heart could take. But how they'd gotten here…

"If you feel the same annoyance and anger I do, I would not blame you," Einar said.

"And yet, it's all come out for the best."

"After much torment and two centuries of waste."

She couldn't blame him for the low growl in his voice. She was torn between her own gratitude and anger. "Will you be able to serve them with the same loyalty as before?"

"My loyalty is to you now, and only you. That hasn't changed. But for you, I will serve them to the best of my ability, with all my strength and honor. They know this."

A tiny thrill of pleasure warred with an even tinier worry that his changed allegiance might not sit well with the sovereigns. But if they knew…

She let the worry go for now. She was too tired to contemplate disasters that weren't currently a problem. Instead, she asked two of the many questions she had about the previous night. "If the queen knew what would become of our bonding, why did she make us wait so long? Why make us suffer for so many years?"

With his free hand, Einar lifted one of her hands and placed a kiss on her palm. The feel of his mouth on her skin sent tingles up her arm.

"I asked the queen those very questions when you and the king were discussing the details of your new arrows."

"What did she say?"

"I quote: 'Your bonding was required at this point in time, my Darkness.'"

Nuala waited a few steps but when he didn't continue, she said, "That's all? Our bonding was required now? Does that mean she knew all along? That she only gained the knowledge of how our bonding would change our magic recently? Was this all hope and presumption on her part? Have they allowed us to remain brokenhearted all this time at a whim or because the movements of the universe required it? I don't understand."

"She said no more on the subject and refused to explain further. I have no clue if she knew all along or if she only realized recently what our bonding would mean. And that it was as important to them as it was to us."

They stopped just outside her front door, and Einar turned her to face him. "I do know that I'm unhappy about being kept from you for so long. But grateful to have you now. Freely. Without any threats hanging over our heads."

"Unless we break our new vow of fealty to the sovereigns," she pointed out.

"Do you intend to? Would you want to?"

Her first response was sharp and sarcastic, but she held that reaction back while she really thought about her feelings on the matter.

"No," she said after a few moments. "No. I'm still loyal to them, despite what's happened. I do want my skills to benefit Glengowyn always. Though I could do without the label of being 'too valuable', I recognize my value to the city and would continue to serve."

"And so long as you serve them, I will without restraint. You were my only point of contention with the sovereigns, ever. I will continue to protect them with all I have." He cupped her cheeks. "But they come second to you. I made that clear to them before we left this morning."

She gripped his wrists as a tingle of fear tickled her nap. Perhaps this disaster was more imminent than she'd thought. "How did they react?" The queen was notorious for taking the elevation of others above her...poorly.

"The king said nothing, only raised his brows."

"As he does," she commented with a sideways dip of her head.

"The queen smiled."

"Smiled?"

"And then said, and again I will quote, 'Why do you believe this is information new to us, Darkness? What has changed to make this different?'"

Nuala gasped. And then she laughed. "She's always known? That you would choose me over them?"

He kissed her lightly. "Apparently, you are my only vulnerability. And she used that knowledge willfully."

Nuala rose up to kiss him this time, letting her mouth slide across his in comfort and love. "I won't take advantage of being your only vulnerability," she promised with her lips close enough to brush his as she spoke. "Just remember, you're mine as well. Take care with my heart."

"Your heart will never be safer than with me," he vowed. "Through all our lifetimes. You're mine, Nuala. My only love. And I'll hold our bonding sacred into the end times."

She sighed and relaxed fully against him, absorbing his kiss like oxygen, like the very essence of her existence. A part of her still couldn't believe they were free, to love, to be together, to live. But the larger part of her rejoiced. Two centuries of pain and loss dribbled away as she led Einar into her home, into her bed, and gave over fully to the perfect sense of their love.

As morning sun spilled across her bed and Einar slid gently inside her, Nuala embraced the man others called Darkness, knowing, to her, he would always be her light.

DAWN IGNITED

DAWN IGNITED

FIRE AND TEARS BOOK THREE

ENEMIES UNITE FOR REDEMPTION

Branded a traitor, Althir of Glengowyn has resigned himself to life as an outcast from his people—until he's offered a chance at redemption. A suicide mission that will finally put an end to the Sinnale war. His companion on the journey is a human woman unlike any he's ever encountered. Beautiful. Brave. Fascinating. And before he knows it, keeping her safe is more important than his own salvation.

Mina Dawnswealth's talent for spycraft has kept her alive even as her dreams—and her family—have fallen victim to the war, one by one. Much as she hates the idea of helping the traitor elf, at least she gets the pleasure of burying a knife in his back should he decide to betray her people again. A much easier task if she didn't find him so damned compelling.

Only when they're beyond the point of no return do they discover just how much blood their mission will cost. And how much love it will take to overcome their pasts for a chance at a future together.

CHAPTER ONE

Althir of Glengowyn stared at Samuel Brightarrow for a long moment after hearing his proposition. The man had aged over the last two years, the ongoing war with the Sorcerers taking its toll on the once large and vibrant human. Samuel and his wife Iona, members of the Sinnale council, were the reason Althir found himself here, a prisoner of the Sinnale.

The reason he wasn't forever dead.

"This might be your only chance at redemption, Althir," Samuel said in his deep, even voice.

Althir snorted. "Redemption." He shouldn't need redemption now. He should have had everything he ever wanted, and instead he spent his days wasting away in this comfortably maddening cage in the basement of the Sinnale council's meeting hall.

"Ulric has spoken with the king and queen. They've agreed to allow you back to Glengowyn if you complete this task."

"And why would I want to go back?" Althir paced away from the man. "Labeled a traitor by my fellow elves for all time? There's nothing there for me."

"Then you'd be free to go wherever you please. Another elven city, perhaps. But you wouldn't be a prisoner any longer."

He didn't bother to answer. His bespelled cage wasn't the worst thing that could have happened to him. And what would he do with freedom? No other elven community would welcome him once they learned of his history.

He glanced out the high window at the sliver of blue sky above the hard lines of brick making up the neighboring building that blocked most of his view. Ah, but he did miss the forest. He'd had enough of this bloody besieged city, the place where his entire life had been ruined.

"Speaking of Ulric," he said to change the subject, and because he couldn't quite help himself. "How is my brother, anyway? Never does come to visit. I imagine he's too busy fucking your daughter. Though, I can hardly blame him. She is infinitely fuckable." He stared at Samuel as he said this last, watching his reaction.

Samuel stared back. His pale skin darkened and his eyes narrowed. Althir smirked.

Rather than the explosion of anger he'd been expecting, though, Samuel calmly said, "You're trying to send me away in a fury. You want me to refuse you this chance. Why?"

Althir curled his lip in a snarl. He'd never hated another being more in his entire life than he hated Samuel in that moment. For being too wise and seeing too much.

He stalked as far away from the man as he could get, keeping his focus on the sliver of blue sky.

"You're mad to trust me with this," he stated flatly, his back to Samuel. "Why would you do that?"

"You know their Citadel. You know where to find what we need."

True. He did. They only knew the List of Names was there—that it existed at all—because of him.

But the mission was suicide. Since he was no longer under the *Or'roan*, the forever death curse that robbed elves of all future lives, ending their existence permanently, death didn't frighten him. He was just infuriated that he found himself in this bloody position.

Suicide or a cage for the foreseeable future? What kinds of choices were those? Although, if he succeeded, he'd be responsible for ending this war once and for all. Would that change anything?

Would that give him back what he'd lost?

"You'll trust me to return if I do succeed?" He was actually quite curious about the answer. He'd been providing the Sinnale with good information for months now, information that had helped turned the war in their favor and put the Sorcerers on the defensive. But the fighting dragged on. Humans continued to die. They wanted the fighting done, he knew. Would that desire override their continued wariness of him?

"You should know better than that, Althir," Samuel said. "Someone will be going with you. Someone who will ensure you return."

"An elf?"

"A Sinnale volunteer."

He laughed, a sharp, bitter sound. "A volunteer? Suicidal, are they?"

Samuel was silent, and Althir didn't push the subject. The "volunteer" hardly mattered anyway. He didn't care who they were or why they'd go on this impossible quest into the section of the city under the Sorcerers' control.

When the silence had stretched for long moments and Althir still didn't turn to face Samuel, Samuel finally said, "You have until tomorrow to consider our offer. I'll return at midday for your answer."

"There's no need," he said, his voice harsh and echoing in the quiet room.

"You're refusing? You won't accept this chance?"

"Oh, I'll go. Suicide or not. I don't really have a choice, do I?"

Very quietly, Samuel said, "You've always had a choice, Althir. It was those choices that got you here."

Althir didn't acknowledge the comment with so much as a twitch of his shoulders. He continued to stare out the window until well after he'd heard the cage door open and close behind Samuel. He stared out his little window until the light faded and the blue sky turned a purple bruised smudge against the hard, sharp city bricks.

MINA WATCHED THE ELF FOR A LONG TIME FROM HER POSITION AT the opposite side of the huge basement. His cage, a literal cage of bars mixed with minerals and magic to keep an elf contained, was furnished with a comfortable bed, a desk, a small bookshelf fully stocked with what the Sinnale had to offer, a washbasin and stand, and another table where he could eat. The trunk at the foot of his bed was full of clean clothes. And the nearest stone walls were hung with thick, colorful tapestries to keep out some of the cold.

She resented all that luxury for a prisoner, a traitor. Yes, he was giving them information to help in the war now. But that didn't forgive the fact that he'd turned traitor to Glengowyn and Sinnale by joining forces with the Sorcerers all those many months ago. She knew the only reason he'd turned himself over to her people was to save his sorry hide from the Sinnale assassins.

She had no sympathy for him, despite how beautiful he looked in the pale gaslight leaking in through the high window that had been his sole focus for most of the afternoon.

In fact, his beauty only made her angrier. How could someone so cruel, so wicked, look so stunning and enticing? It shouldn't have been possible. She shouldn't notice the solid strength of his shoulders, or the firm lines of a body that filled his trousers so nicely. She should be able to see beyond the masculine planes of his face and the stunning contrast of his angled gray eyes against his long, dark hair.

His brother was allowed to be gorgeous. Ulric was actively working with the Sinnale and the human council to help them win the war and rid their city of the invading Sorcerers. She admired Ulric, and a small part of her envied Layla Brightarrow her mate. But Althir was nothing like his brother.

Her fascination with the elf wasn't purely for his looks, though, and she consoled herself with that. She was preoccupied with him for other reasons, reasons that had more to do with revenge and anger than desire. Emotions she would now have to control if she wanted to see their mission successfully completed.

An end to this horrible war, which had robbed her of so much, was worth putting her personal hatred aside. She wouldn't attempt to kill Althir. She would go with him into enemy territory, as she'd sworn to do, and ensure he returned to her people with the List of Names. Once that was done, however, the elf could rot in the worst torments of the sacred hells for all she cared.

He finally turned away from the window, and she caught sight of his profile in the weak light. Her breath hitched. Reminding her once again that the face of a god could hide the soul of a demon.

"You might as well come out of the shadows," he said, staring at her hiding spot.

She knew he couldn't see her. Still, he seemed to look directly into her eyes as he spoke.

"Who are you and why are you here?" he asked, seeming only half interested in the response.

She straightened her shoulders and approached the cage, coming into the weak light filtering through the windows. Before answering, she took the time to turn up some of the small lamps that provided light in the basement. Having this conversation in the dark felt too intimate, and she was in no mood to be vulnerable for the traitor.

When she was comfortable with the bright lighting, she faced Althir. "I'm Mina," she said, answering his first question because it was the easiest.

"What's your family name, Mina?" His mouth remained a flat line, his eyes revealing very little real interest in her.

"I no longer have any family to be named. Thanks to the war." *Thanks to you and the Sorcerers.*

He nodded and sprawled in the chair next to his desk. "Of course you don't. I wouldn't let it bother you much. Family is highly overrated."

She curled her lip, unable to keep the reaction to herself. In her mind, she cursed him into the next world and beyond. Outwardly, she remained silent, not wishing to give him any more reaction than she already had.

He stared at her for a long moment, the disinterest in his gaze sharpening to something more alert. "So what do you want, Mina of No Family?"

"Your death."

She waited for him to react. He didn't. She realized this probably wasn't the first time one of her people had said that to him.

With a shrug, she seated herself on a "visitors" chair outside his cell. "What I intend to do, however, is just the opposite."

That finally earned her a raised brow. "Am I to assume you're the 'volunteer' accompanying me into Sorcerer territory?"

She dipped her head in a single brief nod.

"And what makes you think you'll fare any better than the rest of your family?"

"Nothing."

"You're prepared to die?"

For the first time, he seemed genuinely interested in her response. His head tilted to one side as he studied her, catching the light along his jaw and cheek, highlighting the beautiful masculinity of his face. Mina glanced away, irritated that she couldn't hold his gaze without noticing him as a man.

"I'd rather live," she said into the taut silence. "But I have nothing to lose."

"There's always something to lose," he murmured.

He spoke so quietly she wasn't sure he meant for her to hear him, and that drew her gaze back to him. "There are worse things than death," she said.

He snorted, an almost-laugh. "Yes. Yes, there are."

She held his gaze this time, not flinching under the bitterness of his comment. She had more than enough of her own to counter his. What did he have to be bitter over, anyway? That he'd sought power and failed? That he'd aligned himself with the wrong side in a war? She had no sympathy for him or his bitterness.

"You do realize going on this mission will mean facing some of those things that are worse than death?" he said.

Another short nod. "For you as well. Maybe worse for you. The Sorcerers must hate you now as much as we Sinnale do."

He chuckled, though there was no humor in it. "I imagine they do. And yes, if they capture me, I'm in for much worse than a simple death. But they won't spare you, Mina of No Family. Don't pretend they will. You've too much emotion, too much anger and hatred. If I can see it, they will. That kind of emotion, combined with your terror, will feed their blood magic better than simple fear ever could."

"I have no intention of being taken alive by the Sorcerers. We succeed or die."

"You might not have a choice."

It was her turn to consider him more closely when she said, "There's always a choice."

To her surprise, he turned away from her, his mouth turning down in a very faint frown. So. She'd hit a delicate spot. She put the information away for later use.

"You're not as scrawny as most of the Sinnale women have become," he stated in a blunt change of subject. "You still have meat on your bones. Very nice tits. Makes you more fuckable than the rest of the women here. I imagine the men spend a great deal of effort trying to get into your pants."

This was the kind of behavior she'd expected from him. "They warned me you were charming."

Her response earned her a full-throated, surprisingly deep burst of laughter. The sound was so wonderfully rich and sexy, Mina lost her breath. Her mouth dropped open for an instant before she caught herself and snapped it shut.

When he laughed, when he smiled for real, he moved well past beautiful and into the realms of unreal. She felt stunned by him just then, and for a long moment, couldn't drag her attention from the lush, tempting shape of his mouth.

She blinked and straightened in her seat. Damn the man. Why did she have to react to him this way?

"I have always been charming," he said when his laughter eased. "It's my particular gift."

"Speaking of gifts, elves have magic. What's yours?"

"Why do you need to know?"

"Because we're going into enemy territory together. I need to know what use you'll be, outside of the information you provide."

"And what use will you be in watching my back when you've as much as admitted you'd rather stick a knife in it?"

"I'm not going on this mission to watch your back. I'm going to ensure the List of Names is brought back to the council. But I've been working for the better part of the last year and a half as a spy. I've snuck in and out of the part of the city held by the Sorcerers innumerable times in that period. And I'm still alive."

"Can you fight?"

"If needs be."

"Are you any good at it?"

"I'm still alive."

He tilted his head in acknowledgment of the point. "Weapon of choice?"

"Short swords."

"That gets you in dangerously close to an enemy."

"If I have to pull my swords, the enemy is already too close to avoid."

He leaned forward in his chair, resting his forearms on his thighs, and gave her a thoughtful nod. "You're prepared to fight with me to get the List of Names?"

"I'm prepared to do whatever is necessary to end this war once and for all."

"Do you know why your people want the List?"

"Do you?"

He smiled, a slow and seductive lift of his lips, though she wasn't sure he intended the look to be seductive. "The council had to tell me, or I wouldn't cooperate with their questions."

"Doesn't that go against your bargain with them? The reason you're allowed to live here rather than be executed as a traitor?"

"Maybe. They were too anxious for the information to realize that, though."

She didn't want to admit she didn't have all the details. Not to him. Samuel and Iona Brightarrow had assured her that the List of Names, the list containing all the *real* names of the Sorcerers, would give them the power they needed to end the war. They hadn't told her how, exactly, but she hadn't pushed for an answer either.

It would have something to do with magic—elf magic. She knew enough to realize the real names of a being of power were valuable and dangerous. Most human practitioners like the Sorcerers concealed their real names and instead went by adopted monikers, something that couldn't hold any control over them in a spell.

She also knew why she hadn't been told exactly what magic would be used against the Sorcerers. If she were captured before she could end her life, the less information she had to reveal, the better. As a spy, she'd gotten used to this way of things, because the threat of capture and torture was always a very real possibility.

"They haven't told you, have they?" Althir said after a moment.

She pursed her lips in a scowl and focused on the bars of his cage rather than his face. "They told me everything I needed to know."

He leaned back in his seat again. From the corner of her eye, she could see him studying her.

Finally, he said, "You don't trust me. And you shouldn't. But you'll still travel with me into enemy territory. On the hope that this will end the invasion?"

She nodded.

"Why should I trust you?"

"You shouldn't. But you'll have to rely on me once we cross the border. And you can do that."

"If I betray you?"

"I'll kill you. Happily. That's why I've been allowed to volunteer for this mission." She finally faced him. "Are you going to betray me?"

He held her gaze for a long moment and then dropped his to stare at the floor. "I don't discuss my magic here. When we get into Noman's Land, I'll tell you what I can do, for my part, beyond provide directions."

He glanced up and caught her unawares, capturing her in a look full of something hot and dangerous. This time, she had no doubt he meant the seduction in his eyes. To her horror, that heat and promise made her pulse jump sharply and her breathing quicken.

"Suffice it to say," he murmured, his tone deep and intimate, "my charm is one of my very useful skills."

She stood so quickly she knocked her chair over. "I doubt the Sorcerers will be bothered with that." She tried to keep her tone hard and impersonal, but even she heard the breathlessness, the hint of a tremor. From his ever-so-slight smirk, she knew he did too. "We leave tomorrow noon. We'll spend the first part of the night in Noman's Land. Then we go in."

He nodded, his expression never changing as he watched her hurry from the basement. Even when she disappeared into the shadows, she felt his gaze hot on her skin.

Once out of the basement, she continued up to the streets and out into the cool night air.

For a long moment, she stood beneath a brightly lit gas lamp, breathing in the faint dampness of approaching rain and letting the chilled breeze cool her overheated skin.

She'd known when stepping forward for this mission that it was going to be the most dangerous thing she'd ever done. She hadn't realized just how much of that danger would come from the very elf she was partnered with.

CHAPTER TWO

lthir studied Mina where she leaned against the parapet
watching the dim streets of the Sorcerers' territory. She
surprised him. So much so he was quite fascinated with her. He
hadn't been truly fascinated by a human woman in years.

He wasn't sure if he could call her beautiful. Her features
weren't soft and even enough for that. Her eyes were a little large,
her nose a little broad. But she *was* pretty. And her curves were so
full and lush, he found himself studying her body with great
frequency.

Though his brother's mate was a tasty-enough-looking woman,
Layla Brightarrow was like all the Sinnale—she'd lost too much
weight under the deprivations of war. Althir had felt no real interest
in any of the women he'd seen since turning himself over to the
Sinnale. They'd all grown hard and sharp in the last two years. Not
one with anything soft left for a man to lose himself in.

Except for Mina. She was the only woman he'd seen whose
shape still begged to be touched and explored. On the other hand,
her personality was all edges and bitter angles, a harsh contrast to

her delicious figure. The war had left her as angry and damaged as anyone, and she made no attempt to hide it from him. Her full lips rarely lifted into anything like a smile, and her dark eyes held distance. But also a quick intelligence.

She kept her fair hair pulled into a tight bun at the base of her neck, which did nothing to soften the curve of her cheeks or distinct lines of her cheekbones. Yet, there was a hint of something in her face and expression, something that had once been as gentle and enticing as an early spring breeze.

For some reason, the incongruity between her lush body, her hard attitude and that hint of who she might be if not for the war, struck him as infinitely interesting.

"We won't be able to make the Citadel before dawn," he said into the silence that had accompanied much of their night's vigil. "Not on foot. Not if we want to stay hidden."

"I didn't intend for us to head there directly." She glanced over her shoulder, giving him a brief glimpse of her velvety dark eyes. "You're sure the List will still be in the Citadel? Wouldn't they have moved it when you defected to the Sinnale?"

"They don't know I know about it," he said bluntly. When she raised a brow, he bent forward into a slight bow. "I believe I mentioned my charming personality has come in handy before."

"Meaning?"

"Meaning, you Sinnale aren't the only ones with a talent for collecting information."

She turned fully to stare at him. The intensity in her gaze would have left him more uncomfortable if he hadn't been courting it.

"You're trying to tell me you spied on your allies?"

"Information is always useful," he allowed. "Always."

"And you *charmed* this information, about the existence of the List, from one of the Sorcerers?"

"Hardly. They'd never admit to such a thing. Too dangerous."

He joined her at the retaining wall and stared out over the streets. He felt her gaze on the side of his face.

She was interested in what he had to say, couldn't help herself despite the distance she tried to keep between them. And that only encouraged him to try drawing her out more. There was something so deliciously satisfying about capturing her reluctant attention.

"At least one of their human servants is aware of the List. That particular human was…" He turned suddenly and caught her stare. "She was quite susceptible to my charms."

Mina snorted and looked away. The reaction made him smile. Why he was enjoying this game with her, he couldn't be sure. But attempting to tease and infuriate her gave him more pleasure than anything had in a very long time, so he wasn't inclined to stop.

"Then we can expect the List is still in the Citadel."

"Yes," he said. "But not the one you're thinking about."

She turned back sharply. "What are you saying? I thought there was only one Citadel?"

"The information the Sorcerers allowed to get back to the Sinnale." He leaned against the low wall, crossing his arms over his chest. "Your spies are very good. But the Sorcerers know about more of them than they let on. Though they take and use many, they allow a few to 'escape' with information they want you to have."

Her face seemed to grow paler in the dim light from the gas lamps below.

"Why do you think you've never gotten ahead in the war?"

"They have magic. Once we ran out of elven weapons, we didn't have anything to counter that."

"At which point, they could have initiated a full-on assault and taken all of Sinnale."

She shook her head. "No. We still fought. They never had enough people—"

He lifted one shoulder. "True. They use up as many of the

captured as they turn minion. And the minions are eventually used up as well. They need a constant flow of new blood to maintain their powers and the balance of power between them."

"Which is where you traitors came in," she spat. "Using elf magic to lure my people into their hands without so much as a struggle."

His amusement dropped and his fists clenched. But he continued. "The traitors are a convenience. But hardly necessary to the Sorcerers' efforts. They could take the advantage at any time. Yet they haven't. Why do you suppose they keep the war going?"

"Like I said, they never had enough minions. We have superior numbers."

"But no magic. They're aware of this. Do you think your people aren't tortured when they're taken?"

She spun away from him, her fingers digging so sharply into the brick wall he was surprised she didn't draw blood.

Very quietly, she said, "I know very well what captives of the Sorcerers suffer."

"Then you know the prisoners reveal information," he went on relentlessly. He didn't know why he was pushing this, why he pummeled her with truths she didn't need. But he also couldn't seem to stop himself. "So why didn't the Sorcerers take the city while you were essentially helpless against their magic?"

"We still had blades. Some, anyway." She let one hand fall to the hilt of one of the two short swords strapped her to hips. "Enough to hold them back."

He snorted. "Not nearly enough."

"The minions fell to our regular weapons."

"Again, you're missing the point. Even with elf weapons, you barely have enough to hold the Sorcerers back. Why do you think they let any of you remain free?"

He watched the tension tighten her body and jaw, her chest rising and falling sharply with her increased breathing.

"Why?" she murmured around clenched teeth. "You tell me."

"They need the conflict. The war. The blood. This *feeds* them. And they have every intention of drawing it out until they wring every last drop of pain and terror and agony from your people."

"And then?"

Her voice was so quiet now, he barely heard it.

He straightened and let his arms drop back to his sides. "Then… As my brother always suspected, they will turn their attention to Glengowyn."

Her sharp brown eyes pierced him. "And yet you still joined with them, when you knew they'd turn on your people? How could you?"

In his mad zeal to push her toward the real truth of her war, he'd cornered himself. Disgusted with both his own behavior and this entire situation, he grunted a curse and walked away from the wall.

"There was more to it than that," he muttered, not caring if she actually heard him or not.

What was he doing? He couldn't even explain why he'd pushed her that way. He didn't want to talk about the reason he'd joined with the traitor elves. Not to anyone.

Certainly not to this human woman he barely knew. A woman he had no doubt wanted desperately to stick one of her two short swords into his back right about now.

He was an idiot.

With his back to her, he said, "The fortress where the List is located, its existence isn't information they allow out of their territory. Most of the minions don't even know it exists. Only a handful of the Sorcerers' servants, a select guard and the Sorcerers themselves know where it is. Each Sorcerer maintains their own stronghold. The 'public' Citadel is for show and business. The List fortress is the site of their power. The place where they meet in secret and maintain their alliance."

She was silent for a long time after he'd spit out what he'd started to tell her before getting sidetracked. Though he could usually wait out the silences of others, with Mina he found himself turning to face her, to see if he could read her expression.

She looked thoughtful. Her lips were pursed, her gaze turned inward. When she glanced up, the anger and pain he'd forced her to feel were no longer evident in her expression.

"'Maintain their alliance'. What do you mean by that?"

He took in a deep breath and let it out slowly as his shoulders relaxed, releasing some of his tension. "Do you honestly think so many powerful individuals would work together willingly? Without ever making a grab for all the power themselves? The Sorcerers are selfish and hungry. Each would happily destroy the others if it meant they could walk away with everything."

"Yet they don't." She nodded slowly in understanding. "You know why, don't you?"

"The List of Names."

Her eyes narrowed. He could practically see her sharp mind ticking through the facts he'd just laid out for her, and he watched as comprehension dawned. Confirming what he'd suspected all along about Mina the spy. She was a very intelligent woman.

"They use the List as a…standoff, of sorts," she said. "Is that right?"

"One human was given the job of writing down the names—given to him in secrecy—and another was given the job of guarding the List. The man who'd taken the names was killed so he couldn't be tortured into revealing any of them. The woman who guards them was given a certain measure of power to protect her. Not enough to threaten the Sorcerers' own power. But enough to keep them from bypassing her to steal the List."

"Why would they allow her to know their names, though?"

"She doesn't know. The List was locked away in a bespelled vessel by the original taker of the names."

"Wait." She raised a hand. "We not only have to get around this guardian, but we have to get through a spell to get at the List?"

"You didn't expect this to be an easy mission, did you? That the Sorcerers would just leave something so valuable lying about?"

She scowled but rather than responding to his barb, she said, "So the Sorcerers use the List as a kind of insurance against betrayal. If one attempts to overpower the others, there's some plan in place for that Sorcerer's true name to be revealed?"

He clapped slowly in approval, the sound muffled by his thin leather gloves. "Just so. As you said, a standoff. A way to maintain the alliance. If one tries to betray the others, they risk losing something far more important to them than the power they might otherwise gain."

"Their true names. Which can be used in magic against them. Spells to destroy them."

"Oh more than just simple death spells. They could be turned into slaves if their true name gets into the wrong hands. A fate none of them covets."

"How could the name get out if one of them attempted to overthrow the others? Couldn't that one just kill the guardian, steal the vessel and make sure the others never got his name?"

He walked back to the wall, his earlier tension replaced by a strange need to be near her. "Outside of the guardian's own powers to help prevent that, part of the spell placed on the vessel is tied with all of their blood. The betrayal of one triggers an element of the magic that then whispers that one's name to the others. They would all know of both the betrayal and the betrayer's true name before that Sorcerer could ever make a move. Quite elegant, really. The perfect stalemate."

"I didn't even know there was magic capable of what you're describing."

"It's not common knowledge. And Sinnale had very few practitioners before the invasion. None since. Your people don't know the half of what your enemy is capable of."

He settled his hip against the wall, closer to her than he'd been before. She didn't move away, too caught up in their conversation to notice he'd placed himself so near. The position gave him a chance to breathe in the very faint but deliciously sweet smell of her skin.

He hadn't noticed her scent when she came to speak with him the day before in his cage. She'd kept herself too far away. Now, he was drawn by that elusive hint circling toward him on the chilled breeze. He wanted to nuzzle her neck to better capture and analyze the soft sweetness. But he had a feeling he'd end up with one of her swords in his gut if he tried. For some reason, that thought actually amused him, further lightening his earlier tension until he was almost cheerful.

"Do your people understand fully?" she asked. "You work with magic. You each have some to command."

"Our magic is different. Of the earth and ourselves. Not ripped away from some unlucky sacrifice. Our magic doesn't come from books and spells. It's part of our essence, part of who we are in each life we live."

"That doesn't answer my question," she said, her chin pulled back as she stared up at him.

He allowed a very slight smile. "No. It doesn't." He nodded back toward the currently empty streets. "And we've moved away from our goal. If we enter there now, we'll have to hide inside enemy territory. And we have a slightly different destination to reach than you assumed."

"Are you willing to tell me where we're going before we cross the border? I had planned for us taking at least two days to reach the

Citadel. But now… You should have shared this information with me earlier."

"The council didn't need to know this much detail. I knew we'd have time to discuss it once inside Noman's Land."

"You have a very roundabout way of bringing it up. So…"

"So, the List fortress is located five city blocks behind the Citadel, at the very center of their territory. The building is nondescript, maintains no outward guards—though there are guards inside—and has a vaguely disused look about it. That part is thanks to some elf glamour."

"The traitors help the Sorcerers disguise their true center of power? Isn't that a risk for the Sorcerers?"

He rolled his eyes. "The others never bothered to find out what they were hiding with the glamour. They assumed the Sorcerers were testing their skills. Idiots." He spit out the last through a half snarl.

"The same idiots you joined with willingly," she pointed out. "What does that make you?"

"The biggest fool of them all," he answered without hesitation. Her eyes narrowed, and he knew she'd ask more. Somehow with this woman he kept slipping into a topic he had no intention of discussing. To stave off her curiosity, he returned to their original topic. "Now then, our direction is still generally the same as before. But we'll have to get past the Citadel. And it, along with the surrounding area, is heavily guarded and patrolled. Only partly for show."

Her gaze turned inward again as she considered their options. He watched her thinking, unable to look away even if he'd wanted to. The play of concentration across her face, the way her brow creased and her full lips flattened into a line, continued to fascinate him, holding his attention more thoroughly even than the full bounty of her breasts or the sexy flare of her hips.

Finally, she said, "If we attempt to go too far out of our way to bypass the Citadel, this mission could take at least a week. The longer we're in their territory, the better chance we have of being captured."

"And there's no way to circumvent the Citadel without running into minion patrols. Not unless we attempt to go outside the city limits and sneak back in. But they guard those well with spells as well as minions. I understand the edges of the city in their territory are even more heavily monitored now."

"After the two elves who came to deliver those special arrows got through? But how would you know about their patrols if you've been in our prison?"

"Not all of you Sinnale are immune to my charms," he said with a slight chuckle. In fact, very few humans could resist his particular talent when he really tried. But the king and queen had ensured the magic mixed into the bars of his cage provided some protection for the Sinnale. Fortunately, he'd always found a handsome face and a ready ear went a long way on their own. "Information is always available to someone willing to…chat."

"One of my people told you the city limits were being more heavily monitored. Who?"

He shook his head. "Ah-ah. I could hardly betray that very kind person's confidence by revealing they'd spoken with me."

She narrowed her eyes as if she intended to say more so he held up a hand. "But back to the topic. Moving outside the city limits and then back in again won't prevent us from encountering patrols and protection spells. Any attempt to get around the center of the minion movements will be a waste of time."

She sighed. "I was afraid of that. Well, then. We take my original route, hide in the places I'd planned for. Once near the Citadel, we'll have to gather information, watch patrol movements. This will still take at least an extra day or two. But not as long as a week. Unless you're still not telling me something?"

"I can direct you to the List fortress, and I can lead you to the List of Names inside— if we make it that far. I haven't kept a secret way to get there from you."

"Fine. We'll have to do what we can once we know more."

He edged just a little closer, near enough his hand could easily brush against hers on the retaining wall. He resisted the urge to touch, knowing she'd pull away, but he couldn't resist the need to hover closer to her heat.

"Are you still determined to cross the border tonight, then?" he asked.

"We don't have time to waste. I planned for us going in tonight."

"We'll be to one of your hiding places before dawn? The patrols aren't any larger or smaller during the day, but we'll be easier to spot."

"You forget I've done this before. You haven't. I know what I'm doing. We'll be well hidden before dawn."

She stopped short of asking him to trust her. Which was good, as he didn't trust anyone anymore. But he did believe she knew what she was doing. As she'd pointed out, she was still alive. That spoke well of her skills.

"Well, then," he said, staring into the streets of a part of Sinnale he'd never expected to visit again.

He knew exactly what they were getting into, exactly what dangers lay ahead. Suicide. But he'd made his choice. And sneaking into enemy territory with Mina was infinitely more interesting than his endless days in a cage, reliving and reviling the circumstances that got him there.

He glanced at his companion. Yes, there were worse ways to spend time. "I'm ready whenever you are," he said.

Using the information on the border protection spells another spy had provided, Mina led Althir into enemy territory. Though she hadn't bothered to tell Althir, her real reason for avoiding a delay was that the location of those spells changed frequently, and she didn't want to get caught in one because she was working from outdated information.

Althir was right. Information was a very valuable commodity, and her life revolved around gathering it now. The risks she and the other spies took helped save lives.

Though if Althir was to be believed, not all of the facts they'd gathered were correct. The idea that the Sorcerers had allowed them some of those details made her stomach turn, made her feel like a puppet.

Once beyond the border, she kept to less-used roads but moved slowly and cautiously from point to point. The Sorcerers kept their part of the city brightly lit, which meant there were fewer shadows to hide in. But even with most of the gas lamps turned up, pockets of darkness and unlit alleyways gave them some cover as they made their way toward her first goal.

The building she intended to hide in during the daylight hours had once been a rival chocolatier's shop—one of the few chocolate makers in Sinnale who could claim to be any kind of competition for her family. She knew the shop and its surroundings well. Its small size and uselessness in the war kept it from being frequented by minions. There were two rooms above the shop and kitchen where they could hide, giving them beds to rest in—a rare luxury in her line of work.

Each spy who entered Sorcerer territory had their own hiding places. And they never shared that information with the others. A way to avoid too much movement at those locations, but also, if one spy was captured, they wouldn't be able to reveal the secrets of any of the others. So far, this practice had kept her safe and alive. The real danger arose when she came out of hiding to complete her missions. When she had to walk beside the enemy to collect information.

Althir remained silent at her back as they moved through the cobbled streets. His ability to move so quietly was both a relief and a little unnerving. She found herself glancing back at him every so often just to make sure he was still there. And every time she did, he gave her one of his little knowing smiles, the ones that left her feeling like he could read her thoughts.

Fortunately for them both, he couldn't. Because her thoughts kept fluctuating between a need to hurt him for the way his kind had hurt her family and a fascination with him she didn't want to feel. He was infuriating, arrogant and amoral. Yet… She kept catching glimpses of more, hints that he wasn't what he let the world see.

Ridiculous thoughts. He was exactly what he seemed. And she would do well to remember that. She didn't trust him, no one did, which was why she was here—to make sure he did what he promised to do. That goal had to stay firmly in her mind because forgetting what he really was could get her killed.

Or worse.

As they neared the little shop, she heard the approach of a minion patrol. Without speaking, she motioned Althir into a dark alley, moving them into a large cargo doorway to hide. The patrol marched past without pause. Seeing them made her throat ache. Though she knew better, she still found herself searching for one face amongst them.

He's dead, she scolded herself. *You watched him die.* He was better off dead too. Better than being one of those wretches turned into something no longer human, something that carried the stench of rotting meat and obeyed the Sorcerers without question.

When she was sure the patrol had passed, she continued on, checking only once to make sure Althir followed.

The sky was just beginning to lighten with the coming dawn as they slipped through the kitchen door at the back of the small chocolatier shop. With a gesture, she ordered Althir to remain in the kitchen while she searched the building, verifying that it was still safe and hadn't been used by anyone besides herself recently. The little clues she'd left in place, things that would give away the presence of others, were all still as they should be.

She returned to Althir and murmured, "We'll be fine here until sunset. There are two bedrooms upstairs, both with moderately clean beds. Feel free to use one. Sleep while you can. Time to rest will be rare over the next few days."

"And you? You'll sleep?"

"I'll see to myself," she snapped. Shaking her head, she reined in her temper. Her first view of minions in enemy territory always left her raw. But she didn't want Althir to know or question her about it.

She gestured at a cabinet above an expansive counter. "There's some food stores—dry meats and some dried fruit." She didn't go into enemy territory with much besides the clothes on her back and her short swords, sometimes not even those. The less she had to carry, the faster she could move, and the easier it was to adopt a disguise when she needed one. She left food and other gear scattered around her safe spots. Or she liberated what she required from the Sorcerers.

"Fresh water still comes out of the pumps from the well out back," she continued. The Sorcerers hadn't poisoned any of the water in their own territory, though they'd poisoned or bespelled most of the wells throughout Noman's Land. Once on this side of the border, finding water was never a problem.

Althir nodded, but he didn't look away from her.

"We'll leave as soon as the sun sets. We have a ways to go to reach the next hiding spot and the patrols will be heavier in those areas."

"Do we need to keep watch?"

She shrugged. "I'll take care of that."

She didn't trust him to guard her back while she slept. She would do as she always did—maintain a light snooze while a part of her remained alert to the noises of their surroundings. One of the advantages of having used this location a number of times was that she knew what was normal and what wasn't.

When he still didn't move, she sighed. "Do as you like. But I warn you, you'll regret missing a chance at some sleep."

"I've gone for days without sleep before," he assured her. "And I've had too much 'rest' of late in that cage."

"Your choice." She pulled a small packet of dried fruit from the cabinet. "Don't go into the front of the shop. The windows are dirty but not covered enough to prevent a passing patrol from spotting you." Then she climbed the stairs to the room she always used, the one with the best views of the surrounding streets, and settled in for a day's vigil.

When Althir joined her, she wanted to groan in irritation. She needed to be alone, just for a few minutes. Could he not listen to wisdom and go sleep?

"You're tense," he commented.

She couldn't read anything in his voice, couldn't decipher his tone, but since he hadn't ask a question, she didn't bother to respond. She had no interest in conversation with him outside of what needed to be done.

Or so she kept telling herself.

No, no she really didn't want to talk with him right now. Not when thoughts of her brother were so close to the surface.

"The minions scared you?"

She snorted and shook her head.

"Then it's something else..."

"Althir. Go sleep. Or twiddle your thumbs. Or eat. Or do nothing at all. I don't really care. Just go away."

"Something about the minions...," he murmured, drawing the sentence out, ignoring her pleas.

"We're in enemy territory now. I have every reason to be tense."

"There's a difference since the patrol passed."

She rolled her eyes. "You don't know me well enough to judge my mood shifts. Go away."

"Aren't you afraid I'll sneak out and alert the patrols to your presence?"

"No."

"Why?"

She finally turned from the window to look at him. "Because they'll do much more damage to you, after betraying them, than they could ever do to me."

"I could buy their forgiveness with you."

"I'm not that valuable. And you are many things distasteful to me, Althir of Glengowyn, but you're no idiot."

"If I weren't an idiot, I wouldn't be in this mess."

She wasn't sure which mess he referred to—joining the Sorcerers to begin with, having to turn himself over the Sinnale to save his miserable life, or this current mission to regain his freedom. It was on the tip of her tongue to ask when she remembered she didn't care and had no interest in talking with him. She turned back to the window.

The sound of the bedsprings creaking made her want to screech, *"Go away!"* But she didn't say anything aloud. Engaging him would just draw things out. Showing him her anger and annoyance would reveal more than she wanted a traitor elf to know.

"What other distasteful things am I?" he asked, amusement clear in his tone.

She nibbled on her fruit, ignoring him. At one time, her family had been large and boisterous. She'd learned well the power of silence.

Or so she thought.

"Can't think of any? I suspected as much. I'm too charming and handsome to be distasteful."

That surprised a snort of laughter from her. She cut it off as quickly as she could but knew he'd heard the response and cursed herself. Damn him and his charm to the sacred hells. She preferred the crass, bitter elf she'd met the day before. She couldn't find that elf amusing, even if she did find him beautiful to look at.

"I've visited this chocolatier before," he commented. "Before the invasion. Damned fine sweets they made. Maybe the best truffles in the city."

She shrugged, though it took an effort not to refute his claim. Family pride died hard, even after years of war.

"Another topic then. You never answered my question about how you managed to maintain anything like a figure over the last two years."

She felt her cheeks warming but kept her gaze on the streets below. Discussing her figure wasn't exactly an improvement in topics.

"Oh I'm sure some of it's down to family, right? Your mother probably had great tits too."

She tried not to react or stiffen, but knew she'd failed when she heard his slight hum, as if he realized he'd uncovered something.

"And sisters? Cousins, maybe? Were they as…fully curved as you?"

She continued to munch on her fruit as she tried to ignore him. In the otherwise quiet room, though, the deep cadence of his voice dug its way into her consciousness, leaving her too aware of him.

"I bet they were. With tits and asses to make a man's mouth water."

"Are you attempting to use that vaunted charm on me again?" she asked before she could stop herself. "If so, you do realize you're failing miserably, right?"

Her retort earned her a soft, sexy chuckle. "So, she speaks. Will you answer my question?"

"After all that rot you've just rambled on about, I have no idea what you asked."

"How have you managed to keep from getting too skinny during the occupation?"

She blew out an irritated breath and raised her hands palms-up in surrender. "Fine. If you must know, I was fat before the war."

When he didn't respond, she looked at him over her shoulder. His brows were raised and he was staring at her as if surprised by her outburst. The expression made her want to laugh.

"Gloriously fat," she continued. "So beautifully full and fat I was coveted by many a man in my family's industry." She realized too late she'd said too much. Biting her lip, she faced the window again. "Now go away."

"I've never heard a woman announce being fat with such pride," he said, continuing to ignore her pleas for him to leave. "I like it. I approve."

"I don't care."

He snorted. "No, of course you don't."

The bed creaked, and she held her breath, hoping he was finally going. But after a moment, she realized he'd just shifted positions and was still staring at the back of her head.

"So what was your family's industry that made being fat so valuable?"

Damn, damn, damn. She knew he wouldn't miss her slip. How had he managed to get so much from her, despite her efforts? His "charm" must really have magic to it. Though calling this conversation charming was a stretch. Yet that had to be the reason she found herself revealing details she'd never intended to share with a man she considered little better than an enemy.

"Don't try to ignore the question," he said. "I'll just keep nagging until you tell me. Or I'll guess until I hit on the right answer. Do you really want to go through all that just to keep such an inconsequential secret?"

"Your efforts, not mine," she grunted, slipping a little lower in her seat.

"Fine."

He hummed under his breath and she heard him tapping his gloved fingers against something.

"Pig farmers? No? Something to do with food, though? Cheese makers? Bread?"

She kept herself perfectly still so as not to react to his last guess.

"Or was it simply to do with wealth? Your lush plumpness a sign that your family could afford all the good food they wanted? Bankers, maybe. Loan agents?"

She let his litany roll past her, focusing on the streets. Everything was quiet for the moment. Under other circumstances, that would have pleased her. But at the moment, she wanted something to distract Althir from his attempts at uncovering more about her and her family, so a handy passing minion patrol wouldn't have upset her terribly. At least that would force the damned elf to shut up.

"I know," he said with a snap of his fingers. "And that explains a lot."

She raised her brows though she was still looking out the window and he couldn't see her.

"Your family owned this shop, didn't they? That's why you chose this location."

"No," she stated bluntly because it was the honest truth.

"But you're familiar with this shop. You know the area well."

He paused and she resigned herself to the fact that he'd stumbled onto the truth.

"Your family was in the chocolate business," he stated, his tone deep with satisfaction. "And being too thin would signal to potential customers that the chocolates created couldn't be all that great."

She pulled in a deep breath and let it out slowly. Though she didn't confirm his guess, she didn't deny it either. The bastard had figured it out, but she didn't have to be gracious about it.

"I've got it, haven't I?" he said, sounding inordinately smug. "Now it's a matter of pinpointing exactly which chocolatier."

"Why?"

"Why?" he echoed, sounding confused.

"Why do you care? Why try to figure this out?"

The silence stretched. Mina hoped he'd stop speaking altogether but knew her luck wasn't that good. As the minutes ticked by, though, she started to wonder if he'd actually left without her realizing. She turned. He was still on the bed, leaning against the headboard with his long, well-muscled legs stretched out on the mattress.

His arms were propped behind his head as he studied her. In the morning light, his eyes glittered and the angled planes of his face stood out in sharp beauty. How could such a rotten personality live inside such a stunning body, she wondered yet again.

They stared at one another for several long minutes before he finally spoke.

"I don't know why I care," he murmured. "But you…interest me, Mina of No Family. You had family once. And you refuse to acknowledge them, to the point that you've abandoned your family name. That's a riddle I find hard to resist."

"The answers are nothing I intend to share with you. So leave it alone."

"No."

She raised her brows at his blunt answer. "I was wrong earlier. You are an idiot."

His mouth cocked up at one side, a half smile, half smirk. "Told you so."

With a groan, she turned away from him again. It shouldn't be possible to find him repulsive and be drawn to him all at the same time. Yet that was exactly how he made her feel. He was one of the traitor elves, one of the ones responsible for taking the last of her family from her. She hated him for that. But she also found herself amused by him, interested in what he might say or do next.

No doubt there *was* magic involved. Because she couldn't believe even a small part of her would truly find Althir so absurdly desirable.

She heard him pull in a breath to continue but a slight movement on the street caught her attention and she raised a hand for silence. Edging closer to the wall so no one on the street could see her, she watched as a minion patrol marched into view. In the middle of the patrol, to her surprise, strode the tall, thin form of a traitor elf.

Althir stood beside her in the next instant, his movements so silent she hadn't even heard the bed creak.

He made a noise that sounded suspiciously like a growl. She glanced up and realized he was snarling at the patrol. At the other elf.

"Friend of yours?" she whispered.

He spared her a glare before focusing on the patrol again.

Neither she nor Althir moved as the minions passed beneath them. They kept still and silent. Despite this, the elf paused and glanced at the chocolate shop. He studied the façade, turning his attention slowly to the second story.

Mina held her breath, not moving even to frown. Seconds passed. The minions stopped in their march to watch the elf. Finally, with a slight shake of his head, the elf signaled them all back into motion, and the group moved on, continuing out of sight.

Mina sucked in a deep breath, filling lungs that were burning from the strain. Then she faced Althir.

"He sensed you, didn't he?" There was no other reason for the elf to have paused. She'd watched many patrols just like that pass her while she was in hiding, and not one had stopped before, not while she held her silence and stillness.

Althir scowled, his gaze still on the street. "Shouldn't have. Bastard Liroc. He's picked up something new from the Sorcerers." He met her gaze. "I could sense it. He's been tainted, using blood magic now too." He shook his head.

"I'm not sure I understand. Isn't that why you all turned traitor to join the Sorcerers? For more power? For access to their skills? Haven't you been learning their magic before this?"

He hissed and stalked away, a reaction she hadn't been expecting. It was common knowledge his excuse for turning traitor was power. Maybe he was upset he'd never managed to receive any of that additional magical strength.

He kept his back to her when he said, "The Sorcerers are jealous with their magics. I've mentioned that before. They were protective of it with the traitors too, never giving much, only hinting at more to come. They've never given any of the elves access to the kind of taint I could sense on Liroc. Something's changed."

"You…regret not gaining access to their magic?" She wasn't sure she wanted him to answer that question. She knew he must or he would never have turned traitor to begin with. But somehow, hearing him admit it would disappoint her. Odd.

He spun to face her. "You're not listening. Something has changed. Something I didn't plan for or anticipate. That will make what we have to do even more complicated. If the Sorcerers are sharing their magic with the elves, after all these many months, they're worried. They've uncovered some bit of information that's forced them to an extreme I know for certain they never intended to go."

She tilted her head. "You're saying they never intended to share their magic with you?"

He gave a sharp nod. "They lied. As they are wont to do."

"Then… Why do the other elves stay? Why didn't they defect the way you did if the Sorcerers had no intention of following through with their promises?"

He curled his lip in a snarl. "*They* continued to believe the lies. As I've said before, they're all idiots. They refused to see through the charm."

"But you did?"

With a snort, he dropped back onto the bed and lounged against the headboard. But his casual position belied a tenseness to his muscles, a coiled readiness to jump back into action.

"Charm is what I *do*," he said with no little bitterness. "No one can charm me, not with lies."

"If not, why did you turn traitor in the first place? And why did you stay so long?"

"None of your fucking business," he spat.

She raised her brows and crossed her arms over her chest. "Such venom. So much for charm." She watched his lips flatten into a thin line but couldn't tell what emotion he was suppressing. "So, despite the fact that the Sorcerers hadn't intended to share their magic, they have now."

He jerked his chin down once.

"That elf could sense you. Does that mean the others will too? Have you just become more of a liability than a help on this mission?"

Scrubbing his hands over his face, he growled something in his own language she couldn't understand.

"I don't know," he said from behind his hands, before dropping them to his lap. "I don't know what the other traitors are capable of now."

Mina left her spot by the window and paced across the room, considering this new information. As she walked, she said, "Do you think word of our goal has reached them? Do you think they realize what we might be after?"

"Again, I don't know. I didn't expect the Sorcerers to go this far and share their powers. So whatever they've discovered, it's forced their hands."

Under his breath he mumbled something she didn't catch. "What was that?"

He stared at her without blinking. "You weren't told why your people want the List."

She shook her head. "The less I know, the better. They can't torture anything out of me that I don't know."

"It may be too late for that."

"Meaning you think the Sorcerers know not only that we want the List but why? How could they when barely any of my people know?"

He didn't answer as he continued to consider her. She raised her brows in silent question.

"I'm going to need a weapon or two now," he said, in a seeming change of subject. "If we continue with our plan, we're not likely to get out of this without a fight. I need a weapon."

She pursed her lips. The council had very purposefully not armed Althir. She'd agreed with that decision, not wanting to find a dagger in her back. Though she suspected he could kill her without a weapon, given his superior elven strength, she'd at least have a chance to fight off a physical attack.

But things had changed. In an instant an already deadly mission had taken a turn for the worse. Her job rarely involved engaging the enemy in an actual fight, but now a fight might be unavoidable. She sure as hells didn't want to fend off an entire squadron of minions with only her two short swords to aid her.

"Where?" she asked shortly, her decision made. She just hoped pragmatism didn't get her killed.

"I know a place where there are weapons stored that's not too far off the route to the Citadel."

"It will be heavily guarded."

"I have a plan."

Her stomach dropped at the look on his face. When he smiled, she groaned. "Great. You're going to get me killed, aren't you?"

"We were never likely to survive this anyway," he said, almost cheerfully.

Even better, she thought with a growing sense of doom. She was paired up with a suicidal ex-traitor elf she couldn't trust but found herself having to while in the middle of enemy territory.

Wonderful.

She was not looking forward to tonight.

CHAPTER FOUR

hey left the small shop once full dark took the city, Althir leading the way this time. He still had questions for the lovely Mina, things about her he wanted to know, but he'd left off teasing her after Liroc had sensed him in their hiding spot. Instead, he'd shifted to his wartime vigilance, and even when she'd dozed, he'd continued to keep an eye and ear on their surroundings, watching for the appearance of any other elves.

Not that she realized he'd kept watch too. He'd pretended to sleep. And because he couldn't resist some level of teasing, he'd "slept" in the room she'd claimed for the day. A part of him wondered if she'd go to the other bed. A very specific part of him hoped she might even crawl into bed with him—though he really didn't see that happening. Yet. But he had wondered how she'd handle his continued insistence on remaining in her company.

To his surprise, she simply dozed in the chair by the window. She couldn't have possibly been comfortable. Yet she didn't complain or even comment. He could tell by her breathing and position in the chair, she never did fall asleep deeply either.

Her watchfulness reminded him of other soldiers, other spies, other wars. Over the course of the day, his fascination with her increased.

As they crept through the streets toward the small building housing an emergency store of weapons, he found himself hoping to spend time with her when this mission was done. If they survived. If she'd allow it. Though, he didn't really intend to give her a chance to refuse his company. He was certain he could charm her at least that much before they returned to Sinnale territory.

The real trick would be surviving. That possibility had just gotten worse.

They reached the building without encountering more than one patrol, which passed them without incident. He kept them hidden in a narrow space between two buildings just across the street from the weapons hold, watching the guards and their movements. Mina remained motionless and silent behind him, not even murmuring a question as they waited.

They stayed that way for a long while. Finally, Althir heard the incoming fresh guard approaching. Exactly what he'd been waiting for. Five minions marched up to the main door, their attention on their goal and not the surroundings. When the door opened, they filtered in. Several moments later, five minions filtered back out again and turned in the general direction of the Citadel.

He didn't move even after the off-duty group had disappeared and he could no longer hear the sharp ring of their boots on the cobbles. He continued to watch the building in silence. He was sure Mina must be growing restless behind him, yet there was still no hint of any impatience in movement or talk from her.

Finally, when he was sure the new guards had finished their check of the building and were settling into their posts, he turned to face Mina. The tight confines meant he was forced to press up against her. The feel of her full breasts against his chest was a pleasure he wasn't about to refuse.

She stiffened, attempting to put some space between their bodies, but there wasn't enough room. All she ended up doing was rubbing her breasts against him. As he stared down at her, her breathing increased, just enough to continue the torture of movement, and he felt the stirrings of real lust begin to rise. Despite what they were about to attempt, he smiled.

With a hand on the wall beside her head, he leaned down and whispered in her ear, "We'll go around to the side of the building, to an entrance hidden from the street. It will be monitored by one of the five minions that just entered the building."

"And how do you intend to get past the guards?" she murmured in a brush of hot air against the sensitive lobe of his ear.

He took a deep breath, and their bodies pressed tighter together. Though he enjoyed the position immensely, he was realizing this might be too much of a distraction. He hadn't recognized just how very susceptible he was to the lure of her body. He didn't want to get either one of them killed before he had a chance to thoroughly enjoy her.

Yet he didn't attempt to move away from her. "If you'll allow me the use of one of your swords, I can silence the guard on the door without raising an alarm. That will give us time to retrieve a few more weapons and get back out before anyone notices."

She pulled back to look up at him, holding his gaze. "You're sure?" she mouthed.

Did she realize he could still hear her, even when she spoke so quietly? He nuzzled against her ear again and murmured, "They have a pattern. They won't change the position of their watch unless an alarm is raised. Not for the next hour. We'll have enough time."

She remained still and quiet for long enough he wondered if she'd trust him with the sword. He didn't absolutely need it. He could overpower the minion without it. But that might create more noise, and they were attempting stealth.

Finally, she nodded, her hair brushing against his cheek with the movement, and he eased far enough away for her to pull one sword from its scabbard on her hip. She handed the weapon over reluctantly. When he touched it, he realized why. It was an elf-made short sword. An old one, not one of the more recent additions sent into Sinnale after the Glengowyn king and queen resumed trading weapons with the humans.

Did she know this particular sword held more than the usual elven magic? Did she know exactly how old it was? He glanced at the base near the guard and spotted the telltale elven signature. He raised his brows, momentarily stunned. Not just old, then. Something even rarer.

Whether she realized the true value of her swords or not, her reluctance proved the weapon was important to her. Or maybe she simply didn't like the idea of him having a sword. Though if that were the case, she wouldn't have agreed to this detour to arm him. Either way, he acknowledged her trust with a slight bow of his head and then led the way back down the narrow gap so they could approach the weapons storage facility from a more covert angle.

As they neared the building again, Althir stopped where he could see the door through which he intended to gain entrance.

Leaning near enough to speak into Mina's ear, he said, "Wait here. If you hear anything at all, I've drawn too much attention. Get back to Sinnale territory."

She pulled away and looked up at him with her eyebrows raised and her eyes wide. "No," she mouthed flatly. Then closer to his ear, "I go in too. That's why I'm here, to make sure you don't return to your former colleagues."

Irritation bit deep into his gut, even though he recognized her logic. Her distrust made sense. She was here to keep an eye on him.

He knew that. The Sinnale council had made it very clear. So he wasn't entirely sure why her lack of faith in him grated against his pride so sharply. He didn't expect her trust. In fact, he'd probably think less of her if she did trust him too easily.

Still… His logic didn't seem to be communicating with his instincts, and his instincts were annoyed beyond measure that she refused to listen to him.

"Fine. But keep quiet. Let me do what I need to do. We're finished if we're discovered."

She released a mostly silent breath that sounded suspiciously like a snort and turned back toward their goal.

He led on silent steps to the door, then motioned her back against the wall while he turned the knob. A minion stepped through with his sword pointed at Althir. Althir stared down his nose at the thing that used to be a human man until the minion lowered his sword and bowed his head. With a quick nod, and an even quicker flick of his wrist, he swept the short sword upward and sliced neatly through the minion's throat. He didn't even have a chance to gurgle a dying breath before collapsing face first onto the cobbles.

The stench of rotting meat, which permeated all minions, increased as the man bled out. Althir curled his lip at the noxious smell and moved inside, not waiting to see what Mina did.

She followed as silently as he could have hoped. For a human, she moved with a great deal of control and stealth. Years working as a spy had obviously trained her well.

Once inside, he went to the smaller of the two weapons rooms. Rather than take from the main stores, he raided the watches' supply, knowing those weren't monitored as closely, or counted as accurately, as the main collection in a much larger room deeper in the building. A further advantage of stealing from the guards' supply—the room was very close to the door they'd entered through and not secured with a complicated locking system.

He concentrated on listening to his surroundings as he moved, waiting for any sign the other minions were moving from their stations. The house remained eerily, but blessedly, quiet. At the door to the weapons room, he dropped to one knee to study the simple key lock. He could force the door easily enough, but doing it without making noise would take some finesse. As he studied the knob and frame, Mina dropped down to her knees next to him and shouldered him over a few inches.

She put her mouth against his ear and said, "Any spells?"

He shook his head.

She pulled two long, thin needles from inside one of the sleeves of her tunic and proceeded to pick the lock with a dexterity that both surprised and impressed him.

"Thief," he mouthed around a smile as the door clicked open.

"Spy," she corrected in the same near-silent tone.

They scooted inside and Mina pulled the door nearly closed, leaving an inch of space so she could watch the hallway. Althir went right to the rack of swords, bows and arrows.

He fingered the arrows, thinking of his cousin and her special arrows just delivered into Sinnale hands. He could use some of those about now. But, then again, they made a lot of noise when they exploded. Better the stealthier, if less elegant, human-made arrows.

He picked up a full quiver and bow, dropping both over his head so they rested at an angle across his back. Then he turned to select a sword. Just one. He didn't want to weigh himself down, and he also didn't want to take so much that it made the theft obvious.

The swords weren't nearly as well made as Mina's, but they were sturdy and would do in a fight. They weren't elven either, of course. During the neutrality, Glengowyn hadn't traded weapons with either side. And now that the elves had gotten involved in the human war, they sent weapons only to the Sinnale.

He hefted one blade, checked its balance, replaced it and selected another. Satisfied that the second would do, he went in search of a scabbard to hold it. Unfortunately, none of those were in the storage room.

Damn. Well he'd have to make do with his belt. He slipped the naked blade gently through the belt looped through his trousers and hooked the guard on the edges of the leather to keep it in place. Maybe the dead minion had a scabbard, he thought as he joined Mina.

She glanced back, noted his weapons and nodded once, then she eased the door open as quietly as the hinges allowed. Althir continued to listen intently for any possible noise from the others, and it was that attention that kept him hovering in the door a beat before following Mina into the hall.

The minion that came up behind her moved much more quietly than most of them did, though he wasn't as silent as an elf—or even a human spy. Mina must have assumed the noise came from Althir, however, because she didn't turn to face the threat immediately. Her hesitation was only seconds, but those were preciously long seconds that nearly cost her her life.

The minion raised his sword, Mina turned just as the sword speared toward her. She leapt back awkwardly, unprepared for the attack. The sword caught one of her sleeves, slicing through material and drawing blood, though not actually piercing her. She was quick to reach for her sword but not quick enough.

Althir stepped out, using their focus on each other to move up behind the minion in silence. With Mina's short sword, he sliced the man's throat as smoothly and quietly as he'd killed the first minion.

When he looked up from the collapsed carcass, Mina's eyes were wide, her nostrils flaring and her mouth slightly opened with her rapid breath. She met his gaze but didn't bother to mouth any comments. They didn't have time to waste.

Althir stepped over the body, took her hand and hurried toward their exit. He paused before rushing out into the night, listening for signs of ambush from outside or that the alert had been raised inside. When he was sure their exit was safe, he pulled her into the streets. They raced back toward the road Mina needed to get them to their second hiding spot.

Once well clear of the storage hold, though, Mina jerked him to a stop and pulled him into an empty building. He was about to protest, but she put her fingers over his mouth to silence him. The contact was more of a shock than any real impediment to speaking, and he couldn't manage to form a coherent sentence even if he'd remembered what he wanted to say.

Instead, all he could think was that her fingers were warm and held that very faint but elusive scent that defined her. And that it would be very easy to pull one of her fingers into his mouth to taste her. He was surprised at how desperately he wanted that taste. He held her gaze for a long, charged few heartbeats before she finally dropped the touch.

Motioning him farther into the dark entryway, she stopped when they were well out of sight from any of the windows. He glanced around quickly, taking note that they'd ended up inside what seemed to be a house, then he focused on her again.

"There's no one here," she affirmed in a whisper. "I wanted to… With this detour for your weapons, we aren't going to reach the next place I wanted us to hide before dawn. We took too long."

When he would have commented, she raised a hand.

"I'm not complaining. We couldn't have done that any faster with so little complication."

He raised his brows at the "little complication" comment.

She ducked her head. "About that. Thank you. For…"

When she trailed off, he smirked. "For not letting him kill you?

If I'd done that, who would watch me to make sure I didn't turn traitor again?"

She kept her head down so he couldn't see her expression clearly, but he did catch her slight flinch. His satisfaction with the reaction mingled with another emotion he didn't entirely recognize in himself and so didn't bother to analyze.

"Well. Anyway, I do thank you." She held out a hand and finally looked up to meet his gaze. "My sword, please."

He wanted to mock her for the "please" too but didn't as he handed her blade back.

She sheathed it then gestured at his sword hung looped through his belt. "We'll try to find you a scabbard in our travels. That will be too hard to get at if we find ourselves in a fight."

He just stared.

Flicking her tongue out to wet her lips, she said, "Since we won't make our original hiding spot, I have a backup we can head toward. It's closer but a little out of the way given our ultimate destination."

"Fine."

The glint of moisture on her lips from that quick pass of her tongue captured his attention. How this woman managed to irritate and entice him all at once, he couldn't begin to guess. But at the moment, he didn't really care. He was too busy wondering what that full mouth of hers might taste like, and if she'd still stick her sword in his gut if he tried to kiss her. Maybe not, since he'd just saved her life. Though he suspected he'd still get a sound slap for his efforts. He smiled, just a little, certain the sting of that slap would be worth it.

She sucked in a sharp breath and his gaze dropped to her breasts. Ah, but this woman made him forget where they were, what they were doing, the fact that she hated him, that a part of him resented her. Everything that should have put a halt to his growing desire got swept away under the need to touch her. To fill his hands with her full breasts and taste the skin along her throat, searching out her sweet flavors.

He didn't think he moved, not even to step toward her and act on his growing fantasies, but she made a sudden sound and jerked backward a few steps. He met her gaze without even an ounce of guilt for staring at her breasts or considering all the ways he'd like to taste her.

Her pulse was actually visible in her throat, and he could hear the increased speed of her breathing in the otherwise silent room. She was affected by him. That was obvious. Despite her own distrust and hate.

Maybe she wouldn't slap him too quickly if he moved in for that kiss…

Before he could, though, she said, "We need to move. We won't reach our new safe spot if we linger here too long."

"Then why did we stop?"

Her expression shifted through a series of emotions he couldn't follow before she settled her gaze on his shoulder. "I wanted to tell you about the change of plans."

"You could have done that while we moved."

"And I wanted to pause long enough to thank you. For…"

"Saving your life," he finished for her, amused that she couldn't bring herself to say it out loud.

"Yes. Exactly."

"You could have said that once we reached the safe spot."

"It needed saying sooner rather than later." She straightened her shoulders. "Let's move."

Without waiting for his response, she returned to the door she'd so recently dragged him through, studied the street beyond, then slipped out into the night, leaving him to follow.

He didn't let her get too far away before joining her. He had no intention of letting her get too far away from him for the next several days. More often than he should, he caught himself watching her rounded ass as they skirted close to the buildings and down darkened streets. He might still get slapped, maybe even end up with one of her swords in his gut, but he would have the kiss he so desperately wanted.

Sooner rather than later.

And if she didn't kill him, he had no intention of stopping at just a kiss.

CHAPTER FIVE

Mina was so overly conscious of Althir's gaze on her, she moved stiffly, awkwardly, feeling oddly uncomfortable in her own body. Her skin felt too tight, her clothing too confining. A jittery tingle of awareness kept her nerves so alert to his presence, it was almost pain.

She hated Althir. Hated his kind. Resented his masculine beauty that she found so hard to ignore. So why did she suddenly feel this…need? Why couldn't her anger and hate overcome the growing twist of desire tightening in her stomach?

She didn't even like him! He was arrogant. Rude. Presumptuous. Mean.

And he'd saved her life.

Swallowing hard around the thickness clogging her throat, she led him into the former tavern that would be their hiding spot for the day, then motioned him toward the stairs at the rear of the common room.

"Check that floor," she murmured.

As he disappeared up the stairs, she shook her head in an attempt to clear it so she could pay attention to their surroundings.

She searched the ground floor and made sure the place hadn't been used since her last visit. She didn't take advantage of this particular spot very often, so it wasn't as clean as some of her other hideouts. But the dust wasn't thick enough to give away their presence if someone made a pass through the ground floor. From her search, it appeared no one had bothered to enter this building for some time.

Once she was confident they'd be safe for the day, she followed Althir to the second level, the floor with the rooms the former tavern owner had let out to travelers and the occasional overly drunken customer.

Althir met her at the top of the steps. She tried not to react, to give away her growing awareness of him, but he continued to stare at her with the same focus and intensity as he'd kept on her during their entire journey here. And it was getting more and more difficult to breathe normally under that scrutiny.

"This floor is clear," he said, his voice deep and quiet in the silent hallway. "Nothing but a few scurrying mice to keep us company."

She nodded, surprised to find she couldn't seem to speak. He was close enough she could feel his natural heat. It sparked a visceral memory of standing pressed tightly against him in the narrow gap across the street from the weapons storage building. The hard muscles of his chest had felt surprisingly wonderful against her breasts. So much so she'd wished they had less clothing separating their skin. The thought of rubbing her naked breasts over his chiseled physique left her lightheaded.

The fact that she had such thoughts about Althir humiliated her, made her feel weak and vulnerable.

If only he would stop looking at her that way! She needed time to herself, to get her head straight and purge his scent from her nostrils.

"I'll take a room near the front of the building," she managed to say around her dry throat. "You take a room at the rear. That way we can keep watch over more of the area. I'm not as confident of the security of this spot as I was the previous one."

He straightened a little, seeming to loom larger and more formidable before her. She didn't back down, even managed to return his stare, but she could tell he was about to argue with her. She just couldn't allow him to stay anywhere near her for another day.

Not if she wanted to retain her sanity.

Fortunately, she'd presented him with a valid and logical plan. Unless he wanted to put them at potential risk, he had very little room to debate her strategy.

With a slight frown and an irritated grunt, he said, "I'll stay near the room you choose. I hear well. You won't have to speak loudly to alert me to trouble."

Her shoulders dipped in relief. Afraid he'd notice, she skirted around him and ducked into a room looking out over the street in front of the tavern. She went right to the window and tried to ignore the fact that he'd followed her rather than going into one of the other rooms.

When she could no longer ignore his stare, she faced him and raised a brow, trying for irritated but unaffected.

"Did you really think I would let that minion kill you?"

He asked so quietly she had trouble reading his tone. "It never crossed my mind one way or the other. Before it happened, I hadn't thought to be in a position where you might need to save my life. During… I was too busy trying not to get killed."

"And after? You were surprised."

"I was relieved."

"You were surprised."

She huffed out an annoyed grunt. "Maybe. I still haven't really thought about it."

"You thought about it enough to know you wanted to thank me quickly."

"I… I didn't want you to think I was ungrateful for the help."

"Why not? Why would you care?"

"Why do you? Why are you pushing this? And what does it matter? Someone saves your life, you thank them. That's it, all there is to it. It's done. Now go mind the back of the building. Or would you prefer a patrol sneaks up on us while we argue?"

"I'd hear them coming."

That made her frown. "Your hearing is that good?"

"Minions are that noisy. But yes, my hearing is also that good."

Damn. That meant he could hover in her doorway for as long as he liked and she had no real excuse to send him away.

She needed him gone. "I can't hear that well so I need to concentrate. You're distracting me."

His intense stare didn't waver but another of his very slight smiles lifted his lips. She didn't trust that expression. There was something too…purposeful in the look. Like he knew something she didn't and intended to act on it.

A slight shiver tickled her spine. He knew, she realized. He could tell she was having trouble controlling her attraction to him. She wanted to curse, long and colorfully, but didn't want to give him any more information about her state than he'd already uncovered.

"Althir, go away."

"Why are you so intent on being rid of my company? You were yesterday too."

"Because I don't like you well enough to keep your company."

He actually laughed, a surprising reaction that made her cheeks heat—even more surprisingly.

"You like me much more than you want to admit."

"No."

"Yes."

"No," she insisted with an edge of desperation making her voice rise. She quickly swallowed back her need to screech and lowered her voice when she said, "I'm tired. I can't rest with you around and still keep watch. You talk too damned much."

"So I've been told. We still have much to discuss."

Her temper pushed almost beyond her control, she decided to change topics. If he wanted to talk, she would learn more about what they needed to do to finish their mission. "Fine. Tell me about this vessel that holds the List."

His brows rose sharply. "I thought you wanted me to go away."

"I do. But you aren't. So you may as well answer my questions."

He moved from the doorway to the only chair in the room and turned it so he could sit facing her. She glanced around. If she wanted to sit, she'd have to take the narrow bed. The very last place she wanted to be was on a bed while alone in a room with Althir. So she remained standing by the window and turned her gaze out to the street. The rising sun covered the surrounding buildings in gentle, soft colors and darker shadows as the gas lamps winked out.

"The vessel," she prompted when he remained silent. "You said it was bespelled, using the Sorcerers' blood. So if one of them tried to open it, their names would be…whispered magically to the others. What if someone besides a Sorcerer tries to open it? A minion or human slave?"

"All the minions and slaves are tied by blood to a specific Sorcerer, marked as theirs. They can't access the vessel either. They wouldn't leave such an easy loophole in the spell."

"What about the traitor elves? Are they…marked for a specific Sorcerer?"

"Ah," he said. "That's an interesting point."

She heard the chair groan a little under his weight.

"Marking an elf would involve a Sorcerer passing some of their power to the elf. They can't tie us the way they can humans. The necessary blood-sharing has the potential to leave a Sorcerer vulnerable to an elf because an elf can't be completely controlled by the bond."

"So, then, why doesn't one of the Sorcerers get an elf to help them get the List? No blood tie to worry about."

"For the same reason they won't make the blood tie. They can't control what the elf would do once the List was recovered. They certainly couldn't trust elves who turned traitor against their own kind with the knowledge of the List, nonetheless access to it. No, trying to use an elf that way would too likely backfire. The Sorcerers are many things, but they aren't stupid."

She considered this new information, and what he'd told her yesterday. "But the Sorcerers have started to share their power with the traitors. Does this…form a tie?"

"You are such a clever woman," he murmured. "As a matter of fact, it does. And if the Sorcerers have started imparting their powers to all the traitors, then not only have they formed a blood bond with them, they've taken care of any possibility of those elves accessing the List without all the Sorcerers learning of it."

"Do you think they've started passing power for that reason? To tie the elves and protect the List?"

"I'd have to ask a Sorcerer that. If this move is to protect the List, then they've learned something. They suspect the List is in danger. But since very, very few know about it, and even fewer know why the Sinnale might want it, I think there's another reason for their move. Perhaps it's simply that they're losing the war and they need to more securely hold the traitors to them."

She nodded and tapped her fingers on her thigh. Caught up in consideration, she faced him to ask, "You haven't said how we'll break the spell on the vessel. Do you know what has to be done? Or are we to take the whole thing back to Sinnale territory and hope we can break the spell from there?"

His gaze was unwavering. "I know how to break the spell. As it was forged with blood, so must it be destroyed with blood."

She raised a brow.

"A lot of blood," he said. "And all of that blood will have to come from one individual, despite the fact that the blood of many went into making it."

Realization sank in. "That's why the blood ties to the servants and minions prevent the Sorcerers from using their humans to open the vessel. It's not just a matter of being marked as a Sorcerer's property. The blood those humans would use to get at the List is… linked with a Sorcerer."

He nodded and crossed his arms over his chest, looking almost smug.

"How much blood? You said a lot."

"From a human? Virtually all of their blood would be required."

"Someone has to die to open the vessel?" Her chest tightened. Who would do that? Who would they get to make the sacrifice? And how could they ask that of anyone, given what all the Sinnale had suffered during the war? "Does the council know this?"

"Not yet."

"You never told them? Why?"

"They didn't need to know yet."

"But someone will… This can't work, Althir. How could we possibly ask someone to sacrifice their life like that, even if it meant an end to the war?"

"The Sinnale people sacrifice their lives every time they go into battle. Why would this be any different? A noble way to die, as far as I can see."

"It is different," she murmured, though she couldn't say how or why. It just was.

She wouldn't want to be the one responsible for asking this sacrifice of any of their people. The worst part was she knew someone would step forward. One of her people *would* allow themselves to be bled to death if it meant a final end to the occupation. The very idea made her heart ache. She blinked as moisture filled her eyes and turned to face the window so Althir wouldn't see.

"You haven't asked what would happen with an elf," he murmured.

"What?"

"If an elf bled to break the spell…"

"Why would an elf do that? Even though the king and queen are trading weapons with us again, they've still made it clear this isn't their war. They don't send in soldiers to help us fight. They'd hardly ask one of their people to sacrifice their own lives—"

"An elf stands a chance of surviving," he interrupted her. "Our blood is different. It carries that natural magic we all have."

She rubbed at her eyes to keep the tears that had formed from dropping. "But they'd still have to allow themselves to be bled. Would any do that?"

"There are some who would."

She considered that. "Ulric would probably volunteer." Layla's mate didn't remain out of the fighting or pretend the war had nothing to do with him. He might be willing.

A rough growl filled the room, startling Mina into facing Althir again. His brows were furrowed and his lips set in a snarl.

"Of course you would think of Ulric. And why not? He's the

hero. He's the favorite. Why wouldn't such a paragon of virtue be willing to sacrifice himself for his beloved Sinnale?"

"He fights with us where the rest of your people stand back. Or turn traitor." She didn't fully understand his reaction to the mention of his brother. Who else did he think would help them? Ulric was the only elf she knew who might be willing. She couldn't imagine any of the others going to such extremes for her people.

Althir stood so abruptly his chair tumbled backward, crashing loudly to the floor. She winced at the noise and checked the street. Not every building around them was empty. When she was sure no one had heard anything, she faced Althir again, ready to scold him.

Her voice caught in her throat at the sight of him.

He stood at his full, imposing height, glaring at her, his fists clenched at his sides, his jaw locked, and his angled eyes narrowed to slits. "You have your answers now," he grated out. "I'll go to my watch."

He stalked from the room, leaving her openmouthed in surprise. What had just happened?

Well. Had she known all she had to do was mention Ulric and Althir would leave the room, she would have mentioned his brother earlier.

Though, as she retrieved the chair to use for her watch, she felt a niggling of guilt and regret. For upsetting him? She didn't want to believe that. He hadn't shown any compunction about upsetting her since they'd first met. In fact, he'd gone out of his way to irritate and anger her. She shouldn't care that she'd finally managed to upset him. He deserved it, after all.

Still, as she settled in for her vigil, that hint of guilt stayed with her, adding to her already confused feelings for Althir.

She'd already thanked him for saving her life. She was not about to apologize to him. Not all in one day. Especially since she wasn't entirely sure what she wanted to apologize for.

CHAPTER SIX

althir paced the room across from Mina's, moving silently, keeping back from the window so he didn't inadvertently make himself visible to someone on the street. But his irritation wouldn't allow him to sit still.

Ulric. Always fucking Ulric.

His perfect, honorable, flawless fucking brother!

As he paced, he glanced back toward Mina's room and realized he was angrier than her comments really warranted.

But she had thought of Ulric first. Turned to Ulric as a possible savior.

When Althir was right here with her! Doing what needed to be done to end the war. Did she even for one moment consider that *he* might be willing to help her people? To help her?

Why would she? his own thoughts mocked him. *As far as she's concerned, everything you do is selfish and self-motivated. She has no reason to think you'd bleed for her.*

Except that he'd just saved her life. And *he* was the one here risking his life to recover the List. Risking more than a simple bleeding if the Sorcerers caught him.

He flexed his fists, and with a grunt of irritation, pulled his gloves off in a rough jerk and tossed them into a corner of the room. Mina's lack of faith in him was infuriating. Yet the more logical part of his brain understood her reaction perfectly. Knowing that didn't stop him from feeling betrayed. And that just made him angrier.

Why should he feel betrayed by a woman he barely knew? One who hated him, even if she also wanted him. Just because he intended to fuck her before all this was over didn't mean he expected her to suddenly trust in him.

Did it?

No, he was a fool many times over, but he'd hardly be that stupid. He couldn't expect such a clever woman to be that stupid either.

He slowed, easing from a fast stalk to a more thoughtful circuit back and forth across the wooden floor. Finally, he dropped onto the edge of the bed and scrubbed his hands over his face. He'd spent too much time in that damned cage. And before that, he'd been too long with the Sorcerers. He'd lost all sense, all perspective. That was the only explanation for this visceral reaction, this illogical sense of betrayal.

He did not expect Mina to trust him. He did not expect her to believe in him. She had less reason to than anyone. When even his closest family thought so poorly of him, he would be a madman to think a stranger, a human woman, might see more in him than that. He'd hardly given her reason to, either.

He did not *need* her to think well of him. He didn't need anything from her at all.

He lowered his arms, letting his hands flop onto his lap as he stared at the doorway leading back toward her room. Maybe he had gone mad. Just one more thing to berate himself for, one more idiocy to add to the growing list.

The sooner this mission was over, the sooner he could be gone. Putting clever, curvy, sharp-tongued Mina of No Family behind him for good. His discomfort at the thought of never seeing her again would go away quickly enough too, he was sure. No reason to think otherwise. She was no one to him. Just another human woman. A possible fuck, but nothing more. A means to an end.

And he'd do well to keep reminding himself of that fact, or he risked far more than he was prepared to sacrifice.

The sound of a minion patrol several blocks away pulled Althir out of his light doze. Without moving from his perch on the bed, he listened intently to their movements. Heading this direction, he thought. Fast.

He hurried to tell Mina, but she was already on the way out of her room, meeting him in the hall.

"Minions approaching from the east," she murmured.

He scowled. "More are coming from the southwest. Fast."

"Toward us? They know we're here? How?"

"Someone saw us enter the building? I don't know. But two patrols heading directly for us is too much of a coincidence. We need to leave."

She nodded but frowned as she glanced toward the stairs leading up from the tavern's common room. "It's still daylight. We won't be able to hide well."

"The roofs? We can get away from immediate danger before we hit the streets."

She shook her head. "Too far away or too tall. There's nothing close enough to get to. And most of the buildings around here have at least a few people in them—mainly Sorcerer servants."

He could hear the patrol she'd spotted just a few houses away now. The one he'd heard was only a block or two away and spreading out, covering escape in that direction.

"We're being surrounded," he said. He cursed in his own language because the situation called for it. He was about to suggest another exit when they both heard the front door of the tavern creak open.

On silent feet, he moved to the top of the stairs and crouched low, risking a glance at the commons. Four minion soldiers crept inside, swords unsheathed and held at the ready. Slipping back into the second-story hallway, he rejoined Mina.

With a finger to his lips, he edged into the room he'd been using, retrieved his bow and quiver, dropping them over his back, then took up his sword. He could kill four minions. Maybe even without alerting the approaching patrol. But that still wouldn't give them enough time to get out of the area before the second patrol reached them.

After collecting his weapons, he went into Mina's room to check the direction from which the first group of minions had approached. If necessary, he could jump from the second floor without injury. He could carry Mina easily enough too. But when he studied the street below, he spotted the two minions left there to guard against just such an escape. By the time Althir hit the ground, set Mina down and pulled his sword, the minions would sound an alarm.

Cursing silently, he hurried across the hall. The patrol from that direction was just beginning to enter the lower level of the tavern, through the kitchen. A creak on the stairs confirmed at least two minions had already started up to the second floor.

The second patrol left a single guard, posted at the kitchen door, to watch the street while the rest disappeared inside. More footsteps sounded on the stairs. A quick glance around confirmed Mina was right. There were no rooftops within easy reach from here. Oh, he might be able to make the one just across the back alley from the tavern, even though it would require leaping up. But he'd have difficulty doing that with his weapons and Mina in tow without attracting attention. Alerting the patrols to their escape would defeat the purpose.

More footsteps sounded on the stairs.

They were out of time.

Pulling Mina close, he set his lips to her ear. "We're going to jump to the ground. There's only one guard on this side. I'll kill him as quietly as I can." He felt her begin to pull back but he held her close. "I'll hold you as we jump so you don't get hurt, but you'll have to release me the instant we're on the street. Understand?"

She nodded.

He started to open the window, but a sound in the hall stopped him. Reacting instantly and on instinct, he turned to grab Mina and pull her under the bed. To his surprise, she was already disappearing beneath. He joined her faster than a human could move and they both held absolutely still as several booted feet entered the room.

The minions searched without speaking, checking the single wardrobe, the small closet that served as a washroom and then the window. One even opened it and looked out. The second paused at the foot of the bed.

Althir concentrated, calling up a magic he rarely used. He grabbed Mina's arm and focused as he stared at the minion's boots. A face appeared far enough back to avoid the swing of a weapon. The wash of that rotten-meat scent filled Althir's nostrils, but he ignored it, continuing to concentrate, his fingers digging into Mina's arm so she wouldn't react. The minion scanned their hiding spot, his near-empty gaze skimming over them several times. Then he straightened.

Holding his breath and his concentration, Althir waited until he heard them reenter the hallway. Then he let the spell drop. Exhaustion swamped him instantly, making his limbs as heavy as oak. He continued to keep a hold on Mina and forced himself to listen, to pay attention to their surroundings despite an almost overwhelming need to sleep.

Several minions collected in the hallway, just outside their door. "No one," one said.

"They must have left already."

"She said they were still here. She's been watching the building all day."

"Did you find anyone?"

"Evidence someone was here."

"But no actual people."

"They snuck past her. She probably wasn't watching as closely as she claims."

"Search the surrounding buildings. If the elf and spy are still in the area, we'll find them."

The footsteps shuffled back down the hall.

Althir remained motionless, breathing silently and slowly. His eyes drifted shut and he snapped them open as he listened to the movements from downstairs.

"Watch the two exits while we search the area," one of the minions who'd been speaking in the hallway ordered.

Moments later, silence descended over the tavern, but Althir could still hear the sharp strike of their boots on the cobbled streets. He glanced at Mina. Her eyes were wide, her breath barely audible even though his head was so close to hers, but she didn't move so much as a lash as she stared at the slice of floor they could see from their hiding spot.

From his grip on her arm, he could feel her pulse racing. She controlled her body outwardly, though, keeping a careful stillness that wouldn't alert those below to even a hint of sound.

It felt like they held their positions under the bed for hours, waiting as outside Althir heard the search move from building to building. There was an argument in the street, one female voice raised in outrage and threat. The male voice of what Althir assumed was one of the patrol leaders carried a calm, almost disinterested tone. Althir could detect a few of the woman's words but none of the man's.

"I will tell her of your failure," the woman shouted. "They are still there! How could you miss them?"

A scuffling sound from the front of the tavern sent Althir's already alert nerves into overdrive. He was too exhausted now to utilize the camouflage spell again, so exhausted only adrenaline and knowing Mina was in danger kept him from dropping into a deep sleep. If the minions searched the tavern again, Althir wouldn't be able to hide himself and Mina. They'd have to fight their way out. And he wasn't sure how well he could fight while still suffering the aftereffects of that casting.

Another argument sounded from just inside the tavern, this one more easily heard.

"Mistress, we have searched the building thoroughly. There is no one here. They have already left."

"It was that elf, that Althir who turned himself over to the Sinnale. I know it was," the woman hissed. "Do you know how much he's worth to them? We must find him."

"He is not here. He is not in the surrounding buildings," the same calm male voice from the street assured her.

"Did you check the closets? Under the beds upstairs?"

"Yes."

"How could they get away? They couldn't have known I spotted them, couldn't have known I was watching."

"You could not monitor both exits by yourself. They left through the one you weren't watching."

The minion's voice was so reasonable it was an almost comic contrast to the woman's rising screech.

"No! I would have noticed. I would have seen. He's worth a fortune. She would have ensured I lived as well as they do for the rest of my life."

"He is not here."

"He's an elf. He could have used a spell."

Althir didn't move or make any outward sound, but he did feel Mina's arm muscles flex beneath his touch, just once.

"We can see through elf magic," the minion said with absolute surety and no real emotion.

The woman cursed loudly, her voice echoing through the tavern. "It's not fair! I know I saw him. I know it was Althir. The woman… She was human but maybe she has magic? Maybe she's keeping them hidden. Something she got from the elves. The king and queen have started trading in weapons again. Maybe they're trading in more now."

"No spells. Elf magic doesn't work that way."

"How would you know, you mindless slave? Who are you to tell me anything? Take me to the mistress. She will listen to me. She will believe me and punish you for your failure."

There was a long silence. Then the sound of a dull thud, like a body hitting the floor.

"Carry her," the man who'd been speaking so calmly with the woman ordered. More scuffling and grunting and then the same man ordered, "Back to the Citadel."

Marching boots echoed out into the streets. The minions made no effort to be quiet or conceal their movements.

Even when Althir was sure they were several blocks away, he remained perfectly motionless under the bed, his hand on Mina's arm. She didn't move either. They remained that way for what felt like a long time, and to Althir's horror he did drift off to sleep once. He blinked his eyes open to see Mina staring at him.

She whispered, "I think we're safe enough for now. But we need to stay here until sunset, in case the woman left someone to watch the building."

He nodded.

"I think we can come out from under the bed," she continued. "Stay away from the windows."

He followed her as she agilely rolled out from their hiding spot. His movements were stiffer, less graceful as exhaustion continued to drag at him.

Mina didn't bother to stand but propped herself against a nearby wall, watching him through narrowed eyes. He remained sitting on the floor too with his back against the bed. He mustered enough energy to remove his quiver and bow, keeping them close, opposite the sword he still held in one hand, then settled against the mattress again. Unable to hold his head up anymore, he let it fall back against the side of the bed and closed his eyes.

"What did you do?" she murmured.

"When I'm not in danger of falling unconscious, I'll explain." He swallowed hard and tried to clear his throat quietly. His voice sounded rough and gravelly.

"Are you okay?"

"Need sleep. Hard to stay awake now."

"Sleep, then. I'll wake you if the patrols return."

"Can't. You need my help."

She snorted. "You're no good to me in the state you're in. Rest. We still have a few hours before the sun sets and another hour after that before full dark. I'll keep an eye on things. Will those hours be enough for you to recover?"

He moved his head in a bare nod and finally let go of consciousness.

CHAPTER SEVEN

Mina studied Althir's face as his breathing deepened into obvious sleep. His cheeks were hollow and there were strain lines around his eyes and mouth. Whatever he'd done to keep them hidden, it had cost Althir dearly.

She berated herself for not knowing he could do this sooner. Or what the effects of using this magic would be. She should have pushed him for this information yesterday, or the night before while they were in Noman's Land! This was just the kind of detail she needed and had intended to get from him right from the beginning. Yet she'd let him distract her. Let her attraction and anger override her sense.

Shaking her head, she eased up from the floor and edged carefully to a window to search the streets. She was going to get them killed by not remembering why they were here. Her job during the war had always been to obtain information. She'd failed miserably at doing that with Althir. Any more such failures could land them into the hands of the Sorcerers.

She left him sleeping where he was and went to check the other side of the building. The surrounding streets were quiet again, no evidence of anyone watching their location. Though she hadn't been aware of the woman watching for them all day. Another failure on her part. Usually her instincts were better than that, enough to leave her edgy and aware if she'd been spotted.

Again, her only excuse was her reactions to Althir. She shouldn't have taken this mission. The council should have sent someone else. She was making mistakes. Dangerous ones. And if she couldn't trust her instincts going forward, how could she keep them both from getting caught?

With a deep breath, she refocused on her job, or tried to. She needed to get back to doing what she was good at—watching, listening, collecting information. And staying well enough hidden that Althir never had to do again what he'd done earlier. He'd saved their lives. But at what cost? If he tried that at the wrong time, left himself that vulnerable, they were both dead.

Then were would her people be? The war would drag on. They would have lost their best chance at ending it. And they would have lost their best source of information about the Sorcerers.

No, she had to make sure he stayed alive. For her people.

Yes, she assured herself. She wanted Althir alive for the sake of her people. No other reason. No other reason at all.

Once full dark descended and Mina was comfortable they could sneak out of the tavern, she went to wake Althir. He hadn't moved the entire time he slept, still sitting up, leaning against the mattress with his head back. He'd remained so motionless, she'd felt for a pulse once when checking on him. It was there, steady and even. His breathing was slow and deep, and his face muscles were relaxed. She couldn't imagine he was all that comfortable, especially since the wooden floor wasn't exactly warm or padded, but she couldn't see discomfort in his body.

The room was dark now, with only a faint glow of light from the windows of a nearby building. There were no gas lamps lighting the alley on this side of the tavern, but enough ambient light filtered in to give her a view of his profile.

The ethereal smoothness of his skin, the sharp, beautiful lines of his face, reminded her of that day she'd spoken with him in his cell, before they'd set out. He was still more beautiful than any man had a right to be. Yet somewhere in the last few days, she'd stopped resenting him for that.

She was sure, somewhere deep down, she still hated him. But watching him sleep, pushed to exhaustion protecting them from discovery, she couldn't feel the hate anymore. She wasn't sure *what* she felt. Confusion still mixed with anger. Along with that nagging sense that there was more to Althir than anyone knew.

Or was she fooling herself? Falling victim to his beauty and charm?

She set the worries aside. How she felt about Althir didn't matter right now. Getting the List and getting back out of enemy territory alive was all that mattered.

She knelt beside him and placed a hand on his shoulder, already running through the myriad questions she had for him. His eyes popped open suddenly, looking right into hers, startling her into a small gasp. As he stared, she stared back, and everything she'd had in her head, every thought and question, just wasn't there anymore. She couldn't even marshal enough awareness to realize she'd stopped thinking. For several long moments, the only thing in the entire world she was aware of was Althir.

He blinked slowly, leaned forward and pressed his lips to hers, the move so unexpected she simply sat there. Then she closed her eyes.

His kiss was gentle, not asking permission but not demanding either. He kissed her as if they had kissed many times, with his lips a soft caress against hers that sent sharp, heady awareness through her blood, warming low in her stomach. When she noticed the silky glide of desire moving through her, she also realized she was returning his kiss, her mouth moving with his in a slow dance.

His hands came up to cup her face, and he angled his head just a little to better fuse their mouths but still without pushing for anything deeper. Her heartbeat tripped against her rib cage as his scent wrapped around her in the darkness, a warm, rich blanket against the chill in the air. Everything about Althir was warm and rich. His taste, the feel of his bare palms against her cheeks, the firm press of his mouth.

The very brief flick of his tongue against her lower lip startled a gasp from her, not because she was surprised but because the sensation sent a shock of need roaring through her. She heard his faint groan, felt his fingers flex gently against her cheeks, and she opened her mouth to him, taking the kiss further than he'd gone, tangling her tongue with his as she tasted him fully.

She leaned in closer, wanting more, wanting something deeper. And suddenly she was sprawled across his lap, her arms wrapped around his neck, his around her waist. The feel of his erection growing against her hip should have brought her back to the real world, back to their location, the danger. It didn't. It only drove her growing passion closer to frenzy.

Desperation seeped into her body, tingling over her nerves as she pressed even closer, flattening her breasts against his chest. This time his groan was more audible, filling her mouth and vibrating through his chest. The sensation hardened her nipples against the rough material of her shirt. She dragged one of his hands from her waist and settled his palm over her breast, needing the feel of him, almost mindless with a desperation she'd never felt before.

It was like being drunk, out of control. She was so wrapped up in his scent, his heat, the feel and taste of him, she couldn't conceive of anything else in the world existing. He squeezed her breast, his touch rougher now, then found her nipple through her clothing and pinched hard enough to make her moan.

"That feels so good," she panted against him as he tortured her with only his hand and fingers on her breast.

"You feel so good. Perfect."

But the position wasn't perfect, she thought. One of her swords was in the way. She scooted around until she was straddling him, her knees bumping against either side of his hips, her scabbards out of the way. The position pushed his erection tight against her core, adding to the torment and the pleasure. She ground down against him and his fingers pinched her nipple in response.

"Yes," she murmured, then fused her mouth to his again, on fire with a desire unlike anything she recognized in herself.

She hadn't had a man in more months than she could remember. Hadn't wanted sex or intimacy at all for a long time now. Yet she couldn't seem to control herself with Althir, couldn't conceive of walking away from this passion. She pumped her hips against his cock, swallowing his growls, thrilling in the hard grasp of his hands. He cupped her ass roughly and pulled her as tight against him as was physically possible.

And she wanted more. She wanted his mouth on her breasts, sucking her nipples; she wanted his cock inside her, fucking her hard and fast. She wanted to take and take until he had nothing left to give her. And then she wanted to take more.

She didn't even recognize herself like this, this wanton so desperate for a man to fuck her. She'd never felt like this, never wanted someone else with such mindless desperation. That thought managed to creep in past the flood of sensation to sound a slight alarm, a warning she knew she should heed. She didn't. She refused to listen, to let anything get between her and taking what she wanted from Althir.

But when he suddenly pulled back, when he rolled her off him and stood so quickly she barely saw the movement, that faint sense of warning held her still, crouched on the floor, even though every other ounce of her wanted to go to him.

He faced her, breathing hard, his fists clenching and unclenching at his sides. She held his gaze, marveling at the dark heat glittering amidst the gray. She was panting too, which rubbed her nipples against the material binding her breasts, heightening an awareness she was struggling to control.

"What was that?" she murmured. The longer they stood apart, the more certain she was that more than just mutual lust had built that inferno so quickly and suddenly.

"Elf-fire," he said, his voice harsh.

Mina's hands shook as she used the mattress to lever herself up onto the bed. Elf-fire. The pheromone elves gave off when they were in the throes of sexual passion. It was supposed to be addictive to humans. She'd been with an elf once, before the war, but she'd never experienced anything like what had just happened with Althir. She'd assumed the tales of elf-fire were exaggerated. Now she understood why so many Sinnale also called the pheromone elf-tears.

She wanted to ask how this was possible, what it had done to her? Would she experience the addiction now, the withdrawals? And how the hell had she not realized what was going on? If he hadn't moved away, she would have fucked him on the cold floor without any thought to consequences. Then she would have moved him to the bed and fucked him again.

She could still feel the tingling of desperation against her skin, the sharp awareness that made remaining separate from him an act of will. Despite knowing this was nothing more than a chemical reaction, she wanted his hands on her naked skin and his thick cock buried deep inside her.

The thought brought her gaze to his still very erect cock, and without meaning to, she licked her lips. His growl brought her gaze back to his face. He took a single step toward her. She sucked in a breath, only a small part of her *not* wanting him to join her on the bed.

"We need more distance between us," he said and left the room.

His absence was so abrupt she sat stunned for a long while. When she could manage to think even a little, she concentrated on bringing her breathing and body back under control, focusing on slowing her pulse.

She was still a little shaky when he finally returned. He didn't come fully into the room, instead standing stiffly in the doorway, holding himself tall and motionless.

She pulled in a last deep breath. "How did that happen? Why did it happen?"

"I want you. It's what happens when my people want someone."

"Well, stop it."

He snorted without amusement. "I have absolutely no control over the *Shaerta*, the elf-fire. Or the way I want you."

She tried not to react to his statement, but a punch of desire still clenched her gut. She forced it down. "You mean that… That happens every time you're even remotely attracted to someone?" So why didn't she experience it before with the other elf?

"No."

Okay. Then… "Why with me?"

"It happens when we want someone a lot, more than a passing fancy for a quick lay. We can't control it, and we can't fake it."

The trembling started in her body again. She fisted her hands in her lap. "Make it go away."

"Too late now. I'm not going to stop wanting you after that." He gestured to the spot on the floor where they'd both lost control, where his weapons still lay forgotten, framing the place they'd been.

"If we fuck, will it go away after?" She could hardly believe she'd said that out loud, but she needed to know. Needed to find out if she was stuck this way or could work this out of her system. She didn't want to feel this desperation. She certainly didn't want to *want* Althir with such intensity it overrode all other concerns.

He stared back at her, and she saw his jaw clench as he considered her question.

"With you? Probably not."

She swallowed and tried for another calming breath—which didn't work. "Why did you stop?" she asked the other question she needed answered. "I couldn't have." The admission cost her, but at the moment, she needed truth between them. On this, at least.

"That's why I stopped."

She frowned. "I don't understand."

"Which is the other reason I stopped."

He finally entered the room and stalked toward the bed. He snatched his bow, quiver and sword off the floor then straightened and stared down at her for a long moment.

His nearness started her heartbeat pounding again. It took an act of will not to lick her lips and lean toward him, to keep her gaze on his face and not let it drop to see if he was still erect. The moment stretched until her nerves felt raw. Finally, he returned to the doorway, his movements stiff.

"Come on," he said over his shoulder. "We need to move before the minion patrols return."

CHAPTER EIGHT

hy did you stop? Her question echoed through him as they slinked through the streets, making their way slowly toward their next stopping point. He kept asking himself the same thing. Why had he stopped? He wanted her. He'd had every intention of seducing her in the near future.

When he woke to see her face so close to his, kissing her seemed the only possible thing to do. And what a kiss. It had turned his need from a hungry ache to full-blown madness. He'd controlled the madness right up until she opened herself to him, let him inside.

Then the madness—and the *Shaerta*—took over.

He had to taste more, feel more, *have* more. She was his to have, eager, as caught up in the fire as he'd been.

So why in the name of the goddess had he stopped?

The rise of the *Shaerta* had surprised him as much as it did her. He hadn't felt the effects of the pheromone in…longer than he cared to admit. For a long time now, sex had been little more than exercise to him, something to work off needs or a way to get what he wanted from someone. He barely had a thought for the person he was with most of the time.

Mina was different. He wanted her more than he wanted air and food. He wanted *her*, not just the physical act of sex. So much so, he could still feel the tingling of heat over his nerves.

So why stop? Why deny himself something he'd been missing for centuries?

She paused at the side of a building to study the street, and he leaned against the wall a foot behind her. Still too close. The need continued to ride him. But it was the best he could do.

He stared at the nape of her neck, where it was exposed by the now-tight knot of her bun. The soft skin called out to him, demanding to be tasted, touched. He lifted a hand toward her, then made a fist and dropped his arm back to his side. He realized as he did he'd lost his gloves somewhere along the way, but it was a small irritation compared to the compulsion to reach toward Mina again and loosen that tight bun, run his fingers through her silky hair, tug her head back so he could taste her lips…

Closing his eyes and cursing himself, he forced the image away. Now was not the time to lose himself in thoughts of her.

Would this be easier if they'd fucked? She'd almost broken him asking that same question. He felt the already thin threads of his control snapping until only the barest of sense kept him from tossing her back onto the bed and doing exactly what they both wanted.

And again he had to ask himself, why? Why did he *not* take her while he could?

He stared at the wall across from him, knowing he'd told her the truth. Even fucking her then and there wouldn't have been enough to dampen the elf-fire. In fact, it might well have heightened the reaction since he hadn't experienced it in so long. But now that the elf-fire had risen, he knew he would only have two, maybe three times with her before he risked her sanity. And more.

The pheromone was so addictive to humans most elves restricted their sexual activity with human partners to a single night. He knew for sure now that once would not satisfy his need for her.

He didn't want to waste one of those precious nights in a frantic coupling that would have to be silent and fast. He wanted to take his time with her, explore her, bring them both all the pleasure he knew was available to them. He wanted to savor every moment and wallow in the intensity.

Rolling his head against the wall, he stared at the back of her head again. But that wasn't the only reason he'd stopped. It wasn't even the real reason, though now that he could think, he acknowledged that not wanting to waste any of their time together was important to him.

The real reason he'd stopped was the very reason he'd given her. She hadn't understood what was happening between them, hadn't been aware of the elf-fire or its effect on her. She didn't understand. And he didn't want her that way. When he finally took her, he wanted her aware and eager to be with him—not because some pheromone was driving her, but because she needed him as desperately as he needed her. He wanted her to admit to the need, not have an excuse to dismiss it.

He *needed* her to be fully aware of their attraction and take him willingly.

Why, he couldn't say. He'd never cared before, with any other human woman. Or elf for that matter. Sex was sex. He'd never considered the underlying feelings of his partners. Nor they his. It had never mattered before.

But Mina's opinion of him, her feelings for him, mattered. And for the life of him, he did not understand *why*.

She motioned over her shoulder without looking at him, and

they moved out again, hurrying across a brightly lit street into another dark alley.

The closer they got to the area surrounding the public Citadel, the slower their progress. Regular movements of both patrols and servants along the streets at one point made it impossible to move for nearly an hour. Finally, Mina took them through the back door of a small building and up a set of narrow stairs to the roof. From the cover of the small retaining wall, they watched the street below.

The night was waning, sending most of the servants back to their homes, but the minion patrols continued to march through the area. After studying the scene for several long moments, Mina finally spoke.

"We're close to our final goal. We can stick to the roofs from here. But we need to wait for the predawn lull in patrols."

He nodded, turning back to stare at the city rather than risk looking into her eyes too long. The *Shaerta* still stirred just beneath the surface, despite the more pressing rush of adrenaline and readiness. He couldn't afford to let his attraction to her rise now, when they weren't safe.

Over the tops of the surrounding buildings, he could just see the gold-and-red dome at the center of the Sorcerers' Citadel. They'd occupied one of the most beautiful buildings in the city. Before the invasion, it had served as a university. Soft gray stone from the Arei-atun mountain range made for a smooth façade behind the marble pillars, arches and statues that decorated every niche of the building. It was even built in an unconventional shape—a series of interconnecting towers, the center one topped with the huge golden-red dome. Before the occupation, gardens had softened the landscaping around the building, and many Sinnale used the area during good weather.

After the Sorcerers claimed the University for their own, they'd allowed most of the grass and greenery to die. Only one small, isolated, walled-in area was kept rich and verdant—the Sorcerers' garden of herbs. All the deadly little plants they needed for different spells and torture methods.

None of the traitor elves had found the need to spend time in that garden. Althir had risked seeing it once and never returned. It felt…wrong. A wrongness that went past his conscious mind to grind at the very center of his instincts.

Remembering that garden helped him focus. He hadn't really thought they'd get this far without getting caught. Now, the reality of what they had to do sank in. This wasn't like before. He couldn't bluff his way through the day and intimidate when he couldn't charm. The Sorcerers had placed a bounty on his head, and he couldn't just talk his way out of capture if they found him.

He'd accepted this could well be a one-way journey for him before moving on to the next plane. He hadn't expected to feel so fiercely protective of his companion's life, though. The last thing he wanted was to watch Mina fall into Sorcerer hands.

Somehow, things had gotten worse without changing much at all.

He was so focused on the dome of the Citadel and his own musings, he nearly missed the next patrol that passed beneath them. Mina's very faint inhalation caught his attention and he glanced down. Three of the traitor elves marched at the center of the patrol, their heads bowed together.

Althir tried to catch some of their conversation but the distance, the sound of marching boots and their quiet tones kept him from overhearing anything. He held his breath as they passed, waiting for one of them to look up, to realize he was here. Liroc wasn't among the three but that didn't mean the others hadn't acquired similar skills.

The elves only paused once, though, to face each other as their conversation grew more intense, their gestures animated. The minion at the head of the patrol stopped and looked back at them. One of the elves noticed and they all resumed walking. By the time they'd disappeared around a corner, the elves had their heads together again, deep in conversation.

"Wonder what they were talking about," Mina murmured.

"Couldn't hear, unfortunately. Whatever it was, it was serious. More is wrong than we suspected."

"Of course things are wrong. We're winning the war now. They're being driven back by inches and feet every time we face them. The traitors must be wishing they'd defected with you."

His snort was almost silent. "Not likely. Though you have a point, the war has turned and that has to have them worried. But that looked like something else."

"Could you really hear at that distance?"

"If they'd been speaking above a whisper, probably."

"Handy," she murmured. "Good trait for a spy."

Ah, little did she know, he thought. Glancing at her from the corner of his eye, he watched her lips purse as she considered his hearing.

"You have to get closer to overhear information?" he asked.

"Much."

She didn't seem bothered by the risk that involved. He, on the other hand, suddenly found himself angry that she'd placed herself in such danger.

"But there are other ways of collecting information. If you weren't with me, I'd be better able to blend in and function closer to the ground."

"I'm holding you back?" He was both incredulous and amused by her assertion. Especially since he'd saved her life twice now.

"This is a different kind of mission," she said without reacting to his tone. "I'm here to steal something, not gather information. There's no need for me to work as I might normally."

Her calm, even explanation made him frown. She was right. Why was he annoyed? Because the woman annoyed him, he decided and refused to think about it more than that. He didn't want to know *why* he felt as he did when it came to Mina.

"I have a lot of questions for you," she whispered after a few quiet moments and another patrol passed, moving away from the Citadel.

"About?" If she brought up the *Shaerta* again, he was going to have a hard time concentrating. But he didn't discourage her, which confirmed his assessment of himself—he was an idiot.

She didn't speak for another few moments. Then, "The woman who alerted them to our presence. She recognized you."

"There are only so many elves working with the Sorcerers. And I stand out among them."

As he'd hoped, she smiled slightly at his arrogant quip. But she grew serious again instantly. "There's a bounty on your head."

"Also not unexpected."

"True. But you being so recognizable… Why did that minion at the weapons storage building lower his sword when you stared at him, the first one who opened the door?"

He'd almost forgotten about that. "Many of the minions aren't as…fast thinking as the servants. He didn't have time to recognize me as a specific elf, only that I was an elf and they are to defer to us."

"Still? Even after you left?"

He shrugged. "Likely, since he lowered his weapon."

"So that was…intimidation and bluffing. Not magic."

"That wasn't magic, no. You'd be surprised how far you can take bluffing, though."

She dipped her head sideways in acknowledgment. "In the tavern, though, you used actual magic to hide us from the search."

"Yes."

"Is that… What magic can you do? You were going to tell me days ago and never did. Will all of it leave you so…exhausted?"

"You haven't guessed yet? That 'charm' of mine? It's a type of magic. My greatest skill, actually. And so ingrained it doesn't drain me."

"You don't control it?"

"Oh, no, I control it. It's just very natural for me and doesn't require excessive energy. The camouflage, on the other hand…"

"Yes, I saw what that demanded from you. Is that a separate magic?"

"It's actually an extension of the charm, just pushed to an extreme."

"You can work glamour? Like the spells used to keep the List fortress disguised?"

"Not as well as some of my compatriots. That's yet another unique talent. Not something every elf can do. But two of the traitors have some considerable skill in working glamours."

"So…charm is your magic. Your only skill?"

"Not my only skill, by far." He dropped his voice to a teasing seduction and watched her cheeks flush in the dim lights. "But it is my particular magic."

"What other…extremes can you take it to?"

He shrugged. "The furthest is the camouflage. The skill helps me recognize lies and deception in others as well. I'm not easily fooled."

She faced him fully, her brow furrowed. "Then how could you have trusted the Sorcerers? You must have known from the beginning they didn't intend to share power with any of the elves."

He hissed out a curse, too late realizing he was giving too much of himself away to Mina. "That was something different," he hedged. He did not want to discuss the humiliation that was his time as a "traitor".

Her shoulders straightened. "They managed to fool you, is that it? Is that why the subject makes you so angry? They lied to your face and you believed them."

He clenched his jaw to keep from snapping out an answer that wouldn't help either of them.

"That's it, isn't it? They got around your most valuable talent."

"No," he ground out. "And this topic is no longer up for discussion. Next question."

She raised her brows, a gesture he caught from the corner of his eye as he watched the city. Then she shrugged and moved on.

"The woman who recognized you, do you think they killed her?"

"Couldn't tell. Probably just knocked her unconscious to stop her hysterics. They'd leave the choice of killing her up to their mistress."

"Will the Sorcerer kill her?"

"No idea. Depends on if she believes the woman's story or not. And how much power she thinks she'll get from the woman." He shrugged. "Does it matter?"

"Probably not. I just…wondered."

"Anything else? Or can we make our way to our destination now?"

The movement of troops was slower, and he could feel the dawn approaching, just the other side of the horizon. They still had an hour or so before light would start to filter through the streets, but he didn't want to get caught out in the daylight. And he had enough of answering her questions for the moment.

Her brows rose again, and a very faint lift of her lips could have been the beginnings of a smile. He scowled, but her expression remained the same. With a nod toward one side of the building, she moved out, keeping low so they couldn't be easily seen from the street. He hefted the sword he was carrying—easier to use if it was still in hand rather than tucked into his belt—and followed her.

CHAPTER NINE

ina left Althir in the bedroom of the small apartment that was their current hideout and took up vigil in the sitting room. From here, she could see the minion patrols come and go from two of their barracks and monitor movement in and out of the Citadel. Althir had pointed out the direction to the List fortress. She hoped a day, two at the most, of observation would give them a sufficient idea of current troop movements and show her an opening to get them safely past the patrols to their ultimate goal.

To her surprise, Althir hadn't argued with her when she ordered him to remain in the bedroom while she took up watch in a different room. She'd expected him to follow her, pester her as he'd done every day since setting out. Instead, he'd settled in near a window without comment.

She must have hit a very delicate wound when pointing out that the Sorcerers had fooled him. Given the way he'd been tormenting her, on so many levels, she was surprisingly pleased with getting some of her own back. And his distance seemed to keep the elf-fire from rising, which was much more of a relief than she would admit to out loud.

The effects of the pheromone were terrifying. She'd felt completely out of control, out of her mind with desire, too caught up in lust to recognize the dangers. The last thing they needed now, this close to the Citadel, was to fall victim to that compulsion again.

She needed her wits, her sense, her instincts under her own control or they would never survive.

The day's vigil kept her occupied and her thoughts focused on something other than Althir—for which she was grateful. He remained in the bedroom, making so little noise she frequently forgot he was there. Or at least tried to.

The movements of the patrols were well organized and consistent throughout the day. If they remained this way tomorrow, she could work out a way to slip past the Citadel and reach their real destination tomorrow night.

With her attention on the filtering of servants into and out of the Citadel's main entrance, she took her hair out of its tight bun and let the mass fall lose over her shoulders. She'd had her hair so tightly contained for so many days in a row, her scalp was getting sore—a sensation she was used to after the years of working as a spy but one she still didn't much like. She scrubbed her fingers over her head and left her hair down for a bit.

If she were smart, she'd cut it short, like so many of the other women had done. But she'd discovered having longer hair gave her more flexibility when she hid in plain sight as a servant or a newly brought-over slave. Her looks in general were just generic enough to allow her to blend in without necessarily calling attention. That had served her well in her job.

New movements from the barracks caught her attention, and she stood, flattening closer to the wall beside the window to better see what was going on. The sun had dropped low, covering the area in shadows, though they were still a few hours from full dark.

To her surprise, five Sorcerers marched out of the Citadel behind an armed contingent of minion soldiers. A few broke off from that group and headed toward the barracks, marshaling the full complement of soldiers within. Soon the entire courtyard outside the Citadel was crowded with fighters, their weapons catching the last glints of sunlight.

Without thought, she rolled her hair back up into a bun and studied the movements. She'd only seen this happen once or twice before. Every time, it had been preparation for an assault. Were they launching an attack on Sinnale territory?

A runner charged through the crowd, carrying a message to one of the five Sorcerers overlooking the army. After reading the note, he crumbled the paper and started shouting and pointing. The minions began a steady, mostly organized march away from the Citadel.

Mina turned to get Althir, but he was already standing in the doorway staring at her. She ignored the unreadable look in his gaze and motioned him close.

"The entire army is pulling out, heading toward the border. One Sorcerer just got a message that started the actual movements." She murmured her observations to him.

"A battle."

"Yes, but who's starting it? Is this a defensive movement? Or are they attacking my people?"

"Does it matter?"

His question made her scowl up at him. "Of course it matters. If they're attacking, my people are in danger."

"There's nothing you can do about that now except to complete your mission." His logic didn't make her feel any better.

"And if your people have started the attack, they've given us a much-needed opening," he finished. "Either way, we have an opportunity here."

She faced the Citadel again. Four of the five Sorcerers followed the army, climbing into a carriage that had been brought around for them while she'd been speaking with Althir. The fifth Sorcerer turned back into the fortress where two others stood just inside the door.

"Do you know what the ones remaining behind will do?" she asked.

"Likely, they'll involve themselves in the fight from here."

"Meaning?"

"They can cast their essences outside of their bodies and watch the movements of the battle without actually being in danger."

"Why don't they all do that?"

"Those that went with the army, their skills are more heavily weighted to fighting and destruction. The three that went back into the Citadel are better at the soul-casting."

"And the rest?" The number of actual Sorcerers had never been something her people could pinpoint. Their movements were too covert, their ability to disguise themselves too good. It was only when Althir started feeding them information that they learned only twenty-five Sorcerers had invaded the city and created such destruction. Of those, twenty-one still lived. In more than two years of war, only four Sorcerers had ever been killed.

"The rest will either join those at the Citadel or join the battle—if it's big enough," Althir answered. "At least one or two will remain in their own strongholds and aid the battle from there."

"So...given the size of the complement that just marched, I would assume this is no little skirmish."

"Not likely."

"And if it's large enough, every Sorcerer will be occupied with it."

"Yes."

"You're right. We have an opportunity. Especially if the fighting lasts most of the night." She considered their options. "We should move out soon, even before the sun sets."

"We'll be spotted too easily. The servants are still about."

She acknowledged his point with a vague grunt as she watched people continue to move around the area—though in much fewer numbers.

"Will the elves join the fight?" She realized that outside of the two she'd spotted earlier entering and then leaving the Citadel, she hadn't seen any of the other traitors.

"They'll be ordered to, yes," Althir said.

He leaned in close enough at her back to get a different view of the street, and suddenly she was too aware of his presence, his heat. *Not now, Mina!* She had no time to think about Althir, not when they had to alter their plan.

"Do we risk running into them if we leave before sunset?" she asked to keep her mind on the issue at hand.

"Only if they're sent back to the Citadel for some reason. They all have their own accommodations in parts of the city overlooked by at least one or two Sorcerers. They'll have been ordered directly from there into the battle."

"How long do we wait?"

Adrenaline flooded her system. She didn't want to delay. But he was right. There were still too many people in the area. Slipping past them without the cover of darkness would be impossible—especially with an elf in tow.

She still itched to move out now, though.

Even after recovering the vessel with the List in it, they still had to get all the way back to Sinnale territory. The distraction of even a large battle probably wouldn't give them enough time for that, which meant their return trip would be even more difficult than this infiltration had been—especially if the Sorcerers realized too quickly that the List had been stolen.

When Althir didn't answer, she glanced over her shoulder. He was staring out the window, but his gaze was distant, as if he wasn't actually seeing anything.

He blinked and looked down at her. "The sun will be down shortly. We can slip around easier once it sets, even before full darkness. If we give the appearance of heading someplace but don't show our faces to any of the servants, they'll likely let us pass without taking notice. Battle breeds chaos. And servants aren't soldiers."

"But that woman today, she recognized you and we didn't even know she'd spotted us. Someone else is likely to recognize you too."

"They won't try to stop us on their own. With everyone occupied in the fighting, it will take a servant time to draw his master's or mistress's attention to the presence of an elf who shouldn't be here."

"You're counting on the mayhem to help disguise us."

He smiled, very slightly. "Oh, it will. That's the nature of battle."

She wasn't so sure of his plan, mostly because he was too recognizable. If that woman hadn't spotted him last night, Mina might be happier with his strategy. In fact, if he wasn't with her, she'd make herself appear a servant and do exactly what he was proposing to reach the List fortress. No one would take notice of a servant on an errand at a time like this.

But with a wanted elf in her wake…

"We'll stick to the shadows as much as we can," she decided. "Only using your more brazen method if we have no choice. I'd prefer to alert as few people as possible to the direction we're heading."

"Fine. But be prepared to look like a new minion."

She nodded. She'd played that role before—new because the stink of rotting meat took time to build, the yellowish skin and red glint over the irises requiring continued exposure to Sorcerer magic. She couldn't pretend at either the smell or the eye color and her face was still too fresh and alive. No one would believe she'd been under a Sorcerer's control for longer than a day or two.

New minion was better than servant in this case too because she could move about armed. A servant wouldn't carry weapons.

"I need to ask…" Althir started, then trailed off.

She waited him out, afraid he'd bring up the elf-fire and she couldn't discuss that now.

"Your swords, do you understand their providence?" he finally asked.

The question surprised her, especially since she'd just been thinking about them.

"Meaning?"

"You know they're elven?"

"Yes." She debated telling him more but couldn't see any immediate harm if she was vague. "Passed down from mother to daughter in my family for generations."

"Old. Old is good. Remember that."

She scowled at him before facing the city again. "What the hell are you talking about?"

"Old elf magic is strong. Old elf weapons are very strong. Stronger than even the weapons your people use now." He nodded to one of the swords on her hip. "Those are…particularly fine instruments that can cut through a lot of magic."

That caught her attention enough to face him. "Really? How do you know?"

He gave her a look, as if her question was self-evident. "I can sense the magic. And my profession for the last two centuries has been weapons trade with Sinnale. I know swords." He ran a finger down the scabbard. "Those blades were made by one of our greatest smiths, many, many centuries ago."

When she frowned her question, he shrugged.

"I spotted his signature when you loaned me one. There aren't many of these blades left in existence. A true treasure."

He jerked his hand away and faced the window. She waited for more but he remained silent.

She bunched her brow in consternation. Why had he told her that? She'd valued the weapons before this because they were one of the few things she had remaining of her family. But now he'd made them something even more, something she'd be devastated to lose. She couldn't afford to worry about such things, not if she wanted to live. She had to be willing to sacrifice even these heirlooms.

Damn him, he just kept complicating her life.

CHAPTER TEN

he hour they spent in the window, waiting for the sun to set, watching the Citadel, dragged on. But they did see two runners enter the Citadel and confirmed that none of the elves were being called in this direction.

As twilight darkened the streets, in those moments before the gas lamps brightened, they left their observation post and headed out.

To Mina's surprise, they managed the journey with very little difficulty. The fighting had everyone left in the area distracted, and with no minion patrols forcing them to hide frequently in alleys and doorways, she and Althir covered the five blocks to the List fortress quickly.

The building was exactly as he'd described—ordinary, even dilapidated. Nothing that would draw attention or make a passerby look twice. A perfect example of hiding in plain sight, she thought as they edged around to a side door.

"The front is spelled," Althir murmured near her ear. "It's not the real entrance."

She nodded, relying completely on him to get them inside now. Having to put her trust in him during this part of their mission was less daunting than she'd expected it to be. When she had time to consider that, she'd probably be terrified of what she'd opened herself up to. But for now, she followed his lead, trusting him to get them inside and back out again.

He took several long moments outside the door, studying it. There was no visible lock, but that didn't mean the door was open, or that an alarm wouldn't be triggered.

Finally, he gently turned the knob and let the door fall inward. Then he waited another moment or two before going inside.

"Was that very easy," she whispered, "or have we just started a countdown before someone comes to check a breach?"

"We've started the countdown," he murmured back. "Couldn't be helped."

Great, she thought, but kept her mouth shut. The less noise they made now, the better.

He didn't hesitate in the path he took through the building. Inside, everything was much cleaner and richer. The hallway Althir led her down was decorated with thick carpets, rich paintings hung on the walls, and the walls were half wood paneling, half silk paper. Bright gas lamps lit the corridors, reflecting off mirrors interspersed with the paintings.

Mina hadn't seen anything this well maintained since the war started. But then, she'd never been into the Citadel. She'd heard from other spies that the public building was kept at the height of luxury. And from the outside, it was obvious each of the Sorcerers kept luxurious accommodations. Most other buildings, even the places important to servants or housing minions, had been allowed to lose any glory they might have claimed.

Noman's Land was worse—everything dirty and worn. Sinnale territory was kept...as best as they could keep it, under the pressures of the occupation. But nothing was maintained to this standard.

A faint scent of some sweet-smelling incense permeated the air, something she couldn't completely identify, but there seemed to be hints of cinnamon and clove within the larger smell. It reminded her of her family's bakery in the weeks before the Winter Festival, and her chest tightened.

To offset the sudden pierce of pain, she returned to studying their surroundings. No guards hovered in the hall or stood sentry outside any of the few doors they passed. She couldn't hear much noise either. The thick carpets muffling their footsteps. She reached out to touch a doorknob, to test if the room was locked, but Althir stopped her with a hand on hers and a sharp shake of his head.

She frowned but dropped her arm. Questions could wait until they were back on the streets, or, better, when they were somewhere safe and hidden again. If she couldn't risk opening any of the doors, though...

They were too exposed in the corridor. She unsheathed one of her swords, knowing if they came across any guards now, they'd have to fight. There was nowhere to hide without going into a room.

But to her surprise, no guards came running to stop them. Althir paused often, listening. Then continued straight, never veering into another hallway or room. They reached a spot she roughly calculated to be the rear corner of the building farthest from their entry point. And Althir finally opened a door.

From behind it, two large men stepped out with their swords at the ready. Mina took a single step back, raising her weapon and preparing to fight. These were no minions, she realized, staring at their very serious expressions. They attacked Althir without a word or shout, and Althir met the attack in the same way. Outside of the clash of metal on metal, none of them even uttered a grunt.

The lack of noise was so unique and unexpected, she didn't

react immediately, a lapse that meant she was almost caught when one of the two men broke from his launch at Althir to come at her.

She skittered back from his first swing and found her footing before he could attack again. He was agile for a man so large, and his reach, and sword, were significantly longer than hers. She focused first on avoiding his attacks, ducking and backing up, using her smaller size to keep her distance while she waited for an opening. She'd noticed large men underestimated smaller women in fights, and she had no trouble taking advantage of that when he finally lunged forward, attempting to spear her, and opened himself up to her counterattack.

She slid inside his guard and drove her sword into his vulnerable side, then disengaged and leapt away. The wound slowed him. But it wasn't a killing shot.

Her fight with the single guard moved her so that her back was to the door Althir had opened. She heard the sound of clashing metal, more than should have sounded with only two combatants, but she couldn't risk taking her eyes off her opponent to check on Althir.

The hair on her neck rose, a warning that she needed to move. Without taking time to analyze the impulse, she dove toward the man she'd been fighting, swinging her sword wildly until she got past him. He'd responded to her sudden lunge and answered her attack, but awkwardly because of his wound. When Mina whirled to face him again, this time looking back at the door, she saw the knife sticking out of the wall close to where she'd just been. It quivered at a level even with her throat.

She swallowed, hard, and met the next attack. Her own grunts under the weight of deflecting the man's sword were still the only sounds of effort coming from any of the now many guards in the cramped corridor. Her own attacker didn't give her time or an opening to see how Althir was doing, but it only took a brief glance to see there were a lot more guards surrounding him.

A second guard approached her fight, and Mina's adrenaline and fear ratcheted up. She'd barely been holding her own against one. Two would overwhelm her quickly.

This wasn't like fighting minions. These men were trained, efficient and very good. She'd learned to fight out of necessity. Because of her particular skill set as a spy, though, she wasn't actually called on to fight often. She wasn't up to the level of these guards. Which meant she was in serious trouble.

Her entire focus shifted to just keeping them as far away from her as she could. She drew her second sword and used both to deflect each attack. The men fought well together, not getting in each other's way, and she started to take hits. A cut on her forearm, a slice through her biceps, the tip of a sword piercing her thigh when she didn't move fast enough. She could feel the blood dripping, feel her strength waning.

From the very brief moments when she looked toward Althir, she couldn't even see him for all the guards.

So desperate to keep from being skewered, she didn't have time to be afraid, to recognize death so near. Part of her acknowledged this was probably her last fight. But too much of her brain was focused on the swords swinging relentlessly at her to worry about that.

Conscious thoughts dropped away and she shifted to instinct and motion, moving, lunging, striking when she could, sucking up the pain when she wasn't fast enough.

Her muscles trembled, her weapons felt too heavy to hold and her reactions slowed. The little cuts and slices started to come more frequently. They were playing with her. She recognized that. They were too good, and she should have been dead already. But she took the small blessing and kept fighting. If they wanted to play, she'd see it through until she could no longer lift her swords.

As that moment approached, another fleeting glance toward Althir made her frown. There seemed to be fewer guards now. She could actually see the elf. She risked a closer look and realized he was silently slicing through men, working his way toward her own attackers.

He was magnificent, his speed and skill unlike anything she'd ever seen in battle. The fighters before him were well trained and yet they fell one by one, none of them rising in his wake.

Her second look at him, the time it took her to appreciate his skill, cost her. She stared a split second too long. A sword whipped toward her neck. She acted on instinct, falling back to avoid the cut, but she wasn't prepared and ended up falling onto her back, one sword flying from her hand to hit the corridor wall. She didn't even have time to scramble back and had to raise her remaining weapon in a hurry to stop a downswing.

She looked into the dispassionate gaze of the guard as he pressed down with his superior strength, forcing both his and her sword toward her throat. She gripped the tip of her own in a vain attempt to hold him off, ignoring the sharp edge cutting into her hand.

The pressure eased as the guard pulled his sword up just a bit. She watched his next strike coming, knew she couldn't hold him off this time.

And then blood splattered across her face.

CHAPTER ELEVEN

Mina gasped, unable to control the reaction, and rubbed a sleeve over her eyes. The guard who had been on the verge of killing her was pushed sideways into the wall, his throat sliced open, revealing things Mina preferred not to see.

In the next breath, Althir stood over her, his hand out to help her up.

She blinked and took his offered aid. He pulled her to her feet with ease. Panting, she rubbed her shirtsleeve across her face again, smearing the blood. Althir wasn't even breathing hard. She looked down the hall and saw no less than twelve dead men laid out. Her eyes widened as she looked back into Althir's face. His gaze was dark and intense as he looked down at her, his mouth set in a line.

She motioned toward all the dead guards. "You did that alone?"

"Ulric isn't the only warrior in the family," he said, his voice deep.

She shivered.

His gaze moved over her. "How much of that blood is yours?"

"Enough. But it's all superficial. They were playing with me up to that last part."

He grunted and took a step toward her, taking her chin in a gentle hold that belied the intensity of his expression. He moved her face from side to side, then glanced lower.

With a touch far softer than she expected, he rubbed some of the blood from her cheek. "Come. We don't have a lot of time."

She nodded and when he turned back toward the door, she followed, retrieving her dropped sword along the way.

"More are coming?" she asked as they stepped around the bodies.

"Probably not too many more in the building," he murmured. "Those aren't regular troops. If you didn't notice."

She huffed out a rude noise.

"They're the List Guardian's soldiers. But the Sorcerers only allow her to have so many. A larger contingent and the Guardian might start to consider herself something of a power."

Mina put a hand on his arm before they started through the open doorway. "How many more of her soldiers can we expect? And the Guardian herself? How are we going to get through her and her magic?"

He nodded to a body on the floor just inside the door, one she hadn't been able to see until now. A woman in a simple brown robe was sprawled at the edge of a stairwell, a thin red line across her neck. Mina blinked.

"What...?" She looked up at Althir as something like panic started to filter into her blood. This couldn't be good.

"She was dead when the soldiers came through the door," he said. "I didn't spot her at first but saw the body as more soldiers attacked."

"They killed their mistress?"

"No. They'd probably just found her body too."

"Then…what happened?"

"I've no idea. They didn't think we killed her, though, or they wouldn't have 'played' with you. They would have tried to kill us quickly. Or they would have tried to kill *you* quickly. They were trying to take me alive. No doubt to question."

The edge of panic started to get sharper. "One of the Sorcerers?"

"If so, they figured out a way around the Guardian's magic. That shouldn't be possible."

"This isn't good, Althir. What are we walking into?"

"A trap," he said with a shrug. "But if you want the List, this is the way we have to go." He gestured to the stairs that led down into a basement.

"Do you have a plan?" She stared at the dark stairwell, her muscles still trembling from the fight. Panic was a living thing crawling through her stomach now.

Althir didn't ease her growing worry with his answer. "Hard to plan when I don't know exactly what's happened. I'll figure it out as I go."

"Oh, that's going to work out well."

He flashed her a surprisingly sexy smile, one of his real smiles, the ones that stole her breath.

"It'll be fun," he said. "Come on."

Keeping her swords in hand, she stayed close to Althir's back as they started down the stairs. She took a final look at the List Guardian on the way past, but the body gave no clue what they could expect in that basement. As they descended, Mina checked behind them regularly, waiting for more soldiers who never came.

The deeper they moved, the darker the surroundings, until the light from above was no longer sufficient for her to see by. She overstepped on one of the stairs and would have fallen, but Althir turned with amazing speed and caught her arm. When she got her feet under her, he released her. He'd managed to grab her right on one of her many cuts, but since a little sting from the cut was nothing to a broken neck, she bit her tongue on her hiss of discomfort.

She must still have flinched, though, because he leaned close enough to whisper, "Are you okay? I didn't hurt you?"

"It's nothing. Keep going."

He paused half a beat longer, but she gestured him forward, and he turned back toward the slow descent. She did sheath one sword though and put her hand on his back to keep from falling again. He must have been able to see better than her because he continued without any hesitation.

Then a faint light appeared from below, not enough for her to see by, but enough to guide her in a specific direction. She kept her hand on Althir's back, however, and didn't think too hard about why the physical contact made her feel better.

When they reached the bottom of the stairs, the faint light turned out to be a small gas lamp that illuminated a small vestibule. A single, closed door was the only way to continue forward.

She leaned against Althir's back and murmured, "More soldiers?"

He shrugged and studied the door. Then before she could gasp, he opened it. This time, no attack came.

Scowling, she released her breath. "You have to stop doing that," she muttered so low she wasn't sure he'd hear.

He must have, though, because he smirked over his shoulder before moving through the door. She followed slowly, raising her sword just in case.

There was more light through the doorway, but not so much as to temporarily blind her. Where she'd expected more gas lamps, the light actually came from small braziers lit with flickering flame. The scent of incense was stronger now, almost cloyingly sweet. She wrinkled her nose and had to pinch it a couple of times to keep herself from sneezing.

When she looked around, she realized the basement was huge, a lot larger than she would have expected given the size of the building above. Gold inlaid wooden pillars lined the outside of the circular space. The floor was covered in dark green and gold marble, the golden streaks catching the firelight and glittering. At the very center of the room was a simple black pillar. Atop the pillar sat what looked to be a very ordinary ceramic vase topped with a copper lid.

The List, she thought, realizing only in that moment the full significance of what they'd come for. Her heartbeat hammered as she started toward the pillar.

Althir stopped her with a gesture. "Let me. There might be magical traps."

"That you can avoid?" She raised her brows.

"No. But they'll hurt me less."

"Althir…"

He didn't give her time to argue before closing the space to the vessel. Since he still held his sword, he reached toward the ceramic vase with his free hand. She hissed, flinching in anticipation of something nasty happening.

Just as his fingertips touched the copper lid, Mina felt something move behind her.

She started to swing around but was stopped short by a knife at her throat. Then a sweetly feminine voice said, "Step away, Althir."

CHAPTER TWELVE

Mina held her breath as Althir turned slowly to face the new threat. He was smiling, that smug smirk that set Mina's teeth on edge.

"Talliah. Good to see you again." His voice was smooth, his tone light and pleasant.

"Oh, I'm sure it is," the woman behind Mina said with a chuckle. "So eager to see me you went out of your way to find me."

"Well, I would have. But I've been busy."

"So I see."

From the corner of her eye, Mina saw movement. She expected more of the List Guardian's soldiers. Instead, two of the traitor elves stepped from behind two of the support pillars, closer to Althir. She recognized one. He was the first elf they saw after entering enemy territory, the one who'd seemed to sense Althir inside their first hiding spot. He was tall, slimmer than Althir, with pale blond hair, blue eyes and skin a beautiful light brown that only highlighted the lightness of his hair.

"I am less happy to see you, Liroc," Althir said with a sardonic twist to his lips. "Though not entirely surprised." He glanced at the other elf, a tall, red-haired man, with features so perfectly angled he looked unreal. "And Vernil." Quieter, he said, "Not tainted… So. You killed the Guardian, then?"

Vernil didn't respond.

Althir glanced at Talliah. "And you're here for the List. But why? Why now?"

"Preemptive strike," Talliah answered easily.

"At least one of the others is making a play for the List?" Althir asked. "Interesting. Unexpected."

"Oh, given the direction of the war, not so unexpected."

"Is that why you're trusting two elves with the knowledge? Do they know what needs to be done to open the vessel?"

"They know the rewards they'll receive for helping me," she said, her voice silky and seductive.

Althir's eyes narrowed just a little. "They don't know, do they?" But he spoke so softly it was more a comment to himself rather than a question he expected to be answered.

"Drop your sword, Althir," Liroc said in an even voice, his lips lifted at the corners just a bit in a very slight smile. His relaxed body language and raised brow gave off a sense of satisfaction with the situation, but there was a gleam of anticipation in his narrowed eyes.

The other elf looked on without any expression at all.

Althir held up his sword and studied it a moment, lips pursed. Then he tossed it away. "Poorly made weapon anyway," he said. "Nothing like what we'd get back home, eh, Vernil?"

Vernil blinked once, his only response.

Liroc said, "The blade is still sharp."

"But ugly. I hate ugly things."

Something that Mina couldn't interpret passed between the two elves as they stared at one another.

"Enough," the woman behind Mina said. "We'll have plenty of time for questions and insults once Althir is on my altar."

Mina tried not to react but knowing for certain one of the Sorcerers stood behind her sent a jolt of terror up her spine. Her breathing sped despite her best efforts and her hands trembled. She was still holding one sword—the Sorcerer hadn't bothered to disarm her or make her drop the weapon, but Mina had to firm her grip to keep from dropping it on her own.

Althir crossed his arms over his chest and considered the woman behind Mina, his head tilted slightly. "I have better uses than your altar, Talliah."

"True," the woman purred. "And believe me when I say I intend to take advantage of all your uses, dear Althir. But first, a question."

"Ask away."

"You're here acting on behalf of the Sinnale. As soon as I learned you were in our territory again, I knew you'd be after something significant. And based on what Jacine told me when I put her on my altar, after discovering she'd revealed too much to you, I suspected you were here for the List. But why? Why do the Sinnale want it? None of them practice magic. It's of no use to them."

He shrugged. "No idea."

Mina realized Jacine must have been the servant who told Althir about the List, and the Sorcerer had tortured and killed the woman for that slip. The thought made Mina's stomach roll, but Althir showed no reaction to the news at all. Did he even care that he'd cost someone her life like that?

"Come now," Talliah said. "You risked falling into our hands for nothing?"

"Oh, I'm sure they have some use for it. Maybe to hand over to my former sovereigns. I don't really care."

"They offered you more than we could?"

"Of course not. But they offered me what I wanted."

"Which was?"

His gaze flicked to Mina before he looked back at the woman over her shoulder.

"The opportunity to leave this cursed city and be done with this nonsense."

The woman's knife moved ever so slightly against Mina's neck and Mina closed her eyes, a quick blink to control her reaction to the threat.

"Really?" the Sorcerer asked. "You just wanted to go away?"

Althir lifted a brow. "What else would I want, given my options?"

The Sorcerer leaned around far enough to look at the side of Mina's face. Mina didn't glance directly at her but did try to get a look at her from the corner of her eye. She got a glimpse of dark hair, white skin, and full, pink lips.

"And what about her?" the woman said.

"What about her?" from Althir.

"Was she part of the offer from the Sinnale?"

"Not outright. But…" He trailed off and lifted his hands, palms up.

"She's delicious. Have you had her?"

"Not yet."

"What were you waiting for?"

"She calls to my *Shaerta*. I'll get two, maybe three, rounds with her. Look at that body. I'm going to need half a night just to thoroughly satisfy my taste for her tits. I was waiting for a moment when I had enough time to indulge."

"Then what?"

"After I fuck her a few times, she's useless to me."

"So you don't care if she dies now?"

"It would be a waste. But there are other women to fuck."

"Too true," the Sorcerer purred again and straightened away from her inspection of Mina's face.

Mina pressed her lips together, trying not to show any physical reaction to what Althir was saying, but his easy dismissal of her was hard to hear. He sounded like he meant every word. His indifference was so natural it could hardly be feigned.

Had he been pretending at the tenderness she'd seen in him upstairs? Had she fooled herself into thinking he was more than the rude, arrogant traitor she'd thought him before this mission?

He didn't react at all when the knife at her throat shifted so that the sharp edge pressed more firmly against her skin. No gesture, not even a blink to indicate he might care if she died.

"I wish we could keep her," the Sorcerer said, her tone actually regretful. "I wouldn't mind indulging in these beautiful tits of hers either."

Mina jumped when the woman squeezed her breast, but she kept her gaze focused forward, watching everything Althir did. Still no reaction, only a slight head tilt and a disinterested stare.

"But I'm afraid needs must," the woman sighed.

The knife at Mina's throat dug deep enough to draw blood. She held still as all the fear and anger, the sense of betrayal and failure all drained away under the sure knowledge that she was about to die, to finally join her family. There were worse ways to go. And a sliced throat was quicker than a Sorcerer's altar, or being turned minion.

She stared at Althir as she waited to die, a part of her acknowledging how much she hated him in that moment for his betrayal. But even her anger over that couldn't permeate the numbness settling over her.

Because she was watching him, she caught his gaze when he looked directly at her, then ever so slightly nodded down toward her sword. She blinked.

"Are you sure you want to waste killing her here?" he said, his gaze moving back up to the Sorcerer. "Lot of hate in her, for some reason. She'd make a fabulous sacrifice."

"Offering her up to me now?" The woman's voice rose in amusement. "Why, Althir. I didn't know you cared." A very brief pause and then she murmured, "But who precisely do you care about?"

"Oh that's easy. I care about me and only me. You know that."

The woman laughed, a light, happy sound. "My dear, dear Althir. I have never doubted, not once, that your main interest was always you."

He smiled, a sexy lifting of lips that made Mina frown again. Because the knife about to take her life shifted, moving away from her throat this time until the flat side of the blade rested against her chest, just below her collarbone.

Althir's gaze lowered a little, almost coyly, but Mina saw the way he focused in on her sword. Her frown deepened. Her short sword would hardly kill a Sorcerer. They had protections.

True, the swords were elf made, and elf weapons were able to get around a lot of the Sorcerers' spells. But this close, surely the woman behind her had protected herself even from an elf sword.

Then Mina remembered Althir specifically telling her this weapon could cut through a lot of magics. Did he mean something like this? And could she believe him now? She pressed her lips together in a tight line.

If she was going to die anyway, she wanted to go down fighting, not as a blood sacrifice on this woman's altar, and not as an easy, motionless victim. She didn't even bother to tighten her grip. She simply sighed and swiveled around in a tight arc to the Sorcerer's side, plunging her sword through the soft flesh just beneath the woman's ribs.

Talliah's eyes widened at the surprise attack. She glanced at the sword, looked up at Mina with a glare that held the power to kill, and raised her own knife. Mina dragged her weapon sideways, cutting across the woman's abdomen as she ducked under the swing of the knife, working on instinct more than thought. The blade still sliced across her shoulder, but it didn't do any more damage than the numerous cuts Mina had already accumulated.

She continued to drag her sword through the Sorcerer's belly, only pulling free and jumping away from her when she sensed the knife dropping toward her again.

The Sorcerer stumbled a step, the momentum of her lunge with the knife throwing her off balance. She looked down at the gaping wound in her stomach, then up at Mina.

"Shouldn't have been possible," she choked, and blood bubbled out of her mouth. "But my name… Can't use it now."

She lurched toward Mina again, the knife still clutched in her fist, but the wound slowed her and Mina danced away. The Sorcerer fell face first onto the hard marble. Blood spread from her wound in a wide circle that soaked the woman's body and seeped across the floor.

For reasons beyond logic, Mina did not want that blood to touch her. She walked backward, watching it spread and keeping her distance.

She was as surprised as the woman had looked. She'd actually killed a Sorcerer. Shock made her forget for too long that other enemies were still in the room. When thoughts of the other elves startled her back to the present, she spun to face them.

Only to see both sprawled across the marble, Liroc with two arrows sticking out of his chest, Vernil with a single arrow through his throat. Her mouth dropped open as she faced Althir, and her eyes widened when she spotted the bow in his hand.

"But…elves can't kill other elves. Everyone knows that. It's why the Sinnale were asked to kill the traitors, why your king and queen started trading weapons with us again. How…?"

Althir dropped the bow over his head, once again angling it across his back. "Taboo is not the same thing as impossible," he said in a flat voice. "That fact was emphasized to me when my own brother held a knife to my throat."

After everything that had just happened, Mina wasn't sure she could take any more shocks. She wasn't even sure how to process this latest bit of information.

She stared at nothing and shook her head, too stunned to think.

Althir snatched the List vessel off its pedestal while she tried to recover enough to function. "We need to get out of here," he said, gesturing to the Sorcerer's body on the floor. "That made a lot of magical noise. Everyone with even an ounce of magical ability within a hundred-mile radius just felt that."

Her adrenaline jumped again, pushing her to movement finally. She ran back toward the stairs with Althir at her side. Every nerve stood at alert, waiting for the next attack, but none came. They left the List fortress in a rush without encountering any more soldiers or guards. But when Althir would have turned back in the direction of the border, she grabbed his arm.

"This way." She dragged him a few feet, then started to run.

"This is moving farther into Sorcerer territory," he muttered, not even sounding winded.

"I know."

"Which means we're moving farther away from where we have to go."

"I know."

"Why then?"

"Because they will look for us in the other direction first."

The streets were virtually deserted as night had moved on and the battle must still be engaged. Mina was counting on the distraction of that battle to give them just a little time to reach a safe place.

A place she hadn't entered since the war began.

"I hope you know where you're going," Althir grunted.

"I know exactly where I am," she assured. They plunged down the backstreets and dark alleys, covering the short ten blocks that took her home.

CHAPTER THIRTEEN

alking into her former home, Mina's heart ached for all the losses. She hadn't been here since just after the war started, when the initial invasion swept over this part of the city, pushing the populous west if they wanted to survive.

She took Althir in through the back entrance, directly into the bakery kitchen. Her family had owned two shops, a bakery and a chocolatier—the results of a good marriage between her grandmother, whose family were bakers, and grandfather, the offspring of chocolate experts. Each shop had its own kitchen and the family had occupied the two floors of rooms above the shops.

She'd spent most of her time learning how to make chocolates, so that kitchen held the most memories. The bakery was a little less painful, but even less painful was still overwhelming.

The deliciously rich scents that used to fill this building had long since drifted off, though a very faint hint of vanilla and cinnamon hung in the air underneath the aroma of disuse. She tried to keep the tears welling in her eyes from falling as she studied the area.

Dust covered everything. No footprints on the floors. No one had trampled through the place in a while. That was good.

If they were lucky, some of the belongings her family had to leave behind were still upstairs. She pulled absently at her bloody, torn tunic. The way she looked now, she'd never be able to pass as anything but…

As the idea occurred to her, some of the pain of being here eased, giving her something else to concentrate on—doing what she was so good at doing for the war, collecting information.

But first she had to get Althir settled.

"Help me check the second floor," she murmured. "If it's clear, we should be safe here for a while."

He didn't comment, just followed silently. When they were sure the building was secure and hadn't been occupied in some time, Mina showed him to a spare room—not her parents' or her brother's. The idea of Althir in her brother's room made her throat close.

"There might be some spare clothing in that wardrobe. Take what you need. The water in the pumps should be good too, but be careful."

"You're hurt." He nodded to the various patches of blood covering her tunic. "You need bandaging. Your shoulder is still bleeding where Talliah struck you."

She tried to see the wound but gave up when the effort proved futile. All she could see was more blood. "None of it is going to kill me. I'll see if I can find some bandages."

"I'll take care of it. Sit. You need to rest after the blood loss."

"I'm fine, Althir. Just… Just…" She swallowed.

Being in her old home was proving a lot more difficult than she expected. The odd mixture of feeling safe and feeling empty here in this quiet monument to her once loving family had the tears leaking down her cheeks without her permission.

Althir's eyes widened. "Mina. Are you more seriously hurt than you're telling me? Where? What's wrong?"

She would have laughed at the panic in his voice if she had the strength. Wiping the tears off with dirty hands, she shook her head. "It's not the injuries. Don't worry. I'm fine. I'll be right back."

She hurried into the hallway so she didn't have to talk while memories and regret clogged her throat. Somehow, even having an elf here seemed wrong. And yet…

She remembered the way Althir had acted in the List chamber, his casual dismissal of her. He'd looked like he meant every word he said. She couldn't spot any sort of lying or deception in the way he spoke with the Sorcerer. The betrayal of it had cut deep.

But then he'd signaled her to use her sword. And he'd killed the other elves— something that should *not* have been possible. Proving once again that there was more to him than she knew, more maybe than she wanted to see. The elf casually discussing sex and blood magic in the List chamber was the Althir she expected, the man she thought he was before setting out on this mission with him.

She'd started to believe he was different. And she couldn't deny she wanted him to be because her feelings toward him had changed dramatically.

But which Althir was the *real* one? The one who would betray her so casually? Or the one who nearly panicked when she started to cry in front of him?

She had so many questions. She had to get her erratic emotions under control. Then she could talk over what had happened and what they needed to do to get back to friendly territory.

Stepping across the threshold into her former bedroom felt so natural and so odd all at once, she paused for a long time, just staring at the large bed and small desk by the window. A window she'd stared out, entertaining her naïve, innocent dreams for a future that would never be.

With a hard swallow, she went to the wardrobe in the corner. A few things remained, nothing of value—which would have been looted long ago—but a few well-worn garments had been left piled at the bottom of the wooden cabinet. She rifled through the dregs until she came up with a pair of trousers and tunic that would suit once they started back through the city. After a bit more digging, she found a dress that would fit her plan to get the information they needed to get back.

When she came up from the depths to toss the dress onto her bed, Althir stood in the doorway. She jumped a little, then cursed under her breath. "Damned silent elves," she muttered.

"I found bandages and got some water to clean those cuts," he said. "And all the blood."

Self-consciously she touched her cheek. She probably looked like an escaped sacrifice. "You don't have to do that. I can take care of it."

"You wouldn't be the first soldier whose wounds I've dressed. Sit." He nodded to the bed.

"Female soldiers?" She raised her brows.

She'd have to take off her tunic for the wounds to be properly treated. But she did need to get all the blood off and some of the deeper wounds bandaged. The many cuts suited her plan, but the Chemist wouldn't believe she hadn't been bandaged at all before being sent to him.

Still, stripping off any of her clothing in front of Althir seemed a bad idea. Especially now, when she wasn't entirely sure she could trust her instincts about him.

He put a fist over his heart. "On my best behavior. I promise. Even if the elf-fire rises."

She sucked in a breath at the reminder. "What you said in the List chamber…"

"Was necessary to distract Talliah. I was lying."

"Not about everything."

He stepped into the room and motioned her toward the bed again. "Did you think I'd betrayed you?"

"Yes," she admitted. "You sounded very…sincere."

"That's the hallmark of a superb liar. We make it sound like the truth. Now sit."

She finally gave in because she did need help with the slice on the back of her shoulder. Keeping her back to him, she pulled her tunic off and tossed it into a corner. It was useless now. She'd use it as fuel in the heater later. She still had the material wrapped around her breasts, an alternative to a corset. She couldn't function in the restrictive stays of a corset, but she couldn't do without some binding to keep her full breasts from becoming an interference.

Some of the women had been able to toss aside everything besides thin chemises as undergarments. Mina wasn't so lucky, as she was too well endowed to go without. But even with the bindings, she still felt naked. She'd thought she'd lost all her modesty two years ago. Apparently not. At least not in front of Althir.

She heard his audible inhalation and glanced over her shoulder in time to see him scowling at her back.

The look helped ease some of her self-consciousness. "As bad as all that?" she asked, tempted to be amused by his dismay. "Must look pretty horrible for a seasoned warrior to flinch."

He grunted something in his own language that she didn't catch then took up a spot behind her on the bed with the bandages and bowl of water he'd brought.

"I've seen worse," he muttered. "Or so I thought."

She raised a brow. "None of these cuts are that bad. Unless that one on my shoulder goes deeper than I thought."

"It's just a slice, and no bone is showing."

That was a relief. Still, his reaction puzzled her. "Why does it bother you, then?"

"It's deep enough it could get infected," he said.

Something in his tone sounded off, like he wasn't saying everything there was to be said. But she let it go. She didn't feel up to a word duel with him just yet.

The first tap of wet cloth against the cut made her hiss.

"Sorry. Can't be helped."

"I know," she assured. "Just stings."

She flinched a few more times as he worked, but otherwise remained still and silent. All the questions she had seemed to float just beyond her ability to grasp them. She was drained after the night, and she still had a lot to do before she could rest. The one good thing about the pain, it kept her mind off the gentle touch of Althir's hands on her bare skin. Or at least it mostly did. She was still very aware of how exposed her body was to him just then.

"That's the shoulder and arm done," he said, pulling her out of her daze. "The rest aren't deep enough to bandage. But you have a serious cut on your thigh. I need to bind that one too."

"I'll take care of that one," she said mildly.

"Don't trust me?"

There was a wicked, sexy edge to his tone that surprised her. He'd been very careful to remain serious up to that point. She shook her head and flashed him a half smile, which was all the answer she was prepared to give.

"The vessel?" she asked instead, bringing the subject back to their current situation.

"I've got it stored in the wardrobe of the room you showed me to, hidden under some discarded clothes."

She nodded. "Did you not find anything that would fit?" She gestured to the bloody clothes he still wore.

"I'll clean up now. I wanted to make sure we got the bleeding stopped on your shoulder first."

"Thank you."

He held her gaze for a long moment and she stared back. Finally, he said, "I didn't betray you."

"I realize that now. You killed elves."

"Is that the only reason you believe me?"

"It helps," she said with a slight shrug.

"So all the guards before that didn't give you a clue that I was on your side?"

She snorted. "They were trying to capture you and put you at the mercy of a Sorcerer. Of course you killed them. But the elves… I know you said it's taboo, but everyone knows elves can't kill other elves."

"We don't. Doesn't mean we can't. A point made very clear to me by Ulric not so long ago."

She frowned. "What does that mean? You said he put a knife to your neck?"

"Nothing." He tossed aside a cloth he'd been using to wipe blood from her wounds. The now pink rag landed with her discarded tunic. "Part of you still believes those lies I told." He spoke quietly, his gaze on the wooden floor.

She shook her head, but he cut her off with a raised hand.

"It's part of my charm, my magic. A double-edged sword. I can lie very convincingly. It's why I can't be lied to."

She frowned. "You've said that before. Yet, the Sorcerers lied to you. Made promises you later found out they never intended to keep—"

"I knew," he growled and slipped off the bed to pace across the room.

"What?"

"I knew. From the very beginning. From the moment Liroc

approached me to see if I would be open to the Sorcerers' offer. I knew everything was a lie."

"You knew?" She wasn't sure she believed that. "Then…why?"

He waved a hand in the air dismissively. "The rest of them bought the promises, the lies. The idiots never even suspected they were being used." He continued to stalk around the room. "So I played along."

"But *why*?"

"Because Ulric was right! Ulric is always right when it comes to strategy. The Sorcerers were going to invade Glengowyn as soon as they had enough power. So, yes, I went with the traitors, more's the fool me. I had some damned idiotic notion I could get the proof necessary to make the king and queen change their minds about neutrality. I thought I could hand them a neat little box of information, things only I could uncover thanks to my oh-so-charming personality."

"You were working as a *spy*?" That admission was too much to be believed.

He growled. "So deep undercover no one even suspected. Including my fucking brother, who just assumed I'd turned traitor. Bastard."

Mina felt her world tilt ever so slightly to the left. "You're trying to say you were never a traitor? You never lured any Sinnale across the border and into the hands of the Sorcerers?" Doubt laced her words, and she didn't attempt to hide it.

"I never lured anyone," he spat. "I managed a very cute game to avoid it while collecting all the information I could."

"But you didn't stop it." Anger bit hard into her again. "And many of my people were taken because of the traitors."

"If I'd stopped it, I would have given myself away. What information could I have collected then?"

"Information to help your people. Leaving mine to fend for

themselves." Her voice dropped to a lower register in her fury. How dare he try to justify his actions, to make them sound noble!

He stalked close and stood right in front of her, staring into her eyes. "If I'd gotten what I needed to, I would have brought the whole of Glengowyn might into the war. On *your* side of it. Those people lost to the traitors would have been lost anyway. But I wouldn't have just gotten the weapons trade going again. I would have been able to bring our warriors into the fight. Do you understand? The information I was collecting would have turned this war around."

"Then why didn't you go to your king and queen? Everyone knows you turned yourself over to Ulric to save your own life. If you'd done such a great job, why do you have to hide from your own people now? Why do they still think you're a traitor?"

She stood as she spoke, spitting and hissing with her growing anger, anger she couldn't seem to control while in this place. "And those *people* who were lost weren't just random casualties. They had families, people who loved them. People who still mourn!"

She stood toe to toe with him, but he didn't back down under her anger, and he didn't flinch.

"That's what war is," he said with quiet intensity. "Death and loss and devastation. And the reason I didn't turn to my king and queen…" He sucked in a breath and finally looked away. "I never did get the proof that would have convinced them the Sorcerers intended to invade Glengowyn. My word, my suspicions, even backed by Ulric's assertions, were never going to be enough. I needed something solid. And in all the information I managed to accumulate, none of it was *proof* enough for my sovereigns."

"Then why turn yourself in? Why not keep going until you got the proof?" She didn't back down from her anger because too much hurt mixed with it to let her go easily.

He cursed and stomped away from her so suddenly she blinked.

When he whirled to face her, she couldn't read the expression on his face.

"They found out… At least she did. The Sorcerer you killed tonight. She realized what I was doing. Smart bitch, that one. I still don't know how she figured it out. The only reason I'm still alive is because I got word of her discovery before she could send anyone for me. I had time to make alternative plans." He ground out the last two words like they tasted bad.

"Which were?"

"Take what I did have to the Sinnale council and hope it was enough for your people to end the damned war on their own."

She fell silent as she considered his answer. "You thought my people would be gullible enough to trust you?"

"Your people don't have to trust me to take the information I have and use it. And it's been damned valuable too, hasn't it?" he growled. "I have nearly brought this war to an end with what I did. With what we just did tonight, the war will end. If we can get that bloody List back to the council. Because of *me*." He thumped his chest. "And who does every-bloody-one still turn to? My fucking brother—who almost killed me!"

She straightened her shoulders. "Why would he do that? How could he do that?"

"Because as I said before, elves can kill other elves. We just don't. And the why is because he never trusted me, never listened to me, and always underestimated me. The why is because he's an arrogant ass who got every fucking thing he ever wanted."

"Jealousy? Sibling jealousy is behind all this?"

Althir spit out another curse and turned his back to her. "Of course you don't understand. You probably think the sun rises and sets out of Ulric's arse. What the hell do you know?"

"I know what it's like to lose a brother," she said before she realized she would.

The minute the words left her mouth, though, she regretted them. She pressed her lips together and glared at the floor. When Althir didn't immediately say anything, she turned back to the bed.

"You need to leave now. I have to finish cleaning up, bandage the cut on my leg and then get dressed."

"Why get dressed?"

"I can't go out practically naked," she drawled. "That would get entirely the wrong kind of attention."

He was behind her, swinging her to face him without making a sound. "What the hell do you mean 'go out'? Where the hell do you think you're going?"

"To do what I do best. Collect information. We'll need to know what's happening to get back to Sinnale territory."

His hands clenched on her shoulders. "And how do you propose to do that when you *look* like you've been in a fight and there's a dead Sorcerer not far from here? Do you have a death wish?"

At one point, not long after her brother…she'd wondered the same thing about herself. But right now, her mission was too important to risk throwing her life away before she was finished. "The cuts will work for me where I'm going. You've heard of the pain-pleasure servants, I presume."

He sucked in a breath and dropped his grip. "No. Absolutely not. It's too dangerous."

"I'm not going into one of the centers. I'm going to the Chemist. He provides…potions, things to help the injuries heal so a pain-pleasure servant can get back to work quicker."

Althir looked her over, his gaze lingering on her breasts for the first time since she'd stripped off her tunic. She'd nearly forgotten her state of undress. Having his attention shift down to her body brought back her self-consciousness, and she only kept herself from covering her breasts by an act of stubborn will.

Without lifting his gaze from her body, he said, "How will you get information from the Chemist?"

"A lot of information floats around his shop. They'll be discussing the battle—is it still going on, who has the advantage… And they'll know which Sorcerer died. I'll be able to find out what the people are saying about that death."

"You've seen him before? He'll know you?"

"No. I'll be new to the…job. But the cuts, none of them so deep as to be life threatening, will validate my claim. The fact that I know to go to him will also add to the authenticity. Only a pain-pleasure servant would be sent to him for the particular potions I'm going for."

He finally looked up and met her gaze. "You'll get something to heal your wounds?"

She shrugged. "A side benefit. I'm going for the information."

"But the potions…?"

"Will close up all the cuts. Even the shoulder cut, though that will take a little longer."

"How do you know all this?" His voice dropped to a low growl again.

"Because I'm a very good spy," she said. "I have collected a lot of very valuable information in my time." She only realized after she'd spoken that her words could be taken as an insult. He'd failed in his self-appointed mission, if his story was to be believed.

But if he took offense, he didn't show it. "I want to go with you."

"Impossible. No elf would be sent as an escort to a lowly servant. Even the highest ranking servants aren't given guards or escorts."

"I'll follow without being seen…"

"No," she said, putting her hand on his chest to emphasize her point. "You are to stay here and guard that List we've gone through so much trouble to get. If I don't come back before sunset, I've been taken and you'll have to get it to the council on your own."

She dropped her touch when she felt his heartbeat pick up and realized her own had sped too at the brief contact. She swallowed and forced herself to look into his eyes. "Or were you lying about wanting to end the war? You've said you're good at lying. Have you been to me about your motives?"

Althir snarled and ran a hand through his hair. "No. I have not been lying to you."

He stalked a few steps away, then turned back, stopping so close she could feel the heat of his body seeping into her skin.

"If you don't come back by sunset, I'm coming for you. You want to see this through? Make damned sure you get back here safe."

She blinked at his intensity and her mouth dried. Her emotions swung like a pendulum with Althir. One moment, she was so infuriated with him she could hit him, the next…her heart pounded with something other than anger. She inhaled the scent of him, felt the first tingles of reaction along her nerves.

"I have no intention of failing," she whispered because she could no longer pull in enough oxygen to raise her voice.

"Good. Because things between us are not yet settled. And I have every intention of seeing that through."

He left on those ominous words, closing the door very carefully behind him. She stared at the wall, taking in long, slow breaths and swallowing hard to try and rewet her throat. What had she gotten herself into with Althir?

And how would she get out without being damaged?

CHAPTER FOURTEEN

$\mathcal{A}$lthir stalked through the upper levels of the bakery and chocolatier the entire time Mina was away. Once cleaned and changed into clothes that were as close a fit as he could find, he'd searched the entire building. He wasn't sure what he was looking for, but he knew this place was different to her—not just another hiding spot. He suspected it was her family home, but she'd led him to another chocolatier before. He wanted to be sure.

She'd been gone for more than an hour when he discovered the pictograph painting of her when she was younger, at a stage when she was just starting to show the woman she'd grow into. She stood smiling with an older couple and young man nearly a head taller than her. The young man's eyes looked just like Mina's. He had an arm over her shoulder and a crooked smile that also reminded Althir of Mina.

The artwork wasn't done by a great master, but the brushstrokes were sufficient to bring the small family to life. And to show a depth of love and companionship he couldn't quite comprehend. He and Ulric had never been that close. When their parents died during the first goblin war, their relationship had grown even more distant.

Elves rarely had two children as close together as Althir was with Ulric. Usually elven siblings grew up as part of completely different generations. Althir always wished his parents had been smart enough to stick to that pattern. Growing up in Ulric's perfect shadow had been…a lifelong annoyance.

Althir stared at the picture, knowing he was looking at Mina's parents and brother. As he'd guessed, this had been her home before the war. Her earlier tears made sense. Returning home, seeing the remains and knowing what had been lost in the intervening years was never easy.

He returned the picture where he'd found it and continued to stalk through the building, too uneasy to rest. Being forced to wait, not being able to watch out for her, went against the grain. He wasn't sure when it had become so important to him that she remain safe, when he'd started to think it necessary to keep her alive. But he did.

Seeing all the cuts and injuries she'd taken in their fight to get to the List had only intensified that instinct. Letting her leave without him had been one of the hardest things he'd ever done. If not for her reminder that the List itself did need to be guarded, he would have followed her, despite her insistence he stay behind.

He'd lost several hundred years off his long life watching the Sorcerer's knife bite into her throat. Luckily the knife hadn't cut deep. He'd barely been able to keep up his casual façade, though, and for the first time in his life, he wasn't sure his charm—and his ability to lie—would hold out against the raging of emotion he had to contain and hide.

His emotional state hadn't been helped by the sight of all the cuts and bruises decorating her lush body. He'd wanted to break the Sorcerer in half with his bare hands after seeing the angry slice across Mina's shoulder. Yet, he'd seen worse. A lot worse. In previous wars as well as recently while pretending to be a traitor. None of Mina's injuries were as serious as he'd feared. There were just a lot of them, and even one was one too many.

He blamed his edginess for losing his temper with her, and for revealing his humiliation to her. He'd never intended to tell anyone —not the king and queen, certainly not his brother or cousin, and most definitely not Mina. The fact that he'd failed in his self-appointed quest and had to go to his fucking brother for help was probably the lowest moment of his life. Admitting his real purpose in joining with the traitors had never been an option. He'd rather be thought of as a traitor, even a coward, than face his people knowing he'd failed so spectacularly.

If he succeeded now, if they managed to get the List back to the Sinnale council and end the war, he'd at least be able to live with himself. Something of use would have come out of this disaster.

He glanced out a window, gauging the time of day. The afternoon was moving on. His restless movements picked up pace. He knew of the Chemist and had a rough idea where the man's shop was located. Mina should be back soon if nothing went wrong. His hands flexed and he fisted them to keep from snatching up his bow and quiver and heading out after her. She was right—the List needed to be watched. It was the one thing that could redeem him. And it would end the war, thanks to the arrows his cousin had so recently created. Glengowyn would never have to fight. Something his people would celebrate.

As he moved from the residential floors to the two shops on the first floor, careful to keep out of view from the streets, he wondered what Mina would do once the war was over. She claimed to have no family left—which meant those smiling parents and brother from the painting were dead—so would she come back here and try to restart the family business? Or would she move on to something else?

He found himself preoccupied with the thought, and for some reason he couldn't fathom, a little worried too. What if she decided to leave Sinnale? What if she stayed? And why did he care so much what she did after the war was over?

The one thing he hadn't been lying about with the Sorcerer was the effects of the *Shaerta* and the fact that, like it or not, after he seduced Mina, he'd only have a few nights with her before he risked her sanity. Given that fact, her future plans were irrelevant to him. Still…he wondered.

The thought that she might find a human mate and get married stopped his pacing. The very idea sent a flare of anger through him, hard and fast and strong.

But it shouldn't. Why would he be upset with her finding a life after all she'd lost? She deserved to have a family again. He shouldn't resent the metaphorical man who would make that happen for her.

He shook himself hard, a full-body jolt to pull him out of his own thoughts. Enough. He'd spent most of the day brooding and he was sick of his own head. Months in a cage had given him more than enough time to brood. Now he had to be ready to help Mina if she needed him.

He glanced at the ceiling, in vaguely the direction of the room where he'd hidden the vessel. There was also a List to free. He didn't dare try to do that here—it would leave him too weak from the blood loss—but he intended to be the one to open that vessel once they were back in Sinnale-held territory. Which meant he should study it while he could, make sure he knew what he was doing when the time came.

He started back up the hidden stairway at the back of the bakery when he heard the kitchen door open. Flattening himself against the wall, he listened intently to the sound of approaching footsteps. Light, with a gentle swish of material accompanying the movements. Not a minion patrol or Sorcerer guard. He waited until she moved around the corner, her head swiveling and searching as she walked, checking her surroundings, before he stepped away from the wall.

Mina sucked in a breath at his appearance and the move made her breasts pull tight against the low cut of her bodice. Against his will, the sight captured his full attention.

"Althir, you really have to learn to alert me to your presence with some sort of noise. One of these days, I'm going to stab you on accident," she groused.

"You're not armed, remember? You refused to carry anything."

"A pain-pleasure servant wouldn't carry a short sword. And don't count on me being unarmed to keep you safe if you continue surprising me."

Her tart mood eased some of his worry. She wouldn't be bantering with him if something had gone wrong. "Tell me what you found out."

"Upstairs."

He motioned her to precede him, mostly so he could admire her ass in a skirt. Though the dress covered more than trousers did, it highlighted her most delectable curves and femininity in an unexpected way. For some reason, the thought of stripping her out of that dress did more to fire his lust than peeling off her trousers and tunic had.

With a satisfied grunt, he noted she didn't appear to have accumulated any more injuries either. She even seemed to be moving easier, with less stiffness than earlier in the day.

Once upstairs, she went to the room where he'd stashed the vessel rather than the bedroom where he'd treated her wounds. He'd figured out that was her former bedroom and really couldn't blame her for not wanting to spend too much time there.

"So," he urged when she settled onto a comfortable but dusty chair near the ceramic heater in one corner of the room. He wasn't quite ready to sit yet so he moved close to the window and leaned against the wall, alternating between watching the street and looking at Mina.

"So. The battle is still active at the border. Seems it was a full-on Sinnale assault, and they've pushed farther into Sorcerer territory than during any previous assault."

"That's good news," he commented. "Wonder why, though. Why strike now and risk more lives when what we're bringing back will end things without so many deaths?"

She shrugged. "You can ask the council when we return. I did hear suggestions that an elf was involved on the Sinnale side of things, though."

His lips compressed. "Ulric." Of course. "What else did you hear?"

"Everyone knows a Sorcerer died. The servants are saying two of the traitor elves turned on her and they all killed each other in the ensuing fight."

He nodded. "Makes sense. Even if the other Sorcerers suspect what's really happened—and they'll know the List is gone by now —they won't want anyone else to know about the List so can't even hint at the true story. They probably started the rumors you're hearing."

"Likely," she agreed, shifting in her seat.

The movement caught his attention and he frowned. "Did you get the potion for your cuts? Do you need help administering it?"

She shook her head. "No, the Chemist actually helped with the worst cuts. They just sting a little, is all."

"Oh, *he* helped did he?"

She raised her brows at his tone. "It's one of the things he does for the pain-pleasure servants. Treats the wounds that are the worst. He did tell me the Sorcerer had pushed me too far for someone new to the task and I should be more careful."

Althir snorted at that. "Like the servants have a say."

"My thoughts exactly, though I kept that observation to myself. I was too busy playing humble pain whore to start an argument."

He took a closer look at her neck, but the angle of her head kept him from seeing the thin slice there. Crossing to her, he took her chin in his hand and lifted. She jerked away with a scowl, but he'd seen what he wanted to. The cut on her neck was nearly gone.

"I'll give him this, the Chemist does good work."

"Yes, he does. All the cuts will be healed within the next few hours. Even the worst of them will just be red scars."

"Good," he said emphatically. "What else did you learn?"

"There are whispers…worries among the servants. No one wanted to speak outright for fear of being overheard by the wrong person, but there was a lot of innuendo that the war had gone wrong and the Sorcerers weren't as strong as they used to be. The death of the one last night, at the hands of traitor elves, no less, seems to confirm for them that the occupation is in trouble."

Althir finally sat on the bed. "Seems your people are making an impact."

"Thanks to you."

Her comment surprised him so much he could only blink at her.

She shifted in her seat again and picked at the chair's armrest. "I…I wanted to apologize for…earlier. I was angry about… Well, anyway, I was tired and not thinking clearly enough, and I let my temper get the best of me. No matter what you'd intended when you joined with the traitors, your information since turning yourself over to the Sinnale has been invaluable. I shouldn't have disregarded that."

He narrowed his eyes as he studied her. "I've figured out this was your former home," he said quietly. "I imagine that didn't help your state of mind."

"No," she said with a harsh snort. "No, it didn't. How did you know?"

"There's a picture of you and your family in one of the rooms."

She pulled in a deep breath and held it before letting it out slowly, audibly.

"Why did you bring us here if being here is so hard on you?"

"Because it was familiar and I hoped it would be safe." She shrugged. "I didn't anticipate my reaction to coming back would be so...extreme."

"When were you last here?"

"We left during the first weeks of the invasion, and I haven't been back since."

"Your family was killed then?"

"No. Just my mother."

He watched her throat work as she swallowed. Every part of him wanted to go to her and pull her into his arms. Instead, he stayed where he was, afraid to break the truce they'd managed to strike.

She shrugged and looked out the window rather than at him. "My father..." Another deep breath. "Not long after the traitor elves joined the Sorcerers, my father was taken by one of them, lured across the border and into Sorcerers' hands."

Althir held himself very still as her words washed over him, realizing now why she harbored so much hate for the traitors—why she'd hated him so much at their first meeting.

"After he was taken, my brother decided he could rescue him, that the point of luring him using elven magic was to use him as a sacrifice—he was too old to make a good minion. Tom insisted there was time to get our father out. So long as he was still alive, there was time."

Her mouth trembled. "None of us took the loss of my mother well. Tom maybe worse than my father, though, because he'd been so close with her. I don't think he could tolerate the idea of losing our father too."

"So he went after your father. Alone?"

She nodded.

"He was taken too." Althir didn't have to ask. She'd already told him her family was dead.

"I didn't hear from either one of them for three weeks. And then I saw Tom again." Her breathing shook now, and a gleam of moisture filled her eyes. "He'd been turned into a minion. I watched him march right past me, while I was pretending to be a kitchen wench. He already had the first stink of rotten meat, the faint hint of red in his eyes."

"I'm sorry."

"That wasn't the worst moment." She scrubbed her eyes with her palms. "The worst moment was facing him in a skirmish. I was on my way back to Sinnale territory, in Noman's Land with a Sinnale patrol when the minion patrol found us and attacked. Tom was among them. He looked right at me, stared right into my eyes. And tried to stab his sword through my chest. I was so shocked I probably would have let him but one of the other soldiers intercepted his blade. I just stood there. Watching them fight, watching as my rescuer sliced my brother open, spilling his guts onto the cobbles."

Her entire body was trembling now, and Althir couldn't keep his distance any longer. He snatched her out of the chair before she could protest, returned to the bed and sat with her in his lap, holding her close and rocking her gently. He expected her to push him away. He had no right to presume he could comfort her. Instead, she clutched his shirt and curled against him, pressing her face into his chest.

"My last view of my brother was of his eyes clouding over. And then we were running for the border, most of the minions left dead. I never did see my father again. Something I'm actually very grateful for."

He pressed her close until he felt her deep sigh and her shivering subsided. Then he said into her hair, "You didn't have to tell me that. You didn't need to relive it for me."

"I'm reliving it just being here," she murmured. "And I owed you."

He pulled back enough to frown down at her. "Owe me for what?"

"After I left, after I had a chance to think more clearly, I realized what it meant…you telling me about what you'd been trying to do when you turned traitor. Or pretended to be a traitor."

His frown twisted.

"No one else knows what you were trying to do, do they?"

"I wish you didn't know either."

She snorted a soft laugh. "I thought you'd feel that way. You have no reason to. I promise I'll keep your secret as long as you want me to."

"That's not why I wish you didn't know."

She nodded. "You feel like you failed and don't want anyone to know about it."

With a sigh, he tucked her head under his chin again. "You are far too clever sometimes."

"I feel too worn out to be clever right now. Anyway, when you brought up my family, since you figured out this was our home, I figured I owed you a truth for a truth."

"The reason you hate the traitor elves so much."

"With a passion I can't even begin to describe."

"You don't have to. I understand."

"Having you here… Before hearing your story, having you here was almost as painful as being back."

"Because I was a traitor, one of the ones who destroyed what remained of your immediate family."

"I reacted from that anger earlier. When we first met."

He smiled at the memory. "Threatening to kill me." He felt her cringe, and his smile widened. "You weren't the first to tell me you wanted me dead, you know."

"I know. Still…"

"You believe me, then. That I wasn't really a traitor?"

She was silent for long enough that his frown returned.

Finally, she said, "I'm still having trouble trusting you, Althir. Even though you've proved I can several times now. My feelings for the traitors make it more difficult for me to allow myself to see the man I think you really are under all that arrogance and rude behavior."

He chuckled at that, accepting it as a just statement.

"But I wouldn't have told you about my brother if I truly thought you were a traitor. I believe you were trying to do good, even if your motives are suspect."

He raised his brows. "Suspect?"

"Sibling jealousy? Hardly a good reason to risk everything."

He rolled his eyes, glad she couldn't see his face. When she put it like that, it was even more humiliating than a simple failure. "You haven't had to live with Ulric for more centuries than I care to count."

"I don't know him very well, so I can't really judge that. But I do know you had a good underlying reason for your actions, to help your people. I can't blame you for that, or for the fact that you were thinking of your people before mine. It was unfair of me to expect you to care about us more than you do your own."

"Not unfair. I didn't think enough about your people. My intentions to end the war would have ended it for you as well as prevent my city from being invaded, but that wasn't my major concern."

"It's okay, Althir." She patted his chest. "We get that List back to my people, and the war will end. We'll get the result we all want."

"There's an arrow," he blurted. Then sighed. It really was better she didn't know this if she was captured. But he felt like she needed this truth now.

"An arrow? You mean the shrapnel arrows Glengowyn is trading with us now?"

"My cousin makes those. She's the only one who can. And she's recently invented another type."

He'd talked the details out of the council before agreeing to tell them about the List. They'd been so desperate to find out if there was a way to get the Sorcerers' real names, they'd answered his questions. He'd pushed them, played on their fears, and in that moment, they forgot he'd agreed to give them information in exchange for his life. They weren't required to give him answers. He wondered later if they regretted telling him the truth. Not that it mattered. He'd gotten what he wanted.

"Only a very, very small number of people know about them—"

"Wait." Mina stopped him. "You shouldn't tell me. Until we're safe inside Sinnale territory."

"If you prefer."

Her nod rubbed her face along his chest, and a frisson of desire warmed his blood.

"Just knowing you'd trust me enough to tell me is…nice?" she said. "Stupid word. You know what I mean."

He stroked a long line down her spine and back up again, savoring the feel of her in his arms. He felt the first stirrings of the

Shaerta and wanted to curse the damned pheromone. While it would make the sex between them phenomenal, it also reminded him that they had very little time together.

"I do know what you mean," he said. "And I do trust you, Mina. Probably more than I should."

"Now there's something we can agree on."

"That I shouldn't trust you?" he teased.

She laughed. "That too. But that I might also trust *you* a lot more than I should. We have that in common."

Her statement made his pulse kick over with emotions he didn't bother to analyze. She made him feel better in the midst of all that was wrong with the world. That was enough.

He slid his hand up her spine and stopped when he got close to her wounded shoulder. "How is this doing now?"

"Better. The sting stopped. The Chemist is some miracle worker."

"Are we safe here for the night? I want you to take more time to heal before we try for the border. And don't argue. We won't make it if you're dragged down by injury."

"I think we'll be safe enough. The fighting is keeping everyone occupied. Those that know the List has gone missing will probably be looking for the thieves to make for the border sooner rather than later. And to be honest, I'm not sure if the fighting will make for good cover to reenter Sinnale territory, or if we risk getting caught up in it and killed."

"We'll consider our options in the morning. Then we'll make a plan. Right now, you need to rest and heal."

"And you?"

He hugged her closer because he couldn't seem to help himself. "I'm doing what I need to do right now."

"Althir..."

Her voice was so quiet, if he didn't have elven hearing, he

wasn't sure he would have caught her whispered word, so full of question and trepidation.

"The elf-fire… That part of what you said to the Sorcerer was true. It… It means…"

"Yes. It means. And for now, I don't want to think about it." He stood, still cradling her and turned to lay her down on the bed. "You did good today, my little spy." Pushing her hair back from her face, he held her gaze. "It's my turn to take care of a few things."

She grabbed his hand. "What…?"

"I'm not going anywhere. Just to scrounge us up something to eat. Then you need to sleep." The circles under her eyes made his chest ache. "The outside world, all those decisions we have to make, can wait a few more hours."

She released his hand. "There's more to say."

"And we'll have time for that too." He'd make sure of it.

CHAPTER FIFTEEN

*M*ina woke to the soft feel of Althir's lips on her nape. She knew it was him without having to see him. Though she should probably protest, she didn't feel any need to do so. The effects of the elf-fire were already humming in her blood. Each feather-light touch of his mouth against her skin sent a cascade of chills and heat over her body.

He was lying behind her on the bed, the full length of him a seductive warmth along her spine.

"What time is it?" she murmured, then arched her back so her ass pressed into his groin. The feel of his erection made her moan quietly.

"You've only been asleep for a few hours, don't worry. It's still early in the night."

"Full dark?"

"Full dark. But we're not going anywhere tonight." He settled his palm low on her stomach, keeping her pressed against him to make his point.

She wasn't inclined to argue.

She'd changed from her dress to a tunic and trousers to sleep in and kept her hair tied in a bun—old habits in case she had to wake and move quickly into a fight, or run. But she hadn't bothered to belt the tunic so when Althir began to lift the material over her hips, there was nothing to get in his way. The heat of his palm on the bare skin of her stomach shot another wash of shivers through her, and she ground back against him harder. He nipped at the skin low on her nape in response.

When she would have rolled to face him, to touch in return, he kept her in place with that insistent hand on her abdomen. Again, she didn't argue because the feel of him along her spine, the hard length of his cock against her ass, all felt delicious. And right.

That surprised her. There was no awkwardness, no hesitation. Just a growing need to get rid of their clothes so she could feel all of his firm, muscled body against her naked flesh.

He settled his mouth at the side of her throat, nuzzling her tunic down so he had access to the curve between her shoulder and neck. Another gentle bite made her gasp. She couldn't keep her hands away from him then, so she slid her top arm behind her, rubbing her palm over his waist and hip, around to knead at the firm muscles of his ass. He was still fully dressed and the material was too thick to really feel him as she wanted, but the buck of his hips against her was some reward.

The hand on her stomach finally moved, inching upward in teasing strokes. Her skin felt charged from each caress, building anticipation, making her pant. No caress had ever felt like this, no man's touch had drawn such a sharp, overwhelming response. It was the elf-fire, she knew. She could feel it like a drug flowing through her blood, stealing away all thoughts beyond the feel of Althir.

The effects might have scared her, but she was ready for them this time. Even then, she hadn't realized that a simple caress would light her body on fire. Wetness seeped between her legs, and Althir hadn't done more than kiss her throat and caress her stomach.

Then his hand closed over her breast, palming the fullness, squeezing gently. Mina threw her head back and moaned. She had unbound her breasts, a single concession to more comfortable sleep, which gave him unfettered access to her naked skin. He pinched her nipple, drawing out her pleasure. She bit her lip and ground against him again, unable to control the response.

With her hand on his muscled backside, she had better purchase now, and she held him close, rubbing against his thick cock in a vain attempt to relieve some of the building pressure. He pinched her nipple tighter, almost convulsively.

She gasped his name, pushing and pulling to prevent any space between them, arching into his palm, demanding the increased movement and pressure as he squeezed and kneaded first one breast, then moved lower to the other.

"You are the sexiest woman I have ever had the pleasure of touching," he murmured against her neck, still pulling and sucking on her skin. "You have no idea how desperate you make me."

She rolled her hips against his cock and smiled. "I have some idea."

To her surprise, he suddenly flipped her onto her back and his mouth came down over hers, demanding and hard, the gentleness of his earlier seduction falling to need. She would have laughed, but she was too busy answering his demand, tangling her tongue with his, tasting him fully.

The change in position gave her more freedom to touch him, and she took full advantage, her hands rubbing up underneath his tunic to feel that hard stomach and chest. Then she slid one hand lower, rubbing the rigid length of him through his trousers, squeezing and teasing despite the barrier of soft leather.

He dragged his mouth from hers and moved lower, pushing her

tunic up high to fully expose her breasts. The passion in his stare sharpened her already humming need.

"Beautiful," he whispered. "Perfect."

When the heat of his lips closed over her, she thought her body might come apart. He pulled and suckled at her nipples, licking, nipping, dragging out the exquisite torture. So much pleasure filled her up, she wanted to burst. The tight growing tension at her core built to an extreme with each wet pull of his mouth on her breast.

Her hips pumped against him, as she squeezed his cock more firmly, resenting his trousers but too caught up in her own growing ache to do or say anything about them. His teeth scraped across her overly sensitive nipple, and she cried out, the sound surprising her in the otherwise quiet room.

Too much noise, a small part of her warned. She bit her lower lip to prevent another outburst, but she panted with the effort to hold back another echoing gasp of pleasure when he tugged none-too-gently at her nipple with his teeth.

"Clothes," she managed. She moved the hand on his cock to the top of his trousers and started pushing without much effect.

His grunt was part frustration, part amusement as he rose above her and stripped his tunic off over his head. Her mouth went dry at the sight of all those firm muscles, the thickness of his chest and arms. He hadn't lied about being a warrior. Each ripple of muscle beneath his pale skin was a reminder of all the contained strength of his deliciously masculine body.

She propped herself up on her elbows so she could press her mouth to his stomach, licking a wet line around his navel, tasting salt and sweat and Althir. He dropped a hand to the back of her head, his fingers digging roughly through her hair to hold her in place. She smiled against his stomach before continuing to kiss and lick his skin. His muscles were tight under her caress, his groan low and deep above her.

With one hand still braced behind her, she used the other to tug at his trousers again. "There's a lot more I'd like to suck here, Althir," she murmured and reveled in sound of his harsh curse.

He moved away so quickly she dropped back against the bed with a bounce and a giggle. His gaze fixed firmly on her breasts and darkened when she cupped herself, pinching her own nipples because she knew the move would push him further out of control.

"Strip," he ordered, his voice rough and quiet.

It never occurred to her not to follow that order. She sat up long enough to pull her tunic off over her head, then wiggled her trousers over her hips, tossing them alongside the bed to join her tunic. The worn material of her underwear came next.

Finally, fully exposed to his hot gaze, she thought she might feel some self-consciousness. But none surfaced. Instead, she felt lush and sexy, too consumed by her own desire to care about anything beyond Althir, dizzy with the effects of lust and elf-fire.

Althir's trousers joined her pile of clothing and then he was on the bed, stretching his body along the length of hers, his mouth closing over hers. She dropped her fingers to his cock without hesitation, wrapping him in a firm, insistent clench that made his body convulse.

He felt exactly as she'd expected, hot and hard, thick and silky in her palm. She rubbed her thumb over the tip of his erection, gathering the moisture there and using it to smooth over his skin as she stroked and played with him. His hips pumped against her hand, creating a rhythm and friction that echoed through her to her core. His hand found her breast again, hard and rough to match the pressure of his kiss, the demands of his mouth and tongue.

Mina's every nerve screamed with the raw intensity of having his skin rub against hers, the texture of his hard muscles, the light hair on his legs and chest scraping over her curves, across her thighs and stomach. The sensations were so much more than anything she'd felt before, overwhelming, beyond imagining.

Althir growled against her mouth and gripped her wrist to still her pumping fist.

"Too much too soon," he said.

"Not enough," she argued, and his growl turned to a chuckle.

He lifted away from her just enough to slide farther up her body. "Press your breasts together," he instructed and when she did, he slid the length of his cock between them, pumping between the soft mounds.

She'd never had a man fuck her breasts before, though many admired them. The sight, the feel was more erotic than she could have guessed. He braced one hand on the bed and the other against the wall above her head. When she glanced up, he was watching his cock slide between her breasts, his eyes dark, his jaw clenched. He glanced up, caught her gaze, and it was like touching lightning. She felt that look everywhere. So raw, so open and needy. The awe of his beauty in that moment stole her breath.

Could he see those same things in her expression?

She looked back to where he continued to stroke between her breasts. Her head was braced at just the right angle on a pillow, and he was just long enough, that when the tip of his cock slid between the top of her breasts she could reach him with a quick swipe of her tongue. His entire body shuddered, his hand fisted beside her on the pillow. When he surged forward again, she tasted the tip of him again.

"Goddess, Mina," he moaned. "You're going to kill me."

"I seem to recall promising that."

Her comeback earned her a gravelly chuckle before the sound dissolved into a moan when she licked him again. The brief tastes weren't enough for her, though. She wanted him in her mouth, as much as she could take. She released her breasts and slid down the bed far enough to wrap her lips around the head of his cock. She gripped the base and slid her mouth lower, humming in pleasure as his taste hit her tongue fully. The hand he'd kept clenched in the pillow moved to her hair, loosening her bun, holding her head as she sucked him in long, pulling strokes. His fingers tightened against her scalp, the sensation adding to her pleasure, the erotic control of having him at her mercy.

The sounds he made, the harsh breathing and grunts that filled the quiet room, the wet suck of her lips over his cock, sent Mina's own desperation over the edge. She squirmed beneath him, her body writhing out of her control against the mattress as she sought a way to relieve some of the building pressure. When she felt Althir's body stiffen, she thought she'd pushed him too far and he'd come in her mouth. The idea appealed to her so much, though, she sucked harder, keeping her hold on the base of his erection when he tried to pull away.

With gentle but firm insistence, he slid from her mouth and shifted lower. "A torture I hate to give up," he said, kissing her on the mouth before moving his lips lower, back to her breasts. "But I have oh so much more I want to do with you tonight. And coming too soon isn't one of those things."

She tried to pout, but the expression vanished beneath her gasp as he tongued her sensitive nipples. He moved too low for her to keep her hold on his cock, his lips pressing hot, wet kisses down the line of her stomach.

Then he looked into her eyes. "So you're prepared, though, the elf-fire means I can come and only need a short recovery time before getting hard again. I intend to take advantage of that fact tonight."

"Oh," she breathed, stunned by the erotic promise.

He turned back to her body, trailing more kisses down her abdomen until he licked the crease at the top of her thigh, then over her hipbone. She bucked against his mouth, unable to control her reaction.

"I'm not sure… I usually only… Oh…" Her thoughts scattered when his mouth brushed ever so gently against her wet heat. Then he licked into her and she arched off the bed, her teeth clenched against a scream. She was beyond sensitive now, riding that fine edge between pleasure and pain without dropping over to the pain. His kisses and licks were soft, gentle, teasing without pushing, and it drove her wild.

She couldn't remember once, in her entire life, feeling this out of control with a man, so aware of her body, each sensation sharp and bright. The soft moans and pants escaping her, each plea for more, for less, for everything barely sounded like her, her voice was so full of need and desperation.

Althir built the pressure threatening deep inside until she was so tight and ready she couldn't even move. And then his lips closed over her clitoris and he sucked just hard enough to break through the tension, sending her spiraling off into an orgasm that seemed to last forever. Her body convulsed with the release before she finally relaxed, limp and worn against the mattress, breathing so hard it felt like she'd run for miles.

She blinked into the dark room several times, clearing the spots dancing in front of her eyes. "That has never happened before," she gasped.

"A man's never made you come?" His breath brushed her heat, making her jerk in reaction.

"Not that." She smiled a little through her panting. "The length, the power… I've never had an orgasm like that before." She lifted her head enough to look down at him.

His eyes were dark gray pools of desire in the dimness.

"The elf-fire?"

He nodded and pressed his lips to her again, a closed-mouth kiss that nevertheless sent more aftershocks rippling through her body.

She dropped her head back to the pillow. "I see why it's addictive now."

The rumble of his laugh vibrated against her skin as he kissed her lower stomach and moved up the bed to lie next to her. She was still too spent to do more than savor his touch when his hand closed over her breast.

"You've never been with an elf before?" he asked before dipping his head to suckle her nipple.

"I was once, actually. Long time ago. Before the war."

He raised his head to stare at her, his eyes narrowed. "Oh. And who would that have been?"

She grinned. "I think maybe it's best you don't know his name, given the look on your face. Even though it was a long time ago. But needless to say, I don't remember things feeling like…this."

"Then he was doing something wrong."

"Maybe he didn't want me that much so his elf-fire didn't rise," she murmured. Althir pinched her nipple, rolling it gently between his fingers and she arched against the touch, surprised she could tolerate any more stimulation.

"It happens. We can have sex without the elf-fire. But how he could *not* want you enough for the fire to rise, I can't imagine."

He moved to her other breast, continuing a gentle torture that started the climb of desire deep inside her all over again. She'd felt so sated after that last orgasm, she hadn't realized it was possible to feel the build again. At least not so soon!

"You are the most stunning woman I've ever seen," Althir murmured. "With a body designed for loving. How anyone could resist you is beyond me."

She snorted. "I'm not even close to being stunning or I wouldn't be able to do my job."

"I'm stunned by you."

His gaze flicked up to hers, holding, the intensity stealing breath she'd only just recovered.

"Althir…" She wasn't sure how to respond, because he'd stunned her too.

He kissed her, his lips that sweet combination of gentle and firm. She tasted a hint of herself on his tongue and shuddered at the eroticism of it. Finally, her limbs obeyed her commands, and she wrapped her arms around his shoulders, pulling him over her as she spread her legs wide to welcome him. He rocked against her, his cock teasing at her entrance without slipping in. That tease shattered what remained of her control. She reached between them, gripped his cock and angled until the head dipped into her wetness. With a solid roll of her hips, she took him farther, sighing as he slowly filled her.

Her muscles clenched at him, tightening around his thickness, and he buried his face against her neck.

"Mina…"

The sound of her name murmured in that guttural tone was as seductive as the feel of his erection easing into her, opening her. She was tight enough to enjoy every rigid inch of him, but her body yielded to his length and thickness easily, past ready to have him fully inside her. The final bump of his groin against her as he settled deep inside sent a sharp shock of pleasure through her.

And then he moved. The slide and thrust created a friction so exquisite, Mina lost all sense of the surrounding world. Every fiber of her being drew down into a tight focus on Althir, his rhythm, his scent, the texture of his skin under her roving hands, the sharp sting of his teeth when he bit her shoulder, the tension and heat rolling through her. She matched his pace, clenching her muscles tighter around his cock to increase the friction. She'd never felt anything quite so perfect. Sensual beyond words, sexier, more intense than any experience in her life.

She held him, rocked with him, and when his demand built, when he thrust into her harder, faster, she followed. Scraping her fingers across his back. Sucking at his tongue the way she'd sucked his cock. Demanding more with each breath, each moan. Her orgasm broke through her suddenly, taking her by surprise so that she cried out, the sound muffled by his kiss. Through the waves of pleasure and shock, she felt him stiffen, felt the hot pulse of his release, and greedily swallowed his groan.

This time, her limbs didn't relax beyond her control immediately and she was able to hold him tight, his body heavy on top of her. He nuzzled her neck, his breath hot and harsh. His heartbeat pounded against her breast.

When she felt she could summon enough strength to speak, she said, "I usually don't come more than once. That was amazing."

He kissed the skin along her throat before rising onto his forearms to look down at her. His smile was smug, but she couldn't begrudge him that expression now. He'd earned every ounce of smugness as far as she was concerned.

"And just think," he said, dropping a fleeting kiss onto her lips, "we don't have anywhere to go for hours and hours. Lots of time for more."

Her eyes widened. "I can't keep this up for *hours*."

"You can. You will."

She shook her head. "Althir, I don't have an elf's stamina."

"You're going to surprise yourself, love. Elf-fire does more than just make the encounters intense."

She nibbled her bottom lip a moment, before saying, "Do you think it's safe? Here, I mean. Shouldn't we…pay more attention to possibly being discovered?"

"The battle at the border is still in full swing."

She opened her mouth, and he quieted her with another quick kiss.

"While you were sleeping, I overheard a few passing servants. Every solider has been called to the front. Every elf, every Sorcerer is required to fight right now. I'm not sure what your people are doing, but whatever it is, it's keeping the enemy well occupied. Too occupied to search for us and that missing List."

"Do you think they're doing that on purpose? Maybe we should try to make for the border tonight." Though the thought of getting out of bed and actually walking seemed impossible at that moment.

"We won't get that far in what remains of the night."

Her eyes widened. "How late is it? I thought…"

"Late enough." With a sigh, he said, "But I wanted to keep you here so you could rest and recover from the fight before we made for the border. I'm not letting you do that right now, am I?"

She almost giggled. "No, I'm not exactly resting. But I do feel a lot better."

He smiled, but resignation settled over his expression. "The real world is a harsh mistress. You're right to remind me."

She didn't want to break their bubble of sex and elf-fire-induced madness either. She hadn't felt so relaxed, so free in forever. But the reality of their location, their situation couldn't be ignored, no matter how much she wanted to.

"I wish we didn't have to think about this right now," she said. "I'd rather worry about being able to keep up with you here in this bed."

Her admission drew a small sigh from him, and he set his forehead against hers.

"Mina. You tempt me beyond any woman I've ever known. When we're back inside Sinnale territory, we'll return to this. I am not nearly done with you yet."

The feel of his cock starting to harden again inside her

emphasized his statement and made her gasp in surprise. "The elf-fire really does help you recover quickly."

He nodded then closed his eyes briefly when her hips jerked convulsively against his. "The journey back to friendly territory is going to be torture," he said.

She tried not to laugh but a soft chuckle escaped anyway.

"Minx," he accused, kissing away her amusement.

The kiss turned her own body against her, and before she realized what was happening, they were moving together again, his long strokes taking her beyond whatever limits she'd thought she had. He dipped low to suck her nipple into his mouth, licking and nipping until the line of sensation between her breast and her core drew taut, bringing another build to another crest of impossible pleasure.

She didn't bother trying to control her descent this time, didn't have the strength to hold back or resist. She gave herself completely to Althir's sensual attention and discovered she did have the stamina he promised.

The real world, the dangers beyond this quiet room, remained at bay for just a little bit longer, and Mina fell back into the bliss of freedom, taking the satisfaction only Althir could give her. While she had the chance.

CHAPTER SIXTEEN

In the end, Althir did let her sleep for another couple of hours, insisting she needed some rest before they started to plan their return to safety. He woke her just before dawn with a small meal of dried fruit and a surprising loaf of fresh bread. "Where did you get this?"

"I snuck out and stole it," he said.

"Althir! You shouldn't have done that."

"I didn't go far. I wouldn't leave you alone and unguarded like that." He scowled at her as if she should have known better.

"I was more worried about the List." But the fact that his first concern was for her sent warmth spreading through her body.

"As I said, I didn't go far. And I was able to overhear a little gossip that confirmed the battle is still going strong. Whatever is happening on the front, it's not easing up."

She swallowed a bite of the dark bread. "We need to get back. As quickly as we can. They're giving us a distraction."

He frowned down at the sheet between them where he'd placed the small meal. "It's a distraction, all right. Until we get close to the fighting. Then we'll have to work our way through the enemy lines to get into Noman's Land. That's not going to be a simple task, Mina."

She nodded. "But we just need to meet up with a group of Sinnale and we'll have an escort, someone to cover our backs."

"Again, that's not going to be easy."

"I know. But we can't plan until we get close enough to see exactly what's happening."

He shrugged, but she could tell his attention was turned inward, thinking ahead to what they had to do.

"I'm not particularly happy you did it, but since you did go out without being spotted, what did you see? How many people are left in the area? Can we move during the day or do we need to hold out until tonight?"

"There weren't many servants about, but it was pre-dawn. There wouldn't be. We'll still have to contend with them during the day."

"But minion patrols? Sorcerers?"

"From what I overheard, and what I know of minion numbers, I doubt the Sorcerers had enough bodies to leave any behind. Your people do still outnumber them, even if their magic makes it an even fight. But if the Sinnale are making a serious push to regain more territory, the Sorcerers won't be able to spare minions to search for us or patrol the streets. Not if they want to keep from losing more ground than they already have."

"They know about the List by now. Won't that worry them?"

She was trying to work her way through every possible scenario. With the fighting still such a distraction, she wanted to take advantage of it, but she was afraid in her hurry she'd sacrifice her usual cautious approach and get them both killed. It was always better to move around at night if she wasn't moving in disguise. But the thought of waiting out another day made her antsy and restless.

"Which is why making our way through their lines and into

Sinnale territory won't be easy. They'll be watching for us—for anyone they think might have stolen the List."

"Can we get from here to Glengowyn?" she said suddenly. "I know it's more roundabout. But if we can reach Glengowyn, the king and queen can help us return to friendly territory with the List."

His mouth twisted in a faint snarl. "I won't find any help from that direction. I'm not welcome back yet. If I go into Glengowyn now, I'll be taken before the sovereigns still a traitor and subject to their full wrath. Until I put the List into the council's collective hands, and they speak to the king and queen on my behalf, the elves consider me a criminal." His scowl cleared. "But for you…"

She shook her head. "No. It's not an option then."

"They would look after you, ensure you got back safely." He nodded as he considered the possibility further. "Sneaking past the city limits might be a little easier now. There's still the spells to consider. We'd risk triggering something. And there's at least two miles of open grassland between the city this far east and the edge of the forest."

"Althir, no. We'll find another way."

He continued as if he hadn't heard her. "We'd probably be safer in the open grass, though, than trying to move farther west through the city to get to a place where the crossing to the forest is shorter. And if we don't start out into the open until after nightfall…"

"Althir!" She grabbed his arm to get his attention. "It's not an option. Not if it means your sovereigns will turn you back into a prisoner. Or worse. I don't know what their 'wrath' will entail, but after all you've done to earn your freedom, I won't have you throwing that away."

"You're more important than my freedom. Taking that List to the council safely is more important."

She swallowed hard, emotions she refused to examine clogging her throat. "No," she said firmly. "You've risked everything for this. Too much to throw it away now and be labeled a traitor forever. Especially when you never really were."

She wasn't sure exactly when she started to believe in him, to be certain his story was true. Sometime during her trip to the Chemist? Her belief had started then. Making love to him had somehow solidified it. She didn't know if what she felt could be called trust yet. But she was positive he'd been honest about his original intent in joining the traitors. He was too humiliated by the failure for it to have been a lie. Because of that, she couldn't stand to see him fail again. Not when he was this close to doing exactly what he'd set out to do.

"Althir, we'll find our way through enemy lines and back to Sinnale. Glengowyn, the king and queen, they can wait until you're no longer labeled a traitor."

He cupped her cheek, a gesture that surprised her. "We'll try the front first, because you ask it of me. But if we can't find a way through safely, we go to Glengowyn for help. No arguments," he said, cutting off her attempt to interrupt. "I will not have you fall into the Sorcerers' hands under any circumstances. And if that means I live the rest of my life as a traitor, so be it."

His declaration robbed her of the ability to speak, but she knew, deep inside, she couldn't let him fall victim to that fate. Not anymore. They would find a way to save them both. And to end the war that had brought so much suffering.

ALTHIR KNEW SHE HADN'T GIVEN IN EVEN THOUGH SHE'D STOPPED arguing with him. She had no intention of using the option of Glengowyn, no matter how much he insisted. That only made him more determined to protect her.

He couldn't pinpoint the exact moment when everything

changed, but everything had sometime in the last day. His priority wasn't to get the List to the Sinnale anymore. It was to get Mina to safety. He wasn't interested in examining his change in motivations either, or the meaning behind it. He refused to look too closely at his own feelings. They were irrelevant at the moment anyway. All he knew was that Mina's safety was paramount, and he intended to do whatever it took to return her alive and well, mission accomplished, to the human council.

The rest… He'd worry about that some other time.

They compromised between getting back to the Sinnale quickly and the dangers of moving through Sorcerer territory in the day by leaving late in the afternoon. The information they'd both gathered proved true. The streets were deserted of everyone but servants and those kept their heads down, moving about their tasks hurriedly. Althir could practically feel the nervous tension in the air. Mina had been right, the servants were worried.

The battle probably wasn't going well for the Sorcerers. The satisfaction that gave him was mitigated by the fact that Ulric had probably provided the battle plan. But he had no doubt the plan came out of information he'd provided. Even if Ulric ended up the celebrated hero and people still considered Althir a traitor, he'd know he'd done more to end the war for Mina's people than his bloody brother.

Full darkness meant he and Mina could move faster through the streets, so when the gas lamps started to light, they increased their pace, circling around areas most frequently used by servants. The journey took them most of the night, but before dawn started to light the sky, they'd made their way unhindered to within hearing distance of the battle.

The sounds of the clashing, the cries of the wounded or dying, were faint echoes on the wind, but Althir heard them clearly enough. Even Mina, with her human hearing, caught the distant noise.

"Do we risk getting closer?" she murmured.

They stood on a dark side street, tucked into the shadows, her arm pressing against his as they spoke. The contact warmed him.

"We need to see what's happening so we can plan a way through," she said.

He agreed. But the sun would be coming up soon, making it infinitely harder to sneak through the chaos of the fighting.

"They're only five, maybe six blocks in front of us. Do you know anywhere in the area we can post ourselves to watch without being spotted? Remember, the Sorcerers will be using rooftops to monitor the battle as well. Though some of them will be there as a projection only, not in reality."

She pressed her lips together as she thought. While he'd spent months in this territory, he hadn't been here to hide from anyone, so convenient places to remain unseen hadn't been high on his list of information to collect. This was her specialty.

Finally, she nodded. "If we head parallel to the fight, about six blocks that way and two down is a building high enough to give us a vantage while still inside. Even if the Sorcerers are using it, they'll be on the roof."

"Dangerous," he muttered.

"It's all I can think of. Every other building in this area is too low. We either cross the breadth of the city, or we move to the very edge of the fighting. Even then, we'll likely only see a few blocks around the immediate area. But it's the best we can do."

"Moving too far across the city will take time." He flexed his fists. "Fine. We'll check the building. If it's being used as a strategic monitoring point for the enemy, we leave it and move farther south.

I won't risk you being discovered." He looked down at the side of her face, but she wouldn't meet his gaze.

"I'll agree to that. But here…" She pulled one of her short swords from the scabbard at her hip. "Your arrows won't help us in close combat."

He'd left the human-made sword behind in the List chamber after their confrontation with the Sorcerer. The weapon had been damaged during his fight with the guards at any rate and wasn't much use to him. He'd intended to get another sword off a dead body as they moved through the battle. Her offer, freely given, of a sword she now knew to be invaluable, humbled him.

"Thank you." His fingers brushed hers as he took the offered weapon and she glanced up, fleetingly. Her dark eyes were serious and fathomless in the faint glow from the nearest gas lamp. "I'll return it once we're safe," he promised.

She nodded, her smile forced, and then she looked back at the empty street. "We need to move now. In case my people manage to push farther in and we get overrun by the fighting."

She adjusted the straps of the backpack they'd found in her former home, a habit she'd fallen into as they traveled. The pack carried the List vessel. He'd wanted to take it himself, but she'd pointed out that he carried his weapons over his back. He wouldn't be able to do that and carry the pack at the same time. Reluctantly, he let her take up the duty, but it rubbed him wrong that she was so vulnerable. She'd be the one to suffer if they were caught and she had the List in her possession.

"The pack is secure?" he asked because she was still fidgeting with the straps.

"It's fine. I'm ready when you are."

"Lead the way."

She hurried through the lit cross street, and they ducked back down a dark side road. With the battle so close and the possibility of running into minions high, they moved more cautiously over the last few blocks. By the time they reached their destination, the sunrise had turned the eastern horizon pink.

Althir pressed her back against a wall out of sight and studied the six-story structure for a long time as the area grew lighter and lighter.

"Althir, we need to get inside soon," she whispered, rising up on her toes to speak near his ear. "It's getting too bright."

He didn't answer immediately but kept his focus on the building, on the rooftop, his senses stretched to hear any telltale noise of occupation. Finally, silently, he motioned her forward and they hurried in through the front door.

Once in, however, he held her back near the doorway, listening more intently for any sounds coming from inside. He could hear the battle better now, since they were closer to the center of the fighting, but he blocked out that noise as he concentrated on their immediate surroundings.

The main floor was a huge, open area that had probably once been either an indoor market or a storage area. Above their heads, a gallery walkway circled the main floor, making for a truncated second level. To his left, the stairs that led to the gallery, seemed to continue up into the darkness of the third floor.

Against her ear, he said, "Do you know this building? The upper floors?"

She nodded and turned to speak into his ear. He worked hard not to be distracted by the hot brush of her breath against his sensitive lobes.

"The stairs to the left lead all the way to the top floor. There's another set at the back of this floor that will take us to the very top. The rest lead to the gallery and we'll have to walk along it to reach a set of stairs going higher."

He was reluctant to take the nearest set of stairs because anyone coming in and out of the building would take that more direct route. Even the stairs to the rear, with their direct path up, were too dangerous. "How open is the gallery? Will we be very exposed if we have to use it to get to a second stairway?"

"It's pretty open, not a lot of nooks to hide in. If anyone is here and they stick to the direct stairs, though, they won't likely see us."

"The better option then." He pointed to a stairway to their right, farther away than the one to their left. She nodded and they edged toward it, sticking close to the outer wall.

Once they reached the stairs, Althir went up first, sword in hand. Mina followed with her sword also drawn, watching their backs. The gallery was as she described, mainly an open walkway, though a handful of doors were visible. The doors were widely spaced, so unless they were right next to one, they wouldn't provide much cover.

The wooden floor was fortunately silent underfoot, no telltale creaking, but if they weren't careful, even light footsteps might be heard. And getting too close to the outer railing would make them visible to the first floor as well as from every point along the gallery.

He headed toward the nearest set of stairs going up, on alert to movement and noise. So far, the building sounded empty, but he didn't trust that silence. When they made the stairs without incident, he heard Mina let out a soft breath. He wasn't nearly as relieved. They had four more floors to cover.

The third level consisted of corridors and closed doors, but the next set of stairs was closer and he hurried up, not trusting all those closed doors. The two floors above that were much the same. On the fifth, they had to walk almost to the back of the building before finding another stairwell. Althir's nerves were stretched tight by the time they reached those stairs, and his ears were ringing from listening so hard.

For all the battles he'd been in, all the sneaking around he'd done trying to find proof the Sorcerers intended to invade Glengowyn, he'd never felt the tension quite this acutely. Having Mina at his back raised the risks beyond anything he'd had to face before. His every instinct screamed to get her out of this building and take her to the forest where she'd be safe.

But getting there wouldn't be any easier than crossing through the battle. The knowledge didn't help him relax.

On the top floor, a single corridor circled the building, with doors branching off toward the interior and exterior. They followed the route until they were at the side of the building facing the battle, and then, after much hesitation and listening at doors, they slipped inside a room that would give them a view of the fighting.

Once the door clicked closed behind them, Mina's sigh was more loudly audible.

"Don't relax yet," he warned. "We could get cornered here if someone discovers us."

"At least we're not so exposed." She took up a spot to one side of a window and studied the city beyond.

She'd been right. They were two stories higher than the highest nearby building. The view gave them a vantage over several blocks. The roof would have been better but also infinitely more exposed. Outside, the sun was high enough to fill the streets with light and morning shadows. Under that soft pink glow, he could see pockets of fighting in the streets below.

As he'd worried, the fighting was moving deeper into Sorcerer territory, the Sinnale pushing them back, forcing them to retreat. While that was good for the war effort, it meant they'd been dangerously close to getting caught up in the chaos before they were ready.

Mina, however, only saw the progress her people were making.

"They're much deeper than ever before," she murmured, her tone filled with satisfaction. "They're winning."

"The Sorcerers are likely strained between the knowledge of the missing List and the heavy surge. I'd bet Ulric planned this."

"Why?"

"Because attacking while we're stealing their most valuable possession is strategically brilliant. Their attention is divided, their level of worry high, and after knowing them, I'd bet their infighting and arguing has grown worse. It's hard to plan an effective defense under those conditions. Just the kind of thing Ulric would take advantage of."

Mina glanced at him and her direct focus pulled his attention to her. She was looking at him with a strange expression.

"I think that's the first time I've heard you speak of your brother without bitterness or resentment. Not even sarcasm."

He scowled and turned back to monitoring the streets. "Even I can give him his due," he grumbled. "Sometimes. And if nothing else, the bastard is a brilliant tactician. That's his magic." His scowl deepened when she chuckled.

"I think maybe you like Ulric more than you let on," she said.

"I absolutely do not. Especially since he would have killed me."

"Why did he threaten to kill you? You never said. Just because you were a traitor?"

He felt his skin heating at the memory, a mixture of anger, embarrassment and resentment. "I might have been…taunting him. About Layla. He deserved it. But I didn't realize how he felt about her, or that he'd take me so seriously. Never has before."

Althir felt her studying him but this time didn't look at her. He'd admitted enough humiliations to her. He didn't need to know what she thought of him for this one.

"My brother used to dig at me too," she said quietly. "Used to infuriate me—just for the fun of it sometimes. We fought a lot before the war. And once or twice, I might have goaded him in front of a woman he'd fancied himself in love with. I wasn't always a very nice little sister."

Her admission surprised him and softened his mood. There was humor and regret in her tone. He knew a lot about that latter emotion.

"Brothers," he snorted in disgust, a gesture that earned him a soft laugh.

They watched the fighting for hours, gauging its ebb and flow.

"The defenses seem to be holding where they are," he murmured, rolling his shoulders to loosen muscles.

"Damn. If they could push the fighting farther this way, they might even move past us and we could slip into the ranks of our own army."

He didn't correct her assumption that the winning army was "theirs", but he doubted the Sinnale would claim him so willingly. "That might have worked against us if the enemy decided to bring the fight inside this building."

He'd observed several of the separate skirmishes moving inside as minion patrols tried to take cover from the exploding arrows being loosed on them. He watched the destruction arising from his cousin Nuala's specially designed weapon, something only she could do, and felt a sense of familial pride he rarely experienced. But the shrapnel-carrying arrow bombs were another very dangerous impediment to them getting through enemy lines. Those arrows killed indiscriminately and at a distance. Everyone within the circumference of their landing spot ended up shredded.

"The new arrows are really helping us," Mina murmured, her comment echoing his train of thought. "But they're going to make it harder for us, aren't they?"

He grunted. "Our best option will be to stick close to the buildings. If it weren't for the Sorcerers, I'd suggest roof-hopping.

We'd reach your people quicker and stay above the majority of the fighting."

There were only a few fights that he could see taking place on the rooftops. There might be more of those farther back where the Sinnale archers were heavily clustered, but in their immediate vicinity, rooftop skirmishes were rare.

Unfortunately, he'd spotted at least four Sorcerers throughout the day, each from a rooftop vantage. Too many to risk a rooftop run.

"Are any of the Sorcerers we're seeing the ones that aren't really here?" Mina asked. "The ones sending their souls out? Can you tell at a distance?"

"I can't tell. They can appear very real, even up close. We wouldn't know the difference until we were right on top of them and then it'd be too late."

"Damn." She was quiet for a few minutes before saying, "Do you think they realize you had a part in the theft of the List?"

"Oh, I have no doubt they suspect me. Talliah was expecting me in the List chamber. She figured out what I was after first but wouldn't have been the only one suspicious of why I'd returned to their territory."

"So one of them seeing you, or one of the traitors spotting you, is likely to cause us even more trouble than if we were just random enemies."

She wasn't asking a question. They both knew his notoriety worked against them.

"I could always draw their attention away," he muttered as he considered their options. "Take one route, purposefully draw them off, giving you a way through the lines with less difficulty."

"No," she said firmly. "That plan isn't any better than the Glengowyn plan. Besides, if they catch you, they'll torture you."

"True." But they would have done that even if he hadn't stolen the List. He wasn't sure why that was her objection.

"You know why the Sinnale need the List. They'll make you tell them."

Ah. "You're afraid I'll give under the torture." For some reason, her very practical logic irritated the hell out of him. "Think I can't keep my mouth shut, huh?"

"That's not it. But under torture—"

He glared at her, stopping her in midsentence. "I'll take my knowledge into the afterlife with me, Mina. No need to worry about that."

"Althir, I didn't mean…"

He turned away. "If we wait for a break in the skirmishes, while they're still working out a way to beat the Sinnale back, I can distract them before the shrapnel arrows start falling again. That'll give you an even better opportunity to slip through." To his surprise, she actually stomped her foot.

"No! You are not setting yourself up as a sacrifice. I won't allow it. We stick together and get back to safety together."

He didn't look at her, but the venom in her voice eased a little of his irritation. Still… His plan would give her the best chance.

"Althir," she growled. "If you try to do this anyway, I will follow you and stick to your side. Do you understand me? If they take you, they'll take me too."

"Mina, don't be an idiot. This might be the only chance to get that List to your people."

"We have other options. The sun will set in a few more hours. We'll take our chances then. Fight our way through if we have to. Avoid the elves and Sorcerers as much as we can and stick to fighting the minions. We just have to make contact with the Sinnale army and we'll be okay."

He shook his head. "Not that simple. Not with an elf in tow."

"You're as notoriously well known to my people as you are to the Sorcerers. They'll recognize you too. And I have no doubt the word has been spread that if I come through the ranks with you, I'm to be let past."

"What if they think it's a trick? That we're actually disguised minions or under an elf glamour to look like…us?"

"The enemy doesn't know what I look like. They couldn't send in a pretend me."

"And your entire army does know?"

She frowned, and he knew he'd hit on a flaw in her thinking.

"Fine, they don't all know me. But even if they're suspicious of us, they'll take us to Ulric, under guard, to confirm who we are."

He wasn't so sure they should count on that logic, but time was running out.

Unfortunately, and he hated to admit it, strategy wasn't his strongest suit. That was Ulric's talent. Althir's magic worked better in face-to-face encounters. And Mina was no warrior, though she'd fought and killed before out of necessity. Taking her into the heart of the battle risked her life more than he thought he could tolerate.

But they couldn't stay hidden in this building forever.

"Come dark, we take our chances on sneaking through the fights." He pointed out a route. "We'll stick to those streets that aren't being used much." They were all too narrow and strategically dangerous to both sides. "And yes—" he raised a hand before she could speak, "—we'll stay together. Fight when we have to. I can't see any other option than to just work our way through—at least not anything one or the other of us won't object to."

She snorted her agreement.

"So we'll take the direct approach." He shrugged. "A rare method for me, but it's been known to work."

"When do we start?"

"As soon as the sun sets, we make for your army. And hope we don't get killed along the way."

It wasn't a great plan, he knew that. But he also knew neither she nor he would accept an option that put the other in specific danger. They'd make a run for it and hope for the best.

And if things turned against them…well, he did have one or two tricks up his sleeve. Another option Mina would object to, so this time he kept the backup plan to himself. For once, what she didn't know might just save her life.

CHAPTER SEVENTEEN

They took advantage of a lull in the fighting to make their move into the heart of the battle zone. Mina let Althir lead while she watched their backs. They slipped down the darkest, narrowest pathways they could find but still had to hide from small groups of minions loitering in buildings, watching for the next assault.

The Sinnale had fallen back just a little, so she and Althir were deep into the battle zone when they came across the first group of humans. The soldiers were huddled around a map, murmuring and occasionally pointing to nearby buildings.

Mina edged in front of Althir, knowing she would get a better reception than he would—even if they recognized him. But just as she was about to move out of the shadows, a volley of arrows arched overhead, coming from the Sinnale lines. Moments later, the streets filled with running Sinnale and minions, the clash of metal and screams. Mina cursed silently.

The fighting erupted all around them, turning their escape route into a melee of chaos. She and Althir stayed hidden, watching for an opening to move to another area of cover, still going in the direction they needed to go.

The sound of a much louder, closer clank of metal had Mina spinning around to see Althir fending off two minions who'd snuck up on them. Or at least on her. Althir looked in perfect control of the fight. He sliced through the two enemies quickly, with so little sound she could barely hear it over the rest of the battle. She faced the bulk of the conflict again and spotted an opening.

"Come on." She reached back, grabbed his arm and tugged him forward. They crouched and ran, staying close to the buildings, then ducked into the next recessed doorway without being stopped by either human or minion.

Another line of humans marched up the road toward them, their numbers superior to the minions, but as they approached, a blast of magical fire melted the cobbles in a line in front of them.

"Fuck!" Mina couldn't contain the curse. "Where are the Sorcerers?"

Althir tapped her shoulder and pointed to a building less than a block away. "There's one up there. And another there, and there." He pointed to flanking rooftops.

Mina watched in horror as the three Sorcerers launched deadly magical attack after attack, fire and bolts of lightning covering the street. Another volley of arrows arched overhead, toward the Sorcerers.

"We are not in a good spot right now," she hissed.

"No, we're not. Come on."

He pulled her behind the building they'd been using for cover, on the Sinnale side of the fight but out of view of the soldiers in the streets, then hurried across the next road. The fighting was just as heavy there.

The sound of brick and mortar giving way startled another

screech from Mina. She looked back to see a corner of the building they were hiding behind collapse.

Althir cursed this time as he searched the streets. He pointed through the smoke from a burning line of cobbles. "There's a line of humans that way. If we can reach them, we'll at least be on the right side of the battle."

"If we can get through without getting killed," she muttered.

"I offered other options," he reminded her without looking back.

"None of them any better." She took a breath. "At the next arrow volley, we run."

He reached back for her free hand. She grabbed hold because she needed the contact. Her heart pounded so hard in her chest, it knocked against her ribs. This wasn't her first fight. But it was the first time she'd tried to get through major battle lines from the wrong direction.

She hated being in the middle of these conflicts anyway. Each scream, each death, the scent of blood and burning things assaulting her nose, coating the back of her throat.

She hated this war to the very depths of her soul. But never more than when she found herself in the middle of all the fighting.

Althir's hand clenched tight around hers, and she looked up just as more arrows arched into the air. Even before the arrows peaked over their heads, Althir took off into the streets with her close on his heels.

Some of the arrows must have been shrapnel ones because the sounds of screams and shattering glass exploded behind them. Mina didn't turn to look. She kept her head down and ran for the line of humans.

As they approached, several broke off from the line to face them, swords raised. She tugged Althir a little then moved around in front of him, releasing his hand. When she was close enough for them to hear her over the other noises, she shouted, "Friendly! Sinnale spy. I need to get to the council."

The soldiers didn't lower their weapons, but they didn't attack either when she and Althir stopped in front of them. They looked between her and Althir for what felt an inordinately long moment.

"He's the traitor that turned himself in to the council," one woman said, her voice harsh. "What's he doing free?"

Mina patted her pack. "We had an assignment from the council. Retrieved something to put an end to the—"

Her sentence was cut off as minions roared up behind them and her people had to break off the conversation to defend themselves. Althir faced the minions too, sweeping them aside with an awesome ease. Mina managed to drive the one minion who turned on her back, and he fell to Althir's sword.

Not far away, more minions pointed toward them, heading in their direction. The soldiers around her were too occupied to see the reinforcements coming.

"Althir!" She moved to his side to face the newest threat. To her surprise, he handed her the sword he'd been using, slipped his bow over his head and started firing arrows into the approaching group. Half a dozen minions fell before the rest took cover.

He continued to fire until his quiver was empty. In the end, more than a dozen minions lay in the streets, bleeding or dying from Althir's arrows.

He replaced the bow across his back and, without even looking down at her, held his hand out for the sword. She passed it to him as they returned to the other Sinnale. The woman who'd recognized Althir stared at him with wide eyes.

A man Mina vaguely recognized from the council's meeting hall motioned them to follow. "Word's been left with the regiment commanders about two spies coming from enemy territory. I'll take you to my commander. If she can verify who you are, we'll see you get to the right side of the fighting."

Althir walked beside her without comment. His face was set in hard lines, his expression impossible to read. As they passed through the soldiers that had stopped them initially, she noticed all the stares he drew and wondered if he was bothered by those looks or if he even noticed. Given the fact that he'd just singlehandedly leveled a small contingent of minion soldiers, she thought her people should show him a little more consideration.

They jogged two blocks closer to what had been the border to Noman's Land, and their guide led them into a small building with a gaping hole in one side. At the center of the damaged room stood another group of Sinnale bent over a table with yet another map of the city.

Mina and Althir's guide approached a tall woman at the center of the discussion and murmured something to her Mina couldn't hear.

Mina looked closely at the woman. She also looked vaguely familiar. A face she'd seen in and out of the council's meeting hall. But still no one Mina knew well, unfortunately.

The commander's gaze jumped between them before she motioned Mina closer. "Mina Dawnswealth. I knew your brother once upon a time. I was very sorry for his loss."

Mina swallowed and nodded. The comment hit a still painful wound that kept her from speaking.

"You have his eyes. And I've seen you at the council's meeting hall."

Relief made Mina's shoulders sag just a bit.

The commander glanced back at Althir, and Mina felt a new wave of tension.

"Althir," the woman greeted as if they knew each other.

"Commander Reginaldson." He gave a slight bow. "You seem to be doing well here." He gestured at the half-collapsed building.

She barked out a sharp laugh. "We're fortifying our position in what used to be Sorcerer territory, so, yes, we are doing well. Thank you for noticing."

Her response brought an answering chuckle from Althir.

"Samuel Brightarrow said to look out for you. Didn't say why, but I assume you're helping and not hindering our efforts?" She didn't bother to hide the suspicion in her tone.

"Helping, Commander, I assure you. And if you have a way we can get back to the council as quickly as possible, we might be able to help sooner rather than later."

She gestured two soldiers forward from the opposite side of the damaged room. "Take them to the rear lines." To Mina and Althir, she said, "You'll have to make your own way through Noman's Land. We can't spare even two soldiers for long enough to get you all the way home. Good luck."

With that she turned back to the map and those standing around the table. Mina and Althir were led out the hole in the building's façade and taken to the rear of the Sinnale army.

Seeing how far forward her people were holding the line sent a rush of pride through Mina. They would win this war, drive the Sorcerers out and take back their city.

At the edge of what had been Noman's Land, their escorts left them and returned to the fighting.

"You know the way back from here?" Althir asked as they trotted down the dark streets.

"I do."

Beyond the light and noise of the battle, Noman's Land felt like a black, still wasteland. Mina slowed to a walk when the quiet and shadow closed in, making her feel she'd finally reached safety. They wouldn't be safe, not really, until they crossed into Sinnale territory. But they wouldn't run into any minion patrols here tonight.

Althir must have felt a similar sense of relief because he stopped walking altogether and pulled her into a tight hug. The gesture startled her so much she stood stock still for two heartbeats before wrapping her arms around his waist.

"See," she murmured as she pressed her face against his chest. "You didn't need to sacrifice yourself to get me to safety."

"Not yet," he murmured.

But he spoke so quietly she wasn't entirely sure she heard him right. She wanted to ask what he meant, then decided they'd have time for that later. "Apparently your notoriety served you well too. You knew the commander?"

"She was one of the soldiers allowed to question me when I started handing your people information."

"Lucky."

"Probably not. I'd bet the council scattered the commanders who would recognize me all along the lines just in case we managed to do what we did. She knew who you were too."

Actually, she'd known Mina's brother, but since Mina didn't want to talk about her brother, she kept silent.

"Your family name is Dawnswealth," he said into her hair. "I've heard of them. Renowned for their chocolate and pastry."

She smiled but didn't look up for fear he'd see the wetness filling her eyes. "Yes we were."

"Many Sinnale have names related to their profession. Why Dawnswealth for chocolatiers?"

A few tears leaked over her cheeks as she grinned wider, thinking of the old family story. "Years and years ago, one of my ancestors invented a truffle so spectacular it sold out before dawn every time she made it. One of the old nicknames for chocolate was king's gold, so…"

"Gold…wealth. Dawnswealth." He chuckled. "I like it."

She hugged him tighter and soaked in his heat, glad for the moment of peace, grateful he'd brought up a pleasant memory of her family to counter all the death, madness and heartache of the last few days.

They remained quiet for several long minutes, then he pulled back and lifted her chin so she was staring at him. She assumed he wanted to say something so waited for him to speak first. Instead, he just stared down at her.

"What's wrong?" she asked after the silence stretched her nerves too tight.

"When we get back… I don't know what the council intends for me once we return. I'll probably go back into my luxurious little cage until they've cleared my release with the king and queen."

"But you've done what you promised. Why wouldn't they simply release you?"

"They still have to open the vessel."

She frowned, her brow lowering as she considered how that could have anything to do with Althir. Then she remembered what he'd said about getting through the magic to the List. "You think they'll make you… Against your will?"

"Not against my will." He raised a hand to her cheek, running his fingers across her cheekbone as his gaze roamed her face.

"You planned from the beginning to use your own blood to open this? Why didn't you tell me?"

"What would you have said? You assumed Ulric would sacrifice so much, risk his own life. Why are you surprised I'd be willing to do the same?"

"Ulric's been…" She cut herself off when she realized her previous arguments no longer applied now that she knew what Althir's motives had been from the beginning.

"I wouldn't have believed you were serious before," she

admitted. "That's the only reason I thought of your brother. It never occurred to me the man I assumed you were would bleed to help my people."

"Which is why I didn't bother to tell you." His lips closed over hers gently, but before she could fully take in his kiss, he raised his head again. "I want you to know now because…because I'll have to open the vessel immediately. That List is my only hope of getting out of the cage. So…"

His lips compressed into a line before he finally said in a rush, "I didn't want you to think I'd just disappeared and forgot you existed. I…I won't ever forget you, Mina. I just needed to tell you that. Before we get back."

His admission stabbed into her heart, surprising her with the combination of pain and bittersweet joy. "Are you saying goodbye to me already, Althir?"

She waited so long for his answer she finally decided she wouldn't get one and started to pull out of his embrace. He jerked her close again, his muscles bunching.

"Not yet," he said. "No goodbyes yet."

And then his mouth was on hers, hard and demanding.

CHAPTER EIGHTEEN

lthir's kiss was the kind of kiss that overwhelmed instantly and swept Mina in before she could begin to think. The heat and passion, the edge of desperation, called to her own growing sense of loss. She pushed him against the nearest wall and splayed her body across his, leaving no room between them.

The elf-fire rose immediately, and all the fear, tension and horror of the past days fed the call, turning her need into a living, breathing beast too hungry to be denied.

Althir shifted the pack on her back, stripping it down her arms and tossing it over one of his own shoulders. Then his arms were around her again. She gasped when he turned her so her back was to the wall, but she didn't stop kissing him. Running her hands over his chest, his shoulders, up into his hair to hold his head close.

His tension was her tension, the flex of hard muscles a complement to her soft curves, the darkness around them a blanket of comfort that only made each caress, nip and kiss more intense. His lips on her throat started a shiver down her spine. His hand closing over her breast made her arch into his touch, grinding her hips against his erection.

The speed, the angry insistence of her need, might have scared her if she wasn't more worried about letting him go. If knowing this was goodbye wasn't so devastating.

Part of her wondered when all this had happened. When had she gone from hating him to wanting him so desperately? When had that hate turned into feelings she couldn't begin to face because she knew her heart couldn't take them? That part of her still wanted to hate him—for making her feel anything but anger again, for forcing these emotions on her. She wanted to blame him, the elf-fire, the war…

That edge of confusion and blame only added to the fire raging through her, making her touch rough. She wanted him in her control, all hers for a few hours more. She demanded his complete focus with every caress, every kiss. She sucked at the skin where his throat and shoulder met, then bit down, and he groaned, grinding against her hard enough that the wall scraped her back. She didn't care. She wanted that reaction from him, she *needed* him to be as out of control as she felt.

"Inside," he muttered, his lips nuzzling the soft skin under her ear. "I don't want to fuck you on the street."

She wanted inside too. Because she wanted to do much more to him than she could do up against a building. His mouth closed over hers, a momentary distraction, then she dragged her mouth away and looked around. She knew where they were in Noman's Land. And she knew a building not far from here that they could escape into. It didn't have a comfortable bed to take advantage of, but it would be empty and open and warmer than a brick wall at her back.

She grabbed his hand from her breast, despite his mild protest, and tugged him the block and a half they needed to go.

"No beds," she muttered. "Might still be a couch…" She

couldn't concentrate enough to remember. The fact that she could think at all was something of a surprise.

"I don't care," he said, his voice gravel harsh. "Just inside."

She nodded to the building, so caught up she didn't take the time to study her surroundings. The entire Sorcerers' army could descend on them now and she'd never see it coming.

Even that knowledge wasn't enough to jerk her out of her erotic haze. She did open the front door to the building carefully, focusing just enough attention on safety to assure herself the place was empty. It had once been a small house but was now stripped bare and deserted.

"Hear anything?" she asked Althir, knowing he'd hear more than her even in his current state.

He shook his head, closed the door with a firm click and pulled her back into his arms. She melted against him, as if the few minutes of separation had been years. With the silencing buffer of walls, Mina felt the outside world fall away. Nothing existed to her now but Althir's hands and mouth, his scent and taste.

She'd never wanted a man more, needed the feel of him inside her so desperately. She knew the elf-fire was feeding these feelings with Althir, but somehow it was more than that too. She couldn't imagine ever feeling this way with any other man. The reality of that tightened her throat, and her kisses grew frantic, her need to memorize every inch of him driving her.

She tugged at the quiver strap along his chest until he stripped off his weapons and the List pack, but he didn't set them aside immediately. With a hand around her waist, he moved deeper into the house's entryway, kicking open doors until he found a room that, while unfurnished, did still have a half-decent rug across the wooden floor. He set his bow and quiver down just inside the door, gently settled the pack next to the quiver, then pulled her to the rug.

To her surprise and pleasure, he dropped to his knees in front of her and stripped her scabbard belt from her waist, moving away enough to set the swords on the floor beyond the rug. Then he was back to her, still on his knees, stripping her trousers down over her hips. The care he took removing her boots, her trousers and panties was belied by his shaking hands. She knew she was trembling too but didn't care. Having Althir on his knees in front of her was one of the sexiest things she'd ever seen.

He leaned forward and set his lips gently against her lower abdomen, still covered by her tunic. Irritated with the clothing, she reached down and pulled the material over her head in a single move. He smiled up at her before kissing the skin just above her navel, then below it. As his lips moved over her, deliciously light, wet caresses, she unwound the material holding her breasts in place and tossed it aside. He approved the move with a sharp nip of the skin across her hip. She jumped and moaned, bracing one hand on the side of his head to keep from falling. He wrapped his arms around her, his hands moving to squeeze her ass and hold her up all at the same time.

Slipping lower, he nuzzled her thighs farther apart, his breath hot against her heated wetness, sending her body twisting tight with so much tension she thought she might break from it. When his mouth closed over her and he licked into her, she shuddered, clenching her jaw against a scream. The gentle, insistent caresses of his tongue pushed her to the edge so quickly she couldn't begin to slow down. Without thought, she brought her free hand to her breast and squeezed, pinching her nipple into a tight bud. His appreciative growl vibrated against her sensitive skin, dragging out a gasp.

Too soon, too soon, she thought, but couldn't pull back. And she didn't really want to. She wanted to come against his mouth, even if it was the only orgasm she got tonight. His hands on her ass flexed, pulling her closer, his tongue moved inside her once, and then he closed his lips over her clitoris, pressing his tongue against her with exactly the right amount of pressure. Mina clenched her eyes shut as the tension broke open and shattered her, jerking through her body in a hard wave of devastating release.

When the wave ebbed, she folded forward, collapsing over him because her legs couldn't keep her upright any longer. He eased her down to the rug, stretching out beside her while she heaved in air. She glanced over and realized for the first time he was still fully dressed. The fact that she hadn't even noticed made her chuckle.

"This won't do," she said, tugging at his tunic. "Off."

He kissed her on the mouth for a slow, drugging moment, then rolled away and stripped out of his clothes quickly. The sight of his pale, naked skin in the darkness awed her once again. So much muscle and strength, such masculine beauty. She doubted she'd ever seen a man so perfect.

He stretched out alongside her again, and she curved into his warmth, touching, caressing, tasting every part of him she could reach. His cock jumped in her hand when she closed her fingers around him. Ah, that reaction…to control him as thoroughly as he could control her was as satisfying as any orgasm. She stroked him, long, firm pulls, as she continued to taste the skin over his chest and arms.

His muscles tightened against her, around her, circling her with heat and power. He raked his mouth along her neck, before capturing her lips. The tension in his touch, his kiss, only softened her further against him, filling her with an awareness of her own femininity in a way she'd never experienced before. Rubbing her nipples against the light hair on his chest shot bolts of sensation through her body. As if in answer, he scooted lower and took one of her nipples into his mouth, sucking hard enough to make her moan.

When he rolled onto his back so that she splayed over the top of him, she followed eagerly. Straddling him, she sat up, pulling her nipple from his reluctant mouth. The movement of air against the wetness on her breast made her shiver. His hands closed over both her breasts then, squeezing and fondling, and she closed her eyes to savor the feel of him.

"So beautiful," he whispered.

When she looked down, he was staring at her face, his gray eyes dark with more emotion than she could read. She didn't need to know or understand just then, though. She just needed him. She dipped down long enough to kiss him, then sat up and reached between their bodies, taking hold of his cock, positioning him against her entrance and then easing down. He stretched her, filled her and left her breathless.

Her rhythm started slow, slower than she would have thought herself capable of at that point, but she needed to feel each stroke, each hard inch of him sliding against her, into her. She watched him watching where their bodies joined, and the look in his eyes drove her movements. The tension in her core built again, tightening with each thrust and roll of her hips. Unexpected and yet somehow right with Althir.

He pulled gently at her breasts, and she leaned forward, low enough that he could lick and tongue her nipples. So much sensation ravaged her nerves, she wanted to scream. Instead, she threw her head back and groaned between clenched teeth, increasing the speed of her thrusts.

The burst of another orgasm tore through her in a hard jerk and shiver that left her boneless, helpless to him for the second time that night. When he lifted her up and repositioned her on her hands and knees, she went without thought, so caught up in her sensual daze, he could have done anything to her and she would have complied eagerly.

He closed one hand on her hip and used his other to guide his cock into her heat. She was so wet he slid in fast and easy, but the position made him feel even larger and the friction of his entrance made her gasp.

As he moved, his fingers dug into her hips, telling her more than anything what little control he had left. She looked over her shoulder at him. He was watching their joining, watching his cock pump in and out of her. Again she was swamped by a dizzying eroticism that overwhelmed her. Then he looked up into her eyes, and the look of possession, the heat and ferocity of his gaze pierced her heart.

In that moment, as he thrust faster, his skin slapping hot and hard against hers, his gaze holding her captive, she belonged to him completely. She was his. In every way. Caged by her emotions as surely as he would be caged by the prison he was returning to.

The knowledge would hurt later, she knew. But then, in that heated instant of perfection, she knew she loved him. He was hers as much as she was his—even if it couldn't last, even if they never saw each other again after tonight. She gave herself to his keeping and took him into hers.

He finally broke eye contact, closing his eyes and throwing his head back, the muscles across his neck, shoulders and chest tightening, his jaw clenched, his hips thrusting so hard against her she could barely keep her balance. She watched his orgasm take him, his cock pulsing inside her as he shook and groaned in release. *Hers.* In that heady instant, he was all hers. And it was a possession she would keep close in the years to come, a reminder, a memory of something too precious to let go—even if it broke her heart into tiny, aching pieces.

SHUDDERING WITH THE LAST OF HIS RELEASE, PUMPING A FEW MORE times into her because he didn't want to lose her heat, Althir met Mina's gaze again. She was the most beautiful woman he'd ever known. And the thought of never seeing her again made him so angry, his body trembled with it.

Wordlessly, he slid out of her, wrapped his arms around her waist and chest and pulled her upright so that her back was pressed against his chest. He hugged her close like that for a long moment, nuzzling his face against the bend between her shoulder and neck. He could smell himself on her, mixing with her faint vanilla scent and the musk of sex, like he'd branded her as his. The thought made his arms flex and he tightened his hold. He wanted her to be his, to belong to him. She *was* his.

He might be able to see her one more time after this, to make love to her once more. But beyond that, he risked her sanity. The elf-fire, addictive and dangerous, would drive her mad. He didn't want her obsessed with him just so she could get a hit of the pheromone. He wanted…more. Deeper. He wanted things he hadn't ever wanted before in his long life.

He couldn't have those things. Not with a human woman. Not with Mina. The knowledge was infuriating. And more painful than any battle wound he'd ever received.

Because he could feel her trembling, he settled back onto the rug, lying down with her curled against him, his hand stroking long lines up and down her back. He stared into her eyes, wondering what she wanted from the future. What she wanted from him. Did she want more? Or had she accepted their necessary separation in a way he couldn't seem to manage?

She cupped his cheek and he rubbed his face against her palm, savoring the soft feel of her skin. Words escaped him. All his charm, all the witty or clever things he might normally say, were lost to him in the face of losing her. The only thing he wanted to say, the one thing he *needed* to say, stuck in his throat and refused to come out. To speak those three words out loud would only hurt them both. But keeping them to himself caused an ache that robbed him of all other speech.

She leaned forward, placing her lips oh so gently against his, and then she started to pull away. He couldn't let her go. Not yet. Not so soon. His arms tightened and he held her close, her head tucked under his chin. A few more minutes, he thought. Then they'd get dressed and finish what they'd started, handing the war-ending List over to the Sinnale council. But for now, he just needed a few more minutes with her all to himself. Maybe then he could say goodbye and actually mean it.

For once in his life, his wants and needs took a backseat to someone else's. For Mina, and Mina alone, he'd walk away. For her own good, he'd give her up.

What happened to him after that…

He no longer cared.

CHAPTER NINETEEN

Althir and Mina were almost to the council's meeting hall when they were met by a handful of the council's assistants, people too old to fight who helped run things behind the lines. The sun had risen, but the day was cloudy and dark, the scent of rain hanging in the air. Althir loved that smell. It covered a multitude of sins.

One older woman stepped ahead of the others, wringing her hands as she hurried up to them. "We've been watching for you," she said. "The council asked that you be brought to them immediately if...*when* you arrived." She cut a strange look at Althir then focused on Mina as she led them back into the midst of the other assistants.

"Thank you," Mina said quietly.

She walked close enough he could feel her heat even though she wasn't touching him, and Althir's pulse jumped. He studied the side of her face for a beat, then focused on those around them. Despite her nearness, he sensed her pulling away, putting distance between them. He wanted to shake her and make her stop. Yet he understood. He hated that distance, the necessity of it, but he understood.

As soon as they entered the meeting hall, a small group of armed soldiers surrounded them. Althir raised his brows.

The woman who'd greeted them cringed a little, but said, "The elf must be returned to his cage. On order of the council."

The fact that she didn't sound entirely comfortable with this order surprised Althir. He didn't have any friends here, outside of Mina, and he was certain he was still considered a traitor.

Mina scowled at the armed guards. "He has information for the council. We both need to see them."

"I'm sure the council will call for him when they're ready," the woman said. "In the meantime…" She gestured to the guard, and they moved in closer to Althir.

He gave them a cursory glance but most of his attention was on Mina. She looked like she wanted to argue. "We knew this would happen," he said, dipping his head to catch her gaze. "It's fine."

She swallowed visibly. "It's not right," she muttered.

He was so tempted to reach out to her, to touch her chin and rub his fingers across her cheeks. "Everything will be fine," he assured her again. He frowned a little at their company, then as vaguely as he could, "Tell them *not* to try anything without talking to me first."

"Of course," she said, quiet understanding in her tone.

Now the harder request. "When the time comes, I don't want you there."

She jolted her head up, her eyes narrowed.

"I mean it, Mina. Stay away. Promise me."

She stared at him with a stubborn expression, her lips a flat line and little creases at the corners of her eyes. When she nodded in agreement, without actually speaking, he knew she was trying not to give herself away. Did she really think silence would prevent him from seeing the lie?

He shook his head. "Mina… Promise me."

She grunted something that sounded like, "Damned lie detector." Then she straightened her shoulders. "Fine. Just… Just be careful, okay?"

Ah, how could he resist this woman? He gave in to his need to touch her, just a little, and set his fingertips gently against her cheek. "Thank you."

So much more he wanted to say. But not now. Not in front of this avid audience. Maybe not ever.

He stepped away, and without waiting for his guard, started back toward the basement and his little cage. The soldiers hurried to catch up. The sounds of clanking swords made him smirk. They were lucky he was cooperative. They hadn't even taken his bow yet, though since the quiver was empty maybe they assumed the weapon wasn't dangerous. Little did they know.

He wanted to turn and see Mina one more time, in case it was the last time, but he resisted the impulse. He had to focus now, to clear his mind and prepare for what was to come.

For Mina's sake.

HE WAS ONLY LEFT IN HIS CAGE FOR AN HOUR BEFORE SAMUEL Brightarrow joined him. Althir turned away from the high window to face the older man.

"She told you what needs to be done?" he asked without waiting for the councilman to speak.

"She did. She said you were willing to do it too. I didn't believe her."

Althir expected as much. "I don't need your belief. I need you to set up a safe place for me to work. I need a clean knife. An elf dagger would be best, and as old a one as you can find. I need dark and quiet. Some clean water and salt. Purple salt from the Areiatun…" He paused and corrected himself, using the Sinnale name for the nearby mountains so there was no confusion. "The Burrows Range, preferably."

"Wait." Samuel held up a hand. "Mina said this might kill you."

"It will kill a human. I have a chance at surviving."

"Why?"

"Because I'm an elf." Althir frowned at the older man. Mina must have explained that.

"No, not why might you survive. Why are you willing to do this? You've fulfilled your part of the bargain and brought us the List—even if we can't access it yet. We'll send a runner to Glengowyn as soon as the sun sets. You'll be a free man by tomorrow, day after at the latest. Why risk your life further?"

Samuel studied him with that damned intelligent gaze. Althir wanted to say something flippant just to get the man moving. But he already knew that wouldn't work with this particular human.

So he decided to go with absolute honesty. "I have to finish what I started."

Samuel's eyes narrowed. "You delivered the List. That was the only thing you were supposed to do."

"Arguing with me is wasting time. Do you want the vessel opened or not?"

To Althir's annoyance, Samuel continued to stare at him for another few moments. What did the man want him to say? He sure as hell wasn't going to admit the full story, even if he had given Samuel the complete truth. He'd started all this, from the very beginning, to stop a war from coming to his city. He'd see it through, even if no one but Mina knew everything.

Then, if he survived, he'd be able to live with himself.

Finally, Samuel straightened his broad shoulders and said, "Do you need anything else? Another elf to help? Assistants?"

"No. The fewer witnesses the better. In fact, I'd prefer only one member of the council be present, to collect the List once the vessel is open. Have a medic stand by but somewhere outside my work area."

"Do you want Ulric to attend you?"

Althir scowled. "Absolutely not." He softened his expression. "And ensure Mina stays away too. She doesn't need to see this."

Samuel blinked at the second request but said, "I'll see to it." He went to the cage door. "I'll have everything prepared and be back for you within the hour."

"Good." When Samuel turned to close the cage door, Althir said, "Thank you."

Samuel's head tilted as he considered Althir. "Thank you," he murmured.

AN HOUR LATER, TRUE TO HIS WORD, SAMUEL RETURNED. He escorted Althir to the second floor of the meeting hall. Few people were around, giving the large building a deserted feel.

"Have you emptied the hall?" he asked Samuel.

"Not completely. But the battle continues so there are fewer people here anyway."

"If this fails…" Althir flexed his fingers. "If I can't get the vessel open, the king and queen should be able to make it happen. Don't try to do it yourselves. No human will survive the bleeding."

"I understand," Samuel said without glancing at him. Quieter, he said, "I would prefer if you didn't fail."

Althir snorted. "Me too."

This earned him a half smile from the councilman.

Samuel led him to a large, empty room with heavy curtains

covering the windows, leaving the area dark and quiet. In the center of the scuffed wooden floor sat the List vessel, a pitcher of water, a small bowl of purple salt, and one of Mina's short swords.

"Mina's sword?" Althir faced Samuel.

Samuel shrugged. "She insisted. She said the weapon was very old and would bring you luck."

Althir's pulse kicked. Thinking of Mina was a distraction. But her gesture touched him deeply. He wanted to smile at the fact that she'd managed to be here without breaking her promise to him. Clever woman.

"She also made a point of saying this isn't the one she used in the List chamber." Samuel frowned. "Do you understand that?"

He nodded. "She killed a Sorcerer with one of her swords."

"Mina killed a Sorcerer?" Samuel's deep voice rose.

"She didn't tell you?"

"She hasn't given us a full report of the mission yet."

"Well, she ensured you have one less Sorcerer to worry about."

"Would it have affected opening the vessel, using a weapon that's touched Sorcerer blood?"

"If any of the blood was still on the sword, it could mix with mine and trigger the part of the spell that would spread that Sorcerer's real name to the others. It doesn't matter now, as she's dead. But Mina was probably worried it would complicate the opening. A good precaution."

As Althir considered the point, he realized there might be other spells on the vessel he didn't know about, nasty little tricks that would be activated by Sorcerer blood and do more than just release the real names. It was possible there were spells that lashed out at the one opening the vessel. By sending the sword that didn't kill the Sorcerer, Mina made sure he didn't inadvertently trigger something that might kill him. Ah, his woman was smart.

His woman.

Because he was standing next to Layla's father, Althir thought of his brother and his mate. Ulric risked Layla's sanity being with her. Yet they were still together. How could Ulric do that to Layla? How could he take such a chance? Was it possible for Althir and Mina to do the same? Could he take that chance with her? Did he dare?

There were songs written about the few great loves that had stood the test of time, relationships between elves and humans that had actually lasted. Sweeping romances from long ago. Althir had never believed those stories. Most elves didn't. They were simply ballads to make young elves swoon. Althir hadn't even believed in love until Mina. To consider he might experience such a powerful bond had been unthinkable. That true love between a human and elf was even possible seemed ridiculous.

Now…

Althir stared at the vessel. Considering any kind of future just then would only keep him from focusing on what he had to do. First, release the List. If he survived this, he could consider everything else. *If* he survived this…

Althir nodded to one wall. "Stand over there, Samuel. And don't interfere, no matter what happens. I will pass out at the end. Do not do anything until the lid comes off the vase."

"If it doesn't?"

"Then I've failed. Go to the king and queen."

"Just let you die?"

"If the lid doesn't come off before I die, you won't be able to prevent me from dying."

Althir pointed toward the wall again, without actually looking at Samuel, then crossed to the vessel. Slowly he paced around the simple brown vase, opening himself to the magics coating the ceramic like water flowing endlessly over the surface. He let his eyes unfocus so he could give himself over to his other senses.

Once he felt centered and in complete touch with the vessel, he picked up the pitcher of water and poured it in a slow drizzle as he went back to walking his circuit. After the outer ring was complete, he did the same thing with the salt, sprinkling it in a steady stream just inside the water's line. He felt the circle close with a solid snap when the last grains of salt hit the wooden floor.

Mixing elf magic with this kind of ceremonial magic was always a tricky thing, but Althir had studied the Sorcerers' process —as much as he was able, given their secretive, guarded attitude about their powers. He could feel the ebbs and flows of the spell that had gone into sealing the vessel. It rubbed against his skin like a brush of lightning. A deeper part of his consciousness detected the low hum of warning. Not actual words and not something he could entirely explain, but the hairs on his nape rose as tendrils of death and pain reached out to tap his soul.

He allowed himself a brief memory of Mina, of her beautiful face and intelligent eyes. Her determination and sorrow.

For her.

He settled on his knees before the vessel, picked up the sword and sliced open one of his forearms from inner elbow to wrist, letting the initial drips of blood roll onto the copper lid. Swallowing down a hiss of pain, he switched hands and sliced a line down his other forearm. More blood splattered onto the copper. The blood soaked into the lid the instant it touched the metal.

Setting the sword gently aside, he pressed his forearms alongside the lid, so his wounds were in direct contact with it. A jolt of pain shot through him, and his entire body stiffened. He clenched his jaw as a basic, instinctive part of him wanted to pull away, but he forced down the need and kept his arms against the vessel. Blood flowed into the lid faster and faster, and a sick, sucking noise filled the air.

Althir started to tremble as his blood rushed out of his body, quicker than the wounds would have allowed naturally, so much blood the vessel couldn't drink it in fast enough. It dripped red over the copper and ceramic, puddled under the base only to be absorbed into the porous pot. Blackness filled the edges of Althir's vision, but he kept his concentration on the vessel, his full focus on the magic he was attempting to break.

In his mind, something unnatural screeched and screamed. The power whipped around him like stinging sand. The spell began to snap, cracking and breaking apart with such ferocity, Althir felt like his very soul was being ripped open.

He put all his focus into the single thought that this vessel *would* open. When he felt resistance in the magic, he growled the words aloud, in his own language. "You will open. You will open." He repeated the phrase until he could no longer speak and then he continued the litany in his head. Everything in him centered on that single purpose.

More blood than he thought he had in his entire body poured out, and the brown ceramic and red copper started to glow white.

The glow was the last thing he saw before blackness closed in on his vision, leaving him blind and close to unconsciousness. He held on to his concentration, his sense of his surroundings, and the vessel for as long as he could. His body felt cold, distant, like it wasn't his anymore, and he couldn't have lifted his arms now if he'd wanted to.

More layers of magic rose up to replace the ones he broke through, resisting, rebelling against his efforts. But the more blood he lost, the more the spell shattered into sharp, cutting pieces.

Numbness closed around him. His sense of himself, his knowledge and focus slipped.

Then he felt one last roar of denial from the vessel.

An earthquake rumbled through Althir's bones. He smiled to himself and forced through that last barrier with what was left of his strength. Inside the darkness of his own mind, splinters of light and screams of agony pierced him.

Finally, he let go. As he slipped away, his last thought was a vision of his beautiful Mina.

Mina stood at the door to Althir's sickroom, staring at his unconscious form. Oh gods, he was so pale, so still. His bandaged arms lay atop the white blanket tucked around his motionless body. She swallowed hard and forced herself close to him.

His handsome face looked ravaged, his cheeks sunken, deep circles under his closed eyes, his lips dry and cracked. His chest barely moved and she had to touch him to assure herself he was really breathing.

A nurse sat quietly in one corner of the room, working on a small swatch of needlepoint as she kept watch over Althir.

"He's really going to survive?" Mina asked the woman. Again.

"Yes, dear. Believe it or not, he looked worse just a few hours ago. Already seeing improvement. Damned elves have some recovery ability. Don't know what he did to himself, but he was nearly bone dry of blood when they brought him here."

Mina let out a very quiet moan. "How can he recover from that?"

"Not sure he'd have been able to, but his brother gave him a transfusion."

Startled by the news, Mina finally looked from Althir to the nurse. "What?"

"Ulric was here right after they brought Althir up. Though maybe I shouldn't have said. Ulric swore me to secrecy, but he was only specific about Althir finding out. Don't tell Althir, dear. I don't want to upset Ulric. He was very insistent his brother not know he was even here."

"Ulric? Ulric helped Althir? They hate each other." But a part of Mina wasn't as surprised by Ulric's behavior as she suspected Althir would be. Or probably Ulric was himself. It had never mattered how angry she was with her brother, she would have done anything to keep him alive if she'd had a choice. Maybe there was hope for the brothers after all.

She almost smiled. Althir would really hate that.

She stood by his bed for more than two hours, watching him breathe, holding his wrist so she could feel his slow, steady pulse. The nurse gave her an occasional speculative glance, but didn't pry into Mina's reasons for being here, for which Mina was grateful. She didn't want to discuss her feelings for Althir with a stranger.

She loved him, more than she'd ever loved a man before. And she couldn't have him.

If she knew them better, she was tempted to ask Layla and Ulric how they managed to sustain a relationship. Was there something different about Ulric, something that allowed him to be with a human where most elves couldn't?

Althir had never even hinted that a future between them was possible. He hadn't tried to delude her with pointless hope. She appreciated that. But it would be hard to see Ulric and Layla, happy and together, knowing she wouldn't be free to love Althir in the same way.

Her hand tightened on his. At least he was alive. They couldn't be together, but she wouldn't have to watch another love die.

The nurse cleared her throat and stood. "Change of shift," she said to Mina's raised brows. The woman glanced at Althir. "Funny, all this care for a traitor elf. Wonder what he did to deserve it?"

Mina bit the inside of her cheek to keep from yelling at the woman and telling her exactly what Althir had done. No one was supposed to know, outside of a very select few. She was too conscious of secrets to risk revealing this one.

But that didn't mean she couldn't do something to help improve her people's opinion of Althir. She considered everyone she knew in the meeting hall, and then went to find the two or three people who liked to…"chat", as Althir would say.

She had a rumor to start.

CHAPTER TWENTY

hree days after handing the List vessel over to the council and then nearly bleeding himself dry to open it, Althir made his way to the room Ulric kept at the Sinnale council's meeting hall. He hadn't spoken to his brother since he officially gave himself over to the Sinnale. But now he had a question for him, and it wasn't something that could wait.

Since Ulric wasn't in his room when Althir arrived, he made himself comfortable in one of the chairs set up near the ceramic heater in the corner and propped his feet up on the small table nearby. He stared out the third-story window at the surrounding buildings, sunlight sharpening the bricks and angles, and waited with forced patience. Only the fact that he still felt a little weak kept him from pacing around the small room.

When Ulric entered, he stopped short and stared. Althir stared back, amused by his brother's surprise. Ulric wiped the expression from his face quickly and stalked into the room, dropping a small handful of letters onto his bed—the only large thing in the room.

"You shouldn't be out of bed yet," he said without looking at Althir. "Even you can't recover that quickly."

"I have a question for you."

Ulric raised his brows. "The king and queen have lifted your banishment. You can return to Glengowyn anytime."

Althir nodded. "Ah. Good to know. But that's not what I came here to ask."

"The label of traitor has been lifted."

With a snort, Althir said, "You know I'll always be looked at as a traitor. No matter what the king and queen say. Our people have long memories."

Frowning, his brother faced him with his arms crossed over his chest. "Why *did* you do it, Althir? And don't tell me it was for the power again. I never bought that story. You've never gone looking for magic beyond your own charm."

He shrugged. "It doesn't matter now."

"It matters to me. I'd like to know why my brother turned against his people."

"Of course you would." He rolled his eyes. "That's not what I came here to discuss."

"You want your question answered, answer mine."

"Ulric, there's no point. It's over." Mostly to himself, he muttered, "And what I'd been trying to do worked out in the end anyway."

Ulric's gaze sharpened, so Althir hurried on. He did not want to discuss his reasons for turning "traitor" with Ulric, of all people. "Will you answer my question now?"

"You haven't answered mine."

"Is it worth it?" he asked before Ulric could attempt more interrogation. "With Layla. Is it worth the risk? To her."

The change of subjects visibly surprised his brother, leaving him silent and blinking for a few moments. Althir would have been amused if the answer to his question didn't matter so much.

"Well?" He waved a hand to get Ulric focused. "Is it?"

"Why are you asking?"

"Ulric, stop being an ass and answer my question."

"Yes, it's worth the risk. But I'm in love with Layla, and she loves me."

Althir huffed out a half laugh. "I should hope so since you nearly slit my throat for her."

He turned back to the window and considered his brother's answer. Ulric was counting on his and Layla's love being *that* kind of love, the kind that would survive through time, the kind those romantic ballads celebrated. Ulric was gambling on the fact that he and Layla loved each other *enough*. He was betting on them having a true love.

A risk Althir had never even considered taking with Mina. Yet…

"Is there someone?" Ulric asked into the quiet. "A human woman?"

Althir didn't respond.

"Mina," Ulric said with a note of understanding and a hint of satisfaction at having guessed the answer.

Althir twisted his lips in disgust but kept his attention on the sunlit day beyond the glass pane.

"Do you love her?" Ulric pressed.

"Yes."

Silence. Then, "You didn't even hesitate."

"I didn't need to."

"Does she know?"

"I haven't told her yet."

"Will you tell her?"

"I don't know."

"Does she love you?"

He did pause a moment before answering that question. "I don't know," he repeated. One of his greatest fears was that she didn't.

"If she's not in love with you, if you don't truly love her, an affair will end badly. For her. You know that."

He hissed over his shoulder at Ulric and finally stood to pace. "Of course I fucking know. Why the hell do you think I'm here asking *you* about this?"

He stalked to the door then turned and paced back to the opposite side of the room while Ulric stood watching.

"How could you be so sure the risk was worth it with Layla? Weren't you worried about…about what would happen to her if things went wrong?"

"Of course. Which was why I explained it all to her from the beginning."

Althir paused to stare at his brother with raised brows. Ulric had the grace to glance away, his frown just a touch embarrassed.

"Okay," he admitted. "I didn't tell her from the very beginning. But before committing fully, before letting her commit to me, I told her everything."

Althir nodded and started pacing again. The only way a relationship between a human and elf would work was if they really loved each other. The negative side-effects of elf-fire were worse on couples not in love because no real bond ever formed. Without that bond, without a true love, eventually things would fall apart, and the human would be tipped into the abyss of madness as a result. Very, very few humans had ever survived a long-term relationship with an elf without ending up insane.

He wasn't sure how his brother could risk that with someone he claimed to love. Yet Althir couldn't imagine never seeing Mina again. But to see her, he would have to risk her sanity in just that way.

She had come to his sickbed after he'd bled to open the vessel. Or so he'd been told by one of the nurses looking after him as he recovered. He'd been unconscious and hadn't actually spoken with her. Since regaining consciousness, he hadn't seen her. But he hadn't gone looking any more than she'd come to him.

"What will you do?" Ulric asked quietly.

"I don't know that either." His circuit took him back to the door and this time he reached for the knob. He had some thinking to do, and he didn't want to do it with his brother staring at him.

"Will I see you back in Glengowyn?" Ulric asked as Althir swung open the door.

Althir faced him and shrugged. "We'll see what happens."

"Good luck."

As he returned to his sickroom, Althir realized that had been the most civil conversation he'd shared with Ulric in years.

THE NEXT DAY HE MOVED FROM THE SICKROOM TO A PROPER, SMALL flat in a complex near the meeting hall. That move was as sure a sign as any that he was free to go his own way now. The fact that the Sinnale were still willing to give him accommodation in the city confirmed what he'd started to suspect over the last few days. The humans he encountered inside the meeting hall didn't glare at him anymore, or spit, or curse. He actually received hesitant smiles, nods of greeting, even one or two of the men had clapped him on the arm and expressed pleasure that he'd recovered from the bleeding.

Most didn't know *exactly* what he'd done, and Althir was sure the council was keeping the details quiet. But something must have gotten out, enough information that those humans close to the council knew Althir had done *something* to help end the war— something he'd nearly died to accomplish.

Whatever the rumors, it was enough to change some attitudes toward him. To his surprise, that change did give him a sense of satisfaction. At least to some he was no longer a traitor.

With his own people…well, he accepted he'd never be fully welcome in Glengowyn again. He could return now. And he'd be safe to live among his own kind for the rest of his life. But they wouldn't forgive as readily as the Sinnale had, even if they understood what he'd done to end the war.

For some reason, Althir couldn't find it in him to care what his people thought of him anymore. There was only one person whose opinion really mattered. And he was going to have to face her soon.

The morning after moving into his new flat, he left the neat but nearly empty home and went in search of Mina. He wasn't entirely sure where to find her. He'd been hesitant to ask anyone where she lived, afraid of revealing things he wasn't ready to reveal to just anyone. He knew she came and went from the meeting hall frequently, though, so he set himself up across the street from the entrance in the common room of what had once been a pub. The room was deserted, but the tables and chairs were still stacked around the edges of the space. He pulled a table and two chairs close to the large front windows and settled in for his vigil.

A few passing humans gave him strange looks. He ignored them. As he waited, he realized he could go find Ulric inside and ask him. But somehow, bringing his brother into his confidence any more than he already had didn't sit well. Years of resentment and bitterness didn't go away overnight.

What truly surprised Althir, though, was how little real anger he felt for Ulric anymore. He didn't think he'd proved himself equal to his brother finally. It wasn't that. It was just…he didn't care anymore what others thought of him in comparison to the glowing icon that was Ulric's fame.

But Ulric didn't need to know that.

Hours passed before Althir finally spotted Mina approaching the meeting hall. The sight of her stunned him, and for a long instant, he could only stare. She was dressed in plain trousers and tunic, both deep brown and formless. But her curvy figure was too hard to hide, even in shapeless clothing. Her swords were strapped to her hips, her hair pulled back into a tight bun. Sunlight glinted off the blond strands, highlighting the color. She looked beautiful.

And tired.

Even from the short distance he could see faint circles under her eyes and her cheeks looked hollow. He frowned, worry thrusting him out of his stupor. He hurried from the empty pub across the street and stopped her just before she walked into the hall.

He cupped her chin in one hand and held her face up for closer study. "Why aren't you sleeping? What's wrong?"

"Hello to you too, Althir." She smiled crookedly, but her brows lowered in confusion.

"What's wrong?" he pressed, too concerned to bother with pleasantries. "Is it the fighting? Has something changed?"

The massive offensive strike the Sinnale had started had ground to a halt two days earlier, according to the gossip he'd gathered from the nurses. But they were holding the retaken territory securely now, forcing the Sorcerers to fall even farther back.

Mina shook her head and dislodged his hold on her chin. "Everything is still quiet on the front, for the moment," she said. "There's something else going on. I don't know the details. Just that there's a mission underway. Something to do with the List."

She murmured most of this in such a quiet voice only an elf could have heard her. She studied the passersby as she spoke. He and Mina drew attention, but no one passed close enough to overhear them. Still, they'd be better able to talk with some privacy.

"The council gave me a flat on the next block. We can speak

more freely there." He took her arm, but she hesitated. "Do you have a meeting inside?"

"Nothing immediate."

He watched her closely but couldn't tell from her slight frown what she might be thinking.

Finally, she let out a sigh. "Lead the way."

Her hesitance gave him even more to worry about as he led her the short distance to his rooms. When he opened the door for her, she walked the full length of the sitting room, going directly to the windows that looked out on a side street.

"You're safe here, you know," he said.

She gave him an inscrutable half smile and turned her back to the window. "A matter of perspective," she murmured.

"Why haven't you been sleeping?" he asked again.

She raised her brows and nodded to his arms. "How are you doing? I thought it would take another few days for you to be fully recovered."

The bandages weren't visible beneath the sleeves of his shirt, but they didn't need to be. "Good enough to leave the sickroom. Elves recover faster than humans."

"You were nearly dead." She swallowed visibly.

"As you can see, I survived."

"I went to see you that evening. You weren't awake yet."

"They told me you came."

"You were so pale, Althir…"

She sucked in her lips and looked away, but not in time for him to miss the moisture in her eyes. He couldn't refuse the need to comfort her pain any more than he could resist her. He crossed to her and pulled her into his arms. She was stiff against him for several torturous heartbeats, and then she softened and her arms circled his waist.

"Scared me to see you that way," she muttered against his chest.

He stroked a hand over her hair, a little ashamed to realize he was pleased she'd been worried about him. "That's why I didn't want you to see," he said. "Why I asked you to stay away."

Her grunt sounded annoyed, and for the first time since crossing the street to her, he smiled.

"Was it worth it?" she asked without loosening her hold or looking up. "The List was there? It will help?"

"I'm sure it already is." He pulled back enough to lift her chin so she had to face him. "Would you like to know what it was for now? Why we did what we did?"

She tilted her head and nodded. "I guess it's safe for me to know now, right?"

"You'll be one of exactly twenty-three people, both human and elf, who know the truth."

He watched her eyes brighten with curiosity, and some of his concerns banked. He still wanted to know why she looked so worn, but that could wait a little bit longer. Holding her to his side—he couldn't seem to let go now that he had his hands on her—he walked her to the couch and they sat.

"My cousin, the one responsible for the shrapnel arrows? She's, inadvertently as it turns out, created a new kind of arrow. One that doesn't even have to be aimed. Once it's drawn, an archer just has to whisper the name of its target and that arrow will fly strait to its target's heart. Even with obstacles in the way."

"It flies through the obstacles?"

"Around them. It's a very directed missile."

She pulled back so she could stare up at him. "That's…that's rather terrifying. Is there any way to avoid it?"

He shook his head. "Not that she's told anyone yet. If there is at all. That's why so very few people know about it. My cousin, the king and queen of course, one of their bodyguards, your council,

Ulric and Layla, three human and three elf assassins. And now you."

"You learned from the council? You said you'd talked it out of them when they were asking about the Sorcerers' real names?"

"And the powers that be are in agreement the information about the arrows is too potentially dangerous to make known to the general public of either city. But I trust your discretion."

Her lips lifted in a brief smile before dropping back to a slight frown. "So the List… With that, the arrows can kill the Sorcerers? The Sorcerers' protections won't prevent the arrows getting through?"

"That was tested last night. Two of the Sorcerers were killed by the assassins, using the arrows from a safe distance. Human spotters in different locations confirmed the kills—they didn't know how the arrows worked or what was different about them. They just confirmed the Sorcerers were shot through the heart and the resultant implosion turned them into little more than bloody chunks."

She cringed at his description but a blink later her expression opened. "It worked. What we did… They can kill them now. All of them!"

He grinned at her growing enthusiasm. Her wide-eyed satisfaction wiped some of the exhaustion from her face. "It won't be long now. The war will be done. Maybe a matter of weeks."

She blinked. "I can hardly believe it. After all this time… It's hard to comprehend the end being so close."

Studying her, he asked, "What do you want to do once the war ends? Will you go back to making chocolates? Do you want to reclaim your home?"

He hoped her answers would help him decide his own next move—whether to let her go or to find out if she returned his feelings. Even if she did, though, he still wasn't sure if he could risk her sanity. Holding her, he already felt the first tingles of the elf-fire, a low burn through his system. He was already playing a dangerous game just seeing her again. If she didn't love him…

He couldn't think about that yet. First, he needed to find out what *she* wanted for her future.

She lifted her shoulders in a little shrug. "I haven't been able to think about the future in so long, I'm not sure what I want. I should reclaim the family home and shops, but…" She twisted her mouth into a half frown. "But there are so many memories there now. I'm not sure I can face it, knowing my parents, my brother won't be coming back."

"Any other family to take up the mantle?"

"Oh there were a lot of us at one stage. But all the ones interested in running the bakery and chocolatier have died in the war. There are some cousins still alive, no one I'm close to. But maybe they'd be interested in having the old place."

"If you had a new location? A new shop, would you want to continue the business?"

"A new shop might help, actually. Start over fresh. But this city is going to need a lot of rebuilding once the Sorcerers are finally pushed out. I think it'll be a long time before I can indulge in my own dreams."

It was on the tip of his tongue to argue her point but he stopped himself. Though the goblin wars hadn't been fought on Glengowyn lands, there had still been a lot of rebuilding of their society following each conflict. She was right, the Sinnale would need time before their lives started to feel normal again.

"Glengowyn will likely help with the rebuilding. It'll make for good trade. Ulric will love that."

"Ulric? Why?"

"He loves bartering and trading—a side effect of his strategic genius." He couldn't seem to help the edge of sarcasm when saying the word "genius". Some habits were hard to set aside.

She smiled at his tone. "Help from the elves would be good. Probably heal some of the tension still between our people."

"Speaking of… I no longer appear to be a pariah, at least within the meeting hall." To his surprise and delight, color rose in her cheeks.

"I might have…mentioned how you nearly died helping us," she said. "No details, of course. Just a few rumors to help right the accounting."

"Mina. You didn't need to do that."

"Yes, I did. You won't tell anyone the truth about why you aligned with the traitors. At the very least, people need to know you contributed—nearly with your life—to end our war."

"My reputation doesn't matter to me." And it didn't anymore. For the first time in his life, acclaim and acknowledgment seemed hollow things compared to what he might lose now if Mina didn't return his feelings.

She pursed her lips and looked down at her hands in her lap. "It matters to me."

Lifting her chin, he made her meet his gaze again. "Why? Why does it matter to you?"

"You're a good man, Althir. I won't tolerate people saying otherwise."

Her defensiveness made him smile slightly. But that wasn't the answer he was hoping for. "You thought I was an intolerable ass when we first met."

"You were," she shot back. "And very rude."

He laughed. "You threatened to kill me."

"And you decided talking about my breasts was fair game."

"Well…" He glanced down, unable to resist. "They are very hard to ignore."

She thumped his thigh, none too gently. He noticed, though, because he was still staring at that part of her body, that her chest rose and fell faster as her breathing sped. It took a great deal of willpower not to reach out and cup one of her impressive breasts. But that wouldn't solve the issue at hand. One he wasn't sure how to raise.

"What about you?" she murmured.

He dragged his gaze back up. "Me?"

"What will you do now? Return to Glengowyn? I spoke with Layla. She said you were allowed. And the king and queen lifted the traitor label."

"When I was in my cage, I did miss the forest. I definitely wanted out of this city."

"So you'll move back." Her gaze danced away as she spoke.

"Not right away."

His answer must have startled her because she looked directly at him. "Why not? This place isn't exactly a comfortable city anymore."

"I'm still deciding if I'll stay here or in Glengowyn. Or…"

"Or?" she prompted when he trailed off.

He hadn't allowed himself to think through the "or" fully, but at the back of his mind, he had been considering that if Mina didn't return his feelings, staying even as close as Glengowyn might prove too much of a temptation for him. To ensure he left her alone, he would have to go somewhere much farther away.

"I've considered…traveling," he said. "It will be some time before the other elves can look at me as anything but a traitor. I might be allowed back to Glengowyn, but I won't be welcomed. And here…" Mina was in Sinnale. Leaving would hurt wildly. But if it meant she was safe from any repercussions, he'd go.

"Traveling where?" she asked quietly.

"I don't know. I hadn't really planned anything out yet. Still have some recovering to do." That last was an excuse. He was a bit weak, but he could travel without risking his health.

He heard her swallow hard and the sound started his heart beating a little faster. Did his leaving make her sad? Would she miss him? Did she want him to stay?

"I'd be sorry to see you leave," she admitted.

"You'd be the only one I'd truly miss."

"Not even Ulric?" She raised her brows, trying to joke, but there wasn't any real humor in her eyes.

He cupped her cheeks in both hands and held her face. "Mina. I'd stay for you. But…"

"But the elf-fire," she said with a nod. "The addiction. You can't be with me anymore. I know."

"There *is* a way." He took a breath and prepared to jump out over the abyss.

CHAPTER TWENTY-ONE

"Ulric and Layla..." Althir started, watching Mina's expression closely. "The reason they can be together is because...because they're in love. Not just a passing love. A true love."

She frowned. "What's the difference?"

"A passing love… It eventually goes away. If an elf and human have maintained a relationship until that point, the separation is extremely dangerous to the human. To their sanity, their health… The effects of the elf-fire addiction do a lot of damage after long-term exposure."

Her eyes widened. "How does a 'true love' change things?"

"That's the kind of love that can last through the years, the kind that strengthens over time, bringing a couple closer. There's no real risk because they won't separate."

"Until the human dies."

He rubbed his thumbs along her cheeks. "That's another...side effect. The human's life is extended to match their mate's lifespan. Another reason the pairings, when ended, can have such dire consequences. If the human has lived long enough, most of the other humans they loved have died. There's nothing left for them once the relationship with their elf lover ends."

"Is this why the pairings are so rare? Not because of the addiction but because of the possible outcome of a relationship?"

He moved his hands from her face to her shoulders, then down her arms in a long caress. He couldn't stop touching her even though the elf-fire was threatening to overwhelm him and throw him off track. He forced his desires down, knowing this conversation was too important to get wrong.

"Most elves aren't willing to take the risk," he confirmed. "It… it's not pretty, the separation, when it happens."

"Does Layla know?"

"Ulric told her."

"And they're willing to risk it?"

"As I said, they have a love they think can survive."

Mina lifted her chin in a slight nod and focused on the back of the couch, her eyes narrowed in thought.

Althir tried to keep his hands from trembling, but maintaining his composure was getting harder by the minute. He wanted her desperately. But he wanted her to tell him she loved him more than he'd ever wanted anything. That need kept him still and quiet while she considered what he'd just told her.

"Not many people know about this, do they?" she murmured.

"No. We don't tell others often. It's considered…elf business. But even inside Glengowyn it's not spoken of much. Outside of romantic ballads."

"Yet you're telling me."

He stopped running his palms over her arms and dropped them to her lap, taking her hands in his.

"Why?" She faced him fully, her gaze assessing.

He didn't flinch away, allowing her to see every emotion he was feeling.

"Why?" she repeated.

"I love you. And the thought of losing you kills me. But…what we have can't just be sex, or you'll be in danger. If you don't… I can't stay here with you so close and not come to you. Not now. I won't be able to resist you, Mina. But if you ask it of me, I'll leave Sinnale and Glengowyn. To keep you safe."

"You think leaving will keep me safe?"

Her tone was flat and even, impossible for him to read. Her expression was as closed as his was open. She hadn't reacted at all to his admission of love either. The faint hope he'd been harboring shriveled, and he straightened away from her.

"Yes. You'll be safe from any dangers brought on by the elf-fire once I leave."

"And if I get involved with another elf?"

The very idea tore open his chest with a pain he could barely fathom. He only realized he was growling and his fists were clenched when he noticed the wary look on her face. He forced himself to relax.

"You'll have a similar issue. If he loves you. If he doesn't, you'll have the kind of affair most humans have with elves—temporary."

"My…exposure to you won't make things worse?"

His jaw tightened but he forced out an answer. "No. Each… encounter is unique."

"So I could sleep my way through the males of Glengowyn, so long as I didn't fuck any of them more than two or three times, and not risk insanity. Correct?"

"Correct." Pushing the single word through his clenched teeth made it sound more like an animal grunt than language.

"And if I only want you?"

"We might be able to risk one more night together. But then…"

"Then you'll still have to leave."

His nod was sharp and stiff from the tension holding his body.

"If I don't love you."

Another single, sharp nod.

"But what if I do love you?"

Every nerve in his body jumped and his muscles flexed. "*If* you love me, you're the one taking the biggest risk. I wouldn't risk your sanity, though, if you have any doubts at all. I'd leave rather than see you hurt."

"Yet you're hurting me now. And still you sit there."

His brows lowered. "I'm hurting you? How?"

"By assuming I don't love you. But assuming what I feel for you is *passing*," she hissed the last word, striking him with it like a slap.

She might as well have issued him a physical blow because her words jolted him back.

She poked him in the chest. "Do you have *any* idea how terrified I was knowing you could die opening that bloody List vessel? Can you even comprehend what your death would mean to me? I have lost *everyone* I've ever loved to this war. And I had to sit by and wait and wonder if I was going to lose another love. A love I never even hoped I'd be able to keep for myself, but at least knowing you were alive would be something. And then you nearly died! I haven't slept in days. I keep waking up thinking I imagined your recovery, that you lied to me about elves being able to survive the bloodletting required. You with your superb ability to lie!"

Her tirade had him so stunned, he didn't think to stop her when she stood and started stalking in a tight circle around the couch.

"Even knowing you were healing in that damned sickroom, *I've* been sick thinking about what could have happened. What might have been. How very close I came to…to watching you die too.

And you sit there and question my feelings for you! You tell me *now* we could have a future! How dare you?"

That brought him to his feet in front of her, stopping her in mid-circuit. "How dare I? What exactly did you want me to do, Mina? Tell you I loved you and we could have a future *before* I opened the vessel? You expected me to make things worse than they already were?"

"Damn you, Althir. If you love me, you should have told me!"

"Why? So you might suffer even more if things had gone wrong and I died? I didn't know *you* loved *me*."

"Well, what the hell did you think I felt?"

"I have no idea. You weren't exactly upfront about your feelings either. At least not since our first meeting and your statement that you wanted to kill me."

"I still want to kill you. For putting me through this. For breaking my heart. And for not trusting me."

"Mina." He took her shoulders and gave her a gentle shake so that she glared up at him. "I trust you more than any other living being."

"Then no more keeping secrets. No more leaving out important information. Like we could be together. Like you do love me. If you really feel that way, you can't keep it to yourself. Not anymore."

His anger and tension and frustration evaporated when he saw the dampness rise in her eyes.

"Mina." He pulled her into a tight hug, refusing to let go when she made an effort to tug away. "I love you," he said against her hair, kissing her temple. "I love you more than I've ever loved anyone. In a way I can't even explain. So deeply it's impossible for me to fathom. Before you, I was so cynical I didn't consider this sort of emotion even possible. Now… I don't want to think about my life, my future, without you."

She sniffled, and he felt the dampness of her tears through the material of his tunic.

"I didn't think a future was possible either," she said. "But… I wanted you nearby, to know you were alive and safe and…that if I really wanted to, I could always say…hi when I saw you passing."

The very idea of her greeting him like an acquaintance struck him as so absurd he started to laugh. "My love, if you'd tried to pass me with just a casual hello, you'd have found yourself up against the nearest wall with my mouth on yours and my hands everywhere. There was never an option of us reverting to virtual strangers."

She hiccupped a soft laugh. "You paint a very sexy picture, though." Turning her face up to his, she said, "I would welcome your mouth, your hands."

What little control he'd had over his need for her slipped away. He kissed her, leaving her in no doubt that he wanted her. Needed her.

Loved her.

And to his awe, she returned his kiss with an equal passion.

"I do love you," she said against his lips. "Don't you dare doubt that again."

"How could I? I'd be able to tell if you were lying."

She took his mouth again, her tongue thrusting against his, and he tasted her like she was the most exquisite of wines. Something to be savored and cherished.

Taking her to his bed, he held her close, for a long time just caressing her through her clothes, kissing her wherever there was available skin. Though the elf-fire was a burning ache in his blood, he felt no drive to rush, no desperation except the overwhelming need to please her. He teased and tempted until she writhed beneath him. With tender care, he took her hair down from its usual bun and let the silky waves of blond fall across his palms.

"I've wanted to do this since I saw your hair down when we were in Sorcerer territory," he said. "So sexy."

She smiled. "I rarely get a chance to leave it down." She closed her eyes as he threaded his fingers through the locks and gently massaged her scalp. "That feels wonderful."

"I plan on doing this a lot," he said.

"Good."

He stroked her hair, enjoying the sensation, the luxury of having her so relaxed and free. Then he stripped her slowly, taking his time with each garment, kissing newly exposed skin for long, drugging moments before exposing more.

She was perfect, beautiful, and his. And he proved his possession with each touch. When he finally freed her breasts, his groan slipped out. "I will never get enough of you," he murmured, then he took her nipple into his mouth, sucking her with an insistence that had her moaning and gripping his hair to hold his head in place.

Though he knew he could spend hours simply lavishing attention on her breasts, he finally pulled away to finish removing her clothes. Then she removed his clothing in another slow and drugging exploration with her mouth on his skin this time. Nothing had ever felt so smooth and perfect as her lips on him, covering him, sucking him into her heated mouth.

They caressed and kissed, licked and teased almost leisurely, time nothing to the need to memorize and explore each other fully. He sought out every spot on her body that made her moan, every soft, vanilla-scented inch of her that made her melt. And she uncovered places he didn't even know he'd find erotic, touched him in ways that left him breathless.

When his tension had surpassed any ability to continue slowly, he cupped her face between his palms and kissed her, hard, as he slid inside her. For a beat, he held still, savoring the wetness and heat that surrounded his cock. Then he stroked out and back in again. Her muscles tightened, drawing out the friction and pleasure. Still he couldn't rush, didn't want to hurry. He rocked into her in a steady, slow rhythm, swallowing her sounds of pleasure, relishing each gasp and cry.

For the first time, they didn't have to worry about making too much noise and he took advantage of that as well, giving pleasure until she cried out, calling his name in a shout that echoed around his room.

"I love you," she said again as she settled from her orgasm.

The statement, so honest and true, robbed him of the last of his control. He pumped into her a few hard times then gave in to the almost painful pulsing gasp of release.

He collapsed over her, his heart racing, and hugged her close, murmuring his own love against her sweat-soaked hair.

"The elf-fire… That was different," she said, her voice a little hoarse.

"Yes. Better even than my ability to spot a lie."

"What?" She lifted his head so he was looking her in the face.

"That kind of elf-fire reaction… That only happens with couples who are in love."

"More than just sex," she agreed, placing a soft kiss against his lips.

"I should warn you, though."

She groaned. "Now what?"

"To make sure you age as I do, that our bond stays strong, it's important for us to make love a lot."

"How much is a lot?"

"A lot. Regularly. Every day."

"Hmm. Are you sure you want to do that? I mean, that could get tiring over the years."

He scowled because he could see the glimmer of humor in her

eyes and knew his expression would amuse her. The sound of her giggle was a reward all its own. "I think I can maintain enough stamina to satisfy you on a daily basis," he said.

Her breasts jiggled with her laughter, drawing his attention. He turned her chuckle into a gasp when he bent and claimed one of her peaked nipples with his teeth. He watched her face while he suckled her, as pleasure made her close her eyes.

"As you can see," he whispered, blowing cool air across her wet nipple, making her shiver, "I'm well up for the job of ensuring our future together through regular sex."

Her hips bumped his and she opened her eyes. He'd grown hard again, still buried deep in her body. "I'm going to enjoy our life together, aren't I?"

"I will do everything within my power to ensure your happiness, Mina." He kissed her softly. "You won't ever have cause to regret the risk you take with me."

She smiled, open and vulnerable, the most beautiful thing he'd ever seen.

"What risk?" she said, before kissing him.

Truly, he thought, what risk indeed.

BOOKS BY ISABO KELLY

Fire and Tears Series

Brightarrow Burning

Darkness Singed

Dawn Ignited

Fire and Tears: Series Collection Books 1-3

Fate's Hand Series

Thief's Desire

Destiny's Seduction

New York Empires Anthologies

Going All In

Icing The Puck

Roughing It

Kellyn's Sacrifice

The Last Guardian

Bonfire Night

ABOUT THE AUTHOR

Isabo Kelly is the award-winning author of numerous science fiction, fantasy, and paranormal romances. She also writes best-selling paranormal romance under the name Kat Simons. Her life has taken her from Las Vegas to Hawaii, where she got her BA in Zoology, back to Vegas where she looked after sharks, then on to Germany and Ireland where she got her Ph.D. in Animal Behavior. Now Isabo focuses on writing. She lives in New York with her beloved family and a library's worth of books.

For more on Isabo, be sure to visit her website or you can find her on social media. She loves hearing from readers!

KATSIMONSBOOKS

WELCOMES

ISABO KELLY

Look out for all of Isabo's books as they make their way to her alter ego's store where readers can buy direct from the author, get cool new merch, special editions, and more! Be sure to check out all Isabo's fiction at KatSimonsBooks

https://www.KatSimonsBooks.com